"YOU DON'T HAVE TO
TO BE WICKED,

He came a step clo[se]
was right behind her—not touching her, but close
enough for her to hear his slow, measured breathing. Close enough to make her tremble.

He wasn't subtle, or shy. With confidence he
rested one hand on her shoulder and slid the other
inside her vest. Later she would feel guilty, Teryl
acknowledged, but at the moment the sensations
were exquisite and only heightened by the fact that
they were standing on the sidewalk where anyone
might pass, where anyone might see them.

Pushing her hair away, he pressed his mouth to
her ear and murmured, "Unbutton your blouse for
me, Teryl. Let me touch you."

Her hands trembled. This was crazy, wrong—
reckless as hell—but it felt incredibly right . . .

ALSO BY MARILYN PAPPANO

In Sinful Harmony

Published by
WARNER BOOKS

MARILYN PAPPANO

Passion

WARNER BOOKS

A Time Warner Company

WARNER BOOKS EDITION

Cover design by Diane Luger
Cover photo by Shunichi Yamamoto/Photonica

Warner Books, Inc.
1271 Avenue of the Americas
New York, NY 10020

Ⓦ A Time Warner Company

Printed in the United States of America

First Printing: April, 1996

10 9 8 7 6 5 4 3 2 1

Passion

Prologue

---

*H*is arm throbbing from the stitches the doctor had put in, John Smith stood in front of his house—or what was left of it—and watched the sheriff and his two deputies walk in a slow circle around it. The fire was out, except for occasional hot spots that still flared, but the heat remained, radiating from the rubble and the ash. It would be tomorrow, the sheriff had decreed, before the debris would be cool enough to allow his men to conduct an investigation, but no doubt, some sort of incendiary device had been used.

No doubt, John drily agreed. Explosions didn't just create themselves out of nothing, and there *was* the gasoline smell that permeated everything. He'd never kept gasoline around the house. He had no gas-powered generator, no yard to require a lawn mower or weed whacker. The only gasoline legitimately on the grounds was inside his truck's fuel tank. No doubt someone had brought his own supply and had used it to destroy his home.

Leaning back against the truck, he shifted his gaze from the three men to the house. Shattered glass covered the ground, and oily lumps—part of the roof—still smoldered, sending a thin smoke into the air. The only thing that remained relatively intact was the foundation, and even that was split by great cracks. Virtually everything he owned had been destroyed by the explosions or consumed by the ensuing flames. The three bombs had done their job well.

Bombs.

Jesus, someone had blown up his house. Having lived through the blasts and staring now at the evidence in front of him, he still found it impossible to believe. Not many people in the county even knew there was a house up here—the sheriff hadn't known; his deputies hadn't—and the few who did know were the closest thing to neighbors that he had. What reason could one of them have for destroying his house?

Maybe it had simply been malicious mischief—nothing personal against him, just circumstance, location, and chance. But almost immediately he discounted the possibility. He could accept a break-in at an isolated house if the intention was robbery. Terrorizing whoever lived there was also possible. But building bombs? Going to the trouble to gather whatever materials were necessary and carting them up into the middle of nowhere? It seemed like a lot of work when a five-gallon can of gasoline and a match would give much the same satisfaction to a pyromaniac.

Maybe the motive had been more sinister. More personal. Maybe someone had wanted to destroy the very things John had come back from Denver for: the evidence of his dual identity. The proof of his career. The paperwork that legally documented who and what he was.

Maybe someone had wanted to be certain that they destroyed him.

Muttering a curse, he remembered the headline he'd read this morning in the hotel. *Reclusive author comes out of hiding.* Each newspaper had had its own version of the publishing world's big news. It was those stories that had sent him straight back home, those stories that had him packing his bags for a trip down South only seconds before the first explosion.

But the stories were a mistake or maybe part of a publicist's game plan to sell more books. They couldn't be connected to this. No one in his publisher's or his agent's office knew where he lived; the only address they'd ever had for him was the post office box ninety miles away in Denver. The post office box to which, he'd discovered yesterday, they weren't sending mail anymore.

Simon Tremont to step out of the shadows.

What if the stories weren't a mistake or publicity hype? What if . . .

The idea forming in his mind was ludicrous, so ludicrous that he refused for a moment to bring the words and thoughts together in a coherent body. But they kept gathering, kept echoing, until finally he was forced to face them. What if it wasn't a mistake? What if Candace Baker, his editor at Morgan-Wilkes, truly did have the latest Simon Tremont manuscript sitting on her desk? What if Simon Tremont really was coming out of hiding?

It was impossible. Simon Tremont couldn't come out of hiding for the simple reason that Simon Tremont didn't exist. It was merely the name John had chosen to hide behind, a name he'd made up, much the same way he'd made up names for his characters. There was no Tremont, no new manuscript.

But Candace had said on the phone that there was a book. She'd said *Resurrection* was the best book Tremont had ever written.

Only he hadn't written it.

Thrills and chills in New Orleans: Simon Tremont speaks.

In spite of the heat from the still-smoldering house, he felt a few chills of his own as he remembered the headline. What he was thinking was so crazy, so implausible, so extraordinary, that even he, who had earned a living the last eleven years making the implausible seem quite plausible . . . even *he* couldn't begin to believe this tale.

But the facts were inescapable. Someone had blown up his house. Someone had written his book. Someone answering to the name of Simon Tremont was scheduled to give an interview in New Orleans next week.

The conclusions, however outrageous, were also inescapable. Someone had taken his name. Someone bright, cunning, and devious, someone talented, tormented, and dangerous as hell, had . . . Jesus, he was crazy to even think it, but he had to.

Someone had stolen his life.

Chapter One

*T*eryl Weaver was disappointed.

She knew it was silly. Just because Simon Tremont had been her favorite author since his very first book had come out was no reason to expect so much from him. And, really, exactly what was it that she had thought he would be?

He was everything that befitted the master of the psychological thriller—dark, brooding, extremely bright, extremely driven. There was an air of mystery about him, a feeling of unpredictability, a sense that this was no common man. He was handsome enough to fuel more than a few female fantasies, with streaky blondish brown hair and a brown gaze so direct that it could bore a hole through steel, and yet he seemed the sort of man other men could relate to. Whether the matter at hand was politics, business, women, or sports, he looked as if he could hold his own.

She couldn't even put her finger on what it was about him that bothered her—the lack of connection, maybe. After years of admiring and idolizing his work, she had expected to admire and idolize the man. She had come to New Orleans to meet him assuming that she already *knew* him, and she had been wrong. She didn't know Simon Tremont at all, and what she had learned about him in this morning's meeting, she hadn't anticipated.

With a sigh, she glanced at her watch. The interview they

had come here for was set to begin in an hour. Simon and Sheila Callan, the New York publicist who was coaching him and smoothing his way, had left for the studio nearly an hour ago in a long, white limo. Teryl could come along whenever she was ready, Sheila had informed her, or she could skip the interview entirely and go sight-seeing. Her implication had been clear: Teryl's presence wasn't necessary, even if Simon had requested it.

Bless his heart for that request, she thought as she rummaged through her suitcase. She had long wanted to visit New Orleans, and the first Tremont book set in the city years ago had served to sweeten that desire. Still, no one had been more surprised than she when he had suggested that she make this trip. After all, she was just his agent's assistant; until his arrival this morning, their contact had been infrequent and limited to a few phone conversations. But, whatever his reasons, suggest it he had, and because he was the sort of client every agent dreamed of representing—because he was the client who had single-handedly made the Robertson Literary Agency such a success—Rebecca Robertson had given in.

In the depths of her suitcase, Teryl found a belt, held it to her waist, and checked in the mirror, then tossed it aside. She should have unpacked when she'd arrived last night, should have set everything out in a neat, orderly fashion, but of course, she hadn't. She'd taken two minutes to hang up her clothes so the worst of the wrinkles would fall out and then she'd been out the door for a quick tour. Her forty-eight hours in New Orleans were too precious to waste with such things as neatness and order.

The belt she was seeking was in the corner of the suitcase, wrapped around a small vinyl cosmetics case. The case and its contents—a gag gift from her best friend—made her pause in spite of her rush, and they brought her a smile. It was a New Orleans survival kit, D.J. had told her. There was a small plastic case of aspirin for the headaches that came from drinking too much. A pack of Band-Aids for sore feet from walking too much. A sewing kit for letting out the seams in her clothes after eating too much. And, tucked in the corner, tied together with a lavender ribbon, four plastic-encased condoms. For getting lucky, D.J. had said with a wicked grin.

Getting Rebecca to pick up the tab for this trip was the luckiest she'd gotten in a long time, Teryl thought, her smile fading as she threaded the belt around her waist. The last time she'd gotten lucky with a man was ancient history.

She gave her hair one last brush, slipped into her most comfortable dressy shoes, grabbed her bag, and left. Maybe she wasn't needed at the interview, but she wasn't going to pass it up. She'd never been in a TV studio before. Besides, she wanted to see how Simon did. She wanted to wish him luck, wanted to let him know there was a familiar face in the room. And, after all, she *was* here officially as Rebecca's representative, even if the only thing Rebecca had asked of her was to not get in the way.

Outside the hotel the bellman whistled for a cab, and less than ten minutes later she was making her way around the crowded backstage area, looking for Sheila or Simon and not even trying to hide her wide-eyed curiosity or to act as if she belonged there. Security was so tight that the only people who could get in were those with a legitimate right to be there, so no one paid her any mind.

The show was called "New Orleans Afternoon"—catchy name, she thought drily. It came on at four o'clock, when most of the city's residents were still at work or fighting traffic trying to get home. They had debated—the publisher, the agency, and the PR firm—making Simon's debut on something bigger, something national, but Sheila had succeeded in choosing New Orleans. Start small, she had recommended. Get him used to the cameras, give him some experience, and then move up.

Besides, she had pointed out, five of Simon's best and most popular books had been set in New Orleans. They shared a common theme, recurring characters, and legions of fans who still clamored for a sixth book in the series. The readers had formed so strong an association between him and the city that any mention of New Orleans and authors always brought Simon Tremont's name in response. For this first time out, he would likely be too nervous to make an effort at being witty, impressive, or even particularly interesting, but for a man who had written about their city with such authority, such familiarity and grace, the locals would overlook his flaws.

The hostess was a former beauty queen and a stereotypical Southern belle, pretty, airy, and about as bright as a ten-watt bulb. A Twinkie, Sheila called her. But that was all right. She wouldn't ask any hard questions—she probably wouldn't be able to think of any, Teryl thought uncharitably. Even if Simon totally flubbed the interview, he would come off looking good in comparison to Miss Magnolia Blossom.

Then, once this debut was out of the way, they would hit the big time. Sheila and Rebecca were sorting through offers, making deals, negotiating. After the press release last week that Tremont was coming out from behind his well-woven cloak of mystery, they had been flooded with requests from the likes of Oprah, "Today," and Larry King.

Of course, while Simon made the rounds of New York, Chicago, and L.A., she would be back at work in Richmond. But that was all right. She'd met her idol in the city his books had made come alive for her.

Spotting Simon in a distant corner, she started his way. The great man—that was what Rebecca called him—was standing alone, his thoughts someplace far from a New Orleans television studio. Fearing the worst from a recluse, Sheila had scheduled time this morning for an inspection and, if necessary, a shopping trip, but Simon had arrived with a wardrobe that was decent by anyone's standards, although maybe a tad casual. But what did it matter if he looked as if he were dressed for a lazy anonymous afternoon with friends instead of a television interview? So what if his shirt was a little loud, if his trousers were a shade away from matching the shirt, or if his shoes were run down, broken in, and worn without socks? After all, writers were supposed to be eccentric, right? And writers who had hidden themselves away in the Colorado Rockies for the last ten years were entitled to be excessively so. Besides, his fans didn't care how he looked or dressed.

Hell, when you could write like Simon Tremont, when you could breathe such power into the written word, when you could bring unrelenting terror to millions of people the world over and keep them coming back for more, you could be flat-out nuts, and no one would care.

"Can I get you anything, Simon?"

He glanced up, his gaze connecting with hers with enough force to make her take an involuntary step back. "No, thanks. I'm just relaxing."

"Nervous?"

"A little. This is my first interview." Raising one hand, he carelessly combed his hair back. "But it'll be fine."

She'd been about to say the same thing, but it sounded different coming from him. His confidence—arrogance, a sly voice whispered in her head—along with the look he was giving her sent a little shiver of uneasiness down her spine. Maybe that was part of her problem with him, she thought—those intense, measuring looks that made her feel much too exposed, like an insect mounted on a presentation slide.

But just as she'd reached that decision, he backed off, even though physically he didn't move at all. It just seemed that suddenly there was more breathing space between them. "Thank you for agreeing to fly down here for this."

A moment ago she would have had to force her smile. Now it came naturally. "Believe me, coming to New Orleans was no hardship. I've always wanted to spend some time here." His books had created the desire, had led her to other books and to movies—mercy, yes, movies—about the city. After seeing *The Big Easy*, she'd had fantasies of traveling to New Orleans and finding a Remy McSwain all her very own—minus the corruption, of course, but complete with the sexy body, the adorable grin, the charming Cajun accent, and—*ooh la la*—the passion.

She needed some passion in her life.

"Mr. Tremont?" With Sheila at his side, the producer gave Teryl a nod before turning his attention to Simon. "We'll be ready to start soon. If you'll come with me . . ."

After they walked away, Teryl wandered off, watching the activity, wondering if the people who worked here found their jobs as interesting and exotic as she did. Probably not. She had friends at home who thought working in the publishing business, even as far out on the fringes as she was, must be glamorous and exciting. Truth was, it was a regular job. Nothing more, nothing less.

The set for the show was on the spare side. There were two big overstuffed chairs that looked wonderfully comfortable for curling up in front of the TV, both upholstered in some nubby black fabric, and a couple of low tables with a matte black finish. The wall behind and the carpet were gray, perfectly neutral and plain. The only real color came from the floral arrangement on the black table in the back—tall, rather sparse, blood red.

"So he's the one."

Glancing over her shoulder, she saw a man standing in the shadows, his hands in his pockets, his gaze fixed on Tremont. He wasn't aware of her, and he didn't seem to notice that he'd spoken out loud. He didn't look like one of the crew, but security had let him in, so obviously he belonged.

"Are you a fan?" she asked, moving a few steps closer to the man.

At first he seemed startled that he wasn't alone, but it quickly faded. He glanced at her, looked at Tremont again, then back at her. "I've read everything he's ever written."

His tone was dry, and he hadn't answered her question—meaning he wasn't a fan? she wondered. "You know, he's probably one of the most talented authors writing in this country today," she remarked.

That earned her a smile every bit as dry as his last words. "So I've heard. Are you his publicist? Cheerleader? Or just a fan yourself?"

She laughed. "I work for Rebecca Robertson, his agent. She let me tag along on this trip on the condition that I stay out of everyone's way, not cause any trouble, and not act like a starstruck fan."

"Are you?"

"Starstruck?" She considered her reaction to Simon—her uneasiness, the intensity of her discomfort beneath that unnerving stare of his, her disappointment—and answered in the affirmative anyway. "Absolutely. I've read all his books numerous times." Finding out that Simon was one of Rebecca's clients had been the highlight of her employment at the Robertson Literary Agency. Actually meeting him was supposed to have been the highlight of her life. Considering how dull and normal her life was, she acknowledged wryly, even with the disappointment, it still might be.

"Tremont . . . I always figured that was a pseudonym. Is it?"

Teryl shifted her gaze to the set, where Simon, Sheila, and the producer were now talking to the beauty queen. Of course it *was* a pseudonym, but few people realized it. Most of his readers assumed there really was a man named Simon Tremont tucked away somewhere, turning out best-seller after best-seller. An enterprising soul could find out the name behind the pen name, but Simon's real name was so common as to be a joke. Every state had dozens, hundreds, of men by that name, and the biography that appeared in his books offered no help. *Simon Tremont lives in the western United States.*

When he had first approached Rebecca weeks ago about doing publicity for *Resurrection*, it had been agreed that his name would remain their closely guarded secret. For a time, until the novelty wore off, he would be in great demand. The only way he could hold on to any sort of peace—other than scurrying back to his Colorado mountain retreat—would be with his real name. Simon Tremont would be famous.

John Smith wouldn't.

That decided, they had gotten into the habit of calling him by his pen name. They didn't want to risk letting his real name accidentally slip sometime. She had gotten so used to it that lately she'd begun thinking of him as actually being Simon Tremont.

"Tremont is the only name I know for him," she lied, turning back to the man. "Speaking of names, mine's Teryl Weaver." She extended her hand, and, after a moment, he shook it.

"I'm John."

What a coincidence, she thought wryly—although John

probably *was* the single most common man's name in the country. "You don't sound like a native—what is it they call people who live in New Orleans?"

"Lucky," came his response.

"Don't I know it. I've been here less than twenty-four hours, and I've got to leave in another thirty or so. I've been thinking about not sleeping tonight so I can use those extra hours for sight-seeing."

He gave her a long look, but didn't respond. It was just as well, because the interview was about to start. The shadowy studio grew even darker, and the lights coned in on the blonde. On cue she smiled a practiced smile and said, "Welcome to 'New Orleans Afternoon.' I'm Tiffany Marshall."

Another smile, a shift to a second camera. "Today we have a very special guest for you. He's been called the master of the psychological thriller. He's one of the top-selling authors in the country. He's written twelve international best-sellers, and lucky thirteen, due in the stores in August, is rumored to be his best work ever. You all know his books and the movies made from them, but until today no one has known the man. Please join me this afternoon in welcoming him for his first interview ever. Ladies and gentlemen, Simon Tremont."

All in all, Magnolia Blos—Tiffany Marshall was pretty good, Teryl decided. She gave the impression that she might actually have even read one of Simon's books, an impression that was no doubt courtesy of the producer, a great fan of Tremont's, who, like John beside her, had read everything Tremont had ever written.

Listening to the interview with half a mind, she turned her head just enough so she could see John. He wasn't drop-dead gorgeous, but he was better looking than anyone she'd seen lately, including Simon. His hair was sandy blond, his eyes blue, his expression intense. This was a man under a great deal of stress—like everyone she knew in business today. There was always a deadline to beat, a meeting to run, an account to land, a promotion to fight for. She wondered if he ever relaxed. She wondered if he ever smiled. He had the sort of mouth that was made for smiling.

She wondered if he was married.

In the dim light, with his left hand in the shadows, it was impossible to see whether he wore a ring, which, of course, meant nothing. She knew enough men whose wedding rings went into the pocket once they'd left the house—she'd known one entirely too well—and plenty of others who didn't care enough to try to hide it.

On the set the hostess was smiling prettily at the camera and asking in an obsequious voice, "Why all the secrecy, Simon?"

He shifted in his chair, just getting more comfortable, but the movement made him look edgy. "The books I write are for everyone," he replied. "They appeal to all ages, all classes, all types. To pull that off, I have to remain in touch with everyday life, with the average American experience. That's far easier when no one knows who I am. Americans tend to make celebrities out of their authors. For instance, it was announced less than a week ago that I would be doing interviews, and now everyone is interested in seeing me on television. Ten days ago no one cared. Now Barbara Walters is asking to do an entire show about me." He looked mildly amazed, but Teryl knew from this morning's meeting that he thought the honor no less than he deserved. His acting skills, it seemed, were almost on a par with his writing skills. "I'm on the network news. And that will surely change the way I see the world, the way I see life. It will surely have to change the way I write."

Teryl shook her head. She recognized the major part of his spiel from an early Tremont novel, the one about the world-famous actor who had lived and worked shrouded in secrecy, who had made a fortune playing anonymous roles behind masks or heavy makeup. Still, there was a certain truth to it. His life *was* going to change. Exactly how depended on him. How much adulation could he embrace? How much worship could he accept without letting it go to his head? Just how much could his ego grow before it became unbearable?

And how would it affect his writing? His books were successful, in part, because he put ordinary people in ordinary situations, then let extraordinary things happen to them.

After all the interviews, all the adoration, all the praise, would he still be able to relate to those ordinary people? Or would he lose touch with them, lose touch with the strength that had brought him such fame?

She waited for the obvious question: *If coming out will change the way you write, then why are you doing it? Why are you tampering with what's proven enormously successful for eleven years?* She assumed she knew the answer already—the man had an enormous ego; he had enjoyed the fortune for eleven years, and now he wanted to bask in the fame—but she would be interested in hearing his answer anyway.

But Tiffany merely continued the interview, harmless questions, harmless answers. It didn't get any better than that one reply, which he'd written years ago and had come close to memorizing word for word. The rest of the questions were simple or silly, his answers stilted and uninspired.

But he would get better. Sheila would work with him, and as he got more comfortable with the interview process, as he graduated to more accomplished interviewers, he would get better.

When it was over, she turned to John. She wasn't sure exactly why—to ask his opinion, to try once again to see if he wore a wedding ring, or just to get another look at him—but he was gone. Somehow, while her attention had been on Tremont, the best-looking guy she'd seen in a long while had slipped away without her even noticing.

That was the kind of luck she had, she thought with a wistful sigh. And D.J. thought two nights in New Orleans and her wicked little survival kit could change all that. Her friend was too optimistic by a mile.

Turning back, she saw Simon approaching her. He didn't look nervous, as she would have, or glad to have the ordeal over with. Instead, there was a hint of annoyance deep in his expression that made her wish, for one uncharitable moment, that she had disappeared along with John.

"What did you think?"

She smiled a bit. "It was fine. You were fine."

"It should have been better."

She was about to reassure him—*Simon, it was your first interview; you'll learn*—when he continued.

"I was all in favor of doing the interview here because of the connection with the New Orleans books, but I should have insisted on a more capable interviewer. They can't expect brilliance when I have to work with talent like that."

Teryl's smile froze in place. His arrogance was another part of her disappointment in him, part of the unpleasant surprise of the man as opposed to the ideal she had admired so long. In reading and rereading his novels, she had never suspected an arrogant Simon Tremont. She had known that he had to be aware of the tremendous talent he possessed, but she had never sensed this.

"Oh, well . . ." He brushed it off with an impatient gesture. "What do you have planned for the rest of the evening?"

"I thought I'd go sight-seeing—head down to the French Quarter."

"Sounds like fun. How about if I join you—"

Rescue came in the form of Sheila Callan. "Not so fast, Simon." Holding a videotape in one hand, she slipped her free arm through his. "A tape of the show. We can use it to prepare for the next interview. We want you to be perfect next time out." The woman spared only the briefest of dismissive glances for Teryl. "We won't need you tonight, Teryl. Enjoy playing tourist."

She was about to make her escape when Simon stopped her. He didn't touch her, but merely raised his hand as if he were going to. It was enough to keep her in place against the wall. "Will I see you tomorrow?"

Another forced smile. "Of course." She was taking an evening flight home, while both Simon and Sheila were scheduled to leave at 9:00 A.M., but she would spare a few minutes to bid them farewell in the hotel lobby.

"Breakfast?" he suggested. "In the courtyard? At seven?"

Inwardly wincing, she agreed, then immediately felt guilty, because that steely gaze of his could see her reluctance. She was convinced of it. Besides, it wasn't as if he were a thoroughly unlikable person. He just had some rough edges that needed smoothing. He'd lived alone up there in his mountains for so very long that he'd forgotten how to relate to people. Maybe he'd never been very good at it; maybe that was partly why he had locked himself in such solitude in the first place.

Compensating, she offered a warmer acceptance. "I'd love to have breakfast with you. I'll meet you there."

After another moment's scrutiny, he nodded, broke the contact, and walked away, Sheila at his side, and Teryl gave a soft sigh of relief. The interview had gone as expected, it was a warm day, and she had the rest of the evening free. She was going down to the French Quarter, and she was going to have some fun. She was going to make the most of her last night in the city.

She hadn't gone more than twenty feet when someone called her name. Turning, she saw John once again. This time they were in the well-lit hallway, and she could see that he definitely was not wearing a wedding band—and, if his tan was anything to judge by, he never had worn one. At least, not in a very long time.

"Where are you headed?"

"The French Quarter."

"Alone?"

She nodded.

"Want some company?"

She hesitated only a moment. She was a bright woman. She knew better than to go off with a strange man, but it was early June in New Orleans and the Quarter was crowded with tourists. They would never be alone, would never be away from a crowd. What could it possibly hurt?

She accepted his offer, and they left the studio together. It was a six-block walk along Chartres Street to Jackson Square, a walk that he didn't seem much interested in filling with conversation. She asked him questions, but his answers were vague and insubstantial. He'd lived in New Orleans a while, he admitted, and had come there from somewhere else. He had moved around a lot. She supposed in the TV business, that was often necessary.

"Are you married?" she asked as they crossed yet another narrow and crowded street.

He looked at her and, for the first time, smiled. It was slow and sweet—and, yes, his mouth was very definitely made for smiling. "No, never have been. Are you?"

She shook her head.

"Too busy with your career?"

That made her laugh. "It's a job, sweetheart, not a career. I'm a glorified receptionist and gofer."

"But it brought you to New Orleans. Not a bad job."

"No, it isn't." She pushed her hands into the pockets of her shorts. She had opted for comfort this afternoon—knee-length shorts in cream, a white silk blouse, and a vest woven in cream, crimson, and green. She was glad now that she had. The clothing was flattering and cool, and John's looks were, sometimes when she caught them, hot.

"So why aren't you married?"

They reached Jackson Square, and for a moment she simply stood motionless on the sidewalk. She could live down here, she decided, in one of those apartments that overlooked the square. She could have breakfast every morning at the Café du Monde, could sit on a bench every day and listen to the music, admire the artists, and watch the tourists. She could be totally lazy. Decadent. Dissolute.

At least for a day or two, before her very small savings account ran dry.

"I met a man," she said at last as they began moving again. "He was handsome and charming, and he swept me off my feet. We worked together, cooked together, and played together. We slept together and, for a while, on a part-time basis, we even lived together. And then he asked me to marry him. I said yes." She gave John a sidelong look. "But his wife said no."

"And so you're never going to trust a man again."

That had been exactly her attitude in the beginning. All men were pigs, all men deserved to suffer, all men were unworthy of her trust. In fact, she *hadn't* trusted a man since Gregory, not fully. "I just use them for sex."

"That must make you real popular back home," he said drily.

"Of course," she replied with an airy smile, although it

was far from the truth. She hadn't been involved with a man in longer than she cared to recall. The last time she'd been lucky in either her sex life or her social life was ancient history, and that, she decided, was too depressing a subject to linger on now. It was a warm summer evening, she was in the exotic French Quarter, and she was with a handsome man.

Maybe, she thought with another long look at John, just maybe her luck was about to change.

She was lying.

John wasn't a great judge of people—it wasn't easy when he was never around anyone—but he knew Teryl Weaver was lying. She wasn't the kind to indulge in casual sex, no matter what she said. It was in her eyes, in her quick but unsteady smile, in her manner. He wished she was, wished he could say, "Let's go to your hotel and fuck our brains out," and know that she would go—damned if *he* wouldn't—but she wasn't the type.

Besides, he wasn't here to get laid. This was business.

But who said business ruled out a little pleasure?

He wondered what she knew about the man passing himself off as Simon Tremont. He wondered just how involved a glorified receptionist and gofer was in the business of the Robertson Agency. At the very least, she would have access to the files. She would be able to tell him where the new Simon lived. She would know where his royalties—where *John's* royalties—were being sent.

That man . . . John hadn't known what to expect when he had bribed his way into the studio—an apology, perhaps, accompanied by an admission from Morgan-Wilkes that it had all been a hoax. He *hadn't* expected that man—that completely normal-looking man who had sat there with the pretty hostess talking as if he were Simon Tremont, acting as if he believed it himself.

Maybe he did. If he was crazy enough to come up with such a plan and crazy enough to put it into action, maybe he was crazy enough to believe his own lies.

He'd looked so unimportant, as unremarkable and every-day-average as John himself. He didn't look brilliant or crazy or tremendously talented. He didn't look dangerous. He didn't look like the kind of person who would even read a book like *Resurrection*, much less be able to write it.

But, according to Candace Baker at Morgan-Wilkes, he *had* written it.

And, according to Candace, it was the best book Simon Tremont had ever done.

He had taken John's book—his story, his idea—his *life*, damn it—and had done it better. *Better?* Hell, John hadn't even been able to finish *his*.

He had looked so normal, so *sane*. Who would believe that he'd moved into John's life? That he had destroyed John's home? Who would believe that he was capable of even formulating such a plan: choose a reclusive writer, learn his books, master his style, locate him, acquire his outline for his next book, write the book, and steal his life? Who would believe that he had—so far—been successful in carrying it out?

John knew he'd done all those things—*knew* it—and even he couldn't believe it. *How?* How had the guy come up with such an outrageous idea? How had he located John when other people had tried and failed? How had he gotten his hands on the outline for *Resurrection*? How had he learned to write like John?

How?

Maybe *he* was the crazy one, John grimly acknowledged. Maybe he had finally snapped. Maybe he had never been Simon Tremont. Maybe it had all been an elaborate fantasy—Simon, the books, the house, the checks. Maybe the burden of guilt he'd been carrying for the last seventeen years had finally become more than his mind could bear, and he had just gone all-out nuts.

Pushing away the headache those thoughts brought, he forced his attention back to Teryl. With her sleek brown hair, brown eyes, and easy smile, she was pretty in a wholesome, innocent way. She was too trusting—her affair with the married man proved that—and too naive. Coming down here with *him* proved that.

And she was, in ways totally at odds with her naïveté and wholesomeness, sexy as hell.

On his one night in Denver last week, he had picked up a pretty blonde—high-priced, charming, dressed to thrill—but she hadn't aroused even the faintest desire in him. Maybe it had been because she was a pro, because he'd known it would be greed, not desire, that brought her to his bed, because he'd known it would be a performance, her movements practiced, her responses rehearsed.

There would be nothing practiced, nothing rehearsed, about sex with Teryl.

And there was nothing realistic in thinking about it, either, he admitted grimly. Her brazen bluff about men aside—*I just use them for sex*—the only way he was going to get into Teryl Weaver's bed tonight was to seduce her, and he had been alone so long that he wasn't sure he remembered how.

She was window-shopping, ignoring the crowds, often looking back to make sure he was behind her. He stayed close, patiently following her inside one shop after another.

"So you're not a fan of Simon Tremont's," she remarked when they turned off onto Governor Nicholls and the crowd thinned enough that he could walk beside her.

"He's written some good stuff."

"Good stuff?" She tilted her head to one side and studied him as they walked. "I've been reading him since I was in college. He's written some of the best 'stuff' out there."

"How about—" John swallowed hard. He couldn't say the title, couldn't bring himself to speak it aloud. "How about the new one?"

"*Resurrection*?" She stepped onto a green-painted stoop, then down again. "You can see for yourself in August. Morgan-Wilkes is really pushing to get it out as quickly as possible. It's scheduled to hit the shelves in about eight weeks."

Eight weeks. That was a major rush. With his previous books, turned in on time, he'd faced a wait of nine to twelve months before they appeared in the bookstores. Was the publisher simply eager to take advantage of all this free publicity Tremont was drumming up?

Or was *Resurrection* really that good? Teryl hadn't said.

"Have you read it?"

"He brought it into the office last week while Rebecca and I were both gone to lunch. I got back first and started reading it, but she came in just as I was finishing Chapter 2. She went home and took it with her, and didn't come back the rest of the week."

"So what did you think of the first two chapters?"

They walked nearly half a block before she stopped and faced him head-on. "It was the most impressive work I'd ever read."

John shifted uneasily. Her manner answered his question far better than her words. People had spoken like that about his own work in the beginning, in that hushed sort of reverent tone. Awed. Admiring and, at the same time, envious. Worshipful.

And now Teryl was speaking the same way about the man pretending to be him.

He ignored the jealousy that sparked, turned her with a touch back toward Jackson Square, and asked, "Is this the first time you've met Tremont?"

"We've talked on the phone a few times in the last couple of months, but today was the first time we'd met face-to-face."

"What do you think?"

She paid the shop windows they were passing more attention than they deserved before finally giving him a sidelong glance. "You know you're asking my opinion of the man who, in a roundabout way, makes my job possible. The commissions he pays the agency would be enough to keep it in business and prospering even if he was our one and only client."

"No, I'm asking your opinion of—What did you call him? One of the most talented—and certainly most mysterious— authors in the country. You've been a big fan from the beginning. Is he everything you wanted him to be?"

She gave him another of those long, studying sideways looks before evenly asking, "Can we go to Pat O'Brien's?"

So she wasn't going to answer, which most likely meant that she either didn't like the man or had been disappointed in him. John found some small satisfaction in that and in the knowledge that she wouldn't have been disappointed by the real Simon Tremont.

They cut through the square again, circled around the cathedral, and headed toward Bourbon Street and, a short distance before, Pat O'Brien's. A waiter seated them in the courtyard, out of the sun but near the fountain. Toying with the souvenir menu, she looked around, smiled at him, and sighed contentedly. Was she really so easy to satisfy? he wondered. A two-day trip to New Orleans, part of it spent working, a walk around the Quarter, and drinks at the district's most famous bar—that was enough to give her that contented look?

"I envy you," she remarked lazily.

"Why?"

"Living in New Orleans, being able to come down here whenever you want. I've lived all my life in Richmond. It's a nice enough place, but you don't hear many people say, 'This year we're going to save our money and spend our vacation in Richmond, Virginia.' I'd love to live here."

Personally, he thought being able to live your entire life in one place was pretty special. He could have happily lived all his life in California if he hadn't screwed it up before it'd barely gotten started.

If he hadn't ended Tom's life before *it* had barely gotten started.

"So why don't you move?" he asked, refusing to spoil the moment with thoughts of his brother and what should have been.

She glanced from him to the fountain, then back again. "You're kidding, right? I can't just pack up and move to a strange city, not having a job, not knowing anyone, not being familiar with the place."

"Why not? You say that you're little more than a glorified receptionist. You could do that here. And we've already established that you're not madly in love with anyone back home. What's keeping you there?"

"It's my *home*. It's where I've always lived, where my family lives. Besides, I'd be lonely. I don't know anyone here."

"You're a pretty woman. You're friendly. And your only interest in men is sex without strings." Just saying it gave him a sharp reminder of how long he'd been without. "You would make friends pretty quickly here."

"I could never afford the kind of life I'd want on the kind of salary I earn. I'd want a place down here in the Quarter, one of these gracious old homes with a courtyard and, of course, the lifestyle that belongs with such a place. On what I make, I'd be lucky to be able to afford a closet somewhere out in the suburbs, and that's hardly worth leaving home for." With a wistful smile, she changed the subject. "Where are you from?"

"Los Angeles."

"How long did you live there?"

"Nineteen years."

"Do you still have family there?"

"A couple of aunts and uncles." And parents who pretended that their second son was dead. Who wished that he'd never been born.

"How long has it been since you've been back?"

"Seventeen years."

"Don't you miss it? Don't you miss your relatives and the house you grew up in and the old neighborhood? Don't you miss the friends who still live there?"

He watched as the waiter served their drinks, then pulled some money from his pocket to pay for them. He missed everything about L.A. It had been a hell of a place to grow up. There had always been something going on, always something to do—either with the whole family or his friends but more often than not with Tom or Janie. Thanks to their parents, they'd been closer than just brothers and sister. Tom and Janie had looked out for him, had smoothed things over for him. They'd made his life easier.

And, in exchange, he had destroyed their lives.

Realizing that she was waiting for an answer, he shrugged. "Things change. I miss the L.A. I grew up in, but there's nothing for me there now." Not his old home. Certainly not his family.

"I bet you were a surfer. You have that beach bum look."

He acknowledged that with a raised brow.

"Were you any good?"

"It was the only thing I did well."

She gave him a long, measuring look, then smiled just a little. Secretively. "I doubt that," she murmured.

He felt the pull of desire again—hard, impossible to ignore. He wanted to prove her right, to show her that, hell, yes, he could do something else and do it damned well. He wanted to see her wearing exactly that same little smile again, and nothing else.

I want you.

How would she react if he said that aloud, if he was that blunt? Would she be put off? Flattered? Insulted? Or maybe tempted? Would she brush him off and dump him as quickly as possible?

Or would she say yes?

Back at the square, he'd thought she wasn't the type for casual sex. Now he wasn't so certain. Oh, she certainly didn't make a habit of one-night stands . . . but if the look in her eyes was anything to judge by, there was a first time for everything. A drink or two, dinner, and he just might have something to occupy his night for the first time in far too long.

And if he was wrong? If he was just so damned horny that he was misjudging her?

Then he would pick up a damned hooker, he thought with a scowl, and take his best shot. It wouldn't be the best time he'd ever had, not by any means, but if he closed his eyes and pretended it was Teryl . . .

Yeah, he could damn sure get off on that.

Chapter Two

They finished their drinks and walked more, talked more. By the time they finally approached Bourbon Street, the sun was setting in the western sky, the temperature had dropped a few cooling degrees, and her hormones, Teryl decided dizzily, were just plain out of control.

And the blatant packaging of Bourbon Street's most popular commodities—women and sex—didn't help any.

Under normal circumstances, she would have been embarrassed by the photographs of naked women, the signs advertising sex acts, the sometimes lurid and all too base come-ons. But the alcohol had taken the edge off any inhibitions she might have had a few hours ago, and she was getting aroused just from the way John kept looking at her. If he didn't invite her home soon . . .

She would be in pretty sorry shape, she thought with a sigh.

The exhalation drew his attention her way. "Something wrong?" As he asked the question, they turned onto a quiet, nearly deserted street that led back toward the river, leaving the music, the tourists, and the hustle of Bourbon Street behind.

"No, nothing."

"Getting tired?"

"No. I'm fine." She offered him a breezy smile. "This has

been a lovely evening, John. It's nice of you to spend it with me."

He gave her a hard look. "Don't think that," he said, his voice low and serious. "I'm not a nice man, Teryl."

His harsh words made her uneasy, and she tried not to look at him, tried not to search his face to see if he meant them. But her gaze kept sneaking his way, darting from the sidewalk ahead or from the storefronts on her left but finding no answers in his scowl. When she responded at last, she kept her voice even, her tone pleasantly stubborn. "You've been nice to me."

"Only for my own reasons."

"And what are those reasons?"

Abruptly he stopped walking, and she drew up short a few feet ahead. She stood motionless for a second, then slowly turned to face him. He looked at her, glanced away, then back again, and, like that, the grimness was gone, but the intensity remained—intensity sharpened by desire. "I want to take you to bed."

Her heart was pounding, and her mouth had gone dry. She could laugh, treat it as a joke, and he would probably let her. He would accept her rejection as if he'd never expected anything else, and he would make some excuse to leave or—if he was a better man than she'd given him credit for—he would spend the rest of the evening with her, being nice, and would say a polite good night when it was over.

She could handle it that way. She *should* handle it that way. Back home she *always* handled things that way.

Just once, just for tonight, couldn't she be different?

Slowly she turned away from him, facing the shop window behind them. The store was closed, but lights shone on the display there—Mardi Gras masks of ceramic and gold and feathers, strings of cheap plastic beads and, on a mannequin, an intricately worked costume. "I always wanted to come to New Orleans for Mardi Gras," she said softly, seeing the items through her own reflection, through John's reflection behind her.

"You like drunken celebrations?" His voice was uneven

and tinged with disappointment. Did he think that changing the subject was her way of politely rejecting him?

"I've never been to one," she replied. She took a deep, shaky breath. "But I always thought it would be fun, just once in my life, to be wicked in New Orleans."

He came a step closer, then another, until he was right behind her—not touching her, but close enough for her to feel. Close enough for her to hear his slow, measured breathing. Close enough to make her tremble. "You don't have to wait for Mardi to be wicked," he murmured.

She continued to stare in the window as he moved that last step closer, but she couldn't identify anything she saw—just blurs. Colors. Shapes.

He wasn't subtle, wasn't at all shy. With that single small encouragement, that single voicing of a vague desire to be wicked, he rested one hand—big, strong, and gentle—on her shoulder and slid the other inside her vest, cupping her breast, squeezing it, gently pinching her nipple. Later she would feel guilty, Teryl acknowledged, but at that moment the sensations were exquisite and were only heightened by the fact that they were standing on the sidewalk where anyone might pass, where anyone might see them.

He moved his left hand from her shoulder, circled his arm around her waist, and pulled her back snug against him so that his erection pressed against her. Nuzzling her hair away, he touched his mouth to her ear and murmured, "Unbutton your blouse for me, Teryl. Let me touch you."

Her hands trembled when she raised them to the first button. This was crazy, wrong—reckless as hell—but, damn it, back home in Richmond, she had never been crazy, had never been reckless.

She'd only been wrong. At least this wrong would, for a time, feel incredibly right.

The blouse had a V-neck with a drapey collar, and she needed to open only two buttons to give him access to her breasts. He covered one with his hand, his palm warm and rough against the softness of her skin. When he touched her nipple, it grew hard, and he stroked it, toyed with it, making it swell even more, making her tremble even more. Oh, hell, yes, this felt incredibly right.

At the end of the block, voices sounded, one calling to another, the second answering. The reality of being discovered made her stiffen, but he didn't release her. He didn't remove his hand from her blouse. He simply moved her a few feet past the store and into the narrow alley. An iron gate, eight feel tall and spiked on top, blocked the way only a few feet back, but it was enough to offer some privacy. It was enough to make her sink back against the brick wall and guide his mouth to hers.

He kissed her, taking her mouth hard, thrusting his tongue back to her throat. She was aroused and wet and he was so damned hard that she was in pain. Whimpering aloud, she reached for his erection, but as soon as her fingers closed around it, he groaned and forced her away.

Grabbing her hand, he moved back onto the sidewalk and hesitated, then started toward Bourbon Street, pulling her along behind. Where were they going? she wondered, pulling her blouse together, making an effort to keep up. His house, her hotel, or someplace anonymous and nearby?

Her question was at least partially answered when he signaled a cab parked on the opposite side of Bourbon. The driver met them at the corner, and John opened the back door, ushering her into the seat. "Where you want to go?" the driver asked in accented English as John closed the door.

He looked at her, waiting for her to answer, and for one moment—one very brief moment—she wondered if he had lied about being married. If he had, she didn't want to know. She didn't care.

Her throat tight, her voice husky, she gave the cabbie the name of her hotel.

Before the cab had pulled away from the curb, John was kissing her again, making his way down her throat. She let her head fall back and bit her lip on a moan when she felt his hands inside her blouse, cupping her breast, lifting it, pushing her nipple up to meet his mouth. To be wicked in New Orleans, she had requested, and surely this had to qualify: riding in a cab down the streets of the French Quarter, letting a man she'd known only a few hours suckle her breast while the driver behind the wheel sneaked leering glances in his rearview mirror.

And she didn't give a damn. As long as John didn't stop . . .

They reached the hotel all too soon—and not soon enough. Her face hot—hell, her entire body was hot—Teryl arranged her clothing while he paid the fare; then he hustled her inside, past the front desk, through the lobby to the elevators. Moments later they were in her room, kissing, touching, arousing. He released her only to move her suitcase from the bed; she withdrew from the daze of need only to retrieve the beribboned packets from D.J.'s zippered pouch.

They undressed quickly, the process made more difficult by kisses and tantalizing caresses, and he took one of the condoms she offered. They barely made it to the bed before he was inside her, deep, damn, so hard and deep inside her, stroking, thrusting, and kissing, hot, greedy kisses that demanded passion and offered satisfaction.

It was wild and frantic, lasting only moments before he came, before she came with him, tremors rocketing through her. They lay for a moment, utterly still, utterly breathless, and then he grinned ruefully. "Damn."

Damn, indeed, she silently agreed as she raised her hands to his face. It had taken only minutes—only *seconds*—and yet her heart was racing. Her muscles were quivering. Her entire body was trembling with such intensity, such fierceness.

As she stroked his jaw, he turned his head and placed a damp kiss in the center of her palm—a small thing to send such a shiver through her. When she glided her hands lower, along his throat, across his chest, over his nipples, it was his turn to shudder. She could feel it everywhere their bodies touched, could feel it best deep inside where her body still sheltered his.

He repaid the pleasure of her caresses with a kiss, long, hard, and intimate, making love to her mouth, sliding his tongue deep inside, arousing hungers just satisfied and new ones not yet experienced. Just that kiss was enough to make her ache. It was enough to make her move restlessly beneath

him. It was enough to make her arch against him, to shamelessly ask with wordless pleas for more, and that was enough
to make him give it. Harder kisses, hot and wet, on her
mouth, her throat, her breasts. Rough touches, squeezing,
rubbing, his hands on her breasts, between their bodies, between her legs, making her groan. Deep, powerful thrusts, relentless, driving, pushing her higher, harder, drawing a
second breath-stealing orgasm from her only seconds before
he came a second time himself.

He withdrew from her body and moved to lie beside her,
gathering her close. Her heartbeat slowed, and her ragged
breathing evened out as hazy satisfaction wrapped itself
around her. If this was what came of being wicked on vacation, she thought, allowing herself one small smile in the
near darkness, she would have to try it more often.

The ringing of the telephone jerked John back from the
drowsy fringes of sleep, his eyes opening wide, his heart, for
a moment, racing. Many were the nights when his old nightmares had awakened him in much the same way, making
him break out in a cold sweat, tightening his chest, and making sweet air hard to come by. Those nights he had usually
found himself in unfamiliar places—he'd spent the first six
years after Tom's death on the run, trying to hide from the
horror and the guilt—and he had always been alone. Tonight
he was once again in a strange place.

But he wasn't alone. Teryl—long, soft, naked—was
curled at his side.

Shifting away from her, he reached for the phone on the
night table, cutting off the second ring in mid-peal, and answered with a sleep-roughened hello.

There wasn't silence on the line—he could hear slow,
steady breathing and, muted in the background, the sound of
a television—but the caller didn't speak. There was a sense
of surprise, as if he—John knew it was a man, knew it with a
certainty he couldn't explain—as if the man had been so
completely unprepared for anyone but Teryl to answer that
he couldn't quite deal with the fact that someone else had.

John didn't repeat his greeting, didn't ask if anyone was there. He simply listened to the measured breathing and the frenetic commercial for the latest in new cars until, after a moment, the man broke the connection.

After hanging up, John slowly resettled in bed, and Teryl snuggled right up against him, as if it were the most natural thing in the world. How natural would it seem to her, he wondered, if she knew how rarely he had shared his bed with a woman? How comfortable would she feel if she knew that the only woman he had been intimate with in the last five years had taken her payment in cash rather than pleasure?

Not to imply that Marcia had been a prostitute. She'd been a nice enough woman, alone after three bad marriages, with two kids practically grown, and trying to make ends meet on a waitress's salary. Their arrangement hadn't started as business. She'd been working the evening shift at a nameless little bar about twenty miles from John's house, and he had been trying to drink enough to take the edge off the loneliness that sometimes seemed to envelop his life. When he had been the only customer remaining at closing time, she had invited him home with her, and, desperate to avoid his own company, he had gone.

He had returned time and again, not often but regularly enough. She had never asked for money, had never hinted that she wanted anything more than he did—a connection, however brief, however meaningless, with another human being—but he had offered the cash and she had accepted. It had developed into a mutually satisfying agreement: the generosity of her spirit repaid by the generosity of his wallet.

Then, after a time, she had told him not to come back. She had met a man and was giving marriage another try. By that time he'd been so caught up in the misery of *Resurrection* that he had barely missed her. He couldn't even remember now how long ago it had been. Six months? Eight? Twelve?

Too damn long.

And now here he was with Teryl.

For a moment he allowed himself the pleasure of stroking her hair. It was soft, reaching almost to her shoulders, and so fine that when he tangled it around his fingers, as soon as he released it, the strands slithered free again. Softness—feminine softness—was one of the textures missing from his life, and it fascinated him in all its forms: the silkiness of a woman's hair. The gentleness of a womanly smile. The soothing timbre of a woman's voice.

The warm and infinitely soft welcome of a woman's body.

Teryl had certainly welcomed him.

Leaving the television station with her had been a mistake, he acknowledged grimly, and seducing her had been a major mistake. If not for the fact that he had misled her about himself from the beginning, he would say that neither of them was more responsible than the other for what had happened here—the attraction had certainly been mutual—but he *had* misled her. He had concealed his identity, had lied to her all evening, had taken her to bed under false pretenses. She would never willingly help him now.

So he would accept her unwilling help.

He would *force* her help.

He would give her no choice.

Deliberately he chose to ignore the discomfort those thoughts brought. He was intimately acquainted with guilt; he had lived with the emotion for so long that it had become a part of him. Guilt over his own failures, guilt over Tom, over Janie, over the irreparable harm he had done his family . . . He could bear the added burden for using and abusing Teryl Weaver. If he accomplished his goal, he would salve his conscience by rewarding her for her help. Marcia had often told him he was a generous man. He would make things right.

And if he didn't accomplish it . . .

Trapped in the softness of her hair, his fingers curled into a tight knot. He would do it or die trying. It was as simple as that.

After a moment, he pulled away and sat up, then swung his feet to the floor. It was cool in the room—the air-conditioning had been turned low to combat the muggy June heat—and chills rippled along his skin as he tucked the covers securely around Teryl. Gathering his clothes from the floor, he carried them into the bathroom, where he flipped on the light and dressed without facing himself in the mirror. He didn't need to see his reflection. He didn't want to look into the emptiness that was his own face, that reflected his soul. He didn't want to face himself, knowing what he was planning, knowing *how* he was planning to use an innocent woman.

After a moment, he returned to the bedroom, standing for a moment in the doorway, letting his eyes readjust to the lower light. One lamp, its bulb dim and shaded, burned on the corner desk, and at the single wide window, the drapes were open, the sheers closed, softening and diffusing the light that spilled in from outside.

The room was reasonably neat, as if, beyond sleeping last night and dressing this morning, she had spent little time here. A few pieces of clothing were scattered across the dresser, and two pairs of shoes—three-inch heels and thick-soled sandals—sat underneath the desk. One of the heels stood perfectly balanced on the plush carpet. The other lay discarded on its side.

Everything else, except the clothing she had hastily stripped off a few hours ago, was still in the suitcase. There was no briefcase to be found, and her shoulder bag, barely bigger than his palm, had room only for a compact, a tube of lipstick, what looked like about two hundred dollars tucked into an inside pocket, and a packet of tissues.

Lifting the suitcase to the dresser, he made a quick search, hoping for something, *anything*, that might give him a clue about the man she had come here with. He found lingerie, a pair of walking shoes and cushioned socks, a cosmetics case, a bottle of reasonably expensive cologne whose fragrance now clung to his own skin, and a couple of Mardi Gras masks wrapped in newsprint and secured with masking tape. He didn't find an organizer, a notebook, or anything interesting beyond her return ticket home. It was still in its original envelope, bearing the airline's return address in the upper left corner, and was for a flight scheduled to leave New Orleans late tomorrow evening.

He was returning the ticket to its envelope when writing on the back of the envelope caught his attention. Moving closer to the window, he pushed back the sheer curtain so a little more light fell on the hastily scrawled notes. There was the name of the hotel, the TV station, and the time for this afternoon's interview. Underneath that, she had written, *Simon, Wednesday, 9 a.m. Sheila??*

Was the man masquerading as Simon Tremont flying out at nine tomorrow morning, or did her note have some other meaning—a meeting, perhaps, or another interview? There was one way to find out: to be downstairs long before nine o'clock tomorrow morning. If the guy checked out before then with suitcases in hand, John would know he was leaving, and he could . . .

He could do what? Follow him to the airport? Try to find out what airline he was flying, what flight he was taking, and where it was taking him? That wasn't much of a plan. If they didn't get separated in morning rush hour traffic, if he somehow stayed close enough to find out which airline the cab—or, more likely, the same white limo that had delivered the guy to and from the television studio—took him to, if he somehow managed to follow him to the proper gate and get a flight number, all he would learn was where that particular flight was going—and with his luck, it would be to some busy hub like Dallas or Atlanta. He wouldn't find out anything about the guy's connecting flights. He wouldn't find out the man's ultimate destination.

Or there was his other option. Teryl. Letting the curtain fall, he returned the envelope to the suitcase before turning to look at her. She was so slender that it seemed she made little more than a long narrow mound under the rumpled covers. She was lying on her stomach now, her arms folded beneath the pillow, her face buried in its softness, her hair spreading out like rich, glossy brown silk. He swallowed hard as his arousal, so recently sated, returned again as strong as ever. He would like to take her like that—to undress and raise the covers and slide over to her, to kneel behind her, to lift her just enough to slip inside. She would have to rise to her knees to accommodate him, would have to tilt her hips back to allow him entry, would have to press her body downward to hold him there.

Just the idea—her bottom pressed snug against his groin,

the long downward curve of her spine stretching out in front of him, as intimately joined as a man and woman could ever be without any other contact—was enough to make him hard. Contemplating actually doing it was almost enough to make him come.

Again he swallowed hard as he turned away. His face was hot—with guilt, with shame, and the damnedest hunger he'd experienced. His body was even hotter.

He would be downstairs in the lobby tomorrow morning, and he would wait—but not for the man claiming to be Simon. He would wait for Teryl, and he would tell her his story, and he would try to persuade her to help him.

And when she didn't believe him? When she got angry, when she realized that she had spent her evening indulging in intensely passionate sex with a man who was certifiably nuts and the anger turned to fear?

He would do what he had to do, and may God forgive him, because Teryl never would.

Celebrity was going to be a wonderful thing, the man calling himself Simon Tremont acknowledged as a young brunette, dressed all in white and just a tad too eager to please, escorted him through the hotel restaurant and outside through broad French doors. The courtyard beyond was a popular place for hotel guests to breakfast on an early summer morning, when the sun hadn't yet risen high enough to clear the building next door, when it was still reasonably cool, when the splashing of water in the stone fountain still sounded refreshing and the fragrance of the flowers planted in pots and beds around the tables hadn't yet become overpowering in the heavy air.

It was a truly lovely place . . . and for the next hour or so, it was off-limits to all hotel guests except those he had invited to join him.

Ah, yes, after a lifetime of obscurity, celebrity was going to be fun.

The others were already seated at the table closest to the fountain: Sheila Callan, looking tough and brittle in spite of the elegant cut of her clothing; her fair-haired assistant whose name he couldn't recall, whose jobs included running interference and satisfying her boss's every need, including, Simon suspected, those of a sexual nature; and the gum-chewing photographer with the expensive cameras that, as far as Simon could tell, hadn't once in twenty-four hours come off from around his neck. They were all there and waiting. Waiting for *him*.

All except Teryl.

His jaw tightened. He didn't need to check his watch to know that she was late. He had been deliberately late himself, had wanted to play the star role and keep them waiting just to prove that he could. Yes, he thought with a faint smile, it was petty, but he was Simon Tremont. He could be petty if he wanted.

But Teryl wasn't here. Teryl, who was along on this trip only because *he* had decreed it, had stood him up.

He sat down at the table, accepted the damask napkin that the pretty hostess offered, and took the menu that she'd opened to the breakfast selections. So what was sweet Teryl doing this morning that precluded her from keeping their breakfast date?

Most likely getting laid.

He'd been surprised last night when he'd called her room on the off chance that she might be in, that she might be interested in meeting him in the lounge for a drink. The man who had answered had sounded barely awake . . . or barely recovered from a bout of hot and heavy sex. His presence there had been so unexpected that Simon had hung up without saying a word, which had been best since the only ones in his mind at that moment had been angry.

It wasn't that he begrudged a woman her fun. He just hadn't expected it of Teryl. All of his contact with her—admittedly, little enough—had led him to believe that she was quiet, a little reserved, less than sophisticated. He had figured her for the type of woman who valued commitment ahead of physical pleasure. He had certainly expected some measure of caution from her; she was too smart to pick up a stranger, to invite him back to her hotel, to take risks with her safety, her health, and even, in these times, her life in exchange for one night's diversion.

But, apparently, that was exactly what she had done. She had gone to the Quarter, picked up a total stranger, and let him screw her.

If Sheila hadn't interfered and insisted that he return to the hotel with her yesterday afternoon, *he* would have gone to the Quarter with Teryl. Maybe *he* would have been the one in her bed last night. He *should* have been the one. After all, wasn't he her only reason for even being here?

Frankly, though, when he'd come up with the idea of having her come along for this interview, it hadn't been with the intention of bedding her. It had been, plain and simple, a test of his power. Coming out in the open after eleven years of hiding behind his pseudonym, after eleven years of living in anonymity, had been a new, frightening—and heady—concept for him, and he had wondered just how far he could push it. How much could he ask for? How much would being Simon Tremont get him?

And so he had made his first request—Teryl's presence— and Rebecca Robertson and Sheila Callan had agreed without so much as a blink of an eye. Next he had asked for a limo. For a suite in this, one of New Orleans' oldest and finest hotels. For first-class, red-carpet treatment from everyone at the TV studio and everyone at the hotel. For the courtyard to be barred to other guests while he dined this morning.

Little things, little wishes, and every one of them granted. Every one of them an affirmation of the power Simon Tremont wielded. Would that power have gotten him into Teryl's bed last night? Maybe, he thought as a white-jacketed waiter served him champagne in a delicate flute and a plate of fruit—fresh, exotic, prettily arranged on a crystal dish. Or maybe not. Someday . . .

He speared a plump strawberry with his fork and watched as the red juices dribbled onto the plate, then lifted it to his mouth.

Someday he might find out.

*   *   *

Teryl was slow to awaken, in spite of the steady, annoying beep of the alarm clock on the nightstand. After a minute or two, she flung one arm out from beneath the covers, searching for the clock in its usual spot between the lamp and the phone, only to belatedly remember that she wasn't in her bed in her tiny little house in Richmond. This was a hotel room, and the city was New Orleans. The Crescent City. The Big Easy.

The city, she thought with a drowsy smile half-buried in the pillow, where being easy could help good little girls be very, very bad.

Then she realized that she was alone in the bed, and her smile slowly faded. Lifting her head from the pillow, she listened for a moment, but the only sound was the soft whoosh of the air conditioner. She would have to leave the warmth of the bed and go around the corner to see if the bathroom was occupied, but already she knew that it wasn't. John's clothes were no longer scattered around the floor with her own, her suitcase had been retrieved from the floor where they'd dropped it and placed on the dresser, and the room simply felt empty. No one else was sharing the space with her.

John was gone.

Pushing her hair from her face, she rolled onto her back, tucked the covers securely around her, then felt the sheets on the opposite side of the bed. Even under the blankets, they were cold. Other than the crinkled plastic packets on the opposite nightstand—*three* of them, she thought, her amazement tempered only slightly by shame—there didn't seem to be any sign that anyone else had ever been there.

She sighed softly. In a way, it had been sweet of him to make his exit while she was asleep. After all, waking up for the first time with someone you knew wasn't always easy; she imagined it could be pretty darn uncomfortable with a stranger. So he had saved her from the awkwardness of dealing with him in the bright morning light—of dealing with the morning-after regrets. Right now he was probably home, showering, getting dressed for work, likely giving no thought at all to her.

Which was exactly what she should be doing. Simon was expecting her downstairs for breakfast, and she—

Rolling over, she snatched up the clock, then swore aloud. Simon was expecting her at seven o'clock, and *she* had forgotten to reset the alarm last night. It was already seven-forty-five.

Throwing back the covers, she got quickly to her feet, allowing only a moment to wince at her body's soreness. She'd been so long without passion in her life that she'd forgotten the residual aches and pains that could accompany it. The discomfort was shameful, because she hadn't even known the man, and wicked, because she had certainly enjoyed learning the few things she did know about him.

It was also bittersweet, because she would never have such an experience again. Once she returned home to Richmond, she would go back to being the same old Teryl, the one who still, in spite of last night's pleasure, believed her mother's teachings about sex, that bad girls did and good girls didn't. D.J. had been bad since she was fifteen and couldn't imagine any other way to be, but Teryl had always been good—good enough, D.J. had always gently taunted her, for both of them.

But just this once, she thought with a self-satisfied grin, *she* had been the bad one.

And it had been very, very good.

She adjusted the thermostat as she passed it, then went into the bathroom. It was empty, confirming her suspicion that John had been long gone. She wondered when he had left, it he had lain with her most of the night or if he had simply waited for her to fall asleep before he made his exit. She would have liked to say good-bye, she thought wistfully. She would have liked one more kiss, one more appreciative look from those hazy blue eyes of his.

She would have liked to thank him.

Quickly she brushed her teeth, then dressed in one of her two remaining outfits, a sundress that was light and cool. It was long enough that she needn't worry about hose, bright enough that for a quick trip downstairs she didn't have to bother with makeup to put color in her face. She would find

Simon, she planned as she slipped into a pair of sandals, and apologize profusely for missing their breakfast date. She would see him off to the airport, then come back up, shower, and head off to explore the city again.

She intended to play the I-can't-believe-I'm-actually-here tourist role to the hilt. She was going to ride the St. Charles streetcar, gawk at the beautiful houses in the Garden District, take a buggy ride around the French Quarter, eat beignets at the Café du Monde, and walk until she could walk no more. After sitting by the river to regain her strength, she would venture out again, would eat too much and listen to the musicians in Jackson Square, watch the street performers and shop for souvenirs.

Then tonight, like Cinderella, her magical time would end. At nine o'clock she would board a plane bound for Virginia, and tomorrow morning she would be plain Teryl Weaver again. She would go to work every day, meet friends for lunch, and spend most evenings home alone. She would occasionally wonder why there were no men in her life, and when one did eventually come along, she would wonder why she had wanted him in the first place.

But, she thought with a melodramatic sigh, she would always have New Orleans.

And one wicked night with John.

Sliding her room key into her pocket, she left, taking the elevator to the lobby. It was a cavernous place, the marble floor softened by Oriental rugs, the high ceiling decorated with ornately carved moldings and medallions, and the walls painted with thirty-foot-tall murals depicting scenes from the city's history. Lush plantings created small islands of privacy for the sofas and chairs scattered about, and the babble of water from a central fountain served to mute the sounds of guests coming and going.

She was passing the massive marble registration desk when she heard her name. Turning, she found the man she was looking for standing beside one of the free-form beds that provided the lobby with its rich, earthy scent. With the fronds of a fern providing the perfect backdrop for his bright-patterned shirt and faded khaki trousers, he looked more at home, she thought, than he had anyplace else since arriving in the city. He looked more at ease. More handsome.

Less threatening.

She approached him, her apology bubbling over before she reached him. "Simon, I'm so sorry about this morning. I forgot to set the alarm last night, so I overslept. I'm really very sorry. You should've called and awakened me instead of waiting."

"It's all right. We barely missed you."

His expression, as close as it had come to friendly since they'd met, didn't waver with his last words, which somehow served to make his barb a little sharper. Holding her head a little higher, she smiled coolly. "I'm glad I didn't inconvenience you, but I do apologize. So . . . what did you think of your first foray into the world as Simon Tremont?"

"It's been an experience."

"A pleasant one?"

"For the most part, yes."

"You know, what you talked about in the interview yesterday will come true. People will recognize you wherever you go. Fans will want your autograph. Your life is bound to change significantly. Are you prepared for that?"

His direct blue gaze locked with hers, making her feel once again like an insect under observation. "I've been preparing for that for eleven years," he said with a quiet, and not entirely pleasant, intensity. "I've lived and worked in obscurity, Teryl. The time has come to accept the recognition that's rightfully mine. I've earned it." Before she could think of a response to that, he continued in a more normal tone. "I understand you're staying over in the city."

"Only until this evening. I want to see everything I can. I may never get the chance to come back." Glancing around the lobby, she saw Sheila at the cashier's end of the registration desk. Any moment now the other woman would finish and would join them, offering her a totally disinterested farewell and hustling Simon outside to the limo that was probably already waiting.

It pained Teryl to admit that she wouldn't be sorry to see them go.

"You must have spent a lot of time here," she remarked, watching as Sheila and the clerk apparently debated some charge on the bill.

"Why do you say that?"

Her gaze shifted back to him. Her first thought was that he must be joking, but his expression proved her wrong. He was asking the question in all seriousness, and, for a moment, all she could do in response was shrug awkwardly. "The books. The Thibodeaux books." The five books that had won him throngs of fans. The five books that, more than anything else, had stirred her interest in New Orleans. The five books that had been the reason for making his public debut here.

He shrugged, too, brushing off the books as inconsequential. "You can learn an awful lot about a place without ever going there, Teryl."

"But you captured the city so perfectly—the atmosphere, the feel, the flavor."

"Do you think a writer has to experience something to write knowledgeably about it? That a romance author writes all those love scenes from her own personal experiences? That a mystery author has to commit a murder to be able to describe one? That a science fiction author has to interact with aliens—" He let his question trail off, then shrugged again before continuing in a condescending tone. "It's imagination, understanding, attention to detail, and a way with words. It's called talent, Teryl. I travel some, but most of my research is done at home. I watch travelogues and read travel magazines. I get specific information from local tourism offices. Talent takes care of the rest."

Another disappointment, Teryl thought, even though her expression didn't reveal it. Each of his books was so intense and so well done that she'd always read them with a mental image of Simon in the places where his stories unfolded. She had just *known* that he had lived for a time on the same rugged Maine coast where the protagonist of his first book had lived, that he was intimately familiar with the stately old mansion in the Florida Keys that dominated his third book, that he knew every inch of the Georgia swamp covered by the characters in his sixth book.

And she was wrong. As D.J. had predicted, another illusion was lost.

When Teryl had first found out that she was being included in this trip, her friend—ever more sensible, always more cynical—had tried to warn her that she was setting herself up for disappointment in a major way. Simon Tremont was just a man, she had lectured, and New Orleans was just a city. It was unlikely that either one could live up to Teryl's sky-high expectations. In D.J.'s opinion, she had romanticized the hell out of both of them, had built up their virtues and denied them their flaws, and she was going to find reality one hell of a disappointment.

At the time, Teryl had argued the point. She was realistic. She knew Simon had flaws, and she knew that the grace and elegance, the history and the romance and the exotica, of New Orleans were balanced by the seamier side intrinsic to any big city.

So she'd been half-wrong. She *hadn't* been prepared to allow Simon his flaws. She had wanted him to be exactly as she had imagined him for eleven years, and he wasn't. He wasn't even close.

But she had also been half-right. The city, at least, was everything she could have asked for and more.

"So, Teryl, you finally made it," Sheila said in greeting as she and her assistant joined them. "Have a late night?"

"I overslept," she replied unnecessarily.

"Overindulging can make you do that," Simon responded, his tone mild, his expression smug. As if he knew—not suspected, but *knew*—what she had done last night.

For a brief moment Teryl met his gaze. Controlling a shiver of uneasiness, she evenly asked, "What makes you say that?"

"This is N'Awlins, darlin'," he replied in a creditable imitation of a Cajun accent. "Overindulging is a way of life down here."

And had he learned *that* from a book? she wondered cynically.

"We'd better be going." Sheila gestured toward the entrance, and her assistant left, most likely, Teryl thought, to summon the limo right up to the door. After the woman disappeared, Sheila extended her hand. "At least you weren't a problem," she said brusquely, giving Teryl's hand a quick squeeze.

"From anyone else I would think that was rude," Teryl said. "Coming from you, I'll take it as a compliment. Have a good flight. Simon." She didn't intend to shake hands with him, but he had other ideas.

Holding her hand firmly between both of his, he offered her a smooth smile. "Thank you for coming."

"Thank you for inviting me. I'm sure I'll be talking to you sometime."

"Oh, I'm sure you'll be seeing me around. After all, I'm going to be famous." He gave her a mocking smile, then lifted her hand and pressed a kiss to the back of it. When he released her a moment later, he walked away without a backward glance.

Teryl remained where she was, watching through the glass doors as the limo glided to a stop and the doorman hurried over to open the rear door. His bearing imperious in spite of that damned silly tropical shirt and the rumpled pants, Simon climbed in as if he were well accustomed to such luxury, then disappeared from sight behind the heavily tinted windows.

"It's nothing that a bar of soap and some hot water won't wash away."

The voice came from behind her and sent a shiver of recognition up her spine before she turned around. Leaning against a pillar there, hands shoved in his pockets and most definitely a sight to behold, was John.

She had a number of expectations regarding last night's brief encounter: regret, embarrassment, guilt, even—the use of condoms notwithstanding—a little worry about safe sex and pregnancy. But she hadn't expected, after awaking alone, to see John again.

And she hadn't expected such pure, simple pleasure at the sight of him.

She moved a few steps toward him before stopping. "What was that about a bar of soap?"

He nodded downward, and she followed his gaze to her hands. The fingers of her left hand were rubbing hard at the back of her right hand, as if she could erase the fact of Simon's kiss, as if she could wipe away the feel of his touch. Flushing, she pushed her hands into her pockets. "I didn't think . . ." That she would ever see him again. Obviously, she'd been wrong, she thought, feeling again an intense rush of pleasure. Here he was, handsome, sexy, and waiting for *her*.

"So the great Tremont is on his way back to . . . Where is home these days?"

She opened her mouth, then closed it and smiled wryly. "You know I can't tell you that."

"I figure it never hurts to ask. Sometimes you don't get an answer, but sometimes . . ." The look he gave her left no doubt what he was thinking as he softly finished, "Sometimes you get lucky."

Like last night. *She* had sure as hell gotten lucky last night. She was flattered that he felt the same way.

Before she could find words to respond, he went on. "What are your plans for the day?"

"Sight-seeing."

"Anything in particular you want to see?"

She answered with a shrug and a grin. "Everything I can cram into the next twelve hours or so."

"Want an expert tour guide?"

Just as she'd done yesterday when he'd offered to accompany her to the Quarter, she hesitated, momentarily considering the wisdom of going off with a stranger, and then, just as she'd done yesterday, she dismissed any reason for concern. After all, after last night, he wasn't exactly a stranger. Not anymore. "I'd like that, if you're sure you can spare the time."

"I have all day." Moving away from the pillar, he came to stand in front of her, very close, and raised one hand to smooth a tucked and pleated strap on her sundress that was already perfectly smooth. She knew the action was deliberate, allowing him to touch her in a manner that was both circumspect and intimate, his intention to remind her of what had passed between them last night. But she carried all the reminders she needed: the memories, the utter satisfaction, and the stiffness of a well-used—and appreciative—body.

Resisting the urge to lay her hand over his, to guide it lower, to do something bold and brash and potentially embarrassing, she cleared her throat and took one step back, placing a little breathing room between them. "I'd like the company," she murmured. "Just give me time to change, pack, and check out so I won't have to come back later this morning."

"Good idea. We'll leave your bags in my truck; then I can take you straight to the airport when it's time."

She nodded her agreement; then, on impulse, she asked, "Do you want to come up to the room?"

For a time, he remained silent, his gaze directed at the murals high above the lobby. Finally, with an awkward glance, he shook his head. "I'll wait here."

Nodding again, she gave him a regretful smile, then started toward the elevator. Before she turned away, though, she thought she saw a flash of disappointment in his eyes. Real? she wondered. Or merely her own disappointment reflected back at her?

John watched until she stepped inside the elevator and the doors closed, blocking her from sight, and then he squeezed his eyes shut and swore silently, viciously. Why hadn't she turned down his offer to spend the day with her? Why was she making this so easy for him? Last night should have taught her a lesson, should have taught her that he wasn't to be trusted. He had offered to show her the Quarter, but she'd seen little enough of it and all too much of him. If she were a sensible woman, if she would let go for one moment of the image of New Orleans as an exotic, romantic adventure to be experienced to the fullest, she would have told him thanks but no thanks and run the other way. Back home in Richmond, no doubt she was eminently sensible. Here in New Orleans, no doubt she was living for the moment.

Before the morning was over, she was going to regret it.

When she had awakened alone this morning, she had thought she would never see him again. That was what she'd started to say a moment ago: *I didn't think* . . . It had been in her eyes, too expressive by far. She had thought that he'd gotten what he wanted—easy sex—and walked out of her life. It would have been better for her if he had.

He'd left her last night for a number of reasons—so he could move from his hotel into hers, so he could have the peace and privacy necessary to plan his next move, so he wouldn't be distracted by the sweet temptation of her body, and so he could surprise her this morning. Obviously, he had.

Just as she had surprised him. *Do you want to come up to the room?* Jesus, yes, he had wanted to go, still wanted to go. He wanted to lock the door behind them and pull back the curtains and watch her undress in the warm morning light. He wanted to lay her down in the sunlight, wanted to bury himself inside her as he had last night, only this time he wanted more than merely to feel. He wanted to see. He wanted to see her eyes widen when he pushed into her, wanted to watch her nipples harden as he stroked them. He wanted to see her muscles quiver when he moved inside her. He wanted to see her body grow tight and hard in that moment before she came, and he wanted to see it soften afterward.

He wanted to make love to her again. And again. He wanted to forget all the reasons he was there—Simon Tremont, *Resurrection*, and all the other failures in his life— and simply lose himself in her again. He wanted, for the next few hours, to forget about what he was and just be who he was: John Smith, a man with more sorrows than any woman deserved. A man who would give up a good part of his soul for a little more pleasure in her body. A man who would give up a part of his life for a little of the normalcy of hers.

The hell of it was, she would have let him. That shy little look of hers had been as much of an invitation as his blunt words last night—*I want to take you to bed*. If he had accepted, she would have taken him to her room, would have taken him to her bed. She would have satisfied his arousal and eased his hunger for intimacy.

But it would have been wrong. With the plans he had for her, making love to her now would be very wrong.

His muscles stiff and aching from tension he couldn't control, he walked over to the entrance and gazed out at the street beyond. It was crowded this morning as people went about their everyday routines. What was life like for them, for people who worked regular jobs, who lived normal lives with families, responsibilities, and obligations? What was it like to be as ordinary as the parking valet waiting outside the door, as conventional as the cop standing on the street corner?

There had been a time when he had been almost ordinary, almost conventional, when he had worked regular jobs for regular people—eight-hour days, five-day weeks, and a paycheck twice a month. He had almost fit in with everyone else then, although he hadn't had a family, hadn't had anyone depending on him for anything. What he remembered most from that time was the unhappiness. Dissatisfaction. Being unable to find the things he'd wanted most out of life: escape. Peace. Redemption.

Now he had a highly successful career. He had more money than he could spend in a half dozen lifetimes. There were few constraints on him—no time clocks, no money worries, no dealing with incompetent bosses or difficult coworkers.

And still no escape, no peace, no redemption. He hadn't stopped craving them. But he *had* accepted that he would never have them. He had accepted his life as it was. And then someone—that man—had stolen it from him.

With a sigh, he turned away from the doors and went back to the chair where he'd spent the last few hours waiting. He had seen the man claiming to be him come off the elevator and disappear into the restaurant for breakfast. He had seen him come out again less than an hour later, his entourage—minus Teryl—close on his heels. He had watched the man go upstairs, had waited for him to come down again, and had studied him as he stood only a dozen feet and a bed of thick ferns away. He had listened, catching most, though not all, of his conversation with Teryl.

We barely missed you.

The time has come to accept the recognition that's rightfully mine. I've earned it.

It's called talent, Teryl.

Oh, I'm sure you'll be seeing me around. After all, I'm going to be famous.

Arrogant bastard. That was *John's* recognition he was talking about, *John's* talent, *John's* fame. There was nothing about Simon Tremont's career that that son of a bitch could rightfully lay claim to.

Except *Resurrection*. The most impressive work Teryl had ever read. He needed to see it. He didn't want to. He didn't want to read what someone else had made of his life, of Tom's and Janie's lives. He didn't want to find out, God help him, that someone else had done it better, but he had to know. He had to know just how talented this impostor was. He had to know just how much of his life this man had taken.

Getting a copy of the manuscript was one more favor he would have to ask of—would have to coerce from—Teryl. It was one more thing she would do for him, however unwillingly, because he wouldn't—couldn't—give her a choice. It was one more thing she would hold against him.

Across the lobby, the elevator came to a stop and she stepped off, and, at that moment, the only thing in the world he wanted her to hold against him was her body.

His choked-back laugh was bitter. Jesus, that was corny. He was in sorry shape when he could even think such a line.

She had pulled her hair back and clipped it off her neck. The dress was gone, folded away in the suitcase the bellman behind her carried; now she wore an outfit similar to last night's—shorts, shirt, vest, and sandals. It should have looked casual as hell, but the shorts were pleated and cuffed and pin-striped white on khaki, the shirt tailored and crisp, the vest fitted and also pin-striped, khaki on white. She looked very neat, very pretty and feminine in spite—or perhaps because—of the clothes' obvious masculine influence.

She smiled when she saw him, a sweet, welcoming smile that made him feel every bit the bastard. She was happy to see him, happy to be spending the day with him. She expected him to show her the sights, to share the last day of her fantasy vacation with her, and, before nine o'clock tonight, to deliver her safely to the airport.

By 9:00 P.M., he figured, they would be somewhere in Georgia or maybe even South Carolina. By 9:00 P.M., she would be afraid of him . . . or would hate him . . . or both.

It took her a few minutes to check out, took a few minutes more for the valet to retrieve his Blazer from the garage and deliver it to the main entrance. Teryl climbed into the front seat, glancing back as he placed her suitcase on the rear seat beside his own. Why didn't the suitcase strike her as odd? he wondered as he circled around to the driver's seat, climbed in, and closed the door, automatically hitting the lock button as he did so. She believed he was a businessman, an employee at the television station where Tremont's interview had been taped yesterday. She believed he lived right here in New Orleans. So why didn't she find it curious that he would keep a suitcase in his car?

"I really appreciate this," she said, reaching for her seat belt after she watched him fasten his. He had learned seventeen years ago about wearing seat belts. "What are we going to do first?"

"How about breakfast?" He turned onto Canal Street and headed away from the hotel. "I know this little place. It's not too far."

"How about the Café du Monde?"

He forced himself to smile and hoped it bore some semblance of normalcy as he looked at her. "Everybody goes to the Café du Monde. I bet you had beignets there yesterday."

She nodded. "If they hadn't been busy—and I hadn't been meeting Simon—I could have sat there all day and watched the people."

"You'll get to go there again," he assured her. When this was all over and done with, he would compensate her for the inconvenience, for all the lies and the fear, for all the things he was doing and all the emotions he would be putting her through, and he was a generous man. Not that money made everything all right—he was living proof of that—but it could certainly help. "Just trust me on this."

Tilting her head to one side, she studied him for a moment, then smiled. "Okay," she agreed, and that was it. All he had to do was ask, and she would give.

God help her, she was naive, he thought grimly, wrapping both hands around the steering wheel, focusing his gaze on the road ahead as he turned onto the access ramp that led to Interstate 10. It was no surprise that the married boyfriend she had mentioned last night had been able to fool her so successfully, no surprise that the man posing as Simon Tremont could also fool her.

It was no surprise that *he* was fooling her right now. She had been kidnapped, and she didn't even know it.

As they drove, she chatted easily about the shopping she had done yesterday and the places she would like to go today, requiring little in response from him. He had no responses to give, no polite comments to make. All he had was tremendous guilt, tension, and uneasiness over what he'd done, over what he would do in the next few days.

Her voice rose and fell as she gazed out the windows on her side, on his, straight ahead, and occasionally behind them. She was curious about their surroundings, even though there was nothing of much interest along this particular stretch of interstate. All the glamor of the city had been long since left behind.

His sister had once shared the same sort of unapologetic inquisitiveness . . . until she had been forced to do a lifetime of growing up in a few short hours. She had been so young— seventeen, just finishing up her freshman year in college and anticipating summer vacation. Then, on a hot June day, she had made the biggest mistake of her life—a mistake that Teryl had also just made: she had gotten into a car with John.

Janie had survived that trip, just barely. He hoped— prayed—Teryl's chances were better.

By the time they started across Lake Pontchartrain, Teryl had at last fallen quiet. She had stopped looking around and was staring instead at the road in front of them, sneaking occasional looks at him. Her hands were folded tightly together in her lap, and from time to time, she fidgeted in the seat. Finally, she gave in to the doubts that he knew were building inside her. "This place we're going to . . . what's the name of it?"

John glanced at her, but he didn't answer. He didn't have any lies prepared, and, considering the only truth he had to offer, he preferred to delay it.

Nervously she moistened her lips. "Is it much farther? Because, you know, breakfast is no big deal. I'd rather do some sight-seeing than eat anyway."

Looking her way again, he saw the fear she was trying to control. It darkened her eyes and turned her knuckles white. He hated that she was afraid of him, hated that she had reason to be. Offering nothing—neither explanations she wouldn't accept nor reassurances she wouldn't believe—he turned back to the road as they passed a sign welcoming them to Slidell. From there it wasn't far to Mississippi. When would she realize what was happening? When they crossed the state line? Eighty or ninety miles later when they left Mississippi for Alabama? When would she panic? When would he have to tell her the truth?

"Hey, John," she began, a slight wobble in her voice. "There's a McDonald's at the next exit. If you're really hungry, why don't we just stop there and grab something, then head back? There are so many things I want to do today, and—" Breaking off, she watched as they passed the exit without slowing down. She edged around slightly in the seat, not so much to face him, he thought, as to put a little bit more distance, no matter how slim, between them. It was then that she saw the suitcases in the back.

Understanding crossed her face, accompanied by stark terror that drained her of color and made her breaths come in swift, audible little puffs. "J-John, I don't want t-to go any farther. If you don't want to take me back, just stop. I'll take a bus or a cab or—or rent a car or something. Just—just let me out."

"I can't." He stared straight ahead, his features stony, tension radiating from his entire body. "I won't hurt you, Teryl, I swear, but I can't take you back. I can't let you go."

"This is crazy." Her voice rose in the unsteady treble of panic. "You can't do this. You can't just—just—"

"Kidnap you?" He looked at her then, his gaze dark, his mouth set. "I already have."

Chapter Three

*T*hat look was enough to send shivers through Teryl's veins. It was bleak and shimmered with an anger barely controlled. "From the moment you walked out of the hotel with me, you've been my hostage," he said, his voice hard.

Then, abruptly, his control shattered. "Damn it, Teryl, are you crazy? You let a total stranger pick you up, you take him back to your hotel and have sex with him, you go to sleep while he's still there, and the next day you get in his car and drive off with him? Don't you have better sense than that?"

It was ridiculous, so ludicrous that if she weren't so scared, she would laugh. He was *chastising* her. The man who had *kidnapped* her was scolding her because she had made it so easy for him.

But she *was* scared, too scared to be amused.

"Look, John, it's not too late," she pleaded. "You haven't really done anything yet. If you'll just let me out, if you'll just let me go, I won't tell anyone, I swear I won't. I just want to go back to New Orleans. Please, John . . ."

"I told you I can't. I need you."

Images of last night in bed flashed through her mind. That kind of need—was that what he was talking about? Surely not. The sex had been great, but not *that* great. He was a handsome man; he could easily find any number of willing women who could do far more for him than she could.

But what else could he possibly need from her? She had nothing to offer. She wasn't rich or famous or important. She wasn't worth a ransom to anyone who could afford to pay one. What could anyone want with a plain average woman who lived a plain average life in Richmond, Virginia?

"I—I don't—" She drew a breath, but couldn't fill her constricted lungs. "I don't understand."

"You will. We've got a long trip ahead of us. By the time it's over, you'll know everything." Turning cynical, he added, "You won't believe it, but you'll know."

"Where are you taking me?"

"Home." He looked at her again. "We're going to Richmond."

She stared out the window, a dozen hopeful thoughts racing through her mind. Maybe he just had a warped sense of humor. Maybe this was all a joke, albeit a very bad one. Maybe it was a bad dream, one that she would awaken from any moment now with an entire lovely day ahead of her just waiting to be spent in New Orleans. Or maybe . . .

Just ahead the interstate split. Interstate 12, according to the signs, headed west to Baton Rouge, I-59 began its northeast trek toward Meridian, and I-10 curved east. She grew a little stiffer as John changed lanes, as he chose the highway that would take them to the East Coast, the highway that led to other highways that led to Richmond.

Maybe he really had kidnapped her.

Maybe he was crazy. Granted, he wasn't wild-eyed and raving, but that didn't make him stable. There was something too dark in his eyes, something too intense and still about his manner. There was that sudden burst of irrational anger because she'd been so foolishly trusting. There was that bleak insistence that he needed her. Maybe he *was* insane. Maybe he was going to kill her.

Unless she stopped him. Unless she somehow escaped from him.

She acted impulsively, reaching across the console, grabbing for the keys in the ignition with one hand, for the steering wheel with the other. The truck swerved crazily from the right lane to the left, then back again, as John, startled by her

actions, struggled to regain control. It took him only an instant, with his greater strength, to shove her back into her
seat and hold her there with one arm, and only an instant
more to bring the Blazer to a screeching halt on the shoulder
of the road.

Before they were stopped, she clawed free of him, yanked
open the seat belt buckle, and tried to open the door, but it
wouldn't budge. Hearing him swear viciously, she searched
for the button that would unlock the door, her fingers scraping over nothing but the scuffed panel in the place it was located in her own car. At last she found the switch and shoved
it back, then pushed the door open. Her arm was tangled in
the seat belt, though, and by the time she worked free, he had
hold of her again, his fingers wrapped around a fistful of
shirt and vest, pulling the fabric taut against her throat as he
held her dangling, half in, half out, of the vehicle.

"Damn it, Teryl!" With another curse, he hauled her back
inside, leaned across, and slammed the door, then scowled at
her. That look alone would have been enough to pin her in
the seat, but he didn't rely solely on intimidation. He also
used one big, strong hand wrapped around her forearm, forcing her back against the seat.

Breathing hard, she scowled back for a moment; then her
flash of courage gave way to fear. Her heart was racing so
fast that her chest hurt, and the way he was pushing against
her made it hard to breathe, and his fingers—the same fingers that had stroked her so gently just last night—were gripping her arm so tightly that she imagined she could actually
feel bruises forming. He was hurting her, and the certainty
that he would hurt her more if she gave him reason brought
tears to her eyes.

"Please don't," she whispered.

He stared at her, hard and threatening, for a long time;
then, with one more black curse, he sank back in his own
seat, tilted his head back, and closed his eyes. He didn't release her arm, but at least he stopped pushing so hard.

The silence in the Blazer was heavy, broken only by his
breathing and her own occasional sniffle as she fought the
urge to cry. She was in real trouble here, she berated herself,

and all she wanted to do was curl up in a corner and sob like a frightened child. She had to regain control, had to find some way to hold on to it until another opportunity—a better opportunity—for escape presented itself. It helped to focus her attention on her arm, still locked in his grasp, a mix of aches and throbs and blessed numbness. Tomorrow it would be a dozen shades of black and blue . . . but she would be so grateful to have survived today that she wouldn't care.

After a time, she risked a look at John. His eyes were still closed, and his expression was troubled, so very troubled that it sent a shiver through her.

Dropping her gaze lower, she looked for a moment at his shirtsleeve before realizing exactly what it was she was looking at. He wore a dress shirt, long-sleeved, the cuffs rolled up practically to his elbows. The shirt was neatly pressed and pristine white except on the right sleeve, where a line of irregularly shaped stains dotted the fabric. They were like splatters from a child's paint box, red, bright red.

Blood red.

With a heated flush, she remembered the way, only moments ago, she had struck out at him, digging her nails into his skin in an effort to free herself. She could see welts, puffy and red against his tanned forearm, could see a few pale scrapes where she had scratched but done little damage.

And then there was the blood.

"Your arm is bleeding." She said it flatly, without emotion, without the slightest hint of the satisfaction she took in knowing that her frantic efforts to free herself had caused him at least a moment's pain, with no sign at all of the shame that accompanied the satisfaction.

"It'll stop." He sounded just as flat, just as unfeeling, but his fingers tightened briefly around her arm. Then he raised his head and looked at her, his blue gaze locking with hers. "Don't make me hurt you, Teryl." His words were simple, his voice quiet, but it was a plea as surely as her own earlier request—*Please don't*—had been.

"Let me go," she whispered.

"I can't. I need you."

"Please . . . I'm not worth anything to you. I don't have any money. My family doesn't have any money."

"I don't want money."

That wasn't a reassuring response. If he was telling the truth, if he had no interest in making a trade of her freedom for someone's cash, then what did that leave for a motive? Sex? Murder?

Or both?

Choking back another pitiful plea, she forced herself to ask quietly, calmly, "Then what do you want?" It was better to know what she was up against. Better to find out what he intended to do to her than to wait, unknowing and afraid, for him to do it.

On the highway an eighteen-wheeler rushed past, buffeting them, rocking the Blazer from side to side. He glanced in the rearview mirror, then, still holding her arm, awkwardly shifted into first gear and eased the truck farther onto the shoulder. There he shut off the key and turned in his seat to face her. "You never asked my last name."

Teryl felt a twinge of discomfort, tinged again with a sense of the ludicrous. There was an accusation in the cool, weary tones of his voice, a rebuke that said she should have been more careful, should have shown some caution, some morals, some simple common sense. It made her own voice defensive when she replied, "I didn't think it was necessary. I didn't think, after last night, that I would ever see you again."

But when she had, when she had turned around in the hotel lobby and he'd been standing there, she had been pleased. She had been *so* pleased. Now she wished he *had* just walked out of her life. Now she wished he had never walked into it. And the words he said next merely doubled her wishes.

"My name is John Smith . . . but you probably know me better as Simon Tremont."

Teryl stared at him—simply stared. Of all the things in the world he could have said, that was the one she wasn't prepared for, the one she never would have expected. He thought—he believed—he was Simon Tremont.

Oh, God, he *was* crazy. She had been kidnapped by a crazy man. She had gone to bed last night with a man who was absolutely, one hundred percent, certifiably insane, and now he'd taken her hostage. Now he intended to—To do what? To play out his fantasy? Was she meant to be the adoring fan to his Tremont? Was that why he'd chosen her— because she hadn't bothered to disguise her admiration for the author? Or was it simply because she'd been so damned easy?

"If I let go of you," he began haltingly, "will you promise not to try to get away?"

The crazy man was asking for a promise, and she gave it readily, unable to speak over the lump of fear in her throat but nodding instead. He didn't immediately release her, and when he did, it seemed an effort. She could actually see him forcing his fingers to loosen, to uncurl from around her arm. The instant she was free, she drew back as far as possible, and she cradled her arm to her chest, using her free hand to gingerly rub the place where he'd held her. Already her skin had turned red and dark purple. Already there was swelling around the damaged tissue that would soon form ugly bruises encircling her forearm in roughly the same shape as his hand.

And he expected her to believe that he didn't want to hurt her, she thought bitterly.

Staring out the bug-splattered windshield, he drew a deep breath, then spoke in a flat, unemotional voice. "Tell me what you know about Simon Tremont."

Yesterday he had asked if Tremont was a pseudonym, and she had lied. This morning he had asked where Tremont called home, and her only answer had been a nonanswer. She wasn't going to answer this time, either, she decided. She wasn't going to tell him anything he could use to support his delusions.

But, if she was reading the grimly accepting expression on his face correctly, he didn't really expect an answer. His words confirmed it. "Let me tell you what you know about him. He's been with the Robertson Agency from the beginning. He signed with Rebecca while she was still in New York City, and with his first two books, she earned enough to move the agency to her hometown of Richmond. She had never met Tremont, never even spoken to him—until recently, at least—and neither had anyone else, not even his editor at Morgan-Wilkes. All of their contact with him had been by mail."

So far, so good, Teryl thought. But none of this information was private. Every devoted Tremont fan knew that much. It was all part of his mystique.

"He lives—" John broke off with a pain-filled grimace, then started again. "He lived in Colorado in a place so remote that most people in the area never knew he was there, and he got his mail at one of those mailbox places in Denver. At least, he did until a few months ago."

The muscles in her jaw clenched and tightened. How many devoted Tremont fans knew he'd lived most of the last eleven years in Colorado? How many knew his mailing address had, indeed, been a Denver box? For that matter, how many people knew his real name was John Smith?

But none of that would be impossible to uncover, she silently insisted. In this high-tech age, if you were resourceful enough—and fanatical enough—you could learn virtually anything about anyone. And if you were claiming to be that person you were interested in . . . Well, that was fanatical enough for her.

"You want to know how much Tremont made last year? So much that he quit counting the zeroes on his checks. So much that if he quit the business today and never wrote another word as long as he lived, he still couldn't spend all that money."

"You haven't told me anything that isn't common knowledge," she said, her voice quiet and even, carefully pitched not to upset or anger him. "All of Tremont's fans are well acquainted with the mystery surrounding him. As far as the money, he's the best-selling author in the country. Of course he makes a fortune."

He looked at her for the first time since he'd released her, his troubled gaze settling heavily on her. "Are all of his fans also well acquainted with the fact that the Thibodeaux books are your all-time favorite Tremont books? While they're all asking for Philip's story, do they know that you're more interested in Liane's? That you even included a note with one of his contracts asking if he was going to write her story?"

A chill settled deep in her stomach. Her friends who also read Simon's books knew how much she loved the Thibodeaux series. They knew that, while she found Philip interesting, she was fascinated by the younger sister. But he wasn't her friend, damn it, and not even they knew she had written that note. Hell, *no one* knew except her . . . and Simon . . . and this man. *How?*

"It wasn't a contract," she disagreed, hostility—and fear—sharpening her voice. "It was a royalty statement. How do you know about that?"

"Because you sent it to me, damn it!"

His shout, and all the rage behind it, made her flinch, shrinking back against the door until she could retreat no farther. "This is crazy," she whispered. "How could you be Simon Tremont? I've *met* Simon. I've talked to him. I've sat across a table from him. I've *read* his work."

Lowering his head, he rubbed his eyes with both hands, then blew his breath out. When he looked at her again, the anger was gone, not just controlled but completely hidden behind the blank weariness that etched his face. "You've met a man claiming to be Tremont. What proof did he offer? What proof did you ask for?"

"He knew Rebecca. He knew me. He was the man I'd talked to on the phone. He knew everything there was to know about Simon's business. He knew Simon's real name, knew his address—"

Interrupting her, John recited the address—box, city, and zip code—from memory. "Sound familiar?"

Stunningly so. But she responded almost immediately with a stunner of her own. "He wrote *Resurrection*."

The silence that followed her triumphant pronouncement was repressive, and the rising temperature, too warm now and sticky as the heat from outside seeped in, made it more so. She wished for cool air, for a blast from the air conditioner, for noise or music, for anything to alleviate her discomfort and chase away the suffocating closeness in the cab as John stared at her.

"He wrote *Resurrection*," she repeated, her voice softer now, gentler. "You can't explain that away, can you? If he's not Simon Tremont, how did he come up with the story? How did he write the book that perfectly matches the outline that's been sitting in our files for more than a year? How did he write the best book that Simon Tremont has ever written?"

She waited a moment, but when he said nothing, she gave a little shake of her head. "You can't explain it," she said finally.

"No," he said at last, quietly. Defeatedly. "I can't."

Maybe she had won, she thought, hope rising, expanding. Maybe now he would acknowledge that he couldn't pull this off. Maybe he would turn around and take her back to New Orleans. Maybe he would let her go.

But her hopes were shattered as quickly as they had formed. "I need your help, Teryl." Desperation shadowed his voice, made it unsteady and made her skin crawl. "I'm not asking you to trust me. I'm not asking you to believe me. I just need your help to prove that I am who I say I am. I don't want to hurt you. I'm not going to kill you. But I have to have your help."

Her gaze locked fully with his. "And if I don't give it?"

His fingers knotted around the steering wheel, and a corresponding knot formed deep in her stomach. "Then I'm prepared to take it."

"You're threatening me." Her tone was accusatory, her expression belligerent. "You just said you wouldn't hurt me, and now—"

"It's not a threat, Teryl," he said quietly, silencing her. "It's a promise."

She had never been so utterly miserable in her life.

Teryl rested her head so that the shoulder strap from the seat belt offered some support, but with every bump on the narrow road they were following, her forehead banged against the window, and the muscles in her neck were tight enough to spasm any minute now. Her back hurt from long hours in the same cramped position—as far from John as she could get—and she was hungry, sleepy, and needed a bathroom desperately.

She was almost too miserable to be afraid.

But not quite.

Reaching up, John turned on the map lights, then pulled a road atlas from between his seat and the console and tossed it onto her lap. Sometime this afternoon, somewhere south of Montgomery, he had done the same thing, had instructed her to find a route to Virginia that would keep them off the interstates. She hadn't asked why; she had assumed that it had something to do with all those state troopers they kept seeing, first on I-10, then on 65. Maybe he had thought she would do something crazy, like this morning—something to get their attention, something to force a confrontation.

She had thought about it, had thought about it long and hard, especially when one young female trooper had come up alongside them. She had thought about grabbing the wheel again, about creating enough of a disturbance to get the woman's attention, even about forcing both the trooper's car and the Blazer off the road, but she had hesitated, too afraid of failing and rousing John's anger, and after a moment the woman had passed them and disappeared up ahead.

D.J. would have done it. Of course, D.J. never would have gotten herself into such a mess. Oh, she would have picked up John last night; she certainly would have taken him to a hotel room—although not her own—and she would have used him so thoroughly that he wouldn't have had the energy to move for a few days. Then she would have walked away without even a backward look, and if he had dared show up at her hotel this morning, she likely wouldn't have given him the time of day.

But D.J. had guts. Teryl was just a spineless, helpless, sniveling fool.

D.J. took control. Teryl took orders.

She had followed John's orders, what few he had given, all day. Now, atlas in hand, she sat waiting for the next one.

"See how far it is to the next town."

"What state are we in?" she asked wearily.

"Should be Tennessee. The last town was Morrison—no, Morrisville."

She flipped through to the Tennessee map, found the highway they were on, and began searching for Morrisville. When she didn't find it, she checked the index, but it was no help. "There's no Morrisville on this road. Are you sure we're in Tennessee?"

"We have to be. Jesus, we've been driving all day."

She couldn't remember seeing a sign welcoming them to Tennessee, but then she hadn't been paying attention to signs. She had spent most of the day staring blindly out the window, coming to life only when he prompted her for further directions. Now, seeing the white glow of a highway sign ahead, she squinted to make out the numbers underneath the state designation. No wonder she hadn't been able to find Morrisville; she had been looking on the wrong road. She was bending over the map, searching for the new road, when John swore with such viciousness that she flinched, and the atlas slid from her limp fingers.

He brought the Blazer to a stop on the grass at the side of the road and jerked the map from her lap where it had landed. "For God's sake, Teryl, we're in Mississippi," he muttered darkly, flipping through the pages to the M's. "How the hell did you manage that?"

Mississippi. They had left Mississippi behind a long time ago. If they were back in it again, then that meant they'd spent the entire day driving in a giant circle. It meant that after a long, edgy, tense day, they were little, if any, closer to Richmond—assuming that John truly intended to take her there. It meant another miserable long day to make up for today.

The prospect was too disheartening. Feeling as if she just might fold in on herself, she couldn't even find the energy to defend herself. "I'm not the one driving," she said listlessly.

"But you're the one giving directions."

"And you're the one not following them."

"Maybe they're not worth following. Don't you know how to read a map?"

"I've never tried. I've never driven anyplace where I needed a map." The discomfort in her neck was making its way steadily up into her head until even her scalp ached. Forget food. She wanted a bathroom and a bed. She wondered if, while he studied the map, he would let her make a quick trip into the dark woods that flanked the road. She doubted it. He had let her to to the bathroom only once today, when they had stopped for gas, and then only after he had checked out the small, smelly, windowless little room himself. Lunch had been candy bars, chips, and Cokes from the same gas station.

She wished for a little of that Coke now to wash down a handful of aspirin from D.J.'s survival kit. What would her friend think when she found out—*if* she found out—that her gag gift had truly become a small part of Teryl's survival?

What would she think when she went to the airport tonight to pick up Teryl and Teryl never showed? How long would it take her to start worrying? How long before she called the hotel in New Orleans? How long before she found out that Teryl had checked out this morning and disappeared?

Not that D.J.'s concern would do much good. No one had seen Teryl leave the studio with John yesterday. No one in the Quarter would likely remember them, except the cabbie who had taken them to the hotel, and he'd had little interest in her face; they had given him so much more to ogle. Probably no one at the hotel had noticed her with John this morning, not even the valet who had brought the Blazer. She was just so damned forgettable, and John had seemed so normal. There had been nothing about them that warranted attention.

Being forgettable seemed an awfully poor reason for dying—and even though he'd denied it, she wasn't convinced that John wasn't going to kill her. Who could predict what a crazy person would do?

Resting her forehead against the cool glass, she closed her eyes. "If I don't take some aspirin soon, I'm going to throw up, and I can't take aspirin without something to drink, and I can't drink anything without going to the bathroom first."

He glanced at her—she felt the weight of his look—then closed the road atlas, tucked it away, and shut off the lights. "There's a town about ten miles up. Maybe they'll have a motel and we can stop for the night."

Twenty-four hours ago the thought of spending the night with him had been exciting, erotic, pleasurable. Twelve hours ago it would have filled her with fear and loathing. Tonight she didn't care. He could do whatever he wanted, as long as she got access to a bathroom and a bottle of aspirin first and he let her sleep—or went ahead and killed her—afterward.

The town was little, the business district no more than six blocks long. The three restaurants they passed were closed, she noticed, as was the only grocery store. So much for a real dinner. The only sign of activity in the entire place was at the convenience store located at the opposite end of town, right across the street from the lone motel.

Teryl's smile as she surveyed the place was mirthless. It was two stories, no more than sixteen rooms, cinderblock painted an offensive pale green, and ugly, God, so ugly. If there was a name, it was well hidden; the painted sign above the door read simply Motel. Underneath that hung a sign that read Vacancy. There was no way to add a No in front of it, she noticed. The owners probably found the likelihood of ever being completely booked so remote that they hadn't wanted to waste money on something they would never need.

John parked off to the side of the office, shut off the engine, and turned toward her. "You have to come in with me. Stay at my side and keep your mouth shut. Don't even make eye contact with the clerk. Understand?"

When she nodded, he removed his seat belt and got out. She didn't move at all until he came around the truck and opened her door; then she unclicked the belt, gave it a tug to make it retract, and slid to the ground. The parking lot was mostly dirt with a sparse layer of gravel scattered over it. It felt unsteady beneath her feet, and *she* was unsteady above. Her legs were stiff, her muscles protesting the exertion after so many still hours in the Blazer.

He walked at her side, his hand resting lightly on her right arm, just above her elbow. To anyone watching, it probably seemed a courteous gesture, providing a bit of support to someone who was obviously shaky after a long day's travel, but she knew the truth. She knew how quickly the nature of his touch could change from easy to hard, from supportive to restrictive. She had no doubt that if she made the slightest move while inside the office, if she opened her mouth to ask the most innocent question, or if he suspected that she was even thinking about escape, he would retaliate.

The motel office was tiny, three walls of glass and a paneled rear wall with a door that led to the owner's living quarters. The sound of a television, loud and distracting, came through the open door; when the bell announced their arrival, it was muted, then a voice called, "Be right with you."

Teryl rested both arms on the high counter while they waited. She should be thinking about escape, she acknowledged. She should be making plans, seeking opportunities, mentally preparing herself to act when or if fate presented an opportunity. For example, in spite of John's warning, there was no reason why she shouldn't appeal to the clerk for help. It wasn't likely that John would harm her in front of a witness . . . was it? And if the clerk, who was male, happened to be a big, strong male—bigger than John, stronger than John—she would have to be a fool not to appeal to him for help, wouldn't she?

She was saved from answering that question, because right then the clerk came through the door. It was a man, all right—the oldest, tiniest little wisp of a man she'd ever seen. With his frail body and long, thin hands, with his bald head and little eyes and big, hooked nose, he reminded her of nothing so much as a cartoon drawing of a gangly, awkward baby bird. As a final insult, the little old man was practically deaf; John had to resort to shouting to make himself understood.

With a sigh, Teryl leaned on one elbow so she could rest her head on her palm. Pausing in filling out the registration card, John pulled her left arm from the counter, lowering it out of the clerk's line of sight. Apparently he didn't want the

old man—who to her looked about as blind as he was deaf—
to see the bruises and grow suspicious . . . or maybe he
didn't want to see them himself. Maybe he was ashamed of
what he'd done. That would certainly explain the flush red-
dening his face.

The clerk took John's money—far too much for a dirty little place like this—and gave him a room key in exchange.
Room 14, second floor, on the end, as far from the office as
they could get. They returned to the truck to get their bags,
then climbed the rickety steps to the top.

There was a light on in Room 8, Teryl noticed as they
passed, but every other room was dark, the drapes open.
Room 14 had no neighbors, no one whose attention she
could attract with a scream. There was only the one flight of
stairs, and the windows that fronted the rooms all held small
air-conditioning units. John had gotten lucky. Unless he was
very careless, she had little chance of getting away.

And somehow she didn't think he was going to get careless now.

He unlocked the door, pushed it open, and flipped on a
light, then waited for her to enter first. Clutching the handle
of her suitcase in both hands, she stepped across the threshold into a dimly lit, musty, mildewy-smelling room. It was
one hell of an unwelcoming place, threatening in its darkness, sickening in its smell. Suddenly she didn't feel so tired.
Suddenly stopping for the night didn't seem such a good
idea.

Sharing a room with him didn't seem so acceptable.

Using his own suitcase, he nudged her forward so he could
enter; then he closed and locked the door behind him. The
click of the lock made her shudder with revulsion. She was
trapped in an awful place with a man she knew entirely too
well and not well enough, a man who may or may not be
crazy, a man who might or might not kill her, and she had no
one to blame but herself.

Because just once, just one night, she had wanted to be
wicked in New Orleans.

Now she might have to pay for it with her life.

Chapter Four

John stopped just inside the door, setting his bag down, taking a moment to look around. The room was small, the two beds shoved against opposite walls, the space between them so narrow that the bedside table was wide enough to hold a phone and an ashtray and nothing else. The sight of the ashtray made him long for a cigarette—he'd been smoking them by the carton in the last few months, at least until he'd heard the news about Simon. Then smoking had become too nervous a habit, and he was already nervous. Already edgy. He didn't need anything to add to it.

The only other furniture in the room was a dresser with a TV bolted to it, mounted on a black swivel base. Automatically turning it toward him, he pulled out the button that turned it on. The audio came on immediately, but the picture, like a giant Polaroid shot, developed slowly. It was snowy and ghostly, but even with the bad reception, it was easy enough to recognize the show, a replay of "New Orleans Afternoon."

Without hesitation, he pushed the button and shut it off again.

Teryl had stopped at the foot of the more distant bed. She stood there, still holding her suitcase, as if awaiting further instructions. She needed aspirin, she'd said, and something to drink and a bathroom. She also needed food—which he could get from the convenience store across the street, even if it was just packaged honey buns or more candy bars—and sleep. If that weary, bruised look was anything to judge by, she needed rest as desperately as he did.

Sleep she would get. Rest he wasn't so sure about. Somehow he doubted that she would be able to relax enough to get any real rest until he had been removed from her life and put away, preferably someplace with iron bars, strong locks, and soft, padded walls.

With a dispirited sigh, he moved away from the door toward the closer bed, leaning across it to turn the air conditioner to high, then freeing the pillows from the spread. As he did, she abruptly broke her silence.

"I'd like to take that bed." Her thoughts so easily readable in her brown eyes, she offered what was meant to be a logical excuse for her request. "That way the air conditioner won't be blowing directly on me because I'll be more or less under it."

"You get cold easily?"

"Y-yes, I do."

He glanced at her over his shoulder as he began stripping the covers off. "Right. I was in your room last night, sweetheart," he reminded her. "It was cold enough to make ice . . . only you weren't cold at all. You were hot." He remembered just how hot—hot enough to brand, hot enough, it seemed when he had entered her, to steam—and felt his body respond. He felt the tension pooling deep in his belly, felt the hunger licking through him with a fiery rush.

She remembered, too, with a flush that heated her face, that spread down her throat to the soft, fair skin above her breasts. She had flushed like that last night, he recalled, the first time she had come, and the second and the third. Passion had tinted her face, her throat, and her breasts, had given her swollen nipples a rosy hue, had made her so damned hot that they had sizzled where they'd touched.

She remembered.

And he would never forget.

Neglecting his task for the moment, he turned toward her.

"Teryl . . ." His voice was husky, his tone too damned obviously an appeal.

She stiffened and avoided looking at him. "Please . . . I just want . . ."

She didn't finish, but he could think of several possibilities. *I want to be left alone. I want to sleep unharmed. I want to be safe. I want to come out of this with my life and my sanity intact. I want to forget I ever met you. I want to forget last night ever happened.*

There were any number of possibilities, except the one he would most like to hear. *I want you.* His actions this morning had guaranteed that he would never hear that from her.

"You just want the bed closest to the door," he said grimly, trying to ignore the need inside him. "The closer you can get to the door, the less distance you'll have to cover on your way out and the better your chances of escaping once I fall asleep." Leaning over, he grasped the edge of the mattress and half lifted, half shoved it to the floor in front of the door, blocking it completely. Then he faced her again.

"Damn you," she whispered, her voice curiously empty of emotion. But although her curse had been mild and unimpassioned, the look in her eyes was deadly. He recognized disappointment, along with frustration, a little bit of fear, and, overshadowing it all, anger. There was no hint of the desire he had seen last night. No hunger. No passion. Everything soft and sweet was gone—and not just gone, he warned himself. It was dead. It wasn't coming back.

Like everything else good in his life, he had destroyed it.

But he would sacrifice whatever he had to to save his career.

He would do anything short of murder—would use anyone, would hurt anyone—to reclaim the only thing in his entire life that he'd ever done well.

And somehow, just as he had with Tom and with Janie, somehow he would find a way to live with the guilt.

"I've been damned most of my life," he said softly, bleakly, "and I know I'll be damned for this. But when it's over, I'll make it right, Teryl. I swear I will."

Her expression didn't change. It didn't turn hopeful. It didn't soften at all. "You'll let me go without hurting me?"

"I'll let you go as soon as I have what I need."

His words didn't reassure her. Of course, *she* thought he was crazy. She thought he would never have what he needed because it didn't exist, because he wasn't who he claimed to be. She thought he was delusional, and when she was unable to help him prove his delusions, she probably thought he would kill her. That was what *he* would think if he was in her place.

She let her suitcase slide to the floor with a thump. "I have to go to the bathroom," she announced in a numb voice, silently awaiting his permission before she moved from the place where she stood.

He glanced across the room. Straight across from the door was a sink with a narrow U-shaped counter around it, and next to that was an open door that led into the bathroom. He gestured toward it, then turned away and sat down on the bare springs of his bed to wait.

How could he convince her that he was telling the truth? He had tried all day to think of something that might make his story seem more credible, but he'd had so little contact with her in the past. She had, on occasion, sent him little notes—*Your manuscript was received this week* or *Here are copies of your new contract; please initial, sign, and return to Rebecca*—but that was pretty much the extent of their contact, except for the note asking about Liane Thibodeaux's story. She had obviously not been impressed with his knowledge of that little tidbit.

His vision blurred, and for a moment he closed his eyes, rubbing the spot between and above them where a headache had settled. He was tired, Jesus, so tired. His fingers were sore from clenching the steering wheel the better part of the day, and his jaw ached, too—from clenching it all day, he knew. From keeping his mouth clamped shut on arguments that could only hurt him, on insistences that could only convince Teryl that she was dealing with a lunatic. Under the circumstances, small talk had seemed inappropriate, and so he had forced himself to remain silent mile after mile, hour after hour, until he could think of something relevant to say. Something persuasive. Something rational and sane.

He needed her to believe he was rational and sane.

Even though sometimes he had his own doubts.

No. He *wasn't* crazy. He might have been for a time after Tom died, when his parents had banished him from the funeral, when they had refused to let him visit Janie all those months in the hospital. That was when he'd left California, sick with grief and guilt, seeking peace that he didn't deserve, looking for a way out and finding plenty, but lacking the courage to take any of them.

But he wasn't crazy now. He *was* John Smith, and he had created Simon Tremont. *He* had written those books. *He* had filled all those thousands of pages with pieces of himself. *He* had used his grief, his sorrow, his guilt, and his failures—all his incredible failures—to write those stories.

He wasn't crazy.

But Teryl thought he was. It was in her eyes. In the trembling she couldn't control. In the way she cringed whenever he got close. It was in the fear that was as real, as raw, as powerful as her desire had been last night.

He had to give her credit. Under the circumstances, her behavior had been pretty remarkably controlled. She hadn't done any of the things that any normal, rational, sane person would be perfectly justified in doing when she thought her lift was at stake. She hadn't laughed out loud at his story. She hadn't screamed for help. She hadn't tried to escape after that one attempt when he had dragged her back into the seat and forcibly held her there. When he had left those ugly bruises on her arm.

Except for Janie, he had never hurt a woman before, not ever, and with Janie, while he had been solely responsible, he hadn't actually caused the pain. The car had done that, the old convertible that he had rescued from the salvage yard and, with Tom's help, had rebuilt from the ground up. Even that most typical teenage boy's activity hadn't been worthy of their father's approval. No kid of George Smith's was going to be a damned grease monkey, he had announced the day they'd towed the car home. Besides, he had continued,

Tom didn't have the time to waste on such a chore, and John wasn't smart enough to do it on his own.

He would find the time, Tom had replied evenly, and he had. He had given John time, help, even money when his own funds ran low.

And six months after they finished, almost six months to the day after that first celebratory drive down the coast, both Tom and the car—and Janie—had ended up at the bottom of a ravine.

John had been thrown clear.

As usual, their father had been right. John hadn't been smart enough or capable enough or talented enough to do anything on his own . . . except write. Writing was the only thing he'd ever been good at. Those books, those twelve Simon Tremont books, were the only thing he'd ever done right in his entire life, and he couldn't let that bastard claim them as his own.

Not even if stopping him meant hurting Teryl.

Thought of the books—of *Resurrection*—made his head throb worse. *He wrote* Resurrection, she'd said of the man in New Orleans. *If he's not Simon Tremont . . . how did he write the best book that Simon Tremont has ever written? You can't explain that away, can you?*

His mouth thinned into a scowl. No, damn it, he couldn't explain it. How could that man—how could *anyone*—have written *his* book? His very private, very personal book. He had lived with the story—hell, had actually *lived* it—for seventeen years. After years of trying to forget it, he had finally faced the fact that his best chance of forgetting was to write it. To sit down at the computer hour after excruciating hour, to write things he didn't want to write, to remember things he'd never managed to forget.

He had known he could never do it justice as his first book, his second, or his third. He had known it was too powerful, too obsessive, a story for his fifth book or his seventh or tenth. But for number thirteen, he'd thought he could do it. The irony had mocked him—writing as his thirteenth book a story he'd feared so much. Unlucky thirteen. It had seemed fitting.

The outline had been no problem. He had worked twenty hours a day, had replaced his need for sleep with his obsession to put it all down on paper. He had gritted his teeth through backaches so relentless that the pain had never gone away, not until the outline was in the mail and he'd slept for three days straight. He had endured headaches, sore muscles, and eyestrain, had waded through nightmares, guilt, and sorrow. When he was finished, he'd had the cathartic feeling that maybe there was hope for him after all, and so he had titled the book *Resurrection*. It would be his own personal rising from the death that the last seventeen years of his life had become.

Then reality had hit in the form of a hellacious case of writer's block. Intending to write about fictionalized versions of himself, Tom, and Janie and actually doing it, he had discovered too late, were two totally different and totally impossible things. The memories had been too powerful, the pain still too real. The characters he'd created for Tom and Janie had been inadequate; they had both deserved so much more than the best he could give. Colin Summers, the thinly disguised version of John himself, had also been inadequate—too flawed, too overwhelmingly a failure, to carry the story. There was nothing heroic about him, nothing admirable, nothing sympathetic.

But Colin, at least, had been true to life. Anyone who had ever known John could have recognized him in Colin.

Instead of healing old wounds and laying guilt to rest, the book had turned into an exercise in masochism. The way things had gone, *Damnation* would have been a far better title. It certainly described his life, past and present.

He was scared like hell that it also described his future.

Hearing the bathroom door open, he opened his eyes again and glanced at his watch. It was a few minutes before nine o'clock. If she hadn't had the bad luck to meet him yesterday, she would be at the New Orleans airport right now, probably already on board the plane that would take her home to Richmond. She would be regretting leaving New Orleans while at the same time she planned a return trip. She would be tired, satisfied, and innocently happy.

Instead she was exhausted and frightened, and her regrets had nothing to do with leaving New Orleans and everything to do with him.

For a moment she stood at the foot of the bed that would be hers, reluctant to sit down with him so close. When he told her to sit, though, she did so obediently, like a nervous schoolgirl: sitting on the edge of the mattress, back uncomfortably straight, feet together, hands pressed between her knees. He wished she would relax but knew that was hoping for too much.

He had a knack for that—for wanting the impossible. For needing things from people that they couldn't give. He had wanted so much: affection from his mother. Acceptance from his father. He had wanted Tom to not be dead, had wanted Janie to make her injuries go away.

He had wanted to be a normal man with normal feelings and a normal life. But since he couldn't be that, couldn't have that, now he would settle for the life that had been stolen from him. It wasn't much. But it was all he had.

"Your flight was supposed to leave at nine, wasn't it?" He had looked at her ticket last night, had noted the time and the route—New Orleans to Charlotte to Richmond.

She didn't respond.

"Was someone going to meet you at the airport?"

She so obviously didn't want to answer that he knew the answer was yes. Not giving her an opportunity to lie, he went on. "With the hour's time difference between Louisiana and Virginia, your plane would be arriving well after midnight. You wouldn't want to find your car that late at night, not alone. You wouldn't want to drive home so late all alone, either, not if you could avoid it. Who's supposed to meet you?"

Dismay that told him he was right and embarrassment—because she was sensible and predictable? he wondered—warmed her face and made her voice thick when she mumbled an answer. "D.J."

"Who is he?"

"She. She's my best friend."

He pushed the phone toward her. "Call her. Tell her

you've decided to stay over a few days. Ask her to call your boss first thing in the morning and let her know."

She didn't reach for the phone, but she did at last look at him. "I can't do that. D.J. knows me too well. It's not in my character to just decide to stay over a few days, especially when I have responsibilities at home."

He had no doubt that, ordinarily, that was true. But these weren't ordinary times. This wasn't an ordinary situation. "It's not *in your character*," he pointed out, his words deliberately mocking, "to take a strange man to your hotel room and fuck him, but you did it. People do things when they're on vacation that are out of character . . . especially in a place like New Orleans." Then his voice softened, became quieter, smoother, and more threatening. "Call her, Teryl."

Reluctantly she pulled the phone into her lap. "Do I charge it to the room?'"

Standing up, he pulled a well-worn leather wallet from his hip pocket, withdrew his calling card, and handed it to her. She looked at it for a moment, reading the number before looking at him. "Simon Tremont doesn't have a phone."

"You don't know that for a fact, do you? All you know is that Tremont refuses to do business over the phone." Then he sighed tiredly. "You're right. I don't have a phone. But you don't have to have one to get a calling card. Instead of a telephone number, the company randomly assigns a number for your use."

Instead of sitting down again on his bed, he moved across the small space to sit beside her. He didn't want to be that close—especially on a bed—and she obviously didn't want him there, but he needed to hear both ends of the conversation. He needed to know in case she tried to give some sort of message to make her friend suspicious. Picking up the receiver from the phone in her lap, he forced it into her hand and gave a quiet order. "Call her, Teryl. *Now*."

The phone was ringing for the third time by the time D.J. Howell stretched across the bed to answer it, using her sexiest, most sultry Southern voice. The moment she recognized her friend's voice, she traded sultry for everyday normal. "Correct me if I'm wrong, Teryl, but it's after nine o'clock Louisiana time, and you're supposed to be on a plane heading home. Don't tell me you decided to chuck it all and stay."

"Would you believe me if I said I had?"

"Uh-huh. And pigs might fly. What's up?" The flight had probably been delayed, she thought, wrapping the phone cord around her index finger, or maybe it had been overbooked and Teryl had gotten bumped. Those were the only reasons, short of death or disaster, that she could imagine making her oh-so-reliable friend miss tonight's return home.

But even Teryl, she discovered, could surprise her.

"I, uh—I'm really having a good time, D.J., and I, uh . . . I decided to stay a few days longer. I have some vacation time left, and uh . . . money's no problem—there are ATM machines all over the place—and I-I can change my return flight without having to pay a fortune." Her friend paused to draw a loud breath, then rushed on. "I know I should have planned ahead, but I didn't decide until tonight. Anyway, I'm glad I caught you before you left for the airport. Oh, and D.J., I need a favor—"

Eyes widened in exaggerated disbelief, D.J. interrupted her. "Whoa, girl, back up here. You just decided to stay a few days longer? At the very last minute?" Delight coloring her voice, she asked, "Did you meet a man, Teryl?"

"A-a man?" Teryl's voice squeaked.

Grinning, D.J. rolled onto her back, plumping a lace-edged pillow beneath her head. "My, my, you did. Will wonders never cease. And here I was going to ask for the condoms back when you got in tonight. No need to let them go to waste." She chuckled softly. "He must be good—damned good—to make little Miss Goody-goody behave so naughtily. Tell me about him."

"Listen, D.J., about that favor—"

"Huh-uh. No details, no favor."

"D.J., please—"

"Where did you meet him?"

"Pat O'Brien's. D.J., I really need—"

"Getting picked up in a bar. Teryl, you slut. Is he handsome?"

"Um, yeah."

"Well endowed?"

"Come on," Teryl mumbled, and D.J. could easily envision her blush. "Don't do this, not now, please. I'll call you when I have a new airline reservation, okay? And tomorrow morning, can you call Rebecca and explain to her that I'm taking a few days of vacation?"

"You're no fun, Teryl. I tell you everything about my men, and you won't answer even one pertinent question about yours." D.J. sighed her best put-upon sigh. "All right. I'll call Rebecca and tell her that New Orleans has absolutely corrupted our angelic Teryl, that she's taken leave of her senses and is holed up in a shabby French Quarter hotel doing only the devil knows what with a handsome, sexy, and thoroughly dissolute Southern gentleman." Then the humor faded from her voice. "Listen, girl, you be careful. These are *my* games you're playing. Don't let yourself get hurt."

For a moment the silence was so heavy that she wondered if they'd been disconnected. Then came another burst of rapid speech. "D.J., listen to me. I'm in trouble. This guy—"

D.J. laughed. Trust Teryl to complicate even the simplest one- or two-night stand. The most likely trouble her friend was having was reconciling her actions with her oh-so-good self-expectations. She demanded so much of herself, had such high morals and rigid standards. The fact that she'd had sex with a stranger was probably enough to scandalize her. The fact that she had apparently enjoyed it was definitely enough.

"What's the problem, Teryl? So you're finally discovering that sex without commitment can be pretty damn good. Don't worry, little sister. One wild fling isn't going to turn you into a slut like me," she promised. "Have your fun. Use this guy up and wear him out. When you come home, it'll be our secret. You can put your little halo on again, and no one will ever suspect a thing. Okay?"

After another silence, Teryl sighed and murmured, "Yeah, D.J. Okay."

"Hey, I've got to go. Since you're standing me up, I've got plans to make. Enjoy yourself, and let me know when you'll be home."

D.J. listened until a click indicated that Teryl had hung up, and then she returned the receiver to its cradle. For a moment, she simply lay there, thinking about the conversation.

Who ever would have believed that Teryl would one day do something wild and dangerous? For twenty-nine years she had been so safe, so dull, so *normal*. She was as reliable as mosquitos and muggy summer days in the South, as conventional as any middle-class, white-bread kid could be. Not once in twenty-nine years had she ever taken a chance—not with men, not with herself, not with life. She was predictable. Bland and boring.

And now she was off in some exotic city, getting laid by some exciting stranger.

And even in the middle of this hot and heavy affair, her prudish side was trying hard to make her feel guilty for it. How thoroughly, typically Teryl.

Rising from the bed, D.J. returned to the task the call had interrupted. She took a seat at the old pine table she had turned into a dressing table. Rows of frosted lights lit her face mercilessly, but she had no reason to mind. Her skin was damned near perfect, smooth, free of wrinkles—not the pasty, sickly white of so many redheads, but a creamy gold. The only flaw was a sprinkling of freckles across her nose and high on her cheeks, but they could be hidden by makeup. Nature had given her blue eyes, but contacts turned them green. Her mouth was a little too pouty for her tastes, but most men loved it. Most men said it was made for kissing.

Rich said it was made for something a whole lot nastier . . . and a whole lot more fun. Sometimes when he was annoyed with her, he said that cocksucking was her best talent. It damn well ought to be, she thought as she selected a lipstick from the tray on the table and twisted it up out of the tube. She'd been practicing it since she was thirteen.

She put on lipstick, blotted it, then applied it again. Her makeup done, she removed the band that gathered her hair at her nape and the yellow clips that held it off her forehead and let the dark red strands fall around her face and down past her shoulders. Her hair was long, heavy, and thick and could be a real burden in Richmond's sticky summers, but she refused to cut it. She hadn't had short hair since she was a teenager, when she had realized that men—many of them, at least—preferred long hair on their women. They found something sexy and sensual about it. That was the same reason for her curls, wild and unrestrained.

In fact, men—attracting them, seducing them, using and being used by them—were the motivation behind damned near everything she did.

Pushing away from the table, she slipped out of her robe and put on a nearly transparent cotton skirt and a thin ribbed tank top. If she were still going to the airport, she would be wearing jeans and a T-shirt, but if Teryl was getting laid tonight, there was no reason why *she* shouldn't get lucky, too.

It was ten o'clock when she left the apartment, her destination an old farmhouse a short distance outside the city. A single light, glowing yellow against the night sky, showed where the driveway angled off away from the road. She had wanted to come earlier, had wanted to call in sick and come out here with lunch, a bottle of wine, and her always-willing body.

But Rich had said no. He was a hateful bastard sometimes. He'd known how much she always missed him, had known how horny she would be, and he hadn't given a damn. He had told her to wait.

Screw him. She had waited long enough. If he didn't want her, plenty of men in Richmond did. She wasn't going to spend the night alone.

The driveway was rutted, badly in need of repairs. She had to slow her sleek little Camaro to a crawl to avoid the worst of the holes. Rich hardly seemed to notice things like rutted driveways or wobbly steps or leaks in the old farmhouse roof. Of course, he had other more important things on his mind. He had plans. Ambitions.

She parked behind his car and climbed out. A bare bulb burned beside the front door, attracting a haze of gnats and moths. There were lights on inside the house, too, in the front room on the first floor, in the hallway, upstairs in his bedroom.

On the porch, she ignored the doorbell—it didn't work—and knocked instead, three loud thuds that echoed through the door. He was never quick to answer, maybe because he always knew it was her. In all the years he'd lived there, he had once told her, no one but her had ever come to the house. He had no friends that she was aware of, no other women, no family. His life was tied up in her.

When two minutes passed into three, then four, she twisted the doorknob. It was unlocked. She stepped inside, closed and locked the door behind her, then let her purse and keys slide to the floor. Although the front room light was on, she would bet he was upstairs in his bedroom, probably naked, probably in bed. Possibly waiting for her? Had he suspected or hoped that her plans would change, that she would be free to come here tonight regardless of his lack of invitation? Was that why he'd left the hall and porch lights on, why he'd left the door unlocked?

She wanted to think so. She wanted it so badly that she hurt with it.

As she climbed the stairs, she became aware of the sounds of a television show. The voice was vaguely familiar—Tiffany something, the woman in New Orleans who had conducted the Simon Tremont interview yesterday. D.J. had seen clips of it on the news last night, had caught it again on a syndicated entertainment show. Sweet Tiffany had lucked out, the bitch. She'd gotten more exposure in the last thirty hours or so than in the entire rest of her career combined, all because she hosted a silly little talk show in the city where Tremont had set his five best-selling books.

Teryl had gotten lucky, too—a free trip to New Orleans, an introduction to her idol, and a good screwing by a handsome stranger who obviously knew what to do with whatever nature had given him—and all because she had no more ambition than to be Rebecca Robertson's flunky for the rest of her life.

D.J. shouldn't be surprised. Teryl had always been lucky,

ever since she was four years old, and she always would be. If there was a prize to be had, somehow, some way, Teryl would win it. The rewards of virtue, their mother would say if she were here.

Well, the hell with virtue. *She* would take the rewards of sin anytime.

Stopping outside the partially opened bedroom door, she grasped the hem of her shirt and peeled it over her head. She was naked underneath. She found the feel of fabric against her breasts too sensuous to bother with wearing a bra. Holding the shirt by one narrow strap, she pushed the door open the rest of the way and strolled inside.

Rich *was* naked, he *was* in bed, and he was ready for her, evidenced by the bulge beneath the thin cotton sheet. He wasn't as well endowed as she would have liked, but he had other things going for him that made up for the lack of size. Things like passion. Intensity. Unpredictability.

And just the right degree of cruelty.

He spared her only the slightest of glances before turning his attention back to the television. How many times had that Tremont interview been shown across the country? she wondered as she approached the bed. How many more times would they have to see it before everyone tired of it and went on to something new?

The bed sank as she knelt on it, shifted again as she stretched out beside him. He didn't look at her or speak to her, didn't reach out to pull her close or acknowledge her in any way. Sometimes he ignored her to punish her. Sometimes he did it to remind her of the derision he felt for her. Tonight, she knew, his attention was simply directed elsewhere—to the television screen, to the beautiful woman and the handsome man and the interview they were conducting.

She kissed his nipple, licked it, bit it, and felt a quiver ripple through him. She spread the kisses out—across his chest, his ribs, his belly, taking her time, licking, sucking, suckling, as she edged the sheet lower. She was kissing his belly, hard and flat, the skin rough with swirling dark hair that, only inches away, grew thick and coarse around his erection, when finally he responded, tangling his hand in her hair,

pushing her lower. As Tiffany Whatever giggled and asked
another of her inane questions, D.J. took him in her mouth,
and as the camera moved into a tight close-up of a serious,
earnest Simon Tremont discoursing on celebrity, he came,
filling her mouth in a hot rush. She swallowed rapidly, then
sought more, as some idle part of her mind blessed Teryl and
her dissolute stranger. *This* was where she wanted to be
tonight, not at the airport, picking up her friend. *This* was
what she wanted.

This was what she needed.

Damn.

Sitting stiffly on the bed, Teryl stared at the worn box
springs on the other bed and directed angry, silent curses all
around. Damn D.J. for not being able to get her mind off sex
long enough to hear her plea. Damn John for taking her prisoner in the first place, for scaring her enough that she hadn't
tried harder to make D.J. listen, for sprawling over there on
that mattress that blocked her only means of escape.

And damn *you*, she thought blackly, addressing herself,
for being such a fool. For being sucked in by a pair of intense blue eyes and a rare, sweet smile. For being naive and
trusting and such an incredible idiot. For being too afraid to
blurt out a cry for help that D.J., even while playing sultry,
sexy, and naughty, couldn't misunderstand.

Damn, damn, *damn!*

Across the room—that sounded so much better, so much
safer, than saying five feet away—John was half-sitting,
half-lying on the mattress. There wasn't enough room between the bed, the dresser, and the door for the mattress to
lie flat, so one side was level and the other curved up to
block the dresser drawers; one end was flat, and the other
leaned against the door. The only way he was going to be
able to stretch out comfortably was to lie at a diagonal—not
that she gave a damn if he was comfortable. She wanted him
to share her misery. She wanted him to be just as exhausted,
hungry, and despondent as she was.

Judging from the brooding expression he wore and the

weariness that etched his face, at least that wish had come true.

Craving distance, privacy, and an escape from the blue gaze she'd found so flattering last night, she rose from the bed and went to the sink, yanking the plastic wrap off one of the cups there, filling it with tepid water, and taking a long drink. Her scowl deepened as her gaze connected with his in the mirror. So much for distance.

That left only the bathroom. She made a hasty retreat, closing the door behind her. She knew from her earlier visit that there was no lock on the door, but he had been decent enough so far. Surely he wouldn't begrudge her a little time alone. It wasn't as if she could go anywhere or could do anything.

Lowering the toilet lid, she sat down and rested her elbows on her knees. The bathroom was no cheerier, no cleaner or nicer than the rest of the place. A bare light bulb, maybe forty watts, sixty at most, burned overhead, its fixture dangling by a wire from an irregular hole in the ceiling. The walls were ugly powder blue tile, with an alternating border at eye level of pale pink. The tub was old, small, and set against the back wall. A peek behind the shower curtain revealed bits of plaster fallen from the ceiling overhead, a yellow-red stain extending from the faucet down to the drain and two cockroaches, one dead, the other very much alive.

And lo and behold, there *was* a God up in heaven . . . and a window above the tub. It was set into crumbling tile, square, awfully small, but she could wiggle through it. She knew she could.

With a new sense of purpose—with new hope—she returned to the bedroom and lifted her suitcase onto the bed. "I'm going to take a shower," she announced, opening the bag and rummaging through it until she located the zippered vinyl bag that held her toiletries.

John made no response. He just lay there, his head tilted back at an awkward angle to rest against the door, his eyes closed, his breathing shallow but steady.

Back in the bathroom, she closed the door once more, wishing she had thought to grab a shoe from her suitcase to slide underneath it and act as a wedge. But it was too late now, and the shoes she was wearing, chosen for their thick soles so she could do a lot of walking, were too big to be of any use.

Setting the bag on the floor, she chased away the live cockroach, turned the water on full force, then climbed onto the narrow side of the tub. There was scum—mildew, dirt, slime she didn't care to identify—on the lock and around the edges of the window. Grabbing a threadbare washcloth, she covered the lock and began pushing.

After a moment of fruitless work, she sighed. The window obviously hadn't been opened in ages; the scum grew in a continuous spread all along the frame and seemed to cement the lock in place. Changing positions, one foot on each side of the tub, she braced herself against the wall for better leverage and gave the small, slippery lock her best effort.

The metal had just started to budge when an arm closed around her waist, startling her, pulling her off-balance. She struggled instinctively, shrieking as her feet slipped from the tub rim, one landing in the water that had pooled in the bottom of the tub, the other on John's foot. Muttering a curse in her ear, he lifted her with his arm around her waist, then settled her against his hip like a sack of grain, carried her around the corner, and, with more force than necessary, dumped her right in the middle of the bed.

Scowling, she scrambled into a sitting position. "You bastard."

He ignored her and picked up the phone from the night table. As she warily watched, he disconnected the cord from the back, then laid the phone aside on the other bed. So much for the possibility of calling for help, she thought darkly, not that she'd given it much thought. Whom could she call and what could she say? That she was being held prisoner in a motel without a name in a town whose name she didn't know by a man whose name was commonplace enough to be a joke? And did she know this man? No, not at all . . . well, except for getting pretty damned indecent with him on a French Quarter sidewalk. Oh, and behaving shamelessly with him in a taxicab. And, oh, yes, having sex with him three times only hours after meeting him.

Any rational person would think she was crazy and hang up on her. Even D.J.—*if* she could get hold of her again—wouldn't buy this tale.

When he bent down, searching between the beds, then straightened a moment later with the phone cord in hand, hostility quickly gave way to fear. She watched as he formed a loop with the thin wire, then bent again to fasten it around the metal foot of the bed. Dread coursing through her, she began scooting away, scrambling across the bed, trying desperately to avoid him but simply managing to back herself into the corner.

She was trapped.

And he was reaching for her.

"P-please," she whispered, her voice trembling. "Please don't tie me up."

Looking grim and relentless, he grasped her right wrist and began drawing her across the bed. She pulled against him, but the sheet was old and worn thin; her feet couldn't find traction, and the slick, synthetic blend of her shorts and vest slid right across the bed.

The cord wasn't very long, so he pulled her to the edge of the mattress, then forced her wrists together and began wrapping the length around them. When she struggled, he didn't say a word but merely moved so that he was lying heavily against her, his weight forcing her to subside.

She couldn't bear this, Teryl thought. Her heart was thudding, and she felt an all-too-violent churning in her stomach. If he didn't change his mind, if he didn't loosen the cord and free her, she was going to go into a full-fledged panic attack. She was going to start screaming, and she wouldn't stop until everyone in this entire little town had heard her.

Then she felt his erection.

His gaze met hers, and she saw his startled look. His desire had come swiftly. In no more than the space of a moment, he'd gone from sex-was-the-last-thing-on-his-mind to hard enough to hurt where his penis pressed against her hip. Twenty-four hours ago she had been flattered by his desire, but right now she felt only fear—fear and, in some shameful place deep inside, a tiny little rush of heat.

Oh, God, she was as sick as he was. How could she care at a time like this that the sex between them had been good? He had *kidnapped* her, for God's sake! He had taken her prisoner and was planning to tie her to the bed and was getting turned on by it! How could she feel anything less than total revulsion? How could her body betray her this way?

He shifted positions slightly, rubbing against her, and then, holding both of her hands in one of his, he raised the other to lightly touch her face. "Teryl . . . " His voice was hoarse, soft, a needy plea.

Humiliation given life by her own need made her turn her head away, and her response made him stiffen. He slid off of her, sat on the edge of the bed, and began rewrapping the cord around her wrists, working quickly, mechanically. She lay still until he began to tie the ends together; then she twisted her fingers, managing to wrap them tightly around his. "Please, John . . . "

He brushed her away and fastened the ends into a knot, checking to make sure it wasn't too tight—or too loose.

"John, please don't do this." Panic made her voice thin, insubstantial. "I can't . . . Oh, God, I can't stand this. Please, I'll be good. I won't try to escape. I won't cause any trouble."

He ignored her pleading, stood up, and walked away, crossing the room to the television, turning it on, turning the volume as loud as it would go. If she screamed, some rational part of her knew in spite of her fear, it wasn't likely anyone would hear, and if anyone did hear, it wasn't likely they would care. They would probably assume it was just part of the cop movie on TV. Still, that didn't stop her from making one last, whispered, tearful plea. "I'll be good, John. I swear I will."

John went into the bathroom, closed the door, rested his arms against it, and buried his head in his arms. She was crying; in spite of the television, he could hear it through the thin wall. The soft little sobs pricked at his already raw nerves until *he* wanted to cry.

Christ, what was he doing here in a shabby motel in Podunk, Mississippi, with a crying hostage tied to a bed? What in hell could possibly be so important that it could bring him to this?

Simon Tremont. That smug, condescending bastard claiming to be Tremont.

His books. *Resurrection.*

His life.

Without Simon Tremont and the books, he *had* no life. He might as well be dead. And although he had lived half his life thinking dead was the best way to be, he'd be damned if he would die a total failure. He didn't have friends or family to miss him, didn't have a woman who loved him or kids who would mourn him, but he had twelve much-loved books, and he would reclaim them before he died. He would prove to Teryl that he *was* Tremont. He would prove to her that he wasn't crazy.

He would prove it to himself.

The sound of water still running in the tub penetrated his thoughts, reminding him that he hadn't had time for a shower this morning. He'd had too many plans to make—to obsess over. He had gotten to bed late and had been up early to watch for the impostor in the hotel lobby, and now he felt dirty.

Of course, the dirtiness he felt wasn't the sort a person could wash away with soap and water. It came from the inside out, and there was nothing in the world with enough power to make him completely clean again. Still, a shower might help relax some of his tense muscles. It might help alleviate some of his unwanted desire. It would certainly help block out the sounds from the next room.

Closing the vinyl curtain, he switched the shower on, then stripped out of his clothing and stepped under the water's spray. Although the handle was turned to hot, the water was only lukewarm and quickly edging toward cool. Teryl had used all the hot water in the cover-up of her failed escape. He didn't mind the cool temperature, though. It washed away the outer layers of his exhaustion, made him feel not quite so weary, not quite so ragged.

Besides, cold showers were supposed to be good for over-active libidos, and after years of lying more or less dormant, his was certainly making up for lost time. Practically every time he looked at Teryl, he got aroused. Every time he thought about last night, every time he closed his eyes and remembered . . .

That was exactly what he'd been doing earlier when she was in the bathroom. He had been more than half-asleep when she had informed him that she was going to take a shower. He had heard and understood her words, though; the images his brain had immediately conjured up were proof of that—images of her naked, her sleek brown hair wet against her head, her hands stroking her soap-slick breasts, *his* hands buried in a lather of brown curls between her thighs. They were images guaranteed to lead to the vaguely unsatisfying climax of a wet dream, but before he reached that point, something had jerked him wide-awake. Maybe it had been a sound. Maybe it had been a subconscious unwillingness to come while thinking about her when he would much prefer to do it while making love to her. Maybe it had just been in-stinct.

Whatever the cause, he had awakened hard and horny and suspicious, and she had given him reason to be. If she had escaped, he would have wound up in jail—or, worse, the nearest psychiatric facility.

He smiled bleakly. Maybe they would have kept him too sedated to know who he or anyone else was. Maybe they would have kept him too medicated to remember. Maybe, for the first time in his adult life, he would have found peace.

He finished his shower quickly, not because the tempera-ture of the water now was sending chills through him but be-cause Teryl deserved that much consideration. Because the sooner he was done, the sooner he could untie her and the sooner she could calm down. They could both calm down and get some badly needed sleep.

After drying off with a paper-thin towel, he pulled his jeans on and wadded the rest of his clothing into a ball. As soon as he opened the door, the soft, teary sounds coming from around the corner stopped. He tossed his dirty clothes toward his suitcase, shut off the television, then went to kneel beside the bed. There he freed the telephone cord, loosening it from her wrists and from the foot of the bedframe, winding it in neat loops around the fingers of his right hand. When that was done, he finally found the courage to look at her.

She was lying on her side, her knees drawn to her chest, her arms tucked so that her hands were clasped beneath her chin. There was a red streak around each wrist where she had tried to free herself from the cord, along with the nasty bruises he'd left this morning around her left wrist. Her nose was red, and her eyes were puffy, their expression bleak and hopeless. She looked like a woman facing death, dishonor, or worse.

Remembering the revulsion that had colored her expression earlier, when he had been lying against her and she had first become aware of his arousal, he knew she considered him much, much worse.

He reached out, intending only to dry the dampness from her cheeks. She didn't move away—she was all out of fight for the night—but her eyes widened slightly and her breath caught in her chest. He withdrew his hand without touching her and got to his feet, retreating to the mattress blocking the door. "Get ready for bed, Teryl," he said grimly. "We've got another long day ahead of us."

He shut off the lights on his way, sliding down onto the mattress in complete darkness. For a time, the only sound in the room was his own settling in; then the other bed creaked. Her suitcase opened.

He discovered that he could follow her movements by the sounds, that—to his supreme discomfort—his writer's imagination readily supplied pictures to match. That little whoosh was her vest coming off, those soft little thuds her shoes hitting the floor. The metallic rasp of the zipper of her shorts. The delicate rap of the buttons on her blouse coming in contact with the wood of the night table as she draped it over it. The rubbing of something—a T-shirt, maybe—tugged on, the glide of skin against cotton sheet, the rustle of covers being pulled up and tucked, a pillow being plumped.

Then silence.

Not complete silence, of course. The air conditioner was running. Water was dripping in the sink. She was breathing, and so was he . . . barely. He counted her breaths, measuring them as they deepened and slowed, guessing when she finally went to sleep. Then he turned onto his side, facing her in the darkness, and spoke in little more than a whisper.

"I'm sorry, Teryl."

Chapter Five

—◆◆◆—

*T*hursday had started out to be a very good day for Rebecca Robertson. The weather was unusually mild for a Virginia summer day. Her ex-husband Paul was in town on business and had taken her out last night for a dinner date that hadn't ended until morning. Simon's interview on "New Orleans Afternoon" had earned the best ratings in the show's history and was being seen all around the country. The fans' response had been overwhelming, and the media . . . They were getting a national—hell, an international—promotional blitz of the sort money couldn't buy. Simon was going to pick up thousands, tens of thousands, of new readers. *Resurrection* would be the biggest selling release in publishing history.

And Rebecca Robertson would be *the* agent of choice for every soul in the country who thought he had a story to tell. *She* would be the agent to the stars. She would have the power. The clout. The glory. As if she didn't already have enough.

Yes, this morning had started off just fine.

And then Teryl hadn't shown up for work and hadn't answered the phone at her house.

And Lena had just buzzed and told her that Debra Jane Howell was here to see her.

Drumming her nails on the desktop, she waited for the

woman to make the long walk from the front desk through to the big office at the back. She had known when she hired Teryl five years ago that she was getting a good worker. She *hadn't* known she would also be getting regular exposure to a pain in the ass like D.J. Howell. She knew D.J. and Teryl were close—best friends, sisters, stepsisters; she'd never been completely sure of the nature of the relationship and she didn't care. She just didn't understand how someone as sweet, as hardworking, loyal, and just plain *nice* as Teryl could stand to be around a man-hungry bitch like D.J. It was an odd friendship, one Rebecca wouldn't mind seeing bite the dust. Teryl deserved better.

But Teryl's personal life was none of her business. As long as Rebecca didn't have to see D.J. on a regular basis, other than for her weekly lunches with Teryl, she would deal with business and leave her employees' personal lives to them.

The click of heels in the hallway signaled the woman's approach—very high heels. Other than her nickname, D.J. did everything in her power to play up her femininity. She was flamboyant in her dress, outrageous in her behavior. She somehow managed, even when doing absolutely nothing, to exude pure sex appeal. Paul, who had no particular interest in petite women, in aggressive women, in extremely sexually aware women—even Paul, who had *always* preferred women so totally the opposite of D.J., who had *always* found her kind of blatant sexuality unappealing, had been attracted to her.

Even Paul had had a brief fling with her.

The footsteps quieted as D.J. strolled through the door, stepping from hardwood floors to plush cream-colored carpet. She paid no attention to her surroundings. To her, furnishings, lush carpets, and rich wall coverings were merely backdrops to showcase her own assets. She ignored the two chairs in front of Rebecca's desk and went to the sofa against the far wall instead, forcing Rebecca to leave her desk and take a seat in one of the wing chairs that flanked the sofa.

"Good morning, Rebecca." Everything about her was business as usual. Her smile was catty, her hair unrestrained.

Her makeup was artfully applied, her dress outrageously revealing, her manner so perfectly unconsciously seductive that it couldn't be anything but conscious.

Most men didn't see that. Even the few who did recognize it—like Paul—fell under her spell anyway, for a time at least.

She pushed thoughts of Paul with Debra Jane to the back of her mind and coolly, politely asked, "What can I do for you, D.J.?"

"Teryl asked me to come by. She wanted me to let you know that she's taking a few vacation days and staying over a bit in New Orleans."

"That doesn't sound like Teryl."

The younger woman smiled a curious smile, part amusement, part pleasure, and part pure malice. "No, it doesn't, does it? But I'll let you in on a secret: Teryl's found herself a man. She went off on a simple little trip and turned wicked on us. It's funny, you know. It's always the innocent and predictable ones who surprise us the most." The smile took a chilling turn. "Isn't it?"

Rebecca tensed at the pointed reference to Paul. Yes, for a grown man, he had been somewhat naive and comfortably predictable. It had never occurred to him that a sultry, sexy young woman like D.J. could be interested in an older man like him; his first clue had probably come when he'd found her naked in his bed. And yes, news of their fling had come as a major surprise. She had thought Paul was immune to sweet young things and the games they played.

She had been wrong. She doubted any living, breathing male was immune to D.J.

So Teryl was extending her vacation. Rebecca found it hard to believe. In all her years in business—more than she wanted to count—she had never had an employee more reliable, more dependable, or more conscientious than Teryl Weaver. The girl never came in late, and she'd never taken a sick day without having plenty of aches and miseries to go with it. It would be easier to believe that Simon Tremont was giving up writing to become a garbage collector or that D.J.

Howell was giving up men for the church than to imagine the Teryl *she* knew pulling a stunt like this.

But why—for once—would D.J. lie? Why would she tell a story that Teryl, upon her return, would expose as a lie? Why would she deliberately create a situation that would force her best friend to face the truth about her own untrustworthiness?

"And when did Teryl make this decision?" she asked.

"Last night. She called as I was getting ready to leave for the airport. She said she's having a wonderful time with a wonderful man, and she asked me to let you know she was staying over a few days."

"She couldn't call me herself this morning?"

D.J. crossed one leg over the other, revealing a generous expanse of slender, muscular thigh, and swung her foot languorously from side to side. "I don't guess she knew exactly what it was she would be doing this morning. Maybe she thought she would be having too good a time to interrupt for business."

Rebecca smiled faintly. She could relate to that. Leaving Paul's bed this morning to come to work had certainly been one of the harder choices she'd made recently. It wasn't until she'd caught herself wondering whether they should give their marriage a second chance that she'd managed to untangle herself, throw back the covers, and get up. Dealing with their divorce and the problems that had caused it had taken her a long time; getting over the hurt and disillusionment had taken even longer. Sure, these little interludes were nice, but they weren't anything to base a marriage on. Sex, no matter how good, wasn't a reason to get married.

And while many of her more positive feelings for Paul had survived his infidelity, D.J., and the divorce, she wasn't sure love was one of them.

She wasn't sure she wanted it to be.

Abruptly, she forced her thoughts back on track. "When can I expect to see Teryl back in the office?"

D.J. responded with a shrug that made her hair shimmer in the morning light—dark red hair, and so much of it. "She said she would let me know." She gave a lascivious grin. "I imagine whenever this guy's given all he's got to give."

Disliking her response—disliking *her*—Rebecca got to her feet, hoping D.J. would have the courtesy to acknowledge that this meeting was over. "I appreciate your coming by to tell me, but, you know, you could have called and saved yourself a trip."

She was already seating herself behind the desk again when D.J. finally rose from the couch. "Coming by was no problem," she said, moving with such fluid grace toward the door. There she paused and looked back. "Oh, by the way, I hear Paul's in town." Another brief pause, another smile, devious in its innocence. "Give him my best, will you?"

Rebecca felt a surge of anger at the mention of her ex-husband that she concealed only through sheer force of will. Clenching her hands into fists out of sight in her lap, she sat motionless as D.J. walked out of the room, listening until the sound of her heels on the pine flooring had grown too distant to hear. Only then, finally, did she force the tension from her hands, from her neck and her jaw and breathe a sigh of relief.

Why had D.J.'s remark caught her off guard? She knew the woman was predatory, knew she had no class, no morals, no ethics. Debra Jane Howell had a mean streak, a cruelty that hid behind all that blatant sexuality. She took pleasure in taunting others, sometimes brazenly, other times so exquisitely subtly that her poison seeped in, unnoticed and untraceable. Like with Teryl. How many of Teryl's notions that she wasn't pretty enough, sexy enough, ambitious enough, et cetera, were legitimate conceptions formed on her own, and how many had been put into her head by her friend?

Rebecca would bet the majority had come from D.J. She had a need for attention, to be the prettiest, the sexiest, the one people looked at first, last, and longest. It was a testament to Teryl's innate strength that, after a lifetime together, D.J. hadn't done her more harm.

From the parking lot behind her, Rebecca heard the starting of an engine. She didn't turn around, but merely sat and listened as D.J. backed out, then drove away. Only when the other woman was gone did she allow herself to respond, softly, vehemently, viciously, to the comment about Paul.

"Bitch."

*   *   *

Mornings after were supposed to be awkward. Teryl hadn't gotten a chance to experience with John the morning after they'd made love, since he'd left her room sometime in the night, but she thought it might not have been so bad. She would have felt a little shy, of course—after all, they would have been strangers waking up in a most intimate situation—but she didn't think it would have been too awkward or uncomfortable.

But *this* morning—this morning after nothing had happened, this morning after they'd slept in separate beds on opposite sides of the room—was totally uncomfortable. She couldn't even look at him, which was all right, since he was doing a pretty good job of avoiding her. He had already been dressed when he'd awakened her; while she'd gotten dressed in her last clean outfit, he had returned the mattress to the bed, piled the covers on it, and stuffed his dirty clothes into his suitcase.

Now he was standing at the foot of the two beds, the telephone cord in his hands. She leaned closer to the mirror, seeking the best light as she applied blush to her cheeks but at the same time watching him, waiting for him to pick up the phone from the night table, to plug the cord into the jack on the back. As he hesitated, toying with the cord, her breathing turned shallow, and a slight tremble developed in her hand. Please put it back, she silently prayed, feeling once more the queasiness that had assaulted her last night when she'd realized what he intended to do with the six-foot length of plastic-encased wire.

He could rest assured that he wouldn't need it again. She'd decided last night while it was fastened around her wrists that she wasn't going to try any more escape attempts—unless, of course, the good Lord presented her with an opportunity too entirely fail-safe to ignore. It was too hard, getting her hopes up so high and then being disappointed. It was hard physically, too. She had the marks to prove it.

She wouldn't try to get away again, and she wouldn't give him *any* reason to use that cord on her again. She was going to be the most agreeable hostage any kidnapper had ever taken.

When he moved toward the night table, the relief rushing over her was tremendous. She was overreacting, she knew. It wasn't as if the few minutes she'd been tied to the bed had been so terribly bad. He had bound her securely but not tightly. She couldn't have freed herself, but she wouldn't have hurt herself, either, if she hadn't insisted on trying. If she had lain quietly, obediently, the way he wanted, she wouldn't have these reddened ligature marks around both wrists. Her skin wouldn't be tender there. Whatever discomfort she had suffered had been of her own doing.

But she couldn't have lain there quietly. Her fear had been too strong, her response to the restraints almost hysterical in nature. She had lost control in those first few overwhelming minutes, convinced that being tied up was synonymous with some terrible torment.

Returning the blush compact to her makeup case, she forced a faint smile. She didn't know where that fear came from, but if she had learned anything from years of dealing with her family, it was that everyone had fears, rational or not. D.J. was afraid of the dark, and her mother had a terrible fear of drowning. D.J.'s fear stemmed from her childhood, but Lorna's was as groundless as Teryl's newly realized fear of being restrained.

Groundless or not, fear was a powerful emotion. It could drive people to almost any lengths. It could make Teryl behave impeccably.

She was pulling out another compact, this one square and white, containing pressed powder and a thick, soft puff, when movement behind her caught her attention. John had turned back from the night table.

And he still held the phone cord in his hands. He was wrapping the loose ends around the loops to secure it. When he finished, he tucked it into his hip pocket.

Her compact slid from her hands, landing in the sink with a clatter.

The sound made him look at her. "Are you almost ready?"

For a time she couldn't answer. All she could do was stare

at him while her stomach tied itself into knots as neat as the ones that had bound her wrists last night.

Then, abruptly, she tore her gaze away. "Al-almost," she murmured, reaching blindly for the compact. She bumped the makeup bag, knocking it over, spilling its contents over the narrow counter and onto the floor, then hastily began gathering them back up. Her hands were trembling, her legs were none too steady, and her heart was beating an erratic, jerky rhythm in her chest.

When the rest of the cosmetics had been returned to their case, she reached once more for the compact. It lay in pieces in the sink, the lid separated from the case, the cake of powder broken in pieces and spotted darkly where water had touched it. Picking up the pieces, she dropped them into the wastebasket, then wiped her hands on the last clean towel.

It took her only a moment, even though she was all thumbs, to pack everything she'd taken from her suitcase—the makeup, the toiletries, the tank top she used as a nightshirt, and her dirty clothes. She didn't aim for order but rather speed, stuffing everything in together, then hastily fastening the latches.

Finished, she faced him and opened her mouth to tell him so. The wrong words came out, though. "Please don't take that."

For a moment he looked puzzled, as if he had no idea what she was talking about. Then his gaze moved to the side, to the night table and the phone it held, and his cheeks flushed dull red. "It's just a precaution."

"You won't need it. I swear, I won't try anything."

"If you don't try anything, then you don't have anything to worry about, do you?" He paused, letting his words sink in, then picked up his suitcase and gestured toward the door. "Let's go."

She stood motionless, staring hopelessly at the floor; then she turned to pick up her own suitcase. He hadn't carried it last night, and, of course, he wouldn't offer today. If he had both hands full of luggage, he would have less control over her. She might actually make a run for it or scream for help or something.

At least, before last night she might have.

As she hefted her bag off the bed and to the floor, her gaze slid across the nightstand. The phone sat there, minus its cord, and tucked underneath the handset was a ten-dollar bill.

He had kidnapped her, for God's sake, and tied her to the bed last night; yet he was paying—overpaying—for the cord he had taken. Just what kind of criminal was he? A conscientious one? An honorable one?

Or a crazy one?

She wished she knew the answer . . . but at the same time she was afraid to know.

Outside the sun was shining brightly, making her wince after the artificial darkness of the room. The temperature was already uncomfortably warm, and the humidity made the air thick. The town should have come to life by now, but as they descended the stairs, she saw little activity. There were a half dozen cars parked in front of the convenience store across the street, and an occasional car passed on its way into or out of town. From the parking lot, she could see that the nearest shops—a café, a laundromat, and a garage—were open for business, but there was no one on the sidewalks, no one running errands, no one to pay them attention.

John unlocked the Blazer on her side and put his suitcase in the backseat, then reached for hers. She didn't notice, though—her gaze was on the diner across the street—until, startling her with the unexpectedness of it, he took not only her suitcase but also her hand in his.

Stiffening, she fought the urge to pull away, to scream and snatch her hand free and flee for safety, and she forced herself to stand still while he examined the marks that encircled her wrist. His hand was warm, a little damp in the morning heat, and the pads of his fingertips bore calluses that rubbed roughly against her skin as he probed around but avoided touching the abrasions.

"Does it hurt?"

She wanted to answer flippantly. Of course it hurt; he had bruised her wrist, had grabbed it tightly enough to rupture small blood vessels, had left marks that needed time to heal. But she controlled the urge. "Not really," she replied. Then, when he rubbed lightly across the bigger bruise, the one that matched the heel of his hand, and she involuntarily winced, she amended her answer. "Not very much."

With a fierce scowl, he abruptly released her, put her suitcase in the back, then stepped back. "Get in while I take the key inside."

She obeyed, climbing up into the seat, gathering her skirt around her, before he slammed the door with enough force to rock the truck. She tucked her purse on the floor next to the door and fastened her seat belt. She didn't even think about trying to escape, didn't even consider opening the door again and rushing across the street to one of the stores. She knew she wouldn't make it far if she tried. The motel lobby was mostly glass—she wasn't out of John's sight for even a moment—and she would have to run right past it. There was no way he could miss seeing her, no way he could not catch her.

And, in spite of his apparent regret and guilt about the pain he'd caused her, there would be no way, she suspected, that she could avoid getting tied up again. If he tied her hands behind her back, he could fashion a more than adequate restraint using nothing else but the seat belt—she'd seen it on a TV movie—and they wouldn't look particularly suspicious even to someone who walked right up to the Blazer.

Since there was no way she was going to travel hundreds of miles bound like that, her only other option was to sit quietly. To follow his orders. To show him just how good a little captive she could be.

When he returned to the truck, he was still scowling. He climbed into the driver's seat and fastened his seat belt, then backed out and turned out of the parking lot onto the highway. Teryl watched out his window as they passed the café; she was about to venture a timid request when he spoke.

"We'll stop for breakfast in the next town, all right? Can you wait?"

"Sure." Turning to gaze out her own window, she gave a wistful little sigh. She wasn't sure exactly how far it was to the next town, but she did know that she was hungry almost to the point of being sick. After all, she had missed breakfast yesterday, along with lunch and dinner. All she'd had to eat was two candy bars and a small bag of potato chips. That was little more than a late-evening snack in her daily routine.

But yesterday hadn't been one of her routine days, and today didn't promise to be one, either.

John must have heard her sigh, though, because, after another block, he earned her gratitude by turning into the parking lot shared by the town's other two restaurants. Only one was open for breakfast, a place called Mom's. The parking lot wasn't overly crowded, but in a place like this, she imagined it would take every single car in town to make a crowd. He parked near the door, next to a pickup truck bearing a peeling McGovern bumper sticker, a rebel flag, and—God love the South—a gun rack mounted in the back window and bearing arms.

Inside he guided her toward the corner booth. It was unoccupied, as were the other booths and tables nearby, and offered a view of the parking lot and the door. He chose the bench facing the dining room and left her with the bench facing the wall. Good planning on his part, she thought with a scowl. Other than the moment it had taken them to walk in and the additional moment they would need to walk out, no one in the room, other than the waitress, would get much of a look at her. Later, if anyone asked, if D.J. eventually got suspicious and contacted the authorities, if somehow she and John were tracked to this small town, no one would remember her. Even the waitress was more interested in John than in her.

The woman gave them menus and coffee, then took their orders. He ordered biscuits and gravy, but Teryl was too hungry to settle for so little. She asked for that, plus bacon, eggs over easy, toast, and a short stack of blueberry pancakes.

Alone with him again, she stirred sugar and creamer into her coffee, making it rich enough to almost fool her stomach into thinking it was nourishment, but she hadn't tasted it yet. She was waiting for it to cool, waiting and stirring and uneasily ignoring him.

"Tell me about life in Richmond."

The task of ignoring him went right out the window. She looked up sharply, surprised that he'd spoken, wishing he hadn't. At last, with a little shrug, she put the spoon down, resting it on a paper napkin. "Well, it's the capital of Virginia, and it's located a few hours south of Washington—"

He interrupted her. "Not life in general. Tell me about *your* life."

Suspicion entered her eyes. "Why?"

Her question obviously annoyed him. It darkened his eyes, thinned his mouth, and made his voice go flat and empty. "Humor me. I want to have a conversation. Other than Tuesday evening with you, I haven't had a conversation in more years than I can remember. So what do you do in Richmond?"

For a moment she ignored his question and wondered about the statement that had preceded it. How could a person live so totally isolated that he couldn't remember the last time he'd indulged in such a simple pleasure as conversation? More importantly, *why* would a person choose to live that way?

Maybe because he was crazy. Maybe being crazy was easier to deal with when you were never around anyone who was sane.

"I work for the Robertson Literary Agency," she said at last. "I spend time with D.J. and the rest of my family, and I occasionally go out on dates. It's not an exciting life, but I like it."

"I thought D.J. was your best friend, not family."

"My parents take in foster kids—they have ever since I was a kid. D.J. came to live with us when she was nine and I was eight. We've been best friends ever since." Pausing, she sipped the coffee, wrinkling her nose a bit at the taste. "A person can be your best friend and be family, too. D.J. is. My mother is. So is my dad."

"My mother wishes I were dead. My father wishes I'd never been born." Realizing he'd spoken the sullen words aloud, he flushed and directed his gaze to his own coffee. "Are you an only child, other than the foster kids?"

Teryl studied him for a moment. She didn't want to feel

even the slightest bit of sympathy for him, but she couldn't help it. She'd seen too many firsthand examples of the damage uncaring parents could do to their innocent children to feel nothing at hearing his words. But he was embarrassed that he'd said anything, and, while she might be totally sympathetic, she wasn't about to offer the man who'd kidnapped her any of that sympathy.

"In a manner of speaking," she replied. "I'm the only Weaver by birth, but Mama and Daddy adopted eight of the kids they took in. And some of the foster kids, like D.J., lived with us ten or fifteen years or even longer. They're family, too." She paused again, then asked her own question. "Do you have brothers and sisters?"

It was a simple question to cause such pain, but that was undeniably the emotion that crossed his face before he blanked out everything. Again, she found herself wondering, again feeling just a little bit sorry for him. "There were three of us. Janie, the youngest, is a high school Spanish teacher in Florida, in a little place called Verona."

"And the third one? Brother or sister?"

"Brother."

"Older or younger?"

"Older."

"What is he?"

He looked at her then, his gaze unflinchingly steady. "Dead," he said quietly, bleakly. "Tom is dead."

Teryl looked away, and her hands tightened around her coffee cup. At least that explained the pain. Wishing she hadn't asked the first question, she cleared her throat and murmured, "I'm sorry." Then, almost immediately, she asked another regrettable question. "Were you very close?"

He took a deep breath, then noisily blew it out. "He was the kind of son every parent dreams about. He was unbelievably smart. He lettered in football, basketball, and track. He was captain of the football team, senior class president, the most likely to succeed. He went to college on both academic and athletic scholarships. He had a knack for foreign languages, for musical instruments, for machines of any kind.

He was also the nicest guy you'd ever want to meet." He was quiet for a moment; then he finished, "He was incredible."

"Sounds like a tough act to follow."

For a moment he looked as if he wanted to argue, to protest on his brother's behalf, but then he simply conceded. "He was."

"When did he die?"

"Seventeen years ago."

"That's when you left home."

He didn't say anything to that. He had said enough earlier. *My mother wishes I were dead. My father wishes I'd never been born.* Did his parents blame him? she wondered. Did they feel he was responsible for Tom's death? That would explain a lot. The emptiness of the life he'd chosen for himself. The delusions. The need to be someone else.

"Is that when you moved to Colorado?"

"No. I traveled around for a while. I lived in Maine. The Florida Keys. Mexico. Georgia. Louisiana."

She recognized each of those places as the setting for a Tremont book, but she didn't comment on it. She didn't want to bring Simon into their conversation. "Doing what?"

"Running away. I worked when I could find a job. I drank when I wasn't working . . . and for a time, I drank when I was. Then, while I was working on a Liberian freighter, I started writing."

So much for not bringing Simon in, she thought grimly.

Making two trips with their meal, the waitress saved Teryl from having to respond to his last words. The reprieve didn't last long, though. John finished his breakfast before she'd made more than a dent in her own meal. The waitress brought him more coffee, then took away his empty plate. He watched her for a moment before blowing out his breath in a reluctant sigh and flatly stating, "I wrote those books, Teryl."

Her mouth full of pancakes drenched with butter and maple syrup, she looked at him while she chewed, but she didn't say anything. She tried not to reveal her skepticism in her expression, but his growing frustration suggested that she'd failed, and his barely controlled anger proved it.

"I started the first book while I was on the freighter. When I finished it, I picked Rebecca Robertson's agency out of a book in the library. She was still in New York City at the time. I didn't know about querying her first to see if she was interested in seeing the book. I didn't know anything about the way the business worked. I just sent her the completed manuscript. I didn't even know to send return postage. I figured that if she wasn't interested in it, then it wasn't any good. She could throw her copy in the trash, and I would dump mine and forget about it."

She still said nothing.

"I'd given her a post office box for my return address. I was in Colorado by then; I went there to finish the book. I was about out of cash, so I got a job doing road work and was starting the second book when I heard back from her."

"That was awfully optimistic for someone who was ready to give up writing at the first rejection," she said mildly.

"I wasn't willing to give up the writing—just the attempt at selling it. The writing was for me. It always has been. It's a healing process. It's kept me sane." He smiled cynically. "Although I'm sure you have other opinions about that."

She ignored his last comment. "Rebecca wrote back and said what?"

"That she wanted to represent me. That she loved the book. That she thought it was powerful. She included a copy of the agency agreement. I signed and returned it, and, in the meantime, she sold the book to Morgan-Wilkes."

"So Morgan-Wilkes went from an obscure little publishing house to success beyond their greediest dreams. Rebecca Robertson went from being a small-time player to one of the biggest names in the business. And you went into seclusion, hiding behind layer upon layer of mystery, which enabled the man we saw interviewed in New Orleans to convince Rebecca, Morgan-Wilkes, me, and the rest of the world that *he* is *you*."

"I know it sounds crazy—"

She interrupted him. "It sounds like one of Simon Tremont's books."

"But it's not. It's my life."

With a sigh, Teryl gazed down at her breakfast. One biscuit, half a piece of toast, and two blueberry pancakes still remained on the plates. Not knowing when or if he would stop for lunch, she wished she could take them with her and keep them warm and fresh. Failing that, she wished she could finish them off now without making herself sick, but that was out of the question. She felt the way the family's puppy surely must feel—fat, satisfied, and his belly all rounded—after he'd gorged himself on his favorite meal. If she ate another bite, she would pop.

No matter how she might regret it later, she stacked the plates and pushed them aside. "If you're really Simon, then you can prove it. You have contracts, correspondence, copies of checks. You should know that the business of writing produces a ton of paper. Where is your copy of the agency agreement? Where are your contracts with Morgan-Wilkes? You get royalty statements every spring and fall; where are they?"

He looked as if he didn't want to answer, but finally, his mouth set in a thin line, he did. "Gone."

"Gone where?"

"Destroyed. My house . . . My house burned down last Saturday. All of my records were destroyed in the fire."

A little quiver of unease shivered down her spine. She had expected some excuse, some reason why he didn't have access to all the pertinent documents that would prove he was who he claimed to be, but she didn't like the one he gave. Was he being truthful? Had there really been a fire, or was it merely an excuse to explain away the nonexistence of papers that never had, in fact, existed—at least, not in *his* possession?

And if there *had* been a fire? Was he an arsonist as well as a liar? Were his delusions so powerful that he would destroy his own home simply to explain why he couldn't provide proof of his identity? Without proof, he could claim to be anyone he chose. Without proof, he could easily claim to be Simon Tremont.

Or John Smith.

Clearing her throat, she hesitantly asked, "Can I see your

driver's license?" If it said John Smith, it wouldn't prove anything. It could really be his name—it was common enough, after all—or it could simply mean that he'd gone to great lengths to make his charade believable, at least for himself. But if it had any other name on it or if it was issued by any state other than Colorado, it could prove that he had lied about those two details.

He hesitated only a moment, then maneuvered his wallet out of his hip pocket without sliding out from the bench. He tossed it onto the table in front of her.

Teryl wavered. Something about going through his personal things felt wrong, even though he could have easily told her no. Even though he had handed them over without a word. It was a violation of privacy, and she felt funny about it.

Even so, she needed to know.

The wallet was brown leather, bifold, worn and bent and about a million years old. When she opened it, she caught a glimpse of a stash of cash in the back section. It didn't look like a lot, and it made her wonder if that was all he had. Could that be why he hadn't stopped for meals yesterday? Because he was traveling on a tighter budget than even she normally stuck to?

She turned her attention from the money to the vinyl windows. A single window on the right held his driver's license, issued by the state of Colorado to John Henry Smith. The address listed a rural route, a box number, and a town she'd never heard of.

That could fit. Even though Simon Tremont's John Smith had given them a Denver post office box, she knew that, until a few months ago, he had actually lived somewhere in the mountains outside the city. This little town—Rapid River—could be the place.

If she was willing to consider the possibility that he was telling the truth.

She had to admit that this John Smith certainly better fit her image of the man behind the Tremont novels. He was, at times, sweet, gentle, and sensitive. He was interested in things other than himself. He was attentive to the world

around him, to people and places. He was an observer of the
sort that she imagined a good writer to be. And she couldn't
forget that the man she'd met in New Orleans had been such
a total surprise. He had been an absolute stranger, someone
with whom she, with her affinity for the Tremont novels and
her long-standing respect and admiration for their creator,
couldn't connect.

She had certainly connected with this John. Right from the
very beginning.

But his tale was so fantastic. It sounded like some melodramatic TV movie of the week. It was unbelievable, and if
she considered for a moment believing it, she would have to
question *her* sanity, as well as his.

The photograph on the license wasn't a great one, but it
was definitely recognizable. It was definitely John, serious
and grim-looking as people tended to be in official photos.
His hair was shorter, not as shaggy, and with the bad lighting
it was hard to see that his eyes were blue. He wore a white
dress shirt—like yesterday—and, she would bet, jeans and
running shoes, like today. Or maybe hiking boots would
have been more appropriate up there in Rapid River. He certainly looked as if he'd done something physical to stay in
shape.

He was a handsome man, she acknowledged with a twinge
of regret. Handsome, interesting, good in bed . . . and deranged.

He was more D.J.'s kind of guy than Teryl's. D.J. liked
them a little bit out there, a little on the edge, a little bit dangerous. Teryl liked them normal. Predictable. Right now boring sounded awfully good.

When he didn't seem impatient for the return of his property, she took the chance to examine the cards in the windows that fanned out on the opposite side. There were his
long-distance calling card, two gasoline cards and a Master-
card and a VISA, both gold cards, both in the name of John
H. Smith. One was due for renewal soon, she noticed, and
the other had recently been renewed. It was valid for two
years, the imprint read, from March of this year, and he had

been a cardmember, according to the date stamped on it, since 1986.

So if John Smith wasn't really his name, he'd adopted it long ago. Which proved what? That it probably *was* his name? Or that he'd been delusional for a long time?

Flipping the gold card over, she reached the last window. It held a snapshot that had been crookedly trimmed to fit. The color was bad, a symptom of age, maybe, or of too much exposure to the sun or too much handling. It had been taken in the mountains and showed two young men—boys, really— with their arms around a girl. John was easy to recognize, although some hard years had passed since the shot was taken.

In the picture, he was sixteen, maybe seventeen—a big, tall kid, broad-shouldered, darkly tanned, his hair sun bleached. He wore cutoff jeans and nothing else, and he appeared lean and muscled but somehow fragile, vulnerable in the way young kids often were. He was smiling in the picture, but he didn't seem exactly happy. There was a look in his eyes, one that the camera picked up and magnified, a look that she'd seen all too often on her brothers and sisters back home. It was filled with sorrow, with unhappiness, uncertainty, fear, and about a million other emotions. With some of the kids at home, it took only a few months of her parents' unswerving love, support, and reassurance to make the look go away. With others, it never completely left.

She always wondered what traumas such young, innocent kids had undergone to put that expression there, but she didn't ask for specific details. She had learned at a young age that it was usually best not to know.

Now, though, she found herself wondering again. At an age when the biggest worry in his life should have been whether his girlfriend was pregnant or simply late, he looked instead as if he carried the weight of the world on his shoulders but was doing his damnedest to hide it. He looked twenty years older than he was.

He looked wounded.

And the Weavers—her mom, her dad, and Teryl herself— were suckers for the world's wounded.

"Is this Tom?" she asked, directing her gaze to the young

man on the right. He looked like John, though not quite as tall, not quite as husky. He was older, and his hair was a few shades darker, his eyes brown. He looked, with his wide grin and clear, dark eyes, as healthy and well adjusted as any kid could be. He looked happy. He looked exactly as John had described him. *The nicest guy you'd ever want to meet.*

And exactly as she had described him. *A tough act to follow.*

"Yes."

"When did he die?"

"Two years after that picture was taken. He was twenty-two. He had just graduated from college with honors."

"How did it happen?"

"A wreck. The car went off the side of a mountain."

She looked again at Tom, full of life and vitality even in a twenty-some-year-old one-dimensional photograph, and felt a moment's regret that this stranger should have died so many years before his time. He should have been allowed to grow old, to live out his lifetime, to use his talents, to bless his family with his presence, to fall in love, to become a husband and a father, to experience life to the fullest. If only half of what John had said about him was true, he would have been too good a person to lose so young.

Feeling a little blue, she turned her attention to the girl. Janie, no doubt. She bore a strong resemblance to both brothers. Her hair was golden blond, her eyes the same blue as John's, and she was about five-ten, Teryl estimated, maybe a little taller. She was built like an athlete—not just slender but muscular, strong. The clearly defined muscles in her legs suggested a serious runner, one who ran long, hard miles every day, who could set records in both distance and time, one who didn't simply work out but who *trained* in every tough, aching sense of the word.

She didn't have to ask John any questions. Gazing at the photo, upside down from his perspective, he volunteered a little information about his sister, confirming Teryl's guess. "She was a world-class runner. When she was seventeen, she was the fastest woman in the state of California. She used to run five or ten miles a day, sometimes more, then lift weights, swim, ride her bike. She held all kinds of track records—regional, state, national, world. She was a shoo-in for the Olympic team. The only way she could not make it was to not show up for the trials."

"And she didn't show up for the trials," Teryl said slowly, "because she was in the car with Tom when he died."

John nodded.

"But she survived."

"More or less."

She continued to look at the picture, but she saw little now, her vision blurring it into a smudge of colors, of shapes and indistinct faces. She had learned not to ask for details of other people's tragedies, but if she let this conversation continue, she was going to learn the cause behind one of John's greatest sorrows. She was going to ask the wrong question, and he was going to give the wrong answer, the answer she didn't want to hear, the answer she knew he would hate giving. She should close the wallet, give it back and ask about something else—Colorado. The Liberian freighter. Simon Tremont. She should ask about anything else in the world but this.

Damned if she wasn't too foolish to take her own advice. Her voice soft and unsteady, she stared at the photo that she held in both hands and asked what she didn't want to know. "And you, John? Where were you when Tom died and Janie got hurt? Were you in the car with them?"

Reaching across the table, he pulled the wallet from her hands, closed and clutched it tightly. With a look as bereaved as any she'd ever seen, he met her gaze and bluntly, brutally answered, "In the car with them? *I* was driving the damned thing. Tom died because of me. Do you understand?"

She lowered her gaze, made uneasy by the intensity in his eyes, unwilling to witness such grief. She knew too much already about this stranger; she didn't want to know this. She didn't want to face what a terrible burden of guilt he'd been carrying all these years. She didn't want to know that if he had, indeed, lost his grip on reality, he'd certainly had a hell of a good reason for it.

Because she wasn't looking, when he touched her, she

wasn't prepared for it. He reached out, lifting her chin, raising her face until she felt compelled to meet his gaze again. There was a horrible sort of acceptance in his expression, as if nothing he ever did could possibly make this all right. His family would hate him for it forever—*My mother wishes I were dead. My father wishes I had never been born*—but he would hate himself more. He would punish himself more severely, more mercilessly, than they ever could.

"Do you understand what I'm saying, Teryl?" he asked, his voice quiet and empty of emotion, his fingers gentle against her skin, almost a caress.

She wanted to pull away, wanted to break the contact with him, to change the subject or get up and walk away, wanted to do anything that would bring this conversation to an end *now*. But she could do nothing. She couldn't raise her hand from the tabletop to push his away. She couldn't make her brain put together a rational thought. She couldn't give the commands to her body to move, to slide out of the booth and stand up.

She couldn't do anything but sit there and listen to damningly bleak words she didn't want to hear.

He made her hear them anyway.

"*I* killed my brother."

Chapter Six

————◆————

Georgia looked like Alabama, John thought, which looked like Mississippi, which looked much like Louisiana. After only a few days back in the South, he remembered why he'd left the freighter in New Orleans and settled in Colorado to work on the first book. He had come to hate the heat and the humidity, had despised the steaminess of summer and the sameness of winter. He had grown tired of the Southern landscape, the oaks and magnolias, the azaleas and the Spanish moss, and especially the pine trees and the kudzu that crept over everything. He had loathed the lushness made possible by the temperate climate, had found it suffocatingly close, an overwhelming reminder of a South American jungle he had once traveled through. He had craved space, had needed a place where nature wasn't so rich and ripe and threatening to overrun.

He had thought he could find peace in the mountains. After all, many of the best times in his life had taken place in the mountains that ranged through California.

But so had the worst time in his life.

At least he'd found the space he needed. He had found a life he could live.

But it wasn't his life anymore.

In the last fifteen miles he had watched in the rearview mirror as the sun set, turning the western sky shades of lavender and pink that gradually darkened to deep purple. He liked sunsets. He liked sunrises, too. Endings and beginnings. He hadn't had enough of them. When Tom had died and Janie had wound up in a wheelchair, so many possibilities had ended. So many beginnings had been cut off before they'd started.

It was time to stop for the night. He dreaded it—dreaded sharing a room and nothing more with Teryl, dreaded the discomfort and the awkwardness. Most of all he dreaded a repeat of those miserable minutes with the telephone cord. If only there were some other way . . . If only he could trust her . . .

But there was no other way to get the few minutes of privacy he required, and he couldn't trust her. If he left her alone and unbound, she would escape. No matter what he piled in front of the door, she would somehow manage to get out, and without her, his chances of ever proving anything would drastically decrease.

He wasn't sure they were very good *with* her.

They were on the outskirts of Atlanta, traveling a wide thoroughfare bordered on both sides with gas stations, fast food, convenience stores, and an abundance of cheap motels. On his occasional trips into Denver, he usually stayed at the nicest place in the city, with valets to park his truck, bellmen to carry his luggage, and a concierge to fulfill his every request. What a step down the Heart of the South Motel was. They checked in at the office, then went across the street to buy a box of fried chicken with all the trimmings to take back to the room. This time, since Teryl had the food, he carried both suitcases inside.

For a moment they both simply stood right inside the door. The outside hadn't been too promising, he admitted as he gazed around, but this room was, if possible, even smaller, uglier, and drabber than the one last night in Mississippi. The walls were paneled in dark brown, the carpet was threadbare, and one of the two mattresses sagged into a clearly visible crater. There were only two lights in the entire room, neither exceeding forty watts, and even those dimmed when he turned on the air conditioner, which ran with a tremendous amount of noise but produced very little cool air.

Teryl sighed and automatically turned toward the bed farthest from the door. He wouldn't blame her if she complained about the fact that her sandals stuck just a little to the damned carpet or about the heat that the air conditioner was doing little to relieve, but she didn't say a word. She simply sat down on the bed, removed her shoes, drew her feet onto the bed, and began unpacking their dinner on the nightstand.

As meals went, this one was nothing to brag about. The chicken was greasy; when they wiped their hands, little bits of paper from the napkins stuck to their fingertips. The mashed potatoes were instant and the gravy tasted as if it came from a package, too, but the cole slaw was good and the biscuits were buttery and just a little bit sweet.

After a while, he broke the silence. "You like legs, huh?"

She glanced down at the napkin in front of her, where the remains of three drumsticks were lined up. "It's my favorite piece. Mama used to fry chicken every Sunday for dinner; she would do a whole fryer, plus a couple dozen legs so there would be enough for all the kids."

"What do your parents do?"

The look she gave him was on the blank side. "I told you. They raise kids."

"But doesn't one of them work?"

Disdain sneaked into her expression and her voice. "You try raising a dozen or more kids who aren't your own, who have been mistreated or abandoned or abused since they were babies, and see if that's not work."

"I know that's work," he said, his patience exaggerated. "I just meant something outside the home—you know, something that pays a salary and helps support all those kids. Or does foster parenthood pay better than I realized?"

"They get some money from the state to help cover expenses, but it's not enough. They don't do it for the money. No one does." She made an impatient gesture. "There's not enough money in the world to make taking in someone like D.J. or Carrie or Rico worthwhile."

He assumed Carrie and Rico were two of her adopted or

foster siblings. He focused on the one he was already famil- iar with. "What's wrong with D.J.?"

"Nothing."

But she answered too quickly, and there was too much avoidance in her gaze, to be telling the truth. "Was she mis- treated, abandoned, or abused when she was a kid?"

Ignoring his question, she reached for the box of chicken, sorting through it until she found the fourth and last drum- stick, but once she had it, she merely picked at it—peeling off strips of crispy skin, then long slivers of dark meat. He watched and waited for her answer while she scooped a spoonful of mashed potatos onto her paper plate, then claimed one of the last two biscuits from the smaller box.

Finally she looked at him again, her eyes dark, her expres- sion serious, the set of her mouth regretful. "Let's just say D.J.'s parents had a strange way of showing their affection and leave it at that, okay?"

For the first time in months longer than he wanted to re- member, his writer's curiosity was piqued. If he spent much time thinking about it, it wouldn't be long at all before he'd created an entire background for her friend, a history starting before her birth and extending through the present and on into the future. He would create evil—people who should have loved her, people who should have helped her—and balance it with good—people who *did* love her, who *did* help her, although possibly too late—and soon he would have the bare-bones outline of a story. It would be a story of revenge, he thought. A story that everyone appalled by the horrible things people did to their children could relate to. A story of a hurting, helpless, innocent child grown into a strong, pow- erful woman who could make the people who had once hurt her very, very sorry.

But right now he wasn't interested in D.J.'s story—not the real-life horrors she had lived through or the fictional back- ground he could make up for her.

Right now he was interested in Teryl, in learning every- thing he could about her.

"So neither of your parents has an outside job. How do they manage?"

"My mother has some money."

"You told me Wednesday that they didn't," he reminded her. It had been shortly after she'd finally realized that she'd been kidnapped, and they had been sitting on the shoulder alongside Interstate 10. *I'm not worth anything to you,* she had said. *I don't have any money. My family doesn't have any money.* She had been scared and pleading.

So had he. *Don't make me hurt you, Teryl. I need you.*

Now he watched her flush and shift uneasily, obviously fearful that she'd just made a major mistake. "Not ready cash," she said, studying her food intently. "It's in a trust. It's all tied up in taking care of the kids."

He could tell her that he wasn't interested in money, not her mother's or anyone else's. If she didn't believe him, he could even open his suitcase and show her the cash he'd stuffed in a zippered black shaving kit. Last week in Denver, after hearing the news about Simon Tremont and his new book, after discovering that no mail—other than a few cards from Janie—had been delivered to his box in the last four months, he had gone to the bank and closed out the two accounts where he kept ready cash. Unsure of what the problem was and how long it would take to resolve it, he'd taken the money in cash—all $130,000 of it.

But he was pretty sure that finding out he was carrying over a hundred grand in his battered suitcase would have exactly the opposite effect of reassurance on her. She would probably think that he had held up a bank or embezzled it from his employer or some other nonsense. She would probably see it as one more reason why she should be afraid of him.

She *wouldn't* think it just might be a reason to believe in him.

In an effort to ease her wariness, he turned the conversation away from the issue of money and back more directly to her parents. "The decision to take in a bunch of special needs kids can't be an easy one. What made your folks decide to do it?"

She didn't relax right away; there was still doubt and distrust in her movements, jerky and graceless, as she broke her biscuit in half and took a bite from the top half, the crusty, buttery half. But slowly, degree by visible degree, calm replaced nervousness. The guarded air about her gave way to a more natural openness. "They wanted a large family, but after I was born, something happened. They couldn't have any more kids of their own, so they decided to open their home to kids who needed one—to kids who needed *them.*"

"Didn't you resent the other kids?"

Looking truly puzzled, she stopped eating to stare at him. "Why would I resent them?"

"They were *your* parents," he said with a shrug, "but you had to share them with all these strangers who had no claim on them, strangers who needed extra time, extra attention, extra affection. They must have had to spread themselves pretty thin to take care of everyone. Surely you must have felt slighted at some time."

"I never did." Her tone was emphatic, her manner insulted. "These *strangers* were kids, for heaven's sake—sad little kids who'd been through more pain and sorrow in a few years than most adults experience in a lifetime." Then she softened. "My parents had an awful lot of time and attention and love to give. No one got left out. No one felt slighted." She pulled the last piece of crust from the biscuit, then tossed the tender insides onto the napkin with the bones. Before she ate that piece, though, she asked a hesitant question. "Did you resent Tom?"

The unexpected mention of his brother made him stiffen. He had talked more about Tom today than he had in the last seventeen years combined. In the past the things he'd had to say had been too personal, too painful, and the guilt had been too raw. There had never been anyone to listen, anyone to understand or sympathize, anyone to offer something other than damnation for his deeds. There had never been anyone he could trust with his brother's name, with his brother's memory.

But he instinctively trusted Teryl, and because he did, he forced himself to ignore the ever-present pain, the guilt, the damnation. He forced himself to answer, and to answer honestly. "Yes, I did."

"Because he was so perfect?"

Using one of the wet towelettes that had come with dinner, he wiped his hands, then stretched out on the bed, propped a pillow beneath his head, and gazed up at the ceiling. There were water spots there, seeping in from above the window and spreading outward in a yellow-hued stain. "My parents wanted a perfect son and a perfect daughter, and they got them. Unfortunately, they got *me* in between," he said, then sighed. "I didn't resent Tom. I resented that he came first. I resented that he found it so easy to live up to our parents' expectations. I resented that, compared to him, I looked even more incompetent and inept than I actually was—and, believe me, our parents were *always* comparing me to him. I resented that he did everything right and I did everything wrong. But I never resented *him*."

"Any parent can love a perfect child. It takes someone special to love the rest of us." There was a faint smile in her voice when she went on. "Words of wisdom from Debra Jane Howell."

Still staring at the ceiling, he smiled just a little bit, too. "I figured D.J. stood for something like Dorothy Josephine or Dorcas June. Debra Jane's not a bad name. Why does she go by D.J.? Was she a tomboy growing up?"

That earned what was surely almost a laugh from her. He liked the sound of it. He would like to hear her really laugh, would like to see her really smile. He would like to see her smile at *him*.

He'd had so few normal relationships in his life, especially with women. Of course, he'd had girlfriends, back when he was a teenager. He'd gone steady with one girl all through high school, a typical California girl—nearly six feet tall, blond, leggy, athletic. They'd known each other from first grade on. They'd shared friends, hot summer days at the beach, and sex as good as it ever got for most teenagers.

He had liked her a lot, but they had broken up after high school. Chrissy—as smart as Tom, as popular as Janie—had gone to college back East on a scholarship, and he had begun seeing other girls, girls who didn't care about much of anything but sex, which was fair because that was about all he'd been interested in. By the time he'd gotten old enough to appreciate the distinction between girls and women, he'd been out of the market for relationships of any sort. There had been the occasional encounter of a sexual nature, but, except for his arrangement with Marcia, never more than that.

He hadn't realized until he'd met Teryl exactly how much he missed having more.

Across the room, she was answering his last question. "Not in this lifetime. D.J.'s always been a perfect little . . . "

While she decided how to complete the description, he considered a few possibilities. A perfect little lady? A perfect little angel?

But he was way off the mark, he realized, when she finally finished. "A perfect little vamp. Her family had called her Debra Jane, so when she moved in with us, she chose to go by her initials. It was her way of starting over, I guess. A new home, a new family, a new chance, and a new name."

Vamp. It was an odd word, and it seemed even odder coming from Teryl, describing her best friend. It was a word he might use in a book—*a perfect little vamp, a perfect little tramp*—but not in conversation, not to describe anyone he knew. Its connotations were too distinctly negative.

Maybe Teryl wasn't aware of that. Maybe the word, for her, meant nothing more than seductive, feminine, charming.

Or maybe she knew those negative connotations all too well.

He knew from research for one of his early books that there were a thousand different ways for kids to respond to abuse, neglect, and abandonment. Hell, he knew it to some extent from experience. As far as his parents were concerned, they had fulfilled their obligations to him: they had given him food, a place to live, and clothes to wear. They had even helped pay for his two years in college. But if they had ever loved him—truly, unconditionally, the way parents were supposed to—he couldn't remember it. The soothing, the loving, the affection in his life had come from Tom and, later, Janie. He had a memory or two of being cuddled by his mother, but only when he was very young. The older he had gotten and the more obvious it had become that he wasn't another Tom, the rarer those moments had become. Neither his mother nor his father had had any patience with a clumsy, awkward, slow-to-learn kid who reminded them with his mere presence that, yes, they were capable of producing a brilliant child like Tom, but they were also capable of producing an unremarkable, less-than-average kid like him.

It was a reminder they hadn't appreciated.

But his parents hadn't physically abused or neglected him. Oh, there had been that time in the backyard when his father had just finished working out with Tom, pitcher of his Little League team, and had ordered John out into the grass for a little game of catch. The problem was John, five, maybe six years old, was uncoordinated as hell and, worse, he'd had no interest in baseball or any other sport. His father had been unusually patient for the first ten or fifteen pitches, even though John had dropped, missed, or—worst of all—avoided the majority of them.

But then he had lost his patience . . . and his temper. After berating him and calling him a coward, among other names, for dodging some of the balls, his father had fired off a fast one. There was no way John ever could have caught it—no way even Tom, watching from the patio, could have. But then, his father hadn't meant for him to catch it. He had been throwing at a target with the intention of hitting it, and he had succeeded.

John had walked with a limp for weeks afterward.

He could have accepted his father's challenge. He could have practiced, could have worked out with Tom, could have done his damnedest to turn himself into the best jock the Smith family had ever seen. By junior high, he'd had the size for any sport that might interest him; he'd been quick on his feet, and, from his experience as Janie's occasional running partner, he'd known he had strength and endurance.

But he had chosen instead to avoid sports altogether. Going one step farther, he had chosen as his sole physical activity an activity sure to anger his father—surfing—and he had excelled at it. It was a worthless talent in the old man's eyes and just further proof that John was neither the son he wanted nor the son he deserved.

What had D.J.'s choices been? he wondered. What had happened to her to lead her best friend to describe her the way Teryl had? If she had been sexually abused as a child, it wouldn't be uncommon for her to remain sexually active as a teenager and as an adult. After all, Teryl had said that her friend had *always* been a perfect little vamp. Inappropriately seductive behavior in young children was a prime indication of sexual abuse.

On the other hand, a repressive, unloving, unaffectionate upbringing could bring about the same behavior. Maybe her parents had cared no more for her than his parents had for him, but maybe she hadn't had anyone like Tom and Janie to love her in their stead. Maybe after nine years in such an emotionally sterile environment, she had learned to seek affection wherever she could find it—and the easiest place for a young girl to find such affection always had been and likely always would be in sexual relationships with hormonally driven young boys.

The rattle of paper and plastic signaled that Teryl was finished with dinner and gathering the wrappers together. He listened to the creak of the bedsprings as she bent to get her shoes; then she rose from the bed and carried the paper bag to the wastebasket near the door. For a moment, she simply stood there, her summery dress a splash of color in an otherwise drab room. It was the same dress she'd worn to say good-bye to the man claiming to be Tremont—simple in style, bright in color. It left her arms bare, along with a bit of her back, revealing a little creamy golden skin, but concealing more. With its wide straps, rounded neck, and damned near ankle-length hem, it was as modest as a piece of clothing could be. It flattered her. It concealed her body so thoroughly that it made her look sweet. Innocent.

It made him remember her naked.

And under the circumstances, he thought grimly, Teryl naked was a memory he definitely didn't need.

* * *

Returning to the bed, Teryl propped the pillows against the headboard, kicked off her shoes again, and leaned back. It was warm—the air conditioner had clearly met its match in the muggy heat—the room was dimly lit, and she was full and tired. It wouldn't take much at all for her to drift off into dreamland—a few more minutes without conversation. A few more minutes of listening to the rushing sound from the air conditioner's ineffective fan. A few more minutes of fighting fatigue.

All in all, she thought, letting her eyes flutter shut, considering the circumstances, it hadn't been such a bad day. They'd had breakfast, lunch, and dinner. They had talked. John seemed more like the interesting, friendly man she had met Tuesday than the volatile, threatening stranger who had kidnapped her Wednesday. She had behaved, and he hadn't done or said anything to cause her alarm.

Not that she was coming to accept the situation. Given a choice, she would rather be anywhere in the world with anyone else in the world—well, *almost* anyone else, she amended as Simon Tremont immediately came to mind—than here with John. She would much rather be home, living her boring little life, going about her dull routine, doing the drudge work—typing, filing, running errands—that filled her days, and watching TV at home alone, as she did most evenings. She didn't need excitement or thrills or danger in her life, and when they reached Richmond, she intended to do whatever was in her power to remove them—and him—from her life.

Still, she wasn't as afraid of John now as she'd been yesterday. She wasn't so convinced that he was going to hurt her. She was pretty much convinced that he *wasn't* going to kill her. She thought he was probably a decent guy—probably, at some time in his life, about as normal as any man who had been raised the way he had could be.

But she still thought he was crazy.

It was obvious he blamed himself for his brother's death and for whatever injuries their sister had suffered in the accident. Guilt was a powerful force. It could drive a man over the edge. It could rob him of his ability to reason. If a man felt guilty enough—and she suspected that the guilt John carried was as intense, as strong and poisonous, as it could get—it could affect his mind. It could make him hate himself so much for what he'd done that he would choose to become someone else in order to deal with it.

And if you were going to take on a different identity, why not reach for the stars? Why not become a man who was universally known, universally admired? Why not choose an identity that would make people adore you rather than criticize and belittle you? When you'd lived so many years in other people's shadows, why not choose the name that cast the biggest shadow of all?

It was too bad that her parents hadn't gotten hold of him about thirty years ago. They could have undone whatever damage *his* parents had already done. They would have loved him, taught him, encouraged him, praised him. They would have made him feel like the most special little kid in the world. They would have saved him, the way they had saved D.J., Carrie and Kenny, Rico and Allison and Kathy and all the rest. God, there had been so many of them—so many unwanted kids, so many mistreated ones. She couldn't remember all the names now . . . but her parents could. On their walls hung photographs of every single child who had ever come through their home, and they remembered every one. Names. Birthdates. Backgrounds. Problems. Triumphs. Successes. Losses. Deaths.

John could have been one of their successes.

Instead, he was his parents' biggest failure, their loss, and she would bet they didn't even realize it.

With a yawn, she switched mental gears, thinking about getting ready for bed. She should take a shower, but she could leave that until morning. She definitely had to wash her face, though, to remove her makeup, and she had to change into her T-shirt and, because it was too warm in here to cover up with even a sheet, her pinstriped shorts; this dress was all she had to wear until they got back to Richmond It was already wrinkled and in need of a quick wash and a hot iron. A night of tossing and turning would leave her—

Across the foot or so of space that separated the two beds, the springs squeaked as John moved. She heard his tennis shoes hit the floor with a slight thud and wondered drowsily what kind of abuse it had taken to get what once must have been a reasonably decent piece of carpeting into the awful shape this carpet was in.

Then he spoke her name. "Teryl."

His voice was quiet, a testing sort of tone to see if she was awake. She could respond—could open her eyes, could ask what he wanted, could simply move to acknowledge that she'd heard him and wasn't asleep—or she could just lie there, head back, eyes closed, lazy and comfortable, and if he wasn't persistent, in another minute or two she really would be beyond responding.

"Teryl."

This time his voice was closer. Opening her eyes, she saw him crouching between the two beds. His head was bent so that, from her position, she had a good view of his hair, more blond than brown, thick, a little on the shaggy side. When they had made love Tuesday night, she had played with his hair, had stroked it. Once, when he had suckled her nipple a little too greedily, sending a jolt of mild pain through her, she had pulled it, just enough to give him the same little jolt of pain. She had liked the texture of it, coarse and heavy. She had liked touching it.

She had liked touching *him*.

He had been so responsive, so generous, so hot. She had thought he was extremely talented . . . and passionate . . . and hungry. But it had never occurred to her then that he might be unbalanced. Had he hidden it well, or had she simply been blinded by lust?

She didn't know the answer, not even when he abruptly looked up and their gazes locked. His face underwent an immediate transformation. The bleakness didn't disappear, but it faded into the background, replaced by desire. It softened his eyes and his mouth and eased the tension that gripped his muscles while, at the same time, creating a tension all its own. It reminded her how handsome he was, how sweetly he smiled, how needful his kisses were.

Regardless of his illusions—his delusions—his desire was real. She had experienced it for herself two nights ago. She had felt the evidence of it last night when he had pinned her to the bed and gotten hard. She felt it again now—felt it deep inside—with no more than his look.

Maybe he *had* lost touch with reality, but he wanted her. If she gave him any indication that she felt the same need, he would be stripped naked and in bed with her in a heartbeat.

Maybe *she* was the crazy one. She didn't know him, didn't trust him, didn't believe him. She thought the damage his parents had done to him, combined with the guilt and grief he had suffered over his brother's death, had cost him his sanity. She thought he—and she and Simon Tremont and Rebecca and Candace Baker and anyone else affiliated with Simon—would be safer with John locked up and medicated in some soothing, peaceful sanitarium.

But damned if her breasts weren't starting to ache, if her nipples weren't growing hard. Damned if the muscles in her belly weren't tensing, quivering in expectation. Damned if she wasn't hot and getting hotter.

She *was* crazy.

She made the first move—nothing overtly sexual, nothing brash or bold, nothing that she couldn't back down from. She simply lifted her hand from her lap and reached out to touch his hand. His skin was warm, his fingers curled in a loose fist. His hands were big, his fingers long and tanned, his palms callused. Though he'd been reasonably gentle Tuesday night—considering that they had both been too frantic to take care—the calluses had given a rough texture to his caresses, especially on the tender skin of her breasts and inner thighs. With no more than a simple caress across her nipples, he had created such wonderfully pleasurable sensations.

There had been such a long time in her life without sexual pleasure. After she'd found out about Gregory's wife and broken up with him, she'd had dates but no sex. No one had appealed to her in that way. No one had made her knees weak. No one had made her want to be wicked—not even

Gregory, if she was honest. She had believed she was in love with him, had wanted to marry him, but their lovemaking had lacked fire. There had been no passion, no sparks. They had made love because they wanted to or because it was convenient or because that was what couples did, but they had never done it because they had needed it.

John had needed it two nights ago.

She had needed it. She still did.

She had longed to be wicked in New Orleans, but this— wanting him now, wanting him when she was his prisoner . . . *This* was wicked. It was perverted.

And she wanted it anyway.

Still holding his gaze, she began unfolding his fingers, undoing his fist, intending to bring his hand, palm flat, fingers molded around, to her breast. She had reached his third finger before she realized that he wasn't simply clenching his fist. He was holding something. She looked down to see what it was, but her fingertips identified it long before her gaze reached it.

Her desire died an instant death as fear washed over her. She snatched her hand back from his and tried in an awkward rush to scoot away, but he was too quick for her. He grabbed her, one arm around her hips, and pulled her back, holding her forcibly as he pulled the telephone cord into place. "I'm sorry, Teryl," he said, his voice ragged as he began winding it around her wrists. "Just ten minutes—I swear to God, it won't be longer than ten minutes."

"No, no, please . . . I won't try anything! Please, John!" Her voice was breathy, insubstantial. She was having trouble breathing, and her limbs seemed to have taken on lives of their own, trembling and shuddering uncontrollably. "P-please don't do this again, John. I'll stay right here. I promise, I won't move from right here."

He ignored her hopeful pleas and tied the ends securely, then disappeared into the bathroom, pausing only for a moment on the way to turn the television on. She gave the cord a tremendous jerk, which only served to tighten it around her wrists; then, calling on every ounce of strength she possessed, she grew calm—at least, as calm as she could be when she was about to hyperventilate.

Ten minutes, he had promised. In ten minutes or less, he would come out here and remove the cord. That wasn't so long. What could happen in ten minutes?

A person could die.

A person could inflict tremendous pain on a smaller, weaker person.

Horrible nightmares could occur in less than ten minutes. Beatings. Rape. Torture.

But she was alone. John was in the other room, and he had no reason to hurt her. Why would he beat her, when he already felt guilty over the minor bruises he'd caused her? Rape? If he had simply dropped the wire moments ago, she would have submitted to him willingly. Submitted? Hell, she'd been intending to *seduce* him. And as for torture, she couldn't believe he was capable. From her brothers and sisters, she knew more than she wanted about people who *were* capable of it. John wasn't one of them.

But that didn't slow her heart rate. It didn't calm her trembling. It didn't make her breathe easier. It didn't ease this monstrous fear. It didn't wake her from this nightmare.

Nightmares had been a fairly common occurrence in the Weaver household. As a kid, she'd had a few of her own—disjointed, hazy, meaningless frights that had yanked her from her sleep. Her night terrors hadn't been her own, though. They had been born of the stories that D.J. had told her and of other kids' histories that she'd learned in bits and pieces. She was too sensitive by far, D.J. had always said, if she could empathize so completely with them that she shared their dreams.

But it had been Teryl D.J. had turned to when she'd had her own bad dreams. The rest of the kids—Teryl included—had wanted one of their parents, usually their mother, who had held them and rocked them and sung them to sleep. But D.J. had wanted Teryl, at least until she'd turned fourteen or fifteen and had been too tough to cry on anyone's shoulder. Before then, though, she had regularly climbed into Teryl's bed, and Teryl had held her and patted her and sung all the soft, soothing songs her mother had sung to her.

Now she hummed one of those tunes, seeking solace but finding nothing beyond the urge to scream for help, for rescue, to scream and scream and scream. But screaming was a bad idea. It might not bring anyone to her aid, and it would surely anger John. If he was capable of tying her to the bed when he obviously didn't want to, who knew what he could do when he was angry?

The tear that slid down her cheek was hot, and it left a cool, damp trail.

It seemed as if, while she hummed her mother's songs and cried, hours passed before John returned from the bathroom to release her, but in reality she guessed he had probably kept his ten-minute promise. Crouching beside the bed once more to undo the knots in the thin cord, he looked forbidding, full of self-reproach, distant.

She hoped he stayed that way.

Loosening the last knot, he eased the cord enough to slide over her hands, freed it from the bedframe, and wheeled to his feet. As soon as he started off, she slid back into the corner, away from the dim light of the lamp, away from him, curling into the smallest space she could fit herself, and she watched as he got ready for bed. The mattress from the other bed hit the floor, rattling the door, making the television sway unsteadily on its rickety stand. He stripped the bed down to the bottom sheet and left the rest of the linens on the springs, along with the extra pillow. After turning off the lamp that sat on the dresser, he stood stiffly, his back to her, then asked, "Are you going to sleep like that?"

She didn't answer. She simply scooted until her back was against the wall; when she could retreat no farther, she pulled the second pillow over and hugged it to her chest.

After a moment, he turned off the other light, then made his way through the dark to his bed. She listened to him remove his shoes and then his jeans, and she wished with every fiber of her being that she had never heard of John Smith. Or New Orleans.

Or even Simon Tremont.

*   *   *

Lorna Weaver stood at the kitchen counter, a baby on one hip, a bowl of pancake batter in front of her, and an electric griddle heating on the center island. Blueberry muffins were cooling on a wire rack, bacon was draining on paper towels, and the coffee, she knew from the aroma, was just about finished. Any moment now, Philip would herd in the rest of the kids, get them seated on benches, booster seats, and in high chairs around the long table, and the chaos that was a typical breakfast in the Weaver household would be under way.

For the moment, though, she was alone with baby Kesha and D.J., and she could use a hand, but she wasn't likely to get it from D.J. If Teryl were here, she would take Kesha, would sing to her and dance her around the room, and, if the baby cried, she would dry her tears, the way she had dried thousands of tears from countless babies in her life. Or, if she didn't take the baby, she would be happy to cook the pancakes, turning them out in uniform size, color, and texture, buttering them as they came off the griddle, dishing them onto the waiting plates.

But D.J. simply leaned against the counter, a glass of orange juice in hand, and watched as Lorna juggled it all.

She wasn't comparing D.J. unfavorably to Teryl, she insisted, feeling a twinge of guilt that such a denial felt necessary. She had other children who were all thumbs in the kitchen, other daughters who couldn't cook, others who, for one reason or another, had lost their maternal instinct long before it had had a chance to develop.

Still, she would rather be talking *to* her first daughter instead of about her.

"What do you mean she hasn't come back from New Orleans yet?" she asked as she poured the first baseball-sized circles of batter onto the hot griddle. "I thought she was due back Wednesday night."

"She was. But you know Teryl. Rebecca offered her the chance to stay on a few days, and she took it. She's always wanted to see New Orleans, you know."

That was true, Lorna conceded. From the moment Teryl had been offered the trip, she had been brimming over with excitement—although it was a toss-up which had excited her more: seeing the city she'd dreamed about or meeting the author she adored. "What did she think of Simon Tremont?"

D.J. shrugged. "I didn't ask, and she didn't say."

"I hope she wasn't disappointed."

"Why would she be?"

"Because she's admired the man since she was a teenager. Because she tends to have higher opinions of most of us than we deserve. I just hope her expectations weren't so lofty that no mere mortal could live up to them."

"Who says Simon Tremont's a mere mortal?" D.J. scoffed. "To hear Teryl talk about him, he's some god come down from his mountaintop to bring meaning and purpose to our lives."

"That's precisely my point. I like the man's books myself, but I couldn't care less what he's like in person—whether he's young or old, selfless and humble or arrogant and petty. If he turned out to be a perfectly hateful old goat, it wouldn't affect me one way or the other. Teryl, on the other hand, is a fan—"

"As in fanatic."

"And fans usually expect a tremendous amount from the object of their admiration."

"Are you speaking from personal experience?"

Lorna matched her teasing tone. "There was a time, young lady, when I wore silks and furs, diamonds and emeralds and rubies. When I never went out without creating a stir, when young men fell at my feet, when every entrance I made was a *grand* one."

"And to think, you gave it all up—Hollywood, the silver screen, fame and fortune—well, you held on to your fortune," D.J. amended before continuing. "Fame and celebrity, glamor, *stardom.* And you gave it all up for a house full of kids in Richmond, Virginia. Why?"

Using a pancake turner, Lorna flipped the eight round discs so the tops could brown, then shifted Kesha to her other side. D.J. had asked the question before, and she'd always gotten the same answer, but it never seemed to satisfy her. That was one more of the differences between her and Teryl. Teryl thought giving up an acting career to raise a bunch of kids was a perfectly normal thing to do. A career held little interest for her. If she ever found a nice guy, fell in love, and got married, she would like to be a full-time mother herself, provided they could afford it.

A career held little interest for D.J., either, truth be told, but neither did nice guys, love, marriage, and motherhood. The things D.J. had mentioned, though—fame and fortune, celebrity, glamor, and stardom . . . Those things sounded ever so much more appealing than a house filled with kids, with expenses and responsibilities, with tough times and heartache and sorrow. Having a good time, never settling down, never having a child whom she might hurt the way *her* mother had hurt *her*—those were D.J.'s priorities.

And although Lorna didn't approve of her foster daughter's lifestyle, while their definitions of a good time differed vastly, while she thought a good man and the unconditional love of a sweet baby who needed her could do D.J. a world of good, she never said so. Maybe someday the girl would come around, but in the meantime she was still dealing with the first nine years of her life in the only way she knew how. By committing herself to no one and nothing. By flitting from job to job and from man to man. By indulging in countless affairs with countless men. By settling for affection, however temporary, instead of holding out for love.

But it wasn't her place to judge. She hadn't lived through what D.J. had.

With a sigh, she turned her attention to D.J.'s question. Why had she retired at the height of her career and moved all the way across the country to spend the rest of her life as a housewife and mother? Because she had wanted a family. She had needed one in ways that threatened to destroy her.

She had come to a point in her life where her career had meant less every day. Making movies and playing the role of sex symbol had seemed such a waste of time. Keeping her private life—including her husband—secret because the studio didn't want a married bombshell had become wearisome. Philip had wanted public acknowledgment—had deserved it—and they had both wanted a family.

Truthfully, if she hadn't quit the business and moved back

to Virginia, they might never have had that family. They had been trying so long out there in L.A., but moving back here had been magic. One day they had been childless, and the next there had been the promise of the sweetest little baby any mother could hope for. Teryl wasn't their oldest—D.J. was older by a year, Scott by three years—but she was their first, and she was theirs in ways the other kids, no matter how dear, no matter how loved, would never be.

"It's the same old story, D.J.," she said with an indulgent smile. "Philip and I wanted more than we could have in Los Angeles. I wanted to be a wife. I wanted kids. I wanted to get fat and wear my hair in rollers and go to PTA meetings. I wanted to escape the reporters and the fans and the critics and the studio heads and live a happy, healthy, normal life."

D.J.'s response was little more than a snort. "I'd take L.A. over this place any day."

"You know, sweetie, if you really believe you would be happier someplace else, you could always move."

For a moment the younger woman was utterly still, as if such a thought had never occurred to her. Then her expression shifted, changed, all the cynicism and teasing and vitality fading, and she morosely replied, "No, I couldn't." Before Lorna could respond, she came around the island, gave her a hug, chucked the drowsy baby under the chin, and said, "I've got to get going or I'll be late for work for the third time this week. Tell Dad I'll see him soon."

From the door, Lorna watched her hurry across the patio and to the sports car she had treated herself to on her thirtieth birthday.

Tough times, heartache, and sorrow. Debra Jane Howell had lived through her share of them, and she had caused a fair share. Lorna and Philip had done what they could for her, but it hadn't been enough. Over the years, they'd had their failures; she still wasn't sure whether D.J. was one of them. Sometimes all the love in the world wasn't enough.

But sometimes, she thought as Kesha stirred, lifted her head from Lorna's shoulder, and sleepily smiled at her, sometimes it was all a heart needed.

*   *   *

As they crossed the Savannah River from Georgia into South Carolina, thunder rumbled, deep and threatening, loud enough to vibrate through the Blazer. John glanced at Teryl as she stirred. She had dozed the last seventy-five miles, a restless sort of sleep. Now she rolled her head from side to side, then stretched before returning the seat to its upright position. Combing her hair back from her face, she looked around, up the river to the left, down to the right, then twisted to see the city behind them. "Where are we?"

He directed his gaze back to the road and the surrounding traffic. "That's Augusta, Georgia, behind us and North Augusta, South Carolina, in front of us." As the bridge gave way to land, he shifted into the right lane, since he seemed to be the only driver on the road who wasn't exceeding the speed limit. It gave him a perfectly good excuse to look at her again.

"It's going to rain," she remarked, taking a panoramic look around. Her words were barely out before lightning flashed ahead of them. She flinched and reworded her pronouncement. "It's going to storm."

He offered no response.

"I hate storms."

A glance her way supported her words. She looked wary, uneasy. She didn't merely dislike thunderstorms, he realized. She was afraid of them. "Why do they bother you?"

"I don't know. They're violent and dangerous."

"I like them," he remarked evenly. "My house in Colorado is all glass—*was* all glass and wood. Every room had walls of windows for the view, and the most spectacular view in the mountains is a summer storm. There's something more intense about it up there—maybe because of the elevation, because you feel so much closer to the heavens. The lightning is sharper and more brilliant, and the thunder reverberates from valley to peak, and the rain comes down in torrents. It's impressive."

She gave him a long, steady look that prickled his nerves and made him feel edgy and awkward. A measuring look. A judging sort of look. When she spoke, though, her voice was even and hinted at nothing of her thoughts. "This is the house that burned down."

Gripping the steering wheel tighter, he answered with one terse word. "Yeah."

"What happened?"

"Wood burns. Glass, when exposed to high heat, shatters. It was gone in minutes. Totally destroyed." But he knew that wasn't the answer she wanted. She wanted to know what had caused the fire. She wanted to know if maybe *he* had caused it. She didn't want flippancy or deliberately obscure responses. But she didn't want the truth, either. She didn't want to hear that the fire had been caused by three bombs that had demolished the house. She sure as hell didn't want to hear that the man she believed was Simon Tremont had set—or paid someone to set—those three bombs.

Damn the man. She seriously disliked him, but she still admired him. She still had faith in him.

She was waiting for an answer—for a serious answer— and he offered it in blunt terms. "The fire was caused by the explosions. The explosions were caused by three bombs. One went off at the back door, one at the front door, and one upstairs in my bedroom."

It took her a long time to respond. Was she trying to find some truth or logic in his words? Or was she merely finding further proof that she had, indeed, been kidnapped by a raving lunatic?

"And where were you when the bombs exploded?" Her manner was cautious, her tone soothing.

John knew she didn't believe him. She still thought he was crazy. But she was going to play along and avoid upsetting him for fear he could turn violent. The hell of it was he *could.*

Knowing he was wasting his time, he replied in a voice that was little more than a monotone, empty of emotion, stripped clean of hope. "I had just left the bedroom and was on my way into the office. I was going to get my contracts, the correspondence, and tax records—everything I needed to prove to Rebecca and Candace and Morgan-Wilkes that I was Simon Tremont."

He paused, watching as raindrops began splattering on the windshield. He had awakened that morning in a hotel room in Denver—had awakened with Tom on his mind. He must have been dreaming about him. That would have explained the uneven beat of his heart, the unrested feeling, the dampness of the pillowcase.

Sometimes he tried to remember the dreams—whether they were good or bad, whether Tom had been alive, laughing, and so damned real, or dead in his arms—but not that morning. He had deliberately shut his brother out of his mind, had focused instead on what he would do while he was in the city. He had thought about his phone call the night before to Janie, about how good she had sounded and how excited she had been about the working vacation to Mexico that she was leaving on that very day. He had even, for a time, regretted sending away the pretty blonde in the conceal-nothing blue dress whom he'd met the night before in the hotel lounge. They'd had dinner together, had shared drinks in some of Denver's finest establishments. He had paid for her time, and when the evening was over, she had graciously offered an extension. Even though he'd been alone too long, he had turned her down. The next morning, he had regretted it.

With another flash of lightning, the rain increased in intensity to the sort of deluge he liked best, the kind that made driving hazardous, that could flood streets or wash away mountainsides. It was the kind of rain that, he'd often suspected, if he could just stay out in it long enough, could wash *him* away.

Maybe it could even wash him clean.

He braked carefully, slowing the Blazer to little more than a crawl, and, at the first opportunity, he turned off the road into a shopping center parking lot on the outskirts of a town called Aiken. He chose a parking space at the highest point of the lot, shut off the engine, and immediately felt the clammy heat start seeping in.

"You don't believe anything I've told you, do you?" he asked wearily.

She shrugged, bright colors on a gray day. "You have to admit that, so far, it's a fantastic story."

Disappointed again, he stared out the window. "I am not crazy." He had intended the denial to be strong, sure, convincing. Instead, it came out little more than a pathetically pleading whisper.

As if he didn't quite believe it himself.

"Why don't you start from the beginning?" she suggested, her voice still so perfectly calm, so perfectly placating. So perfectly phony. "Tell me the entire story."

Start from the beginning. It was good advice—advice that a writer the caliber of Simon Tremont shouldn't need. He'd been called the country's most powerful storyteller. The master of the psychological thriller. A manipulator of emotions who could make you feel things you had never felt more deeply than you had ever felt.

Start from the beginning. He had done that yesterday when he'd told her about Tom. Tom and Janie were the beginning of *Resurrection.* They were the beginning of his story and the beginning of his life. They had helped lead him to where he was today. The good stuff was all their doing.

The screwups, though, were all his own.

Start from the beginning. Taking a deep breath he did so.

"Over a year ago, I sent Rebecca the outline for *Resurrection . . .*"

Chapter Seven

───◆───

*W*hatever else he was, John Smith was definitely talented in the telling of tales.

He understood the art of storytelling, Teryl thought. It showed in the way he used his voice, in his choice of words, in the pauses that paced his story. Some phrases were pure images. Others were stripped bare, blunt. Almost every thought he spoke of himself was brutal and unforgiving.

And virtually everything he said sounded believable.

He had told her about writing the outline for *Resurrection*, the story that had been born of his brother's death seventeen years ago. It was autobiographical, he said—and the real Simon had also said—but not so clearly autobiographical that she could say with conviction, yes, this book was derived from his life. The feelings were there, though—the emotions, the losses, the grief. Based on what little of the book she'd read, she could easily see John giving life to Colin Summers.

But that didn't mean he actually had.

He had covered up to the point some eight months ago when writer's block had set in, and then he had fallen silent. Now he was staring gloomily out the window, watching the rain that hadn't slackened one bit, thinking about something personal and, judging from his expression, very painful.

She was thinking, too. About the fact that he knew more

about *Resurrection*'s story line than anyone out there should. About the fact that he knew details about Simon's writer's block and his missed deadline that no one else should know. About the fact that everything he said *sounded* true.

It *felt* true, even though it couldn't possibly be . . . could it?

What if this John Smith really *was* Simon Tremont? What if the man in New Orleans really was an impostor? What if *he* was the delusional one?

She wanted instinctively to deny it. It was, as she'd just told John, a fantastic story—too fantastic to believe. But if she believed that *he* could be delusional enough to convince himself that he was really Simon Tremont, why couldn't the same be possible of the *other* John Smith who was claiming to be Simon? If she believed that this John had suffered enough grief, guilt, and sorrow to make taking on a different identity understandable, then she had to believe that the other could also be capable of the same suffering and the same decisions.

After all, this man sitting beside her knew that Simon Tremont was merely a pseudonym. He knew—as so very few Tremont fans did—that his real name was John Smith.

He was from Colorado, where Simon had lived the past eleven years. He knew Simon's Denver address. He knew that it was only a few months ago that Simon had moved from Colorado.

He knew that she was fascinated with Liane from the Thibodeaux series. He knew that Simon had never had writer's block until this book, that he had met or beaten every deadline. He knew when Simon had stopped writing, knew when the deadline had come and gone with no book to show for it. He knew about the notes Rebecca had sent Simon, friendly little reminders at first, only to soon become touched with concern. He knew when those notes had stopped.

But *she* knew that they hadn't stopped. The address had simply been changed from the mailbox place in Denver to a rural route number outside Richmond. Rebecca hadn't stopped the gently prodding notes until the day Simon had shown up at the office to reassure her in person. Teryl had been at a dental appointment that afternoon, and she had deeply regretted missing the chance to meet her idol.

John knew so much. Could he be telling the truth? Was there any chance in the world that he *was* Simon Tremont?

No. Because there was one major undeniable, unquestionable piece of evidence in the other John's favor: back home in Rebecca's office and in Candace Baker's office in New York, there were copies of a manuscript containing over 175,000 words which brilliantly followed the outline submitted over a year ago and which also included changes made to that outline by the author via correspondence with his editor in the interim. Every single word seemed to prove that this man wasn't Simon Tremont. Whatever claims he made, whatever he believed, he couldn't claim ownership of that manuscript.

Despite what he knew about *Resurrection*, he hadn't written it.

That meant he couldn't possibly be Tremont.

A streak of lightning flashed across the sky at the same time the thunder rumbled. It made Teryl flinch, and it brought John out of his preoccupation to wearily continue. "For the last eight months, I've done everything but write. I've hiked so many miles in the mountains that I left trails where none had ever been. I knew every curve and every stone and half the fish in the stream that ran past the house. I watched TV and listened to music and read months-old newspapers. I knew how much I was drinking, how much I was sleeping, and how damned little I was writing." He paused, and his voice grew lower, even more somber. "The book was killing me."

She wondered how it would feel to do the same job and do it brilliantly day after day for eleven years, then to awaken one morning to find out that you could no longer do it. Writers wrote; it was that simple. What happened to them when they no longer could? What happened when they faced a blank computer screen, or pad or notebook, and nothing came out? What became of a writer who couldn't write?

"I kept trying," he went on, "but where I used to write twenty pages a day without stopping, now I was struggling to do four or five. Where I kept ninety-five percent of my original work, suddenly I was doing second and third and even fourth drafts. Finally, last week, I decided I needed a break. I hadn't been in to the city for months. I would go into Denver and relax—do some shopping, pick up my mail, call my sister. I would forget about work for a while, and when I went home, I would be able to work.again. At least, that was what I hoped."

But there was no mail—no Tremont mail, at least—waiting for him in Denver, Teryl knew, because Simon Tremont had sent a change of address to both the agency and Morgan-Wilkes back in February. She remembered getting the note in the mail—remembered wondering briefly why he had chosen to move to Richmond, remembered far more her excitement. Now that he was living in the area, she had thought, maybe she would get to meet him.

Wishes were funny things. Four months ago she had been wishing to meet Simon. Now that she had, she wished she hadn't.

"I drove to Denver Friday afternoon and picked up my mail. Normally, after four months, the mail would fill a couple of boxes. Instead, all I had was foreign copies of two books and a half dozen letters from Janie. There was nothing from Rebecca, nothing but the foreign editions from Morgan-Wilkes. There were no reminders about the deadline, no fan mail, no royalty check. I thought it was odd, but it was too late to call Rebecca. I figured I would take care of it later."

The next morning the announcement that Simon Tremont was coming out of seclusion to do an interview in New Orleans was all over the news. She had seen it on television herself, had read it in the paper. Surely John had seen it, too. Had it pushed him over the edge? Until that time, had he kept his delusions to himself? Had the fantasy that *he* was the world's most popular author been a private one that only he enjoyed, or had he shared it with others? If he had, if he had made claims that were now being publicly refuted, had the news been more than he could handle? Was that what had compelled him to travel to New Orleans, to take her hostage, and make this long trip to Richmond seeking evidence that didn't exist?

He *had* heard the news on television, he acknowledged, and had confirmed it in the Denver, Chicago, and Dallas newspapers that the hotel had obtained at his request. He had known it would be impossible to reach Rebecca at the office on a Saturday and equally impossible for him to stay in Colorado and do nothing, and so he had come up with the plan to go to New Orleans and later, if necessary, to Richmond and New York. He had gone home to pack, to get all the paperwork that would prove his claims—paperwork which was destroyed by fire soon after he got there. Destroyed, along with the house, by a fire caused by three bombs.

So he said.

Fire she might have believed, but bombs . . . Bombs made an outrageous story even more so. People simply didn't go around planting bombs in reclusive writers' houses. The man she knew as Simon, while not the nicest or most likable man she'd ever met, certainly didn't seem the mad bomber type. He didn't strike her as unbalanced . . . although in describing his personality, the word *egomaniacal* did come rather quickly to mind.

So the man held a high opinion of himself. So he was arrogant, obnoxious, and made the hairs on the back of her neck stand on end. That didn't make him an impostor. Or an arsonist. Or an attempted murderer.

When she finally spoke, she made a conscious effort to disguise her skepticism. "So you believe someone destroyed your house in order to destroy the personal records that document your writing career."

He looked at her then, his expression hopeless. "In part."

She didn't want to know, didn't want to hear him say the rest of it, but she asked anyway. It was as if she couldn't help herself. "And the rest?"

"The son of a bitch can't claim to be Simon Tremont if the real Simon Tremont is around to prove him a fraud. In order to continue being Simon, he needed—needs—to get rid of me."

Delusional *and* paranoid. God help her.

Something of what she was thinking must have shown on her face, because unexpectedly he laughed, a bitter chuckle that drained away as soon as it formed. "I don't blame you for thinking I'm nuts. I stood there last week looking at what was left of my house, thinking someone had tried to kill me, and wondering if it had something to do with all those news stories about Tremont. I thought maybe the last seventeen years had finally gotten to me. I thought maybe I really was crazy. But, Teryl, I swear to you, everything I've said is absolutely true. *I* created Simon Tremont. *I* wrote those books. Now someone's trying to take it all away from me, and I've got to stop him. I have to."

She stared silently out the windshield. The glass had been treated with something that made the raindrops bead up and immediately slide away. She could use a coating of the stuff on her own car. She was always having trouble seeing in the rain. D.J., whose prize possession was her black Camaro, said it was because Teryl never washed the car or cleaned the windshield. Her father said it was because wiper blades needed changing at least once in a blue moon. She supposed they were both right. Car maintenance didn't come high on her list of priorities.

And everything on that list had just been bumped one slot lower by one major new priority: getting John Smith out of her life.

Even if some pathetic and traitorous part of her would, in some way, miss him.

No, not exactly miss him. She would miss the potential she'd seen in him that first night. She would miss the charming, interesting, sensual, intelligent man she'd met Tuesday.

Lightning brightened the southern sky, and in the near distance a small explosion sounded as a transformer blew. As the lights on the opposite side of the street went dark, Teryl shivered in spite of the heat inside the truck. When she was a kid, storms had often played a role in those nightmares of hers. At times, the storm merely induced the dream. Other times, it was a part of the dream, the rumble of thunder and the heavy, threatening darkness broken only sporadically by the brilliant strikes of lightning combining to create a menacing atmosphere more than capable of scaring a cowardly small child back to wakefulness.

"Are you okay?"

She felt John's gaze on her, on her hands clenched tightly together in her lap, but she didn't look at him. With the truck's engine turned off, it had taken only moments for the steamy heat to replace the cooler air inside. Now it was hotter inside than out, because they were shut off from the rain's cooling effect. Her skin was clammy, her cheeks flushed, her forehead dotted with perspiration, and the air was almost too heavy to breathe. Was she okay? Not by a long shot . . . but then, she hadn't been okay since Wednesday morning when she had foolishly insisted that he couldn't just kidnap her and he had calmly replied, "I already have."

Without waiting any longer for an answer, he started the truck, turned the air conditioner to high, and directed both center vents her way. The cold air made her shiver and immediately began easing the tightness in her chest.

"Let's go on," he suggested, shifting in the seat, readjusting his seat belt. "We can probably drive out of the storm before long."

Aware that he would rather wait it out—after the accident that killed his brother, he must have a few nightmares of his own about driving in hazardous conditions, about risking the loss of control—Teryl was grateful for his offer.

Although the rain didn't stop, they left the thunder and lightning behind before they'd gone more than ten miles. She let the last taut muscles, those that ran from her shoulders up through her neck, relax and gave a loud, noisy sigh of relief. "Normally daytime storms don't bother me so much," she said, feeling foolish now that the anxiety had lessened. "I think it was just a combination of the storm and the heat and the mugginess." And the conversation she'd been having with the man who had kidnapped her.

John glanced at her but didn't say anything.

"My mother says everyone has quirks. She's afraid of water. I don't like thunderstorms"

"And I think I'm a world-famous author."

Back to that again. No matter how much she disliked the

topic, no matter how uncomfortable it made her, everything led back to it. And why not? It was the reason she was here. It was the reason John had sought her out in the first place. The reason he'd offered to go sight-seeing with her in the Quarter. The reason he'd gone back to the hotel with her. It was the reason . . . She stiffened, not wanting to complete the thought, fighting it and—feeling like an idiot—having to face it anyway.

It was the reason he'd made love to her.

Somehow, in the last few days, that conclusion had escaped her. She had preferred to think that he, like she, had been swept away by passion, that lust had overcome good sense. She had wanted to believe that chemistry had played a part, that two people who had each been alone too long had connected in all the right ways. She had liked the idea of one wicked night, a one-night stand, two ships that pass in the night, and those sorts of things.

But the simple truth was he'd had ulterior motives from the beginning. The moment she had announced to him that she worked for Rebecca Robertson, he had realized that he could use her, and he had set out to do just that. He had probably thought he would have to invest much more time, effort, and energy into his plan, but she had been so easy. All it had cost him was a few hours, a few drinks, and cab fare back to her hotel. Fifteen, twenty bucks, maximum.

He couldn't have bought a hooker so cheap.

No wonder he had left her bed sometime in the night. She had been sorry to awaken and find him gone, but at the same time, she had thought it was sweet of him to spare her the morning-after-with-a-total-stranger discomfort. Sweet, hell. He'd gotten far more than he'd paid for. He had learned one of the most closely guarded secrets in New Orleans at that time: where Simon Tremont was staying. He had probably gone through her things, had probably found the envelope with Simon's departure time on it. He had earned her trust, which had allowed him to walk right out of the hotel with her the next morning, had allowed him to kidnap her with no one—including *her*, damn it—any the wiser.

And he'd gotten laid. Three times. A hell of a return on his

investment. She told herself it didn't matter. So what if
sleeping with her had merely been part of his plan? So what
if he'd taken her one wicked night and turned it into something even tawdrier, something sinister? So what if he'd
screwed her because it was part of his plan and not because
he'd found her enticing and tempting as she'd found him? It
didn't matter.

Oh, but it did. It made her feel dirty. Ashamed. Foolish.

Leaning to the side, she rested her head against the window. Be careful, D.J. had told her on the phone Wednesday
night. *These are my games you're playing.* She had thought
she was grown up enough to play adult games, but she'd
been wrong. The first time in her life that she'd tried to be
daring and a little wild, and she had made big mistakes. In a
city known for its decadence and party atmosphere, she
hadn't even managed to find the right kind of man—a no-
strings, no-commitment sort of guy who was interested first,
last, and only in sex. Instead, she'd hooked up with John,
whose first interest was Simon Tremont, followed by Teryl's
job at the agency, his own delusions, and his plans for her.
Sex had come pretty far down on the list.

This never would have happened to D.J. No man had ever
gone to bed with her feeling anything but desire, wanting
anything but her. Even John would have forgotten Simon
Tremont's name if he'd been with D.J. She was the sort of
woman who drove men to distraction.

Teryl, obviously, wasn't.

They stopped for the night in North Carolina, in an ugly
little town somewhere south of Raleigh. The rain had slowed
them, slacking off for a few miles here or there as they
passed from one cell of bad weather into another but never
stopping, never relenting enough to let John relax.

Teryl hadn't relaxed, either, though there had been no
more storms along the way. Most of the afternoon had
passed in silence while she stared out the window. On the
few occasions he'd tried to start a conversation with her, she
had cut him off with short, clipped answers before returning

her attention to the sights outside. He wondered what she found so interesting there. He wondered why she suddenly no longer found *him* interesting.

This time, for a change, he checked into a reasonably nice motel, the best of the three in town. They ate a silent dinner in the restaurant next door, then walked back to their room, protected by an overhang from the steady rain. He wouldn't mind getting wet, he thought, listening to the splashes and the hollow echo of their footsteps on concrete. He liked walking in the rain, liked climbing to the top of his mountain and staking out a place on an outcropping of rock to watch it fall. Back when he was a kid, he had liked surfing in the rain, too, and the times he had accompanied Janie on her runs had almost always been in the rain. It was refreshing. Cleansing. And a pain in the butt for driving.

Maybe tomorrow morning the clouds would be gone and the sun would be shining. Maybe they would make better time on the remainder of the trip. Maybe he would give up these potholed, congested, meandering two-lane highways and these depressing, shabby little towns and take the interstate the rest of the way in.

And then what?

It didn't take a brilliant mind to know that Teryl was hoping to dump him as soon as she got home. Maybe she intended to go so far as to provide him with an introduction to Rebecca Robertson, but he doubted it. Most likely *all* she intended was to get rid of him. To do whatever was necessary to get him out of her way.

It wouldn't be that easy for her. He wouldn't let it be.

At the last room before the sidewalk took a left-hand jog around a corner, he stopped, pulled out a card key, and unlocked the door. The lamps they'd left burning when they had dropped off their luggage were still on, the television was still tuned to a twenty-four-hour cable news channel, and the air conditioner was humming efficiently. Even without stepping across the threshold, he could feel its cool breeze.

Stepping back from the door, he gestured for Teryl to enter. "Why don't you go ahead and get ready for bed?"

She looked vaguely suspicious. "Where will you be?"

"Out here." He shrugged. "I'm not ready to come in yet."
It was a lame response, but it was true, and he figured it was
safer than telling the whole truth. He wasn't ready to shut
himself into a small room with her again. He wasn't ready to
sit on one of the beds while she took a shower, wasn't ready
to listen to the sound of the water running and know that she
was naked and wet and touching herself in places that he
would sell his soul to touch.

Most of all, he wasn't ready to face the after-shower time.
The time when she was dressed for bed. The time when he
finally got his first real privacy of the day. The time when
he took his own shower. The time when—God forgive
him—he had to tie her to the bed.

After a moment's hesitation, she went inside, picking up
her suitcase as she passed the dresser, lifting it onto the nearest bed. He watched from the doorway as she took out bottles of floral-scented liquids and creams, that damned tank
top, and those pin-striped shorts. He wanted to tell her that
she could sleep in just the top—the shorts were too tailored
to be particularly comfortable—or in nothing at all. He
wanted to assure her that he wouldn't touch her, wouldn't
force himself on her, wouldn't take advantage of her.

But she wouldn't believe him. Hell, he wasn't sure he believed himself.

Besides, if last night was any indication, he wouldn't necessarily have to force her. When he had knelt beside the bed
to bind her hands, before she had realized what he was
doing, she had been aroused. He had seen it in her eyes, had
heard it in the ragged tenor of her breathing. He had noticed
her swollen breasts, had watched her nipples harden until
they strained, visibly taut, against the flowery print of her
dress. She had wanted him, even being his hostage. Even believing he was crazy. Even though it shamed her. When she
had taken his hand, he could have dropped that telephone
cord, and she would have continued touching him. She
would have let *him* touch *her*. She would have let him make
love to her one more time.

He wouldn't have had to force her . . . but he would have

been taking advantage of her, and that was almost as bad . . . wasn't it?

As she turned away from the suitcase, her arms full of toiletries and clothing, she paused, her attention directed toward the nightstand. She was standing so still, looking at the telephone. Remembering what he had used the cord for? Or wondering if she would have an opportunity to use it and call for help while he was outside?

Then abruptly, as if realizing that he was watching her, she moved away from the bed and went into the bathroom, closing the door behind her. A second later, he heard the click of the lock.

He stood where he was for a moment, wanting to trust her, wanting to turn his back and go outside again and not worry that she would try to make a call. But, much as he regretted it, he couldn't trust her, no more than she could trust him. He couldn't leave her and the telephone unguarded in the same room. Crossing to the nightstand in a half dozen strides, he held the phone in one hand and yanked the cord from the wall with the other. Then he tossed the phone on the bed, went outside, closed the door after him, and walked through the rain to the Blazer.

His hands were unsteady; it took him a moment to slide the key into the lock, a moment longer to turn it in the right direction. Once the door was open, he didn't bother climbing in out of the rain, but instead leaned across the seat to rummage in the console for the book of matches he'd picked up at breakfast and the pack of cigarettes he'd bought this afternoon, along with two Cokes and a tank of gas. That had been the only time since her comment about the thunderstorms that Teryl had initiated a conversation with him.

I didn't know you smoked, she had remarked in that slightly smug, slightly condescending tone nonsmokers tended to use with those who did. *I don't very often,* he had replied, which was a lie. He'd started when he was fifteen because the guys he'd hung out with had smoked, because they had thought it was cool, and very much because his parents had denounced it as a nasty habit. He'd taken up swearing about that time—not an occasional damn or hell, but obscenities, every one he'd ever heard, the filthier, the better, and in every sentence—and drinking, too, all in an effort to provoke parents who were already always angry with him.

But eventually he'd grown up. Recognizing swearing for the juvenile act that it was, he had cleaned up his vocabulary. He had realized that drinking was pleasurable enough to become a risk, and so he had cut that back, too—although it was still his strongest temptation when he was stressed out or more morose than usual. But he still smoked—not all the time but more than was healthy.

She didn't like cigarettes, Teryl had informed him, still using that superior tone of voice, and she would appreciate it if he didn't smoke around her. Well, that wasn't a problem, he thought as he held a match to the cigarette between his lips. She was in the bathroom, out of that damnable dress by now and in the shower, water pouring over her head, streaming across her breasts, down the slope of her belly, and between her legs, and he was standing outside in the rain, trying to pretend that he didn't want to be in there with her. The only thing that connected them now was the fact that they were both wet . . . and a certain part of him was bound to get a whole hell of a lot wetter if he didn't quit imagining what she was doing and how she looked doing it.

Hell and damnation.

Backing up, he slammed the door, then headed toward the room again. He didn't pull his key out to go inside, though. He merely stepped onto the sidewalk out of the rain, leaned back against the stucco wall, and took a deep drag on the cigarette.

Why was his luck so shitty? Why wasn't Teryl shallow and self-absorbed or a snooty bitch? Why wasn't she too ditsy to carry on an intelligent conversation? Why the hell wasn't she everything he *didn't* like in a woman? Why did she have to be damn near everything he did like?

If he had met her a year ago—or three or five—maybe they could have had something. If they had met in Colorado instead of New Orleans, if the purpose of her trip had been pleasure instead of business, if her business hadn't been Simon Tremont . . . He still would have thought that she was pretty, innocent, and sexy as hell. It still would have taken him only a record-setting short time to decide he wanted her. He still would have eventually mustered his courage and told her so flat out, and when she agreed, he still would have hustled her off to the nearest bed and crawled deep inside her.

The only difference was that back then something could have come of it. Back then he wouldn't have had to leave her that night or kidnap her the next morning. Back then he wouldn't have been forced to make her hate him before they'd even had a chance to find out if she could ever feel anything else for him.

Of course, back then there hadn't been another Simon Tremont living his life and stealing his glory. Back then he would have appeared a reasonably normal man instead of a raving lunatic.

Jesus, he had the worst luck in the world.

He smoked the cigarette to the filter, lit another, then flicked the butt into the grass. It made little sizzling sounds in the rain; then, with a puff of smoke, the glowing tip went out. He finished the second, the third, and the fourth the same way. He was debating lighting a fifth but decided against it. His clothes were damp and clammy, and his feet were wet inside his shoes. Teryl had had plenty of time for her shower, he wanted a shower of his own, and his need for the bathroom was growing desperate. It was time to face her . . . and the bed . . . and the telephone cord, whether he wanted to or not.

That goddamned telephone cord.

Tucking the matches into the plastic wrap that enclosed the cigarette pack, he unlocked and opened the door and stepped inside. He came to a sudden stop right there.

Teryl *was* finished with her shower, and she was sitting in the sole chair in the room. She had turned the television on its swivel base to face her and had changed the channel to watch a syndicated rerun of "Murder, She Wrote"; although he couldn't see the screen, he recognized Angela Lansbury's voice.

She had turned off all the lights in the room except the swag lamp that hung above the small round table where she sat rubbing expensive-smelling lotion on her legs. Had she simply disliked the bright glare of so many lights? Did she, like him, prefer to watch TV in near-darkness? Had she not taken a moment to consider the scene she had set and placed herself in?

It was damned erotic. A darkened room. A single milky glass–enclosed light bulb casting its softening glow directly on her. The chill that came from the air conditioner, which hadn't yet dispersed the fragrant, steamy dampness drifting out through the open bathroom door. Her wet hair combed straight back from her face. Her legs glistening with sweet-scented lotion. Her cotton shirt, too big, too loose, too revealing by far. The slow, soothing, sensual movements of her hands on her legs.

As she bent to reach her ankle, the tank top dipped forward. It was a man's shirt, scooped low at the neck, cut deep at the arms, not meant to be worn by a woman, at least not without something snug-fitting underneath . . . and Teryl wasn't wearing anything at all under it. The gaping fabric beneath her left arm presented him with a tantalizing glimpse of her breast, rounded and full, and her nipple, small, soft, nearly flat. The last time he'd seen her breasts—jeez, only three nights ago—they had been swollen and her nipples had been as hard as his cock was getting right now. He had sucked them hard, had bitten them, once with enough force to make her gasp. He had made her whimper and writhe and plead in a husky, wordless voice for more, and he had given it to her, had given her everything that he'd had to give.

But she had given him so much more. The welcome of her body. The satisfaction of her release. The comfort of being so deep and snug inside her. His own release. A few hours' peace.

Sweet damnation, he wanted it again. He wanted *her* again. He wanted to touch her, hold her, kiss her. He wanted to fuck her, really fuck her, hard and fast, wanted to come inside her, to fill her until she couldn't take one drop more, and then he wanted to do it again, only different this time. Slower. Gentler. Longer.

He wanted to make love to her. He wanted to make love with her. Sweet, *sweet* damnation.

Finishing with her legs, she sat back in the chair and the shirt fell back into a semblance of modest attire. Rubbing the residue of leftover lotion into her hands, she looked across the room at him. If she noticed his erection—hell, how could she *not* notice when he felt as if his balls just might explode?—she gave no sign of it. She just gave him a cool, distant look and in an equally cool, distant voice said, "Close the door, please."

He reached blindly behind him, shoved it shut, and twisted the lock. He didn't move away from it, though. He simply stood there, forcing himself to breathe deeply, trying not to think about how damned horny he was or what sweet pleasure he could find in her body. He tried not to think about how impossible his need was, about seducing or coaxing or pleading or raping.

When he thought he could safely move closer, he did so, turning his suitcase on its side, opening it and taking out the damned coil of cord. Teryl was still rubbing her hands together when he turned toward her. The instant she saw what he held, though, she froze. All that cool distance disappeared from her expression and was replaced by raw panic. Somehow she had convinced herself that it wouldn't happen again. It was denial, he supposed, a common enough response to something she feared as intensely as she feared this. To something she hated as fiercely, as desperately, as he hated this.

"No." The word was thin, a plea with no more substance than a puff of air, but it echoed through his soul.

"I'm sorry, Teryl."

She found her voice then, along with her anger. "You can't do this to me again. I won't let you."

"I have to." He reached for her hands, but she jerked away. "Please, Teryl . . . You don't have to lie down. Come over here and sit on the floor beside the bed. You can watch television. It won't hurt. I'll make you comfortable."

"*Comfortable*?" she shrieked. "With my hands *tied* to the bed?"

"Don't make this any harder than it already is," he pleaded, reaching for her again. This time she scrambled away, shoving the chair back, struggling to her feet. There was a wild animal look in her eyes, panic and pure terror, as she searched for an avenue of escape. There was none. She had backed herself into a corner. To get away, she would have to climb over the chair and table or go through him, and he was taller, stronger, faster, and outweighed her by seventy pounds. She was trapped, he acknowledged regretfully.

And so was he. Trapped into doing things he despised. Things he would never forgive.

For the third time, he reached for her, catching her wrist, using his hold to pull her to him. She fought every step, scratching at his hand with her free hand, her nails scraping hard across it, tearing off skin, drawing blood. He didn't flinch, didn't relent, but dragged her the few feet to the foot of her bed. There it was a simple matter of using his greater strength to put her in a sitting position on the floor, of kneeling astride her to keep her from wriggling away while he formed the cord into a slip knot, of trying desperately, vainly, to shut out her helpless, breathless sobs of terror.

When he attempted to maneuver the wrist he held behind her back, she fought him, twisting her fingers around, clutching a handful of his shirt. "P-please, John," she whispered, her voice quavering, her muscles quivering. "Please don't do this. I'll do whatever you want, anything you want. I'll sleep with you, I'll give you the best blow job you ever had, I'll—I'll do anything you like, anything kinky. Just please, *please*, don't tie me up again."

He stared down at her, every muscle in his body going taut. "Jesus, Teryl, don't," he demanded. He begged. He was having a hard enough time dealing with what he wanted but couldn't—shouldn't—have. If she offered it to him, offered him what he needed so damned badly that he hurt with it, offered it voluntarily in exchange for freedom from the restraints . . . How the hell could he find the character to turn her down? He wasn't a strong man. He wasn't an honorable man. He was just a weak bastard who'd lived alone so long that an hour's intimacy with her just might be worth sacrificing whatever little bit of self-respect had survived the last few days.

All too aware of her effect on him, she brought her free hand to his chest, then slid it lower, over his belt, past the snap on his jeans, straight down the zipper to his crotch. She stroked him, and his cock twitched, making him bite his lip on a groan.

"Please, John," she whispered, the tremble gone from her voice but the desperation still painfully, shamefully there. "Let me make love to you. Let me undress you so I can touch you, so I can kiss you. Please . . ."

She stroked him again, rubbing hard through the denim that separated them, and he squeezed his eyes tightly shut as he groaned again. If she kept touching him like that, kept talking like that, he was going to come, all right.

He'd never wanted *any* woman this way.

Slowly, one finger at a time, he released his grip on her wrist. His hand was trembling. So was hers. Raising both hands, he cupped her face, bent forward, and hesitantly touched his mouth to hers. She opened to him immediately, accepting his kiss, accepting his tongue. Lower, she was opening his jeans pretty damned quickly, too, not fumbling over the belt, the snap, or the zipper. The mere touch of her hand, soft and cool, on his belly stirred an ache that threatened to never end.

Now his tongue was in her mouth, and her hand was in his jeans, closing around his erection, lifting it for easier access, caressing it. He was so damned close to coming, so pathetically, needfully close to emptying into her hand.

And it was wrong, so wrong. He could spend the rest of the damned night screwing her right there on the floor, and when they were done, she would hate him. He would hate himself, and, worst of all, *she* would hate herself.

She would be so ashamed.

It would be *his* fault, *his* shame, but *she* would feel the guilt. She would blame herself.

With a good deal more decency than he'd thought he possessed, he ended the kiss, drew her hands away, and awkwardly zipped his jeans. For a moment she remained motionless—eyes closed, lips parted, hands resting limply at her sides where he'd laid them—then he slipped the vinyl-coated wire around one wrist, and her eyes flew open. She didn't bargain, didn't plead. She simply looked at him with a steady gaze that spoke eloquently of anguish and fear, a gaze that wordlessly accused him.

Feeling the weight of his guilt all too strongly, he pushed ahead anyway. He guided her hands behind her back, slid the cord over the free one, looped it around both wrists, then tied the ends to the metal foot of the bed. Sliding his fingers between the flexible cord and the soft skin on the inside of her wrists, he made sure it wasn't too tight, made certain she couldn't work her way free but wouldn't suffer any real discomfort.

When that was done, he cradled her face in his palms again. "I'm sorry."

That look didn't waver. "You bastard." Her voice was quiet, empty of any real emotion. But her eyes weren't empty. Her eyes damned him.

Rising to his feet, he grabbed what he needed from his suitcase, went into the bathroom, closed the door, and leaned against it. He felt a hundred years old, a hundred years dead. Some of his aches—like the bloody scratches on his hand or the hard-on that not even Teryl's loathing could diminish—were purely physical. Time—or a little dexterous handwork—would take care of them. As for the rest of it . . .

There was no cure for the pain. For the weariness. For the shame or the dishonor, for the sorrow or the guilt. There was no cure for the miserable man he had become. No cure but death. I'm sorry, he'd told Teryl, and he had meant it with every fiber of his being. He was so damned sorry.

Maybe someday she would believe him.

But she wouldn't forgive him.

Not ever.

Teryl stared at the television screen, but nothing she saw made sense; nothing she heard could penetrate the roar in her ears. She hated this—hated this helpless, degrading feeling and, worse, the fear. Oh, God, the fear. There was nothing worse, nothing more dreadful, than irrational fear. It wasn't as if this were a new and strange thing. It wasn't as if, after tying her for a short time, then freeing her, the two previous nights, John was going to leave her here all night this time. He wasn't going to come back and assault her, wasn't going to rape her, wasn't going to hurt her in any way. She had no reason to be afraid this time. All she had to do was sit quietly, watch the rest of "Murder, She Wrote" and by the time it was over, John would be finished in the bathroom and she would be free.

It was an inconvenience. A little bit of unpleasantness. An embarrassment.

But it wasn't any reason for her heart to beat in her chest as if it might burst. It wasn't any reason for her lungs to be so tight that only the smallest of breaths could squeeze in. It wasn't any reason for her palms to be damp, for sweat to be trickling down her spine, for the muscles in her arms and legs to be trembling with such force.

Oh, God, she wanted to scream. Afraid to do that, afraid of losing what little control she still had, she wanted to cry. To plead. To beg. But she'd already done that, hadn't she? She had pleaded with John not to do this to her again. She had begged him, had offered him anything, had behaved so disgustingly pathetically.

And he had turned her down.

He could have accepted her offer, then reneged. He could have done anything he wanted, could have debased her, used her, then tied her anyway. There was nothing she could have done to stop him.

But he hadn't. Because he'd known he would have to secure her to the bed anyway? Because somewhere inside him the decent, nice, normal man he'd once been still somehow existed? Because he'd been too honest, too fair to take advantage of her when he would still have to subject her to this fate?

Maybe his refusal had had nothing to do with decency, normalcy, or honesty. Maybe he simply hadn't wanted her. Oh, sure, he'd been hard; she'd seen it, had felt it, had wrapped her fingers around the long, hot, solid flesh. But erections were involuntary responses to physical stimulation. An erection simply meant that he'd been aroused, that his body had been ready to engage in sex.

It didn't mean he wanted that sex to be with *her*.

Not that she took his rejection personally, she hastened to assure herself. She wasn't disappointed that he'd turned her down. She knew herself well, knew that if he had accepted, if he had let her do the things she had volunteered to do, when it was over, she would have been humiliated. She would have wanted to die.

Still, honesty forced her to admit that it would have been nice—in some odd, perverted sort of way, the cynic interjected—to think that his lust had more to do with her as a woman and less to do with his long-term abstinence.

When the bathroom door opened, she stiffened. He came out and into her peripheral vision. Without actually looking at him, she could see that he wore cutoffs and nothing else. If she risked a look at his face, she knew she would see that his hair was wet, darkened by the water to a golden brown, and slicked back away from his face like hers.

But she didn't take that risk. She simply stared harder at the television.

He tossed his dirty clothes on the table, set his shaving kit there, then reached for the jeans. He transferred something from the jeans to the right-hand pocket of his cutoffs, something small enough to hide in his hand, and then at last he came to her, crouching in front of her, reaching around without touching her to work loose the knots that held her.

Teryl offered a silent prayer of thanks as the cord fell away from her right wrist. Bringing her hands around in front of her, she yanked it off her other wrist, then clenched it into a tight wad in her fist. "Bastard," she whispered.

He didn't speak. He simply moved, resting one knee on the floor so he could work his fingers into his pocket. Removing the item he had placed there just a moment ago, he wordlessly offered it to her.

It was a few inches long, red and silver, compact. For a moment, she stared at it, not quite comprehending what it was, not quite understanding what he intended her to do with it. Then he pulled out one of the silver blades, held it by the tip and again, handle first, offered it to her.

Fighting the urge to both laugh hysterically and cry great tears of relief, she took it from him, wrapping her fingers tightly around the handle. It was a knife—a Boy Scout knife, for Christ's sake—and it made short work of the damnable cord she was holding. By the time she was finished with it, he would have been hard-pressed to find a piece long enough to make its two ends meet, much less restrain someone with.

When she returned the knife to him, he closed the blade, then slid it into his pocket again. Then he got to his feet and extended a hand, offering to help her up. She got up on her own, though, wiping her hands on her shirt, drying their dampness. She started to turn away toward her bed, but, as relief turned to anger, on impulse, she spun back around. "Don't you ever do that to me again, you son of a bitch," she warned as, with both hands, she struck him a blow on the chest, shoving him at the same time and knocking him off-balance. "If you try, I swear I'll kill you."

The second bed was right behind him, taking up the space he needed to regain his balance. As she watched, he fell backward, making the mattress squeak, banging his shoulder on the suitcase. She heard his curse, low and gritty and underlaid with pain, and for the first time all week she noticed the stitches in his right arm.

How had she overlooked them before? She had been naked in bed with him Tuesday night . . . but the room had been dimly lit and she had been carried away with lust and wickedness. His arm had *not* been the part of his body that interested her most.

She *had* noticed the injury the next morning, she remembered, when she had damn near wrecked them on the interstate; once he'd brought the truck—and her—under control again, blood had stained his shirtsleeve. She had even mentioned it, had pointed out that his arm was bleeding, but he hadn't seemed interested, and, really, she hadn't cared, either. Since then she had seen him without a shirt each night, but always like tonight: after he had untied her. After she'd gotten herself worked into a frenzy. After she'd been incapable of noticing much of anything except that she was *free*.

Now, though, she could see the laceration. It was long, neat, almost as if made by a scalpel. A dozen or more stitches were placed at regular intervals, tidy little knots with the ends sticking up above the skin like little ears. She wondered how he'd gotten the injury, wondered if the fire that had destroyed his house had somehow been responsible, wondered if it had been caused by the bombs whose existence she had so easily dismissed.

Reluctantly, damning herself for caring, she wondered if her actions Wednesday morning—grabbing the steering wheel, sending them careening across the lanes, then struggling to escape the truck—had worsened the injury or the pain.

As she sank down on her bed, across the narrow space, he sat up on his own bed. There were white lines around his mouth that eased when he blew his breath out in a heavy exhalation.

"What happened?" Guilt made her voice sharp, her tone accusatory.

"Why bother asking when you don't believe anything I say?" His own voice was weary. When she didn't respond, though, when she simply sat there and waited, he gave an answer anyway. "I was walking into the office when the first bomb exploded. The concussion blew out all the windows and knocked me to the floor. It happened too fast to remember everything, but I imagine it was a piece of falling glass that sliced my arm open. All I know for sure is the place went up in flames, and I went out through a hole in the wall where a twelve-by-twenty-foot window used to be."

Her gaze shifted to the suture line again. He'd said the house was all glass and wood, wood that would burn like kindling and glass that would burst into millions of shattered pieces. A chunk of window glass could have made a cut like that. Hell, a flying chunk of glass could become a deadly missile. He was fortunate to have escaped with no injuries more serious.

Listening to that last thought echo in her mind, she became still. She sounded almost as if she believed him—about the bombs, at least. But if she accepted that part of the story as truth, didn't she then have to accept that the rest might also be true? After all, bombs were hardly the method of choice among killers today, unless a person was special or the cause was. If he was simply poor deluded John Smith who wrongly believed that he was a famous author, why would anyone want to kill him? And assuming that someone did want him dead, that he did have an enemy or two out there, why would anyone go to all the trouble of building three bombs to take him out? Why not just shoot him, stab him, or run him off the side of the mountain? Why not simply knock him unconscious, then set his house on fire?

Bombs just seemed—to her way of thinking, at least—too much. Overkill.

Unless, as John had suggested this afternoon, the person had had two goals: destroying the proof that the man the world now knew as Simon Tremont was an impostor . . . and destroying all evidence of the real Tremont, including the man.

John could have survived a gunshot wound or a knife wound. To get run off the side of the mountain, the person would have had to catch him out there—not an easy task with someone as much a hermit as he'd been. As for a fire, there was always a chance that could be survived, too.

But a bomb? Three bombs, one at each exit from the house and one in his bedroom? What were the odds that a man could be inside a house when three bombs exploded and escape with nothing more than a gash on his arm?

Astronomical.

And what were the odds that he was lying about the bombs? That he had set the fire himself? That he was, as he had confessed to thinking earlier, indeed crazy?

Pretty damn good.

At least, finally, there was something she could check out. When she got home, she would find out what county Rapid River, Colorado, was located in, and she would put through a

*T*he man known as Simon Tremont prowled the perimeter of his office, pausing in front of a bookcase to pick up an award, stopping at the credenza to study the family snapshot there, resting one knee on the windowseat while he looked out into the darkness. It was the middle of the night, a time when most people were asleep. He didn't need hours of sleep, like those people. When he was writing the last two hundred pages of *Resurrection*, he'd gotten by on little more than a few hours' rest each day. He'd written much of his best, his strongest, most powerful stuff in the middle of the night.

But tonight he wasn't working. He had intended to. He had come in here, switched on the computer, set up a new file, and typed a heading of Chapter 1 onto the first page. That had been two hours ago, and he hadn't yet typed another word.

Maybe it was too soon to go back to work. The mental exhaustion of *Resurrection* wasn't yet far enough in the past. The exhilaration of the interview already completed and of all those scheduled in the weeks to come hadn't yet faded. It tended to go to his head—all those famous, powerful people, clamoring for a little of his attention. It made work hard to think about. It made those bare-bone skeleton characters for his new book tough to care about. It made sitting alone in this office with nothing but the whir of the computer's fan for company difficult to adapt to.

How quickly fame had corrupted him, he thought cynically as he turned away from the window. For years he'd been happy to go unknown. Then the trip to New Orleans had given him just a taste of what he'd been missing, of what had been denied him.

And he had liked the taste. He liked it a lot.

The time was fast approaching when he would never settle for anonymity again. When he would live life the way Simon Tremont should. He would buy a mansion that befitted his status, would buy vacation homes in every place he'd ever thought he might like to visit. He would travel, going first-class all the way, maybe in his own plane, with his own pilot. He would socialize with the rich and the famous, would be the richest and the most famous of them all. People—common people, people who never in their wildest dreams had guessed who they were dealing with—would take notice when he passed. They would want to approach him, but he would be totally unapproachable. Except to a select few.

Moving away from the window, he resumed his exploration of the office. For the last month that he'd worked on the book, this place had been his home. His sanctuary. His life. He had worked at the desk, had paced that long strip of carpet in front of the window, had slept on the sofa against the wall. He had sometimes feared during that frantic, driven, obsessed time that if he left the office, he would cease to exist. But as long as he stayed there, as long as he remained at his computer, as long as he had eaten, slept, and dreamed—oh, God, yes, dreamed—*Resurrection*, he had been safe.

It was still his safe haven—only fair, he supposed, since, in a very real sense, he'd been born there. John Smith, a sorry excuse for a man if ever there was one, had created Simon Tremont, and now Simon had taken over. As far as *he* was concerned, John Smith no longer existed. Now that Simon had come out, as it were, he no longer needed John. Simon was the powerful one. Simon was the rich one. Simon was the one with legions of loyal fans who admired, worshiped, and yes, even loved him. They didn't have the vaguest idea in hell who John Smith was.

Simon was the one every fan, from Teryl Weaver to his editor in France, loved. Simon. *Not* John.

In the beginning, he had thought of himself as John, a relatively normal, anonymous man with an alter ego named Simon. In the beginning, he had thought John was real and Simon was just a pseudonym, just an empty name to hide behind. Lately, though, he'd discovered that he had been wrong. John wasn't the real one, not by a long shot. John had been the puppet who ran things until Simon was ready to take control.

With *Resurrection*, Simon had become ready. Now he didn't acknowledge John. He called himself Simon. He thought of himself as Simon. He was even planning, when the time was right, to legally change his name to Simon. John Smith would cease to exist, and Simon Tremont would live on in his place.

When the time was right.

He passed the file cabinets, four of them, four drawers tall. They were big and old, make of oak, nicked here, scraped there, and they were filled with the life and times of Simon Tremont. Two drawers held blue box folders, expanded to the max to hold his original manuscripts—the *original manuscripts* of Simon Tremont. After he was dead, they would be worth some bucks. Maybe he would donate them to a museum, to some place worthy of Tremont originals.

Investment information—prospectuses, quarterly statements, annual reports—filled an entire drawer of its own. He had more money sitting around in mutual funds than most people could even dream of. The tax records in the fourth cabinet showed how his income had risen from a paltry $13,000 twelve years ago to so damn many zeroes last year that it was hard to count that high.

Other drawers were filled with contracts, research, notes, and correspondence. He had every note he'd ever received from his editor and his agent—and from his agent's pretty, sweet assistant, Teryl.

She wasn't back from New Orleans yet. He'd made it his

business to find that out. Not only had she not come back, but no one knew when she would. Rumor was she was down there getting her brains fucked out, presumably by the same man who had been in her room the night Simon had called her.

If the rumor was true, he had misjudged her. He had been taken in by her sweetness and innocence, when she was nothing but a horny little tramp. If he had known that the day of the interview, he would have ignored Sheila Callan's interference when he'd been about to invite himself along on Teryl's sight-seeing jaunt. He would have sent the publicist off to spend the evening with her butch assistant, and he would have screwed sweet little Teryl every which way but straight. He would have shown her things she'd never known existed, would have done her in ways she'd never been done.

He would have treated her like the slut she apparently was, and she would have liked it.

If the rumor was true.

Soon he would find out. Eventually Teryl would come home, and when she did, getting her into his bed would be a simple matter. After all, he was Simon Tremont, and Teryl Weaver *adored* Simon Tremont. She would do anything for him.

He was counting on that. He'd been counting on it for a long, long time.

In the meantime, his own bed wasn't lonely. Even now it wasn't empty, but for all he cared, it might as well be. The woman there was merely a means to an end. She satisfied his requirements at this time. When that was no longer true, he would remove her from his life. He would replace her with Teryl.

Once again he arrived at the family photo on the credenza. This time he picked it up, holding the silver and brass frame in both hands. It was an old picture, taken long ago on a bright summer day when the sun cast long shadows and cutoffs and T-shirts were the uniform of the day. They were smiling, both of them—happy, healthy people with their entire lives ahead of them.

Now they were dead, and—the woman in his bed notwith-standing—he was alone.

That was the way he liked it, the way he wanted it.

At least, until the time was right to change it.

With a cool smile, he returned the frame to the credenza, but he didn't use the easel back to stand it upright. Instead he laid it facedown. The photograph was one of his most trea-sured possessions, but he didn't want to see it anymore. He didn't want any reminders of what once was. He would focus only on what would be.

Simon Tremont. Author. Celebrity. Star. *Legend.*

Richmond, the highway sign read. Forty-six miles.

John had never looked forward so much to arriving in a city . . . or dreaded it so much, either. On the one hand, he was itching to get into Rebecca Robertson's office. More than anything in the world, he wanted to prove to Teryl that he *was* Simon Tremont. He wanted to prove to her that he wasn't lying, that he wasn't crazy, that he wasn't someone deserving of being warily watched all the time.

And what if all that wasn't enough? What if she still re-fused to believe him? What if the impostor knew as much about Tremont as *he* did? After all, the guy *had* written the most impressive work she'd ever read.

What if he couldn't convince anyone, least of all Teryl?

What then?

The question was too bleak to consider.

Beside him, Teryl stretched, yawned, resettled. Like yes-terday afternoon, she'd been pretty quiet today, though not an angry sort of quiet. Not frightened or moody or pouting. Just thoughtful. What would it take to persuade her to share those thoughts with him?

Things that he didn't have. Such as her trust.

"I wonder if Rebecca's fired me yet."

The look he gave her was sharp, surprised. He had been so intent on taking her home to Richmond and not letting his best chance at reclaiming his life escape that he hadn't thought that far ahead. He hadn't considered the possibility that her boss could, indeed, fire her—missing work for two days without clearing it first certainly seemed good grounds for it—but it was a very real one. If she did get fired, if she was cut off from access to the records in Rebecca's office, where did that leave him?

"Do you think she has?"

She smiled faintly. "No. The job may not be much, but I'm good at it. Before she hired me, Rebecca went through assistants like water. She tends to be a little demanding. She expects a lot from herself and from the people who work for her—too much, I think sometimes. Anyway, I'm a great assistant, I have no ambition to move up and onward, I don't mind running personal errands for her, and I don't mind her demands. Besides, I make amaretto coffee exactly the way she likes it."

His sudden uneasiness calmed, he turned his attention back to the road. "How long have you been working for her?"

"You tell me," she replied, just a hint of a challenge in her voice.

He thought back over the years of correspondence that was now scattered in ashes over the mountains where he had lived. His contact with the agency had never been extensive. When he sent in a proposal for a new book, he had always gotten back a note saying that Rebecca had received it and would be in touch with Candace Baker at Morgan-Wilkes, who got her own copy from him. Between the proposal stage and the completed manuscript, there were more notes, one accompanying the contracts Rebecca sent in triplicate for him to sign and return, another accompanying the copy of the contract that eventually made its way back to him. If Candace wanted revisions either on the proposal or the manuscript, Rebecca sent him notes stating her own thoughts on the matter.

She always sent him copies of the best-seller lists. In more years than he could remember, not a single week had gone by that he wasn't on the *New York Times* list with one book or another; when a movie based on one of his books was released, it wasn't unusual for him to have two, three, or four

titles in the top ten at the same time. She also sent him reviews wherever they cropped up, along with holiday greet-
ings and a card every year on the anniversary of the
representation agreement they'd signed eleven years ago.

The first few years there had also been frequent memos
announcing changes in the agency—the move from New
York City to Richmond, another move from their first Richmond address to the current one, and personnel changes. One
assistant was out and another was in; then a year or six
months or three months later, that assistant would be gone,
too. Until she'd hired Teryl.

"Four or five years," he replied. "You were working there
by the time the fourth Thibodeaux book came out."

She gave him one of those steady, measuring looks that
made him want to squirm, but he didn't give in to the urge.
Instead, he simply looked back at her.

"How do you know that?" she asked, her tone conversa-
tional.

"Because you liked the book enough to say so when you
forwarded some reviews. I'd always gotten plenty of feed-
back from Rebecca herself, but that was the first time one of
her assistants had responded. Until then, I wasn't sure her assistants even read any of the books she handled." He glanced
at her again. "I even remember some of their names. Caryl
with a y and Gina and Mary Kay."

Teryl—with a y, he thought with a faint grin—looked very
serious and just the slightest bit troubled. "I replaced Caryl.
For the first six months I worked there, Rebecca was constantly calling me by her name."

He let a mile or so pass in silence before asking, "So what
are your plans?"

She gave him a blank look.

"You said you have no ambition. You're not interested in
moving up and on. What *are* you interested in? Being Rebecca's glorified receptionist and gofer for the rest of your
life?"

She was quiet so long that he thought she wasn't going to
answer. He wouldn't blame her if she didn't. Answers to a
question like that could weigh heavily on the personal side,

and, God knew, she didn't have a reason to confide anything personal in him. Still, when he was about to give up and find some other direction to send the conversation in, she gave a faintly mocking laugh. "I always thought I would be like my mother. She worked for a while after she was married, but when I was born, she quit. She stayed home and took care of the kids. She was a full-time housewife and mother, a Little League coach, a Girl Scout leader, a homeroom mother—for as many as five or six homerooms at a time. She went on class trips and was a volunteer for all the school plays and pageants. She baked cookies and sewed and taught us all how to throw a mean fastball. She and Daddy have always been the most popular parents in the neighborhood. They loved all the kids, and all the kids loved them."

"So you wanted to get married and devote the rest of your life to taking care of husband, home, and kids. Such a fifties idea for a nineties woman." Her faint mocking was echoed in his voice, although he didn't feel it, not really. It was more of a defense mechanism, he guessed, because the life she was describing sounded damned familiar—and as alien as life on another planet. *His* mother had been a full-time housewife and mother, too. She had also been a Scout leader—for Janie—and a homeroom mother—for Tom. She had gone on class trips and baked cookies, but she hadn't loved all the kids in the neighborhood. Hell, she hadn't even managed to love all the kids in the family.

"True feminism is about choice," she replied, a little defensive now herself. "I don't have to want a career. I don't have to try to prove that I'm equal to or better than the men in my chosen field. I don't have to live up to someone else's expectations. When I get married, if it's financially possible, I can stay home and have a half dozen babies and take in a few dozen more the way Mama and Daddy have, and it's no one's business but mine and my husband's."

That was something he could do for her, John acknowledged grimly. When this was over, if he survived it, he could repay her for her help by making it financially possible for her to take in all the parentless kids in the entire state of Virginia. He could make it possible for her to give countless children the sort of upbringing she'd had—the sort *he* hadn't. He could make it work for her.

And her husband, whoever the lucky bastard might be.

He had never given any real thought to marriage. Back before Tom's death, he'd been too young, had been having too good a time to consider settling down with one girl for the rest of his life. He hadn't wanted to make a commitment in the present, much less one that extended until death. After Tom died, he had suddenly become too old. Spiritually, he had aged a century or two in a twenty-four-hour period. The good times had disappeared while he'd gone off searching for peace, for absolution; not finding that, he would have been grateful for the sweet release of death . . . or so he had thought.

That was the real reason he'd started writing. He'd found himself at sea on that freighter, miserable and dying bit by bit inside while long hours of hard work kept his body stronger and healthier than ever. They had been somewhere in the Atlantic when he'd gone on deck one night for fresh air and a change from the depressing cramped quarters he called his own.

Hundreds of miles from land, his world had consisted of only the ship, the stars, and the ocean. The water had beckoned him, had drawn him. It wouldn't be a bad way to go, the waves had whispered against the hull. Just slip over the side, swim away from the ship to avoid the huge propellers, then float off to oblivion. Soon he would grow tired. Soon, instead of riding the waves as he'd done for much of his life, he would sink beneath them. With each breath water would replace the oxygen in his lungs, and in a very short time it would bring him peace. As long as he didn't panic, as long as he didn't struggle, it wouldn't turn nasty. And why would he struggle? For him, living was the struggle. Surviving the nights, when he was haunted by dreams of his sins and his failures, was a struggle. Waking up every morning, facing another bright sunny day when his brother would never see a sunrise again, getting out of bed and walking away from it when his sister would never walk again—those were struggles.

Knowing that he was utterly alone in the world, utterly unloved . . . That was a struggle.

Dying would be easy.

Only it hadn't been.

He had tried. Looking back now, he could see that he'd been trying from the moment he'd held Tom's lifeless body. He'd taken on risky jobs and made every reckless mistake he could. He'd tried to drink himself into the ground. A time or two he had picked fights that had gotten him beaten senseless. That night on the ship he had gone so far as to climb over the thick cables that served as a railing. The freighter had been loaded with cargo bound for the Port of New Orleans, so it rode low in the water. It would have been as easy as diving into a pool, and he'd been doing that since he was five years old.

He had tried that night to put himself out of the misery his life had become, had stood there leaning over the water, nothing holding him back but his left hand, wrapped tightly around the cable. His brain had given the order to release it, to let go and dive into the blessed dark water, but his fingers had refused to obey. He had stood there one minute, three, five, ten, and then he had climbed back to the deckside of the lines. He had gone below, wanting to put a few thoughts in writing, and had scrounged up some paper and a pen.

Before the night was over, those few thoughts had filled half of a legal pad. By the time they reached port and he'd collected his pay and headed off for Colorado, he'd had the makings of a book. He had discovered that he had a talent for writing—he, who had failed at virtually everything he'd ever tried. More importantly, it made him feel good.

Not being able to write, on the other hand, had brought back all the misery, although this time without the self-destructive tendencies. He had no desire to die—not today, not next week, and sure as hell not so some deceitful, manipulative bastard could claim everything *he* had worked for.

As they drove across a bridge, Teryl spoke again, echoing the question he'd asked her only a few miles back. "What are *your* plans?"

He didn't think he had any long-term plans beyond staying

alive, certainly nothing like hers. He wasn't likely to get married, wasn't likely to meet any woman who thought he was worth spending the rest of her life with. He wasn't sure he was a decent candidate for fatherhood, either, not with the example his own father had set for him. He would rather live alone the rest of his life than make an innocent kid feel the way his parents had made *him* feel.

When he didn't answer right away, she clarified her question. "When we get to Richmond . . ."

Of course. She was interested only in his plans for the immediate future. She didn't care what he might be doing five years or ten or twenty from now, because she wouldn't be around to know. "I'm going to prove to you that everything I've said was true," he replied, wrapping his fingers tighter around the steering wheel.

"And how are you going to do that?" She was using that cautious tone of voice again, the let's-not-upset-the-crazy-man-and-make-him-do-something-rash voice. Christ, how he hated it!

"You have access to Rebecca's files. I can tell you Simon Tremont's career in detail, and you can verify it. I can tell you things that no one but Simon, Rebecca, and the people at Morgan-Wilkes could possibly know. I can give you figures and dates. I can tell you which clauses Rebecca negotiated in which contracts. I can tell you what changed between the proposal and the final manuscript of each book and whose idea it was—Rebecca's or Candace's or mine. I can tell you everything Rebecca has on Simon Tremont." He glanced at her. "Will that be enough to convince you?"

Miles passed as Teryl stared out the window, looking for an answer to his question. She wanted to say yes, and not just to pacify him, not so he would stay calm and not lose his temper. Some part of her *wanted* to believe him. She wanted to believe that this was a lucid, rational man to whom crazy, irrational things were happening.

In the beginning, she had been one hundred percent convinced that he was insane, but since then, he had created a few doubts, and he had the potential if she took him into the agency—if she went through the records with him, if he could do everything he'd just claimed he could—to create many more. But would it be enough to convince her?

"I don't know," she replied honestly. "I'd like to believe you—"

"Why? Because you think it's your best chance for getting out of this alive?"

She looked at him. He was watching the road and the traffic ahead, so all she got was his profile, but it was enough. Enough to see how tense he was. Enough to know that his jaw must ache from being clenched so tightly. Enough to notice all over again—damn her eyes—how handsome he was. "Are you going to kill me if I don't believe you?" she asked, keeping her voice even through sheer will.

He scowled and tightened his hold on the steering wheel a few degrees more. "Of course not. You know that."

Oddly enough, she *did* know. She honestly believed that he wasn't going to hurt her. If that had been his intention, he'd had plenty of chances in the last four days. He could have killed her at any time, could have dumped her body anywhere along the hundreds of miles of highway they'd traveled and driven away. Because they weren't supposed to even know each other, no one ever would have connected him to her. It would have been a perfect crime.

But the only crime he was interested in was the one he insisted the fraudulent Simon Tremont had cooked up, and it was far from perfect. If everything John said was true, Simon had made a major mistake in not making certain his victim died in the explosion. If *she* had been in Simon's place, she would have planned for the remote possibility that John might escape. She would have been tucked away behind some cover up there in the mountains with a high-powered rifle and a scope, and the instant she saw him come out the window, she would have shot him, then somehow maneuvered the body back inside for the flames to at least partially dispose of.

The trail of her thoughts made her shiver. She didn't like

thinking about murders, attempted or otherwise. It was too grisly a subject for playing would-have, should-have.

"When I get home, I'll call Rebecca," she said. "I'll see if I've overestimated her opinion of me and if I still have a job, and I'll arrange to introduce you to her. She can go through the files with you. She can recommend a good hotel, too, and . . ." Her voice trailed off. He was giving her a curiously still look. She knew long before he started to speak exactly what he was going to say. She was even prepared for the apology in his voice.

"It doesn't end that easily, Teryl. Rebecca isn't going to help me. She'll be even more skeptical than you are, and she's got a lot to lose if I'm telling the truth. It wouldn't do much for her reputation if it came out that she released a client's royalties to a total stranger simply on his claim that he *was* the client. She's worked a long time to make a name for herself. She would sacrifice anything—including me—to protect it."

She would like to dispute that, but she wasn't sure she could. Rebecca's reputation *did* mean a lot to her. The agency was the center of her life. It came before all else. Even her marriage had placed a sorry second after business in her priorities. She had survived the breakup of the marriage, but Teryl wasn't sure she could survive the breakup of the agency.

"You may be right about Rebecca. But *she's* the one who can help you, not me. I have no power. I have no authority. I don't—"

"You have her respect," he interrupted. "If you tell her that something's wrong with this whole Tremont situation, she'll listen to you. She may not agree, but she'll hear you out, where she would probably simply throw me out."

"But I can't tell her that something's wrong."

"You can after I convince you."

Teryl thought—but wisely didn't say—that, short of getting the man she knew as Simon to admit that he was a fake, there wasn't anything she could think of offhand that could totally convince her.

"All right," she said, shifting restlessly. "Let's say we go through the files and you know all the particulars of Simon's career. *I* know all the details of my mother's life, but that doesn't make me her."

Once again he scowled. "That's different. You know your mother; you're her only natural-born child; you lived more than half of your life with her. Of course you know everything. But *I* don't know the man who says he's me. Before Tuesday afternoon at the TV station, I'd never laid eyes on him."

Maybe, she thought. *Or maybe not.*

"You don't believe that, either." He muttered a bitter curse. "What do you think, Teryl? That I did somehow know him? Maybe we were neighbors or old buddies, or maybe I worked for him. Maybe that's how I learned so much about him. Or maybe I broke into his house and stole his records so I could familiarize myself with every aspect of his career. Maybe *that's* how I learned so much about him. And then maybe I burned my own house and sliced open my arm to explain why I have no proof of my identity, and then I followed him to New Orleans. Wouldn't that have been a little foolish—risking being seen there by him?"

"You didn't risk that, though," she pointed out in a soft, hesitant murmur. "You didn't come into the studio until just before the interview started, you stayed in the shadows, and you left the minute it was over. The next morning you were in the hotel lobby while he and I were talking. You were watching us, but you never came close enough to be seen. You never got close to him, never got close enough for him to notice you."

His expression darkened. Had he expected her to not notice his disappearing act Tuesday afternoon? Had he thought she would write off both that and the reappearing act Wednesday morning as just coincidence or the luck of timing?

"You're right," he said at last. "I did want to avoid being seen by him. The man was in my house, for God's sake! He tried to kill me! There were photographs in the house, pictures of me with my brother and sister. I didn't know if he'd seen them, if he had taken the time to nose around before or after he rigged the bombs, but I wasn't taking any chances. If he had seen them, then he would have been able to recognize me; you saw for yourself that I haven't changed a whole lot in the last seventeen years. And if he did recognize me there in New Orleans when he thought I was dead . . . It wasn't a situation I wanted to deal with just yet. I want proof before I confront him."

His explanation made sense, she admitted; then she choked back a derisive laugh. *Nothing* in this whole mess made sense. Absolutely nothing.

As they drove into the city of Richmond, the relief she had expected to feel was noticeably missing. She had kidded herself into thinking everything would be all right when she got home, that she would be safe and free, that John Smith would no longer be a part of her life, that his claims would no longer concern her. But it wouldn't end that easily, he'd warned.

How much of a prisoner would she be? Would he insist on sleeping in the same room? Would he allow her to keep her car keys now that her car would be parked right outside the house? Would she be able to go to work Monday morning? To call her mother and tell her she was home? To visit with D.J. the way she always did on weekends?

Would he expect to keep her bound in her own home?

She could kick up a fuss. She could refuse to tell him where she lived. She could develop a little backbone and simply say no. *No, you're not going to stay at my house. No, I'm not going to help you. No, I won't be your prisoner anymore.* She could try again to escape. The first time he stopped for a red light or in traffic, she could jump out of the Blazer and run like hell. She could scream bloody murder. She could get him arrested. She could get him locked away for a long, long time.

Or she could help him. She could do what he wanted and get him out of her life. Although she still thought he was emotionally unstable, she wasn't afraid of him now, not really. He'd passed up too many chances to hurt her. For the most part—except for those few miserable minutes each night—he had treated her well. He had fed her, had allowed her as much freedom as he realistically could. He hadn't kept her tied up any longer than was necessary, he hadn't gagged or blindfolded her, hadn't assaulted or raped her. He hadn't even taken advantage of the sex she had offered.

It sounded crazy—incredibly crazy—but she believed she could trust him, at least to some extent. She didn't believe he would kill her. She didn't believe he would hurt her. She didn't believe he was capable of hurting anyone, with the possible exception of Simon Tremont.

She could help him. She could go along with his plans, could let him stay at her house, could take him into the office tomorrow when no one was working. She could let him try to convince her that his fantastic story was true. When he couldn't prove his claims . . . She wasn't sure exactly what he would do, how he would react, but that would be a good time to take whatever steps were necessary to get him out of her life. Maybe she could get in touch with his sister; maybe Janie could arrange private help for him so they could avoid bringing the police into the matter. At this point—home and feeling reasonably safe—she wasn't interested in seeing him arrested or involuntarily committed to some psychiatric hospital. The idea of John—haunted, wounded, and all too human—locked up with all the other crazies was one she didn't want to face. She didn't want to be in any way responsible for it.

And what if he *did* prove his claims? What if he *did* convince her that he was Simon Tremont and the man in New Orleans was the fraud, the crazy, the criminal?

What a story that would be, worthy of the number one slot on the *Times* list for the next five years.

"Which way to your house?"

She twisted in the seat to face him. "If you're going to stay with me, if I'm going to help you, we have to have a few ground rules."

He gestured for her to go on.

"I'm not going to be a prisoner in my own home. I have to be free to go to work. I have to have access to my car and to the telephone. I have to be allowed to live my life. You trust me, and I'll treat you the same as any other guest in my home." She finished, then remembered the most important thing. "You won't tie me up anymore. You can't. I won't allow it."

"I thought I made it clear last night that it wouldn't happen again," he said evenly.

She remembered his solemn offer of the knife so she could cut the telephone cord to ribbons. She hadn't looked beyond the tremendous relief she'd felt at knowing that that particular wire couldn't be used against her again. She hadn't realized that, for him, the gesture had been symbolic, inclusive of all bonds.

"Do you agree with the rules?"

He nodded.

She glanced around to see where they were, then spoke again. "Take the next exit. My house isn't far."

As he changed lanes, she blew her breath out in a heavy sigh. She was committed now. She had agreed to providing him with a place to stay and to helping him prove—or disprove—his claims. She prayed she wasn't making a mistake.

John followed her directions through a commercial district and into one of Richmond's older neighborhoods. The houses there were gracious, large, and old, most of them built seventy-five to a hundred years ago. There was lots of money in this neighborhood, although, according to Teryl, none of it was hers. When she directed him to turn off the wide, winding street, it was onto a brick drive that passed between two massive brick columns. The gate was ornate, wrought iron with curlicues and lace that formed a fanciful G on each half. A quarter mile in, he turned into her driveway, a broad lane, not quite wide enough for two cars, that wound back a few hundred yards before ending in a clearing at the back of her house.

From the front it was a plain little house, beige stucco, two small stories with a red tile roof, arched windows, and a little square stoop tiled with terra-cotta. In back, there were more arches—over the windows, around the door, and supporting the second-floor balcony that ran the length and the width of the house and shaded the patio on warm summer days.

There was also a courtyard, now doing duty as a parking court, and a fountain, lavishly decorated with thousands of small mosaic tiles in no particular pattern. There was no water in the fountain, though. It had been filled with rich, black soil and served as a planter for lush, red geraniums divided through the center with a swath of white petunias. There were other flower beds nearby, other plantings—vines that snaked their way around the arches and up to the roof, compact trees that were perfectly proportioned to the house, ivies and begonias, periwinkles and lots of roses in red, yellow, pink, and white.

It was a pretty little place, he thought, even if it did look as if it belonged in the Southwest—Arizona, California, or perhaps someplace more exotic, like Morocco—than in Richmond, Virginia.

He shifted into first gear, set the parking brake, and shut off the engine. "Is this where you live?"

She nodded.

"It's a dollhouse."

His pronouncement made her smile. "This estate used to belong to the Grayson family. They were a big name locally in the early part of the century. This was where the groundskeeper lived. The house is a replica of the family home—which is farther down the drive—only, of course, this one is much smaller since a groundskeeper didn't need space or luxury. I don't guess they gave any thought to the fact that Spanish or Mediterranean or Moorish architecture—whichever style it is—doesn't work well on such a small scale."

Unbuckling his seat belt, he opened the door and climbed out. Damp heat and the fragrance of flowers greeted him. "It works well enough," he said, joining her at the front of the truck. "It just looks . . ."

"Like a dollhouse."

As they crossed the courtyard, she dug her keys from her purse and unlocked the back door. The layout, John saw when he stepped inside, was simple. The front and back doors opened into a narrow hallway that ran the length of the L-shaped house. The living room, just visible through the door up ahead on the right, formed the short leg, and the kitchen and dining room, on the left, made up the longer leg. If the upstairs was the same size—and given the width of the balcony he'd noticed, he would bet it was smaller—the entire house was maybe a thousand square feet, probably less. The whole thing would have fitted neatly inside the office and living room in *his* house.

As he closed the door behind him, she adjusted the thermostat on the hall wall, turning it low enough to bring the air conditioner on. Then she simply stood there, looking awkward, apparently feeling uncomfortable in her own home. In spite of their truce, he knew that she really didn't want him here, invading her space, still controlling her life. Would it make a difference to her if she knew she would handsomely benefit from their brief association? If he told her, showed her, proved to her, that she would be a wealthy woman when this was over, would it make her any happier about the circumstances?

Not likely. Especially since she wouldn't believe him.

Probably the only thing he could do that would make her happy was disappear. Then she could convince herself that the last four days were only a bad dream. Then she could go back to worshiping Simon Tremont. Then she could forget that John Smith had ever existed.

Shoving his hands into his hip pockets, he passed her and went into the living room, stopping near the sofa. The room was small, but it didn't seem so. The sense of space was due in part to the three sets of French doors that filled one wall and led outside to the courtyard and in part to Teryl's style. It was comfortable without being cluttered. There was a sofa in wide blue and white stripes and a big armchair in a nubby white fabric of the sort meant for settling in, fronted by a hassock almost as big as the chair itself and in the same fabric. The tables at each end of the sofa were open, two tiers, wood and glass, the same as the shelves tucked in wherever there was space. There were baskets all over, one holding magazines, others filled with books, dried flowers, and fragrant potpourri. The curtains at the door, were white and sheer; he could see the bright reds, pinks, and yellows of the flowers outside through them.

It was an easy room to be in . . . or, at least, it would be if Teryl wasn't standing so uncomfortably at the door.

He turned to look at her. She'd been wearing the same dress for three days now, had sat for hundreds of miles in it, had slept in the less-than-comfortable confines of the truck in it. It was wrinkled and limp and had definitely seen better days, but she still looked lovely in it.

Sweet damnation, how he would like to take it off her.

For a long time he continued to look at her, and after a nervous moment, she looked back. How could two people, each half of the same relationship, see each other so differently? he wondered with regret. He looked at her and saw a beautiful woman, a woman he wanted to be with, a woman he wanted right this moment to make love to, while *she* looked at *him* and saw a man she wished she'd never met. A man she couldn't trust. A crazy man.

Maybe she was right. Maybe he *was* crazy. Living the way he had after Tom's death—drifting from place to place, from job to job, barely living while he tried dying—wasn't normal. Retreating into the mountains and cutting off virtually all contact with the outside world for eleven years wasn't normal, either. Neither was kidnapping an innocent woman, taking her hostage, and forcing her against her will to help him. Or wanting her so damned badly—while she was still his hostage, still his victim—that she haunted his sleep.

Maybe he *was* crazy in those ways.

But not about Simon. He knew *he* had created the pseudonym. *He* had written the books. *His* alter ego was the man Teryl adored, not that arrogant, smug, condescending bastard she had met in New Orleans. He *knew* those things, knew them beyond a shadow of a doubt, knew them as surely as he knew he wanted Teryl.

But *she* didn't know.

She leaned one shoulder against the arched doorjamb and folded her arms across her chest just beneath her breasts. If she knew what a provocative pose it was—fabric pulled taut across her breasts, then falling loosely practically to her ankles, revealing a hint of the loveliness of her body while concealing everything else—she would move immediately. She would pull the material away from her soft nipples, would round her shoulders so the dress fell, unimpeded by curves, all the way to the hem, or would raise her arms higher, providing better camouflage.

She could cover herself in armor from head to toe, but she could never erase the memories he had of her naked in bed beneath him. She could never make him forget how sweetly rounded her breasts were, how taut her nipples had become, how slender her hips were, how soft and tantalizing the curls between her thighs were. She could never make him forget the heat he had stirred inside her or the way she had fitted him so tightly. She could never reclaim from him the sound of the soft whimpers she made or the feel of her body clamping hard around him or the flush her skin took on when she came or the way she turned all soft and weak when it was over.

She could forget, but she could never make *him* forget.

Judging from that hazy look in her eyes, he thought it was a fair bet at that moment that she wasn't trying to forget anything.

"What—" Breaking off, she cleared away the hoarseness from her throat before trying again. "What do you want to do now?"

He knew the sort of answer she wanted—let's unpack, let's get dinner, let's watch TV—but he had no interest in those answers. They had wasted enough time in the last few days packing and unpacking, had eaten enough meals together, had watched enough television together. He wanted more. He wanted activity. Conversation. Stimulation.

He wanted arousal, passion, completion, exhaustion.

He wanted sex.

He walked toward her, covering the distance in his own sweet time, coming to a stop directly in front of her. "I suppose seducing you is out of the question."

His regretful, yet hopeful words took her by surprise, making her eyes widen, her breath catch, her muscles tighten.

She tried to hide it when she spoke, but the slight tremble in her voice gave it away. "That isn't going to happen."

"Why not? You were more than eager Tuesday night. You were agreeable Thursday night. You were pretty damned willing last night. What's different now?"

She didn't answer his question. Instead, she simply repeated her answer. "It isn't going to happen. I can't let it. You can't make it."

He studied her for a moment, then smiled a little. "You're wrong, Teryl. I *can* make it happen." He saw the misunderstanding darken her eyes and immediately dispelled it. "I'm not talking about using force. If I were going to rape you, I would have done it Wednesday morning before we left the hotel. I would have done it again that night, when we were lying in your bed. Hell, we never would have gotten farther than Slidell if that was what I'd had in mind. But I'm not talking about rape. I'm talking about making love. I'm talking about kissing you, about touching you here . . ." He stroked his hand along her jaw. "And here . . ." Just the tips of his fingers brushed across her breast, lingering only long enough to start the sweet rush of sensation that would harden her nipples. "And here . . ."

She caught his wrist before he reached below her waist. Her neat, short nails were pressing hard against his skin, creating four little half-moons of pain. "Another rule," she said, her gaze locked with his, her voice little more than a whisper. "Keep your hands to yourself. I don't want them on me."

He lowered his voice to match hers. The softness enclosed them in an air of intimacy. "You don't? Then why are your breasts swelling? Why are your nipples hard? Why are you getting wet? Why are you trembling?"

Dropping his wrist, she turned away, quickly putting the width of the hallway between them. "You'd better decide what's more important to you: meaningless sex or getting access to Rebecca's files on Tremont."

Mimicking the position she'd abandoned—arms folded across his chest, shoulder braced against the doorframe—he studied her. "Meaningless sex, Teryl?" he asked quietly. "Is that what you think it was?"

Her cheeks flushed, and she avoided his gaze. She also avoided answering. Instead, she climbed the first few steps before glancing in his general direction again. "Why don't you bring the suitcases in, and I'll show you which room you can use." Without waiting for his response, she went upstairs and disappeared from sight.

Meaningless sex.

He had known that going to bed with her when he had lied to her from the start wasn't a good idea. She had believed that he'd gone to her hotel room with her that night for no reason other than lust, for nothing more than a few hours of passionate sex and mutual satisfaction. Then he'd told her his full name, had told her his story, and her insecurities had kicked in. The man she had loved, had lived with and wanted to marry, had deceived her, had merely used her. That experience must have made it easy for her to believe that *he*, too, had used her, that the sex had been simply a means to an end, that—if not for his need to get into Rebecca's office—he never would have been in Teryl's bed.

Insecure or not, if she believed that, she was a fool. He had wanted her in spite of his need for her help, not because of it. He had wanted her—still wanted her—because she was a beautiful woman, because he liked being with her, because he liked the way she smiled, the way she walked, the way she talked, the way she kissed. He had wanted her because he'd gone so damned long without sex, because lust was a powerful need, because her actions had told him that she would be willing, because instinct had told him that they would be good. It had had nothing to do with Simon.

For those few hours Tuesday night, he had forgotten that Simon even existed.

But maybe he was being arrogant. Maybe *meaningless* was how *she* felt about it. Maybe, for her, Tuesday evening had boiled down to one thing: sex, pure and simple. Maybe *he* was the one who had been used. If he hadn't offered to spend the evening with her, maybe the man posing as Simon would have been in her bed instead, or the waiter at Pat

O'Brien's who had served her drinks with more attention than was necessary, or the cab driver who had leeringly watched them in his rearview mirror. Maybe John's presence in her bed that night had simply been a matter of luck that had had nothing to do with *him* and everything to do with fulfilling the fantasy of a nameless, faceless, anonymous fuck.

I always thought it would be fun, just once in my life, to be wicked in New Orleans.

Instead of the desire, instead of the attraction and liking that he'd been convinced was mutual, maybe that was all it had been.

Maybe he'd simply been her *fun.*

Chapter Nine

*S*unday morning D.J. awakened with a headache, bruises up and down her arms, and an overall stiffness that added about ten years to her thirty. Stretching her legs out, she realized that she was lying on a bare mattress, that she was naked except for the sheet wound around her arms and wrists, and she hurt when she moved.

Her memories of last night weren't particularly clear. All she knew was that they'd argued again—she and Rich—as they so often did, and it had ended the way it always did. He had punished her, and in that sick, dark place inside her, she had enjoyed it. She had wanted it. She'd gotten off on it.

Freeing her hands from the sheet, she slowly sat up and shoved her hair out of her face. In the mirror across the room she caught a glimpse of what an unappealing picture she made this morning and resolutely turned away from it. She'd had a rough night. Hell, she'd had a rough *life*. She deserved to look it once in a while.

Leaning across to the nightstand, she opened the drawer and rummaged inside for a pack of cigarettes. Besides the cigarettes and a red throwaway lighter, there was an odd assortment of items in the drawer. They wouldn't mean anything to most people, but for D.J. they held plenty of significance. There was the length of nylon rope that Rich used when he tied her to the bed. There was the belt, brown leather, an inch wide, that he used when he was really angry. There was the bandanna and a roll of duct tape for when he gagged her. Sometimes he liked to hear her cries. Sometimes he liked to make her scream. And sometimes he wanted to hear nothing from her, not even a whimper.

Those were the times, she thought as she held the lighter's flame to the cigarette and inhaled deeply, when he pretended she was just another object—like the rope and the belt—intended for his sexual pleasure.

Or when he pretended she was somebody else, one of her friends. Or Teryl.

He never bothered to deny his interest in Teryl. She told herself he wanted her to believe it, even though it wasn't true, because he was a mean son of a bitch. He understood her conflicting feelings toward Teryl better than anyone else—better, even, than she understood them herself. Their parents thought they were the same best friends they'd been twenty years ago when D.J. had become a part of the Weaver family. Their brothers and sisters believed it, too. Hell, even Teryl believed she'd never had a better friend.

But Rich knew better. He knew that Teryl was everything D.J. wasn't, that Teryl had everything she'd been denied. He knew that her fondest dream, her most cherished fantasy, was to go back more than twenty years ago, back to a time before she'd known the Weavers existed, before the Weavers had known Teryl existed. Then D.J. would somehow slip herself into her friend's place. *She* would be the Weavers' first daughter. *She* would be the one who held a special place in their hearts. *She* would be a real Weaver instead of always being on the outside, part of the group but not a real part of the family, not a legal part.

She would be the one all the other kids looked up to, the one they all envied, the one they all wanted to be like. She had spent much of her life trying to emulate Teryl, trying to make herself over into Miss Straight-A-student, Abide-by the-rules, Never-step-out-of-line, Sweet-generous-and-kind-to-animals, A-virgin-until-she-was-twenty-one-fucking-years-old Goody-two-shoes. She had wanted to *be* Teryl . . . but at the same time she had felt contempt for what

Teryl was. She had hated herself for being so bad, and she'd resented Teryl for being so good. She had craved the respect, acceptance, and love Teryl had always been given so freely, but she had wanted the sex, rebellion, and the inevitable punishment even more.

She had been warped ever since her parents had gotten their hands on her—too warped to ever become Miss Perfect. Like perfectly normal, perfectly average, perfectly well adjusted Teryl.

It had taken Rich about five minutes after they'd met to see and understand those things about her. It had been Teryl who'd brought him into D.J.'s life nine long years ago. It had been Teryl he'd wanted then. Encounters with her in the class he'd taught had made a major impression on him, but Teryl hadn't returned his interest. D.J. had found it amusing to watch him make a fool of himself over someone who clearly would never want him, and, when the time was right, she had offered herself in Teryl's place.

And so love—perverse, sick, depraved—had been born.

At least, it was the closest thing to love *she* had ever known. In nine years she had learned to hate him, to fear him, to loathe the things he did to her, the things she begged him to do. She was miserable with him and even more miserable without him. Like an alcoholic's craving for booze or an addict's hunger for drugs, she needed him—needed the sex, the disdain, the derision, the pain. The few times she had tried to walk away, she had always come crawling back. The few times she had found some pride, some dignity, she had brought it to him to destroy with his sharp tongue and his capable fists.

Her biggest hope was that someday she would escape this unholy, unhealthy hold he had on her.

Her biggest prayer was that someday never come.

Rising from the bed, she found her clothes on the floor where he'd thrown them and quickly got dressed. She would bring an overnight bag with clean clothes, a toothbrush, and other toiletries if he wouldn't mind, so she wouldn't have to go home in worn, wrinkled, and sometimes tattered clothing, but he wouldn't let her. He didn't want her to get the idea she was welcome here. This was *his* home. He would screw her here. He would debase her here. He would hurt her here.

But he would not welcome her.

He could live without *her*.

While she would die without him.

Once her hair was combed and she looked at least presentable, she left the bedroom and went searching for him. She found him in the kitchen, seated at the kitchen table, a bowl of cereal and the newspaper in front of him. Stopping behind his chair, she laid her hands on his shoulders, intending to massage away the stiffness that so often settled there, but he shrugged her away. With a suppressed sigh, she drew back. "Good morning."

He didn't look up from the newspaper as he responded to her greeting with a distracted grunt.

"How long have you been up?"

"A couple hours."

"You should have awakened me. I would have fixed breakfast for you." She wasn't of much use in the kitchen, but she had mastered his favorite foods—eggs over easy, canned biscuits, and cream gravy. It had been one pathetic attempt to make herself useful, one more reason for him to keep her around.

"Cereal's fine."

She circled around to the closest empty chair and sat down. "Want me to make a pot of coffee?"

"No."

For all the attention he was paying her, she might as well not even be there. Of course, that was what he wanted. When he had no further use of her, he wanted her gone. That was the way of their sad, sick romance.

She sat there a moment, considering leaving without another word, but studied him instead. He was handsome, though it had never been his looks that attracted her to him. She had never cared how thick and silky his hair was or what a deep, cocoa brown his eyes were. He'd had a beard when she'd met him, but that had neither attracted nor repelled her. Neither had his body—long and lean, sometimes, when he became absorbed in something, to the point of thinness.

No, what she had first liked about him was the fact that he'd wanted something—Teryl—that he couldn't have. She had liked the fact that he'd taken that desire seriously. She had liked the intensity of it.

And she had particularly liked the fact that he was a kindred spirit. Just as he had so quickly recognized the ambivalence she felt toward Teryl, she had recognized herself in him. She didn't know then—and still didn't now—what had made him the way he was. She didn't know whether someone in his childhood had mistreated him the way her parents had mistreated her or if it was a genetic defect or if he was just plain mean, just plain driven. For a long time, although she had never dared ask, she had cared, just as she had cared why Teryl had turned out as good as she had and why *she* had turned out so bad.

Now she didn't wonder, didn't care. He was beyond saving. And so, she feared, was she.

Finishing the cereal, he dropped the spoon in the bowl with a clatter, set it aside, then pushed his glasses up on his nose. The thick lenses made his eyes appear hazy and somewhat unfocused, but they weren't. He saw life with a clarity that she envied. He saw everything around him and its effect on him. He saw the problems. He saw the solutions. Unfortunately, his solutions weren't always the right ones. They weren't always logical ones.

And sometimes they scared the hell out of her.

As she rose from the chair, she picked up his dishes, taking them to the sink and rinsing them. When they had first met, he'd been as sloppy and messy as any typical young man, but lately he'd changed that. Lately he'd gotten very finicky. He might make messes—might scatter dishes around, might spread newspapers out, or throw clothing to the floor—but he wanted them set right as soon as possible. This old farmhouse had never been so clean as it had been the last week.

Too bad he wouldn't come to *her* apartment and get a little finicky there.

"I guess I'd better be going," she said, standing halfway between him and the hall door, half hoping he would say,

Nah, why don't you stay? even though he never had before, not once in nine years.

This morning was no different.

"Should I come back this evening?"

At last he looked at her. "No. I'll be working."

"I won't bother you."

"No."

"Come on, Rich," she cajoled. "I'll stay in the bedroom until you're finished. I'll be quiet. I won't distract you."

The look he gave her was cold and derisive. "You *couldn't* distract me. You're not smart enough, you're not good enough, you're not interesting enough. I'll let you know when I want to see you again."

"Please, Rich . . ." Calling on her deepest reserves of strength, she bit off the plea. He liked to make her beg in the bedroom. They both derived a certain pleasure from it there. Outside that room, though, it just made him angry.

It got demeaning.

"I'll see you later," she muttered, turning toward the door. All the way down the long hall, out the front door, and across the porch, she hoped he would follow, hoped he would stop her, hoped he would call out, Yeah, come back tonight.

Of course he didn't. He never did. He never would.

But she always hoped.

It felt good being home again, Teryl thought as she sat at the kitchen table, a microwaved bagel and a Diet Coke in front of her. Sitting in her favorite chair instead of in the truck or on a lumpy bed, smelling potpourri and roses instead of must and mildew or gasoline and exhaust, moving about freely without being constantly watched. Sleeping in her own bed, bathing in her own bathroom, drying off with thick towels, wearing clean clothes . . . Those were all little luxuries she had taken for granted, but not anymore.

The only thing that would make it better, the only thing that would make her truly comfortable, was if she were here alone. If John wasn't here. If he wasn't giving her doubts about the Simon Tremont she knew. If she were as blissfully ignorant of his claims as she'd been the last time she'd sat here at this table.

Thanks to John, she might never wear that floral dress again. Or stay in a motel. Or speak to a strange man. She might never venture out of Richmond again. She just might not ever venture out of her house again.

Not that staying locked up at home would keep her safe. After all, the strangest man she'd met in a long time—or, at least, a candidate for that title—was temporarily living with her.

When he had come upstairs yesterday carrying their luggage, she had shown him to the guest room down the hall and around the corner from her own. It was a tiny room, big enough for a double bed, two night tables, and nothing else. Some previous resident had sacrificed a portion of the small closet space to build in shelves since there was no room for even the smallest of bureaus. There was no window, but plenty of light entered through the glass-paned doors that opened onto the balcony.

That damned balcony. From her door to his, more than half the length and about half the width of the house separated them. By way of the balcony, it was just a few yards from French door to French door.

Not that she had felt unsafe last night. They had slept only a few feet apart for three nights, and he'd done nothing. Now that they were in separate rooms, he wasn't going to force his way in. She was much safer now than she'd been the last four days.

Still, there had been something terribly disconcerting about waking up this morning, snug in her own room, lying on her own pillow, tucked beneath her own covers, and looking out one of the three sets of doors that lined her wall only to see him standing out there on the balcony. He had been wearing jeans, no shirt, and no shoes, leaning against the railing, smoking a cigarette, and staring down at the garden.

When he had finished that cigarette, he'd lit another one, then had turned directly toward her doors. She'd known he couldn't see her, had known the shadows were too deep.

Still, she had burrowed a little deeper into the pillow, had snuggled a little farther into the cover, and in so doing she succeeded in reviving an ache that she'd hoped wouldn't come back, at least, for the time being.

That was what she got for sleeping naked. For watching him when he didn't know he was being watched. For letting him touch her face and her breast yesterday, for listening to him say the things he'd said. For bringing him to her house in the first place.

He had been right yesterday. Her breasts *had* been swollen and tender, her nipples had been hard, and, yes, she'd been wet between her thighs. That was why she'd stopped him from touching her there, so he wouldn't feel the moisture and the heat. So he wouldn't know how quickly and how intensely he could arouse her. So he wouldn't know how easily he could seduce her.

She would have been so damned easy . . . if he'd given it any effort.

But he hadn't. Her only satisfaction last night had been self-induced under the cover of the pounding water in the shower. D.J. would say the shower was the only place Teryl could have done it because it was the only place and the only time when it was not only all right but necessary for a good little girl to touch herself there and Teryl, her friend always teased, was *such* a good little girl.

She always had been.

But last night and this morning—and, hell, even right now, alone here in the kitchen—she wanted very much to be bad again.

Even if being bad was what had gotten her into this mess in the first place.

Her sigh was heavy and loud, but not quite loud enough to disguise the sound of footsteps in the hall. In another moment, another second, he was going to walk through the door into the kitchen and tell her that he was ready, that it was time to leave. Time to go to the office. Time to go through Simon Tremont's file and test him on his knowledge of the contents.

The whole idea made her uncomfortable. There was something so sneaky and underhanded in the plan. She would be betraying Rebecca, who had treated her more than fairly, and the real Simon, who had a right to expect confidentiality from *all* employees of the agency. She wished he would give her a chance to sit down with Rebecca and tell her about his claims. She wished he wouldn't insist on being so covert about it. But he'd been right yesterday. Rebecca wouldn't help him. She might refer him to her lawyer or maybe pass him off to Morgan-Wilkes. She would definitely warn Simon, and she might even call the police. But she wouldn't open the files to him. She wouldn't seriously listen to him. She wouldn't give his tale even the slightest consideration.

Not only would she not help him, she would make it very difficult for him to prove anything.

If he really was Simon Tremont, he deserved their help. He deserved *her* help.

He came into the room and sat down across from her. He'd just gotten out of the shower, and his hair was still damp. After silently sliding the untouched half of her bagel across to him, she studied him for a moment. Over the last thirty years, pop culture had elevated California girls to legend status, but there had been few references that she could recall to California boys. Based purely on physical attributes, this California boy—this man—could certainly qualify for at least minor legend status. Golden-tanned, blue-eyed, sandy blond, over six feet tall, broad-shouldered, narrow-waisted, lean-hipped, long-legged, he could certainly have the same effect on the female libido that all those Beach Boys-type, curvy, leggy, busty blond girls in bikinis had on the male counterpart.

God knew, he had a hell of an effect on *her*.

He ate the bagel before speaking. "Does anyone ever come in to the agency on Sunday?"

"No."

"It probably wouldn't hurt to have an excuse ready if someone does happen to come by."

She nodded. "I'll think of something . . ." A sound outside drew her attention to the windows, and she muttered an oath that made him look out, too. He stiffened, just as she did, and rose from the table.

"Who is that?"

"D.J."

"What is she doing here? She shouldn't even know you're back."

Teryl also stood up. "Of course she knows. I called last night and left a message on her machine." She bristled at the annoyed look he gave her. "She's been waiting all week for me to call and tell her when I'm coming home so she could pick me up at the airport. Besides, I would never come back from a trip and just not call her. We talk all the time. We usually spend Sunday afternoons talking."

"Who else did you call?" he asked with a scowl.

"My mother." The slight defiance in her voice faded into defensiveness as she continued. "And I left a message on Rebecca's machine."

"Damn it, Teryl—"

"I *had* to. You're going to take care of your business, then go back to wherever you came from, but *I'll* still be here, John. I *need* my job." She drew a calming breath. "I didn't tell her anything, I swear. I apologized for not coming back when I was supposed to, I promised to make it up to her, and I told her that I would be in Monday. That's *all* I said. I never mentioned you."

After another hard look, he turned his gaze back out to the courtyard, where D.J. had parked beside his truck. Teryl watched him watch D.J. get out of the car, and in his expression she saw the immediate appreciation of a healthy man for a disarmingly beautiful woman. It was nothing new. Every man she'd ever been involved with had been at least slightly smitten with her best friend, but Teryl had never really minded. This time, though, it brought with it an unpleasant twinge of jealousy. This time she wished D.J. was so much *less*—less flashy, less gorgeous, less sexy. She wished D.J.'s hair was less vibrant in color, less wild, less untended. She wished her friend's complexion was pallid and marred with freckles, like so many redheads, instead of rich, creamy gold.

She wished D.J.'s clothes were less provocative, her body less shapely, her voice less sultry.

She wished that just once a man would see the two of them together and would concentrate on *her* instead of staring wide-eyed and hungry at her friend.

They were each a gift, D.J. had told her once long, long ago. Teryl was God's gift to parents—sweet, well behaved, well-mannered . . . meaning boring—while D.J. was Satan's gift to men. Teryl the good little girl, and D.J. the temptress. The seducer.

John, silently watching her move away from the Camaro, was ready, able, and willing to be seduced.

D.J. walked in a slow half circle around the Blazer, then came toward the house. Even if she'd found Teryl here alone, she would have been full of questions about New Orleans, the mystery man, and Simon Tremont. Now, Teryl knew, she would be crazy with curiosity. She wouldn't rest until she got at least a little time alone with Teryl and all the details she could pry out of her.

Teryl found herself hoping that John wouldn't give them any time alone at the same time she wished he would disappear up the stairs in the next thirty seconds and not come down again until D.J. was gone. Then the thirty seconds were up. D.J. was knocking at the back door, and John was still standing only a few feet away.

With a reluctant sigh, she headed for the door.

D.J. wasted little time with hellos. "Whose Chevy is that?" she demanded. "Is it *his*? Teryl, you slut, did you bring him home with you?"

Teryl was stammering through an answer when D.J. abruptly walked away. She approached John, her heels clicking on the tile floor, her movements graceful but calculated, everything done for maximum effect. She reminded Teryl, watching from the doorway, of nothing so much as a sleek, lean cat stalking its prey. Under ordinary circumstances, Teryl found her behavior amusing . . . but there was nothing ordinary about these circumstances.

D.J. didn't stop until she had completed a circle around John, looking him up and down. Teryl recognized that slow, satisfied smile of hers. Her friend found no fault with what she saw . . . but then, she never found fault with *any* male. "I've got to hand it to you, little sister," she said in a honey-smooth drawl, looking back over her shoulder. "This is one heck of a vacation souvenir. Most people who go to New Orleans bring home those gaudy little masks or tacky beads, but not you. You brought yourself a man." She extended her hand. "I'm D.J. Howell, Teryl's sister and friend."

After a moment, he responded. "I'm John."

She released his hand and, taking a few steps back, seated herself at the table. "So . . . how did you two meet?"

Thankful that her friend's attention was focused on John and not her, Teryl stared across the room at him. D.J. had asked the question once before, on the phone their first night on the road, and Teryl had lied. Please, she silently prayed, please let him remember.

He did, and he delivered the lie so smoothly she would have believed it herself if she hadn't known better. "At Pat O'Brien's. It was crowded and we were both alone, so I asked her to join me."

D.J. crossed one leg over the other, and Teryl watched as John's gaze flickered down, then back up again, his expression absolutely blank.

"Funny," D.J. remarked. "You don't talk the way I thought someone from New Orleans would talk."

"A lot of people who live in New Orleans aren't from there," he pointed out evenly.

"And where are you from?"

"Everywhere. Nowhere."

"But you're in New Orleans now."

"Actually, I'm in Richmond now."

Her response to that was a thinly amused smile. "You know what I mean. You live in New Orleans now."

He shrugged. "I'm not living anywhere in particular right now."

If the rest of his story was true, Teryl thought, then that was, too. The closest thing he had to a home right now was *her* home.

Reaching across the table, D.J. picked up Teryl's Coke

can and drained the last of the soda from it before she turned to her. "Come sit down, girl, and tell me about New Orleans," she invited, then added with a lascivious grin, "Tell me about Simon Tremont."

There was nothing in the world that Teryl wanted less than to sit down at that table and talk to D.J. about Simon Tremont in front of John. If only he would leave the room, would go to the living room or outside to the courtyard, so they could talk privately, but she suspected that he had no intention of going anywhere. He couldn't be sure that D.J. wouldn't coax details—secrets—from her. He wasn't sure that he could trust Teryl not to confide in her.

Hell, Teryl wasn't sure she could trust herself not to blurt out everything if she had the opportunity.

Reluctantly, she approached the table, sliding back into her chair. The last bite of her toasted bagel sat on a napkin next to the now-empty Coke can. "There's not much to say," she said, avoiding both John's gaze and D.J.'s. "The interview went okay ... but you've probably seen it by now. I think it's played on every TV station across the country."

"Not much to say?" D.J. echoed incredulously. She directed her next words at John. "The girl has had a severe case of hero worship for the man her entire adult life. He's the standard by which she measures all other writers and most other men. I swear, she thinks he can walk on water. She would have sold her soul to meet him, and once she finally gets to, there's not much to say about him." She mimicked Teryl's less-sexy, less-sultry voice on those last words before laughing. "Reality must have been a tremendous letdown from the fantasy. Poor kid. I'm sorry. So what was wrong with Tremont? Was he a geek? An idiot? Was he stuffy? Obnoxious?" She leaned forward, sending her hair cascading across her shirt, and asked with a conspiratorial grin, "Was he crazy?"

"D.J.," Teryl chided.

"Oh, come on, you've read his books. The man writes about creepy things and creepy places. His books are spooky and totally weird."

Her words made Teryl uncomfortable. Would John take

offense? How would he feel about hearing words like crazy, creepy, and weird applied to the man he was claiming to be?

When she didn't respond to D.J.'s question, he did. He took the seat between them at the end of the table, and he answered mildly, evenly. "What kind of books he writes has nothing to do with what kind of person he is. Do you think romance writers are having all these hot and passionate affairs? Or that mystery writers are killing people? Or that Western authors are saddling up ol' Paint and riding off into the sunset?"

D.J. turned her gaze on him, studying him with an interest that, for once, Teryl noted, wasn't sexual—but it *was* intense. "Did you meet him, too?"

"No."

"But you saw the interview."

"Everyone in the country saw the interview."

"But you were there in New Orleans. Did you see it in person or on TV?"

"On TV," he lied.

"What did you think?"

"That's not a fair question. Unlike Teryl, I'm not a fan." He paused. "But you are, aren't you?"

Abruptly she drew back, just an inch or two, shifted her gaze away, and forced a laugh. "Me? A fan of Simon Tremont's? Oh, please. Teryl does enough hero worship for the both of us. Besides, brilliant eccentrics aren't my type at all. I like *real* men. Attainable men. Men I can reach out and touch."

For a moment there, D.J. looked as if she just might reach out and touch *him*. How would John react if she did? Teryl wondered. Would he welcome her overture, or was he that rare male creature who had no interest in D.J.'s advances? It annoyed Teryl that she didn't know the answer. It annoyed her even more that she cared.

In the momentary silence that followed, D.J.'s gaze shifted repeatedly back and forth from her to John. Teryl could almost see the little wheels spinning in her head, could read the doubt in her expression. Did she suspect something was terribly amiss, or was she simply a little confused by their behavior? After all, they *were* supposed to be involved in a hot and heavy affair, one so intense that sweet, good, and levelheaded Teryl had, for nearly a week, acted totally out of character. She had supposedly become unreliable, undependable, irresponsible.

And yet, since D.J.'s arrival, they had hardly looked at each other. They hadn't touched at all. Even now, sitting there at the table, she kept her hands clasped in front of her, her fingers nervously rubbing back and forth, hating the silence and the discomfort and not knowing how to dispel either one.

D.J. lacked no such knowledge. "So . . ." Her voice was huskier than normal. "How long are you planning to stay, John?"

"I don't know."

"Won't they miss you at work if you're not back soon? Or do you plan to follow Teryl's lead and simply not show up when you're due back?"

"I work for myself."

"Interesting. Doing what?"

"Whatever I want."

She laughed, then cut out the husky voice, the seductive behavior, the smug smiles. "I don't want to be rude, John, but could you give me some time alone with Teryl? I haven't seen her in a week. There are some things I want to discuss with her—personal things."

He hesitated a moment, no doubt weighing whether he should trust her; then he stood up. Before he moved from the table, though, he bent to brush his mouth across Teryl's ear. From D.J.'s point of view, it probably seemed a perfectly normal kiss between lovers. From Teryl's perspective, it was something completely different—an intimate touch shielding a whispered threat.

"I'm counting on you, Teryl," he murmured, little more than a breath giving voice to the words, making her shiver. "Don't let me down."

D.J. listened to the back door close, then watched out the window as John came into sight again at the far end of the courtyard. Sprawling in a big old unpainted chair that was shaded by the overhang of the roof, he lit a cigarette, drew a deep breath, then blew out a heavy stream of thin blue smoke. Cancer scares aside, there was something inherently sexy about a man who smoked, especially a man as handsome as John.

Damn Teryl, she had all the luck. Who else could have picked up a stranger as good-looking and bright as this one was? Who else could have built a relationship out of what had started as a cheap, sleazy one-nighter? Who else could have enticed that one-nighter into pulling up stakes and coming home with her?

Who would have suspected that she could so dazzle a man like John?

And who *ever* would have suspected that, hiding underneath her oh-so-good exterior, beat a heart craving pain?

Finally Teryl quit fidgeting and met her gaze head-on. "What did you want to talk about?"

D.J. settled back in the chair. "Let me explain the concept of pickups to you, Teryl. He comes on to you—or vice versa—you go someplace and get laid, and then you go home. *Alone.* You do not—*do not*—take a strange man home with you. *Especially* when home is a thousand miles away." Then, abruptly, she smiled. "For someone who didn't know what the hell she was doing, you did pretty damned good for yourself. He's *gorgeous.*"

Teryl glanced out the window at him as if to confirm the truth of her words. "He *is* handsome," she agreed quietly.

"What's he like in bed?"

As D.J. expected, Teryl blushed.

"Come on, don't pretend we haven't discussed our sex lives with each other ever since we had them to discuss. Tell me about him. How does he like it?" She paused before slyly adding, "That is, besides rough."

Teryl stared at her, a stricken look in her eyes. "What makes you think . . . ?"

D.J. gestured toward the bruises on her wrists.

"Oh, no, these aren't . . . He didn't . . ."

When she fell silent, D.J. softened her voice. "Hey, kiddo,

it's nothing to be embarrassed about. You're an adult. You want to play adult games, it's no one's business but yours. Just tell lover boy to show a little restraint next time. All you need is for Mama or Daddy to see those bruises, and your halo will be tarnished forever." Which, frankly, was something she wouldn't mind seeing happen. Maybe, if their parents discovered that Teryl wasn't so damn perfect, they wouldn't mind her own imperfections quite so much. "So . . . you like this guy?"

She looked out at him again. "Yeah." Upon hearing her own response, she looked a little on the surprised side. Was the sex so good, D.J. wondered, that Teryl hadn't taken the time until just now to realize that she felt something besides lust for the guy? Was she so deeply under his spell, so enthralled by his games?

Curious, D.J. directed her gaze once again toward John, studying him, this time with the experience of a lifetime of using, and being used by, men. He looked utterly relaxed—long legs stretched out in front of him, cigarette resting between two fingers, head back, eyes closed or nearly so; it was hard to tell from this distance. He wore jeans, faded and snug, and a white shirt, long-sleeved in spite of the heat, the cuffs turned back to his elbows, and he looked as everyday-average as any of a hundred men she knew.

But none of the men she knew could have caught Teryl's fancy so effortlessly. None of them could have seduced her as quickly and as thoroughly as John apparently had. Not one of them ever could have seduced her into games of bondage and submission as John apparently had.

No one D.J. had ever met could have persuaded Teryl that she could find pleasure in pain. But apparently, judging from her bruises and the fact that the man who had inflicted them was now temporarily living in her home, John had.

How? she wondered. He must have seduced her first, all gentle and charming, tender, considerate, generous, and then made his requests. *I did it your way; now will you do it mine? I swear it won't hurt, I'll stop if you don't like it, I promise you will like it.* D.J. knew all the enticements, the words of encouragement whispered softly between kisses and caresses, all the more effective for the intimacy in which they were offered. *Give me your hand. Let me wrap this tie around your wrists. It won't hurt, and you'll like it.* She had seduced more than her share of men into the darker, rougher, crueler side of sex. On occasion she had taken the dominant role, had introduced them to their own vulnerability, but her real preference lay in the reverse. *Just tie my hands, tighter, yes, like that. Now take me however you want. Slap me, rape me, punish me . . . and don't worry. I'll stop you if it hurts.*

Some men had been disgusted by her cravings for punishment—and even more so by the enjoyment they'd found in meting it out. Those she had rarely, if ever, seen again. Some had returned from time to time for a little more guilt-tinged pleasure, and she had developed full-fledged relationships with a few of them, with the ones honest enough, open enough, to admit that they found kinkiness exciting.

But none of them had been as good, as exquisitely talented, at the games as Rich.

What would he think if he knew that sweet, innocent Teryl had been introduced to the sort of sex play that was his own personal specialty? Just how restrained would he be if he knew he could have Teryl in his bed, bound and at his mercy, willing to suffer his pleasure, eager to enjoy his pain? Would the loss of her naïveté and innocence make him want her less . . . or more?

Damned if D.J. would find out.

"So . . . you met John at a bar."

Teryl simply nodded.

"You guys talked, had a few drinks."

Another nod.

"He was by himself?"

A third nod.

"Did he buy you dinner? Take you someplace nice? Show you around the city?"

This time Teryl shook her head.

"Just talk and a few drinks. And this was on Tuesday."

A nod again.

"And you went to bed with him Tuesday night." When her friend gave no response, she laughed. "Jeez, Teryl, this is like pulling teeth. All right, let's try an angle that's a little less personal. What does he do for a living?"

The question may have been less personal, but Teryl's answer came no more easily. "I'm not sure."

"He said he was self-employeed; at some point didn't you think to ask him doing what?" When Teryl shook her head, D.J. grimaced in dismay. "For God's sake, Teryl, he could be a drug dealer or a gangster or a contract killer. He could be a rapist or a thief or a—"

"Or a perfectly normal guy."

"A perfectly normal *stranger*. Did you meet any of his friends? Did you meet anyone who had ever laid eyes on him before? Did you see where he lives, where he works? Do you have any proof that he is who he says he is?" The pauses after each question grew briefer, giving Teryl less of a chance to respond—which was fine, D.J. thought with a scowl, because she didn't *have* any responses. "Is he married? Is he safe? Is he sane? Does he have any money, or is he sponging off you? Now that you've brought him into your house, do you have any reason to believe that he's not going to steal you blind or worse? Damn it, Teryl, do you know anything at all about the guy besides the fact that he likes to tie you to the bed when he fucks you?"

The silence that followed her last question was thick and heavy. Teryl finally broke it when she slid her chair back with a scrape and stood up. "Don't get preachy with me, D.J. I'm an adult, not a kid. You said so yourself not ten minutes ago."

D.J. stood up, too. "This is your idea of adult behavior? You go off to a strange city for two days. The first chance you get, you pick up a strange man, go to bed with him, cancel your trip home, and spend the rest of the week with him. You leave New Orleans with him in his car for a trip halfway across the country, telling absolutely no one anything about the trip or him, and you bring him to stay with you in your isolated little house. You know nothing about him but what he chooses to tell you, which is that he's self-employed at doing whatever he wants, that he comes from everywhere and nowhere and doesn't live anywhere. You don't even know if his name is really John!"

"This is none of your business," Teryl said stiffly.

When she would have moved past her, D.J. moved swiftly, blocking her way. "Something's going on here, Teryl, something weird. You're the most reliable, most responsible, most *normal* person I've ever known. You just don't do this sort of thing. You don't behave recklessly. You don't take chances. You don't have kinky, sleazy, *dangerous* affairs." Then, abruptly, understanding dawned. "It's the sex, isn't it? You like what he does to you, only you're ashamed to admit it. Oh, hell, there's nothing to be ashamed of, girl. You're hardly the first woman to discover that she gets off on something different. But, honey, if it's deviance you want, I know plenty of guys, safe guys, guys you can trust, who will do whatever you ask. Say the word, and I'll call one of them right now. Just get rid of this guy, Teryl."

"I appreciate your concern, but there's no reason for it. I know enough about John for now, and eventually I'll learn the rest."

"Maybe you're right. Maybe there *isn't* any reason to worry. Maybe he *is* just a perfectly normal guy. But my point is you don't *know*. A man like this is fine for having fun with, but you have to balance fun with safety. There are a few rules to these games you're playing, Teryl, and you don't know them."

Folding her arms across her chest, Teryl leaned back against the counter and smiled tautly. "I'm sure with your vast experience, you do, so kindly enlighten me. What are these rules?"

D.J. ignored the sarcasm that thinly veiled Teryl's words. "You don't have sex without a condom. You don't let him make you do anything you're really uncomfortable with. You don't play with a man who might lose control and forget that it's just a game. And you don't bring him into your home. You don't let him get that close. You don't mix him with the everyday-normal part of your life."

For a long time Teryl simply looked at her. When she finally responded, it was in a murmur, soft and thoughtful. "You do have some vast experience, don't you?"

This time it was D.J. who offered no response. While sex had long been one of her favorite topics of conversation with Teryl, there had been much that went unsaid, including virtually all of her experiments with the darker, more daring—less normal?—aspects of sex. She had always feared such confidences would destroy their friendship, that Teryl would begin thinking of her as sick, perverted, or pathetic . . . which, of course, she was. As with everything else in her life, she went too far in her search for sexual gratification. The sorts of little games Teryl was learning from John . . . those were fine, normal, even acceptable. But when it became a way of life, as it had for D.J., when it passed from a natural curiosity to a relentless hunger, when it became a need, an obsession, it stopped being normal. It lost its acceptance. It became a great shame.

Unexpectedly, Teryl smiled the sweet, warm, friendly smile D.J. was accustomed to. "I do appreciate your concern, D.J.," she repeated, "but it's not necessary. You're being overprotective, and you're making assumptions that are wrong. I know this relationship is a little out of character for me, but trust me. I can handle it. I can handle John."

D.J. gave her a long, measuring look before replying. "I hope you're right, Teryl. I hope to God you're right."

Chapter Ten

*F*rom his position on the patio, John watched through barely open eyes as D.J. crossed the paving stones that led from the house to the driveway. She didn't spare him a glance, but he knew she was aware of him. Debra Jane Howell *never* failed to notice a man.

Growing up with D.J. for a best friend couldn't have been easy for Teryl, he thought. Everything about the woman radiated sexuality, from the throaty bedroom voice to the dark, coppery red hair to the impressively long, riotous curls. From the clingy black dress that hugged her stomach and skimmed over her hips to end high on the thigh to the concealing men's shirt worn over it, left unbuttoned, the tails tied at her waist, the cuffs folded back a time or two. From the husky laugh to the loose-hipped walk to the pouting mouth. There wasn't a man alive, he suspected, whose first thought upon seeing D.J. didn't have something to do with sex, and there probably wasn't a woman alive, with the exception of Teryl, whose first thought in the same situation wasn't *drop dead*.

He wondered if Teryl had noticed that he'd taken an immediate dislike to her friend. D.J. was sly and manipulative. She was suspicious of him. She believed he was having an affair with her best friend, and yet she hadn't toned down the seductive signals even in front of Teryl. She thought he'd caused those bruises around Teryl's wrists while seeking a sick sort of pleasure, and she had found pleasure of her own in the idea.

Teryl had missed that brief exchange at the table. She had been nervously rubbing her hands together, and she hadn't seen her friend's gaze settle on them, hadn't seen the recognition in D.J.'s eyes. She hadn't seen the damnably smug, taunting little smile D.J. had given him, one twisted soul acknowledging another. Even now, remembering the smile and the sordid way it had made him feel, John's face grew hot, and the muscles in his jaw tightened.

He had long ago learned that there were no sexual limits between two consenting adults—nothing too kinky, nothing too shameful. If D.J. got off on having sex while she was tied up, helpless, and completely dependent on her partner, fine. It wasn't a desire *he* would want to indulge often, but he had to admit there was a certain appeal to it. The vulnerability. The openness. The sense of power. The *trust*. Damned if he hadn't gotten an erection quickly enough the first night he'd tied Teryl to the bed . . . and the second . . . and the third— although he preferred to think the erections were due more to physical proximity and too many months without regular sex than the kinkiness.

But Teryl didn't get off on being restrained; it scared the shit out of her. She hadn't given her consent for what he'd done, and, his own lust aside, it hadn't been sexual in nature. It had been damned shameful.

And D.J. had found it amusing.

After she'd driven out of sight, he rose from the chair and went inside, as much to escape unwanted thoughts of D.J. as to find Teryl. Had she heeded his warning when he'd bent over her at the table? Had she satisfied her friend's curiosity without further rousing her suspicions? Had she said anything at all to give him away?

The kitchen was empty, as were the living and dining rooms. As he neared the top of the stairs, his steps slowed; he reached the top and simply stopped. Yesterday afternoon, when he had delivered the suitcases upstairs, he had left Teryl's in the hall before carrying his own down and around the corner to the guest room. He had gotten only a glimpse of her room, a fleeting image of soft shapes and softer colors. Each time he had come by since then, the door had been closed, clearly marking it off-limits.

This morning, though, Teryl had left the door open and she was standing at the dressing table against the opposite wall. He stopped in the doorway, unwilling to enter without an invitation but able to see everything from there.

The clutter that was absent in the other rooms was present here. Every available space was filled. Perfume bottles lined the length of the dresser. Belts and scarves spilled out of the wicker baskets where they were stored. Haphazard stacks of CDs flanked the small stereo and miniature speakers on one nightstand. Pantyhose in various shades of tan, cream, and black were draped across the back of a slatted wood chair, while discarded clothing obscured the seat. Purses hung in twos and threes from every knob, and shoes, ranging from hiking boots with ridged soles to comfortably worn loafers to delicately strapped heels, were scattered around the room.

Shoving his hands into his back pockets, he resisted the urge to bring a little order to the room. Straightening up and putting things away were second nature to him. His tendency toward tidiness was the only natural talent his parents had ever observed in him. Tom had been brilliant, Janie had been gifted, and John had been a neat child—such a son to be proud of, he thought mockingly. Still, even now he routinely put things where they belonged. He didn't make messes. He liked things orderly.

Even cluttered, though, Teryl's room was appealing. The walls were painted pale salmon, and the rugs on the terra-cotta floor were a medium shade of the same color. The curtains of the front windows and the French doors were pale and sheer, and the bedcoverings were a pastel print with an occasional slash of vibrant color. The furniture—bed, dresser, night tables, dressing table and chairs—was old but of good quality, and the bed looked damned comfortable . . . and just the right size to keep Teryl close.

She was sorting through a jewelry case at the lace-covered table. She had already put a couple of bracelets, big, wide bangles, on her right wrist. Now she was adding an assortment of smaller bracelets to the watch she wore on her left wrist.

She was trying to cover her bruises.

Feeling sick with guilt, he must have made some noise, because abruptly she looked at him. Her expression was somber and shadowed with shame. She gave up trying to fasten the last chain and, dangling it by its clasp, she moved a few steps toward him. "Would you . . . ?"

He met her halfway and took the bracelet. Though his fingers felt stiff and awkward, he managed to fasten it around her wrist with no more contact than his fingertips brushing lightly against her skin. Finished, he slid his hands once more into the confining safety of his hip pockets. "What did she say?"

She didn't deny that D.J. had had some opinion to voice, didn't feign ignorance for an instant. "She thinks we're into rough sex and bondage."

"You didn't have to let her believe it."

"And what was I supposed to tell her instead? What would you rather have her think, John? That you've tapped into some kinky part of me that no one ever dreamed existed? Or that you kidnapped me? That you held me prisoner and took me from New Orleans against my will and only tied me up so that I couldn't escape from you?" She waited, but when he offered no response, she turned back to the dressing table, bending low to see her reflection in the makeup mirror while she stroked on a dusky rose lipstick.

"It's kind of disheartening," she continued when she straightened from the mirror and began transferring items from the small purse she had carried in New Orleans to a bigger straw bag. "D.J.'s been my best friend for more than twenty years. She knows me better than anyone else, and yet she finds it so easy to believe that I would do that, that I would enjoy being treated badly by a man, that I would find it erotic. I can't even imagine what kind of person would get turned on by being tied up and hurt or by doing it to someone else."

John leaned back against the door frame, his hands cushioning his weight against the rounded wood, and evenly replied, "Of course you can."

She added a few more things from the table to her bag—tissues, a brown leather wallet, and a coin purse—then faced him squarely. "Did *you* enjoy it? Did you get turned on by it? Is that why you . . . ?"

His smile faintly derisive, he answered her unfinished question. "No, I didn't enjoy it. That's not why I got a hard-on when I tied you up. I'm just so damned horny that being close to you is enough to make me hard."

"Then why didn't you . . . ? When I offered . . . ?"

He shrugged. "It wasn't right. You didn't want *me*. You wanted to trade your favors for mine. And it wasn't fair. I could have accepted. I could have made love to you, but I still would have had to tie you to the bed. I still would have had to put you through that." After a long moment's silence, he returned to her earlier statement. "Everyone has fantasies, Teryl."

"But that? What's to like about that?"

Taking another tight breath, he moved away from the door and walked toward her. When he circled around her, she turned, too, always facing him, never turning her back on him. "What would it take for you to let me undress you and tie you to that bed?"

She glanced at the bed, at the carved wooden headboard, at the turned and twisted spindles that would offer no chance of escape; then warily, her eyes big, her face pale, she looked back at him. "Nothing in the world could persuade me to do that," she whispered.

"You're wrong." His voice wasn't much more substantial. "Trust would. If you trusted me, if you believed in me with all your heart and all your soul, if you knew beyond a doubt that I would rather die than let anything hurt you . . . you would let me do it. You wouldn't be afraid. You would let me do whatever I wanted because you would know that you were safe. You would trust me to keep you safe."

He took a step back, put some distance between them, and forced some semblance of normalcy into his voice. "Knowing that I'd earned that kind of trust would give me a tremendous sense of power, and power, Teryl, is one of the biggest turn-ons there is. So ... would I enjoy a little experimentation with bondage? Yes. Would I find it erotic that you had enough faith in me to make yourself vulnerable to me? Absolutely. Would I get aroused playing safe games—*safe*, Teryl—of helplessness and domination with you? You bet. But I would never let it go far enough to cause you pain. I would never try to persuade you to do something you didn't want to do. I would never hurt you. I know you don't believe that right now, but it's true."

She held his gaze for a moment, then turned away, sliding her purse strap into place over her shoulder and moving to the door before stopping and looking back. "You're wrong," she said quietly. "I *do* believe that. It's the only reason you're here right now." After letting that sink in, she turned again and started out the door. "We'd better go now. We've got work to do."

The Robertson Literary Agency was located in a turn-of-the-century Victorian on a quiet, tree-lined block filled with similar old homes turned into offices. Six years ago most of the places had been abandoned, run-down, and only one tax bill away from the wrecking ball; then urban renewal had come to the street. The last of the residents had been bought out, and the houses had been restored, refurbished, and reincarnated. They were beautiful now, neatly maintained, each with a pocket of yard out front and a parking lot around back, but instead of families, they now housed professionals.

Teryl directed John into the narrow paved drive that ran along the side of the agency and around back to the parking lot. It was small, consisting of only a half dozen spaces, but Rebecca's staff was small, as was her list of clients. With the income she derived from Simon Tremont, she had neither a need nor a desire for a large stable of writers.

Digging deep in her purse, Teryl retrieved her keys as he shut off the engine; then she opened the door and slid to the ground. It was a hot, sunny day. On an ordinary summer Sunday, she would be getting ready about now to meet D.J.

for lunch. They would most likely go to their favorite restaurant and sit outside on the patio underneath the shade of a brightly striped umbrella, and they would drink iced tea and eat chilled fruit salads while they talked. D.J. would be her usual outrageous self, and Teryl would spend much of the time listening, laughing, and not even trying to hide her shock at some of the things her friend had to say.

She thought she had hidden that shock pretty well this morning when D.J. had immediately recognized her bruises and their source, when she had so matter-so-factly rattled off her rules for safe, deviant sex, when she had remarked with such understanding, "You're hardly the first woman to discover that she gets off on something different." Teryl had never dreamed that her foster sister, her best friend with whom she'd shared her life and her most intimate secrets, was interested in kinky sex. Of course, she didn't know that for a fact—and didn't *want* to know—but it seemed likely. D.J. had shown no surprise over Teryl's bruises. She'd said nothing that indicated less than total acceptance of what she believed to be the cause. She had certainly seemed well-informed and conversant on the subject.

Did that explain all the men—so damn many of them—in D.J.'s life? Was she looking for men who would do those sorts of things to her? But if John was right, they couldn't be that hard to come by. Everyone had fantasies—and, heaven knew, most men fantasized about D.J. How easy it would be for her to seduce them into playing whatever games her heart desired.

Did those fantasies also explain the long sleeves D.J. had been wearing on such a hot sunny day? And the bruises Teryl had noticed in the past but disregarded on a woman who was far too graceful to be bumping into things as often as she claimed?

The keys slid from Teryl's fingers as she tried to fit one into the dead bolt on the back door. Muttering a curse, she bent to pick them up as John, several steps lower, offered them to her. Instead of trying once again to undo the lock, though, for a moment she simply looked at him. "Do you think D.J. likes . . . ?" Then she shook her head. "Never mind." She *really* didn't want to know.

But that brief glimpse of John's face before she turned away was enough to answer her unfinished question. *Yes.* He thought D.J. liked things kinky.

Damn. How long would it take her to forget *that*?

Inside, the house was quiet and cool. Dim light filtered into the long hallway, spotlighting a few motes of dust that had somehow avoided detection by Rebecca. Her boss was fastidious, both in her appearance and in her surroundings. She didn't tolerate disorderliness or uncleanliness.

She didn't tolerate sneakiness, either, and that was exactly how Teryl felt as she closed the door behind John, then asked, "Would you like a tour?" She didn't really feel like showing him around, but at the moment she was game for anything that would delay the moment when she would walk into the file room, remove Simon's files, and use them to test John's knowledge of their client.

He gave her a look that felt sharp even in the shadowy hallway, then shrugged. "Sure. Why not?"

She led him down the hall to the ornate frosted glass front doors, then gestured to the broad foyer with a wave. "This is Lena's territory. She's our receptionist. The parlor here is our waiting room, for the rare occasions when someone actually comes to visit. The upstairs is mostly empty, although we do use a few rooms up there for storage." Rebecca's original intent when she'd purchased the house had been to live on the second and third floors, but her husband had nixed that idea. Her work infringed on their personal lives enough as it was; he'd known that if she lived above the office, he would never get her to himself. Since they had divorced only a year or two later, Teryl assumed he'd never succeeded at that even living across town from the agency.

She led him back the way they'd come, pausing in the doorway of each office. The first was where Ellie, the agent who handled all of their nonfiction clients, worked. Sue, the agent who worked with the majority of their fiction clients, was two doors down. In between the two was Bridget, the assistant they shared. Next was the kitchen, then her own office, followed by Rebecca's, the supply room, and, at the end of the U-shaped hall, the file room.

Once part of the formal dining room, it was closed off now, windowless and airless. All the business of the Robertson Literary Agency was contained within its four walls, including every piece of paper Rebecca had ever collected regarding John Smith and Simon Tremont.

Resolutely ignoring the uneasiness centered in her stomach, she located the files she wanted, stacked them on top of one of the cabinets, then scooped up the entire bunch. John moved to take them, but she shook her head, tightened her grip, and led the way out again.

If the agency were any bigger or Rebecca any less successful, Teryl would be lucky to be sharing a cubicle with Bridget. But the agency wasn't bigger and Rebecca was successful, and Teryl's office was right next door to Rebecca's. She was close enough to be summoned by intercom or with a shout, if her boss felt like shouting—which, depending on her mood, she often did. She was also close to the kitchen, where, every morning and afternoon, she brewed a pot of Rebecca's favorite flavored coffee, where Lena often baked brownies when no one was dieting, and where Teryl usually ate the sandwiches she bought for lunch at the deli a block down the street.

The office wasn't nearly as big or as beautifully decorated as Rebecca's or Ellie's or Sue's, but considering where she ranked in importance, Teryl was happy to have any private space at all. Besides, she liked the place. The rolltop desk that was pushed flush against one wall had character, and the old leather chair that squeaked whenever she moved was comfortable and big enough to draw her feet into the seat. Built-in shelves were filled with books, many of them written by the agency's clients, many her own personal favorites. When work was slow and the day was chilly or dreary or wet, she liked to close the door, slip off her shoes, curl up on the padded seat that extended the length of the triple window, and read the day away.

She laid the files on her desk, sat down, switched on the green banker's lamp that sat on top, and automatically tucked her bag into the bottom left file drawer. The only other places to sit were the secretary's chair, small and none too comfortable, in front of the computer in the corner, or the window seat. John didn't move in either direction. Instead, he was examining the few personal items on display. She watched him, wondering what he thought of the group picture that looked more like a multinational mob than a family. Did he question the significance of the poster for a movie made before she was born? Did he find it odd that she'd hung a Mardi Gras poster above her desk when she had never experienced Mardi Gras and, at the time she'd hung it, had never even been to New Orleans?

Or did it merely remind him of the wish that had landed her in so much trouble? *I always wanted to come to New Orleans for Mardi Gras. I always thought it would be fun, just once in my life, to be wicked in New Orleans.*

At last he went to the window seat and sat down. Facing her, he leaned back against the wall, stretched his legs out in front of him, and brushed a tendril of hanging ivy away from his shoulder. "I guess we're ready."

She glanced at the folders. Was she ready to betray the trust Rebecca had placed in her? Was she ready to betray Simon Tremont—provided the man in New Orleans was the real Tremont and not, as John claimed, an impostor? Was she ready to prove John right or—far more likely—to prove him wrong? Was she ready to convince herself that he was, as she had feared the last four days, crazy as a loon?

Instead of reaching for one of the files, she picked up a pad and pen and offered them to him. "Write your name for me."

He leaned forward to take them, scrawled his signature across the top sheet, then moved to hand them back.

"Write his name, too."

His gaze narrowed. "I never sign anything with that name."

"Humor me."

With a disapproving scowl, he obeyed, handed the pad over, then sat back again.

There was nothing distinctive about the signatures, either

220

Marilyn Pappano

his own or Simon Tremont's, Teryl thought. There were no swirls, no left-handed slant, no peculiar habits in dotting the *i*'s and crossing the *t*'s. It was just an average signature, not too neat, not too controlled.

But, she discovered a moment later when she opened the top file, it was an exact match for the signature on every contract that filled the folder.

It was also an exact match for the change of address form delivered to the agency four months ago—the change of address form that John claimed not to have sent.

She'd proven nothing. He'd suggested an explanation himself only yesterday: maybe he knew Simon. Maybe they'd been neighbors or buddies. Maybe he'd had access to Simon's house and to his records. Maybe he'd gotten hold of Simon's signature and had learned to copy it so perfectly that even Simon would be hard put to tell them apart.

Or maybe the reverse was true. Maybe John was telling the truth. Maybe his signature matched the contracts because he had, in fact, signed them all. Maybe the man who was masquerading as Simon Tremont was the one who had learned a perfect forgery, and maybe *that* was why the name on the change of address form matched everything else.

Putting the question aside for the time being, along with her guilt, she began combing through the records, searching for questions to ask, for details an impostor shouldn't know. With each answer he gave her, she grew less and less certain of anything.

The man had a terrific memory. Whether he was relating dates and information from his own life or retrieving memorized facts from someone else's life, he was incredibly accurate. He knew Simon's income for the last eleven years, down to within a few thousand dollars—mere pocket change for an author of Tremont's stature. He knew the terms of Simon's contracts. He knew the contents of correspondence Rebecca had sent Simon and knew more than Teryl about the other publishers who had, on two occasions, tried to woo Simon away from his publisher. He knew the sweet deals they had offered, knew Rebecca's response—stay on the first one, go with the second—and knew the reasons Simon had outlined in his letters for choosing to remain with Morgan-Wilkes.

He knew too much. But there was still one answer he couldn't give her.

"How did he do it?"

John simply scowled, but she continued anyway.

"If the man in New Orleans is an impostor, how did he write *Resurrection*?"

His voice taut with barely restrained frustration, he answered in clipped, sharp tones. "Obviously, he stole my outline."

"Stole it from where?"

"From here. From Morgan-Wilkes. From my house. I don't know!"

"So you think someone broke in here or at your house or at the publisher, and you or Rebecca and the rest of us or the Morgan-Wilkes people never noticed."

He moved abruptly, from a comfortable sprawl on the window seat with a tapestry pillow beneath his head to an upright position, leaning toward her, his arms resting on his thighs. "If someone got access to my outline in one of those three places, he would also get access to my records. He would find out my real name, my mailing address. He could get everything he needed to convince Rebecca and Morgan-Wilkes that he's me."

Everything, Teryl thought doubtfully, that John had just provided her. All the details. All the figures. All the evidence. Had he come by the knowledge legitimately, or had he gained possession of it in exactly the way he had just described? Had he staged a break-in that had gone undetected and gathered the material he needed to make his claim? Did he know so much about Simon Tremont because he *was* Simon Tremont . . . or merely because he *wanted* to be him?

"You have to admit, it would explain a lot," he said.

"It doesn't explain one thing, John. The book. You admit yourself that *you* couldn't write it. *He* did. He delivered it to the office in person. Maybe he could have stolen your idea. Maybe he could have stolen your outline. But, John, how could he have stolen your talent? If you really are Simon

Tremont, if the man in New Orleans really is an impostor, how could he have written the book that the real Tremont couldn't write? How could he write it in Tremont's style? How could he write it with Tremont's talent?"

In the stillness that followed her questions, the old grandmother clock out in the hall chimed the hour. Two o'clock. She was hungry, tense, and tired of thinking. Tired of wondering. Tired of asking questions and finding no easy answers.

"I need to see it," he said suddenly. When her only response was a blank stare, he went on. "The manuscript, Teryl. I need to see it. I need to read it. I need to know how he did it."

She numbly shook her head. "I can't help you with that."

"Rebecca has a copy. You saw it. You read—"

She interrupted. "She took it home with her. I told you that. It's somewhere in her house, locked safely away."

"Ask her if you can read it."

"I can't. No one gets an advance look. Morgan-Wilkes isn't even doing advance reading copies for the reviewers. They want the release date to be the great unveiling."

His shoulders sagged just a little; then, once again, his determination abruptly renewed. "What about my bank?"

She settled more comfortably in the chair. "What about it?"

"I can get a statement from my banker. He handled my accounts, my investments."

"He knew you were Simon Tremont?"

"No. But he knows I cashed big checks from the agency three or four times a year. I can get some sort of affidavit from him to that effect."

"And what will that prove?" she asked, regretting the doubt that crept into her voice. "That you know where Simon banked? That you know his account numbers?"

He glared fiercely at her. "I'll send him a copy of my damned driver's license photo. He knows my name. He knows my face. He can tell you that I'm the same John Smith who's cashed a few million bucks' worth of checks drawn on the Robertson Agency. He can tell you that I'm the only one authorized to conduct business on those accounts. Would that convince you?"

"It would certainly help." *If* he could get such a document. *If* the bank that cashed Tremont's checks could verify that John was, indeed, the man they had cashed them for. It would go a long way toward making a believer of her.

Rubbing the stiffness from her neck, she asked, "Are you hungry? There's a deli down the street. We can get some sandwiches and bring them back here."

"Why?"

"We're not finished. There's still—"

"You don't believe me, do you?" he interrupted.

She looked guiltily at the floor.

"You sit there asking questions, trying to placate me, and all the time you're looking for some rational, logical way to explain all this. What have you decided? That I knew Simon Tremont? That I learned to copy his signature? That I got hold of all this information about him and memorized it? That I avoided him in the studio in New Orleans and the next day in the hotel because I was afraid he would recognize me? What are you going to say when the bank comes through? That maybe I worked for him? That I conducted his personal business for him in order to protect his privacy?" He was silent for a moment; then he quietly, pleadingly asked, "Can't you even consider the possibility that I'm telling you the truth?"

She left the chair and walked to the far end of the window to stare out. "It's the book, John. I *know* the man in New Orleans wrote it." She sighed and looked at him. "I don't know if you can write anything other than your name."

He sat motionless for a long time; then, from the corner of her eye, she saw a blur of movement as he got to his feet. Instinctively she tensed, hoping he wouldn't come too close, hoping he wouldn't get too angry.

He walked to the door, paused there long enough to say, "Let's go," then walked out. She listened to his footsteps moving down the hall toward the back door. A moment later she heard the door click shut, and a moment after that he came into sight again as he approached his truck.

Feeling far wearier than she could logically explain, she went to her desk, gathered the folders there, and returned them to their proper place in the file room. She came back to her office, intending to get her purse and to shut off the lights, but as she stood there in front of her desk, keys in hand, she hesitated. She knew what she was about to do was foolish and irrational. It would prove nothing. Still, she sat down in the big old chair and, bending forward, used the small silver key on her ring to unlock the bottom right file drawer. It glided out smoothly, automatically stopping, and she reached into the small compartment in the back, into the deep space unused by the hanging folders that filled the front. Her fingers closed around the slick paper of a book jacket, and she carefully lifted it and the volume it protected out of the drawer and laid it on the desk.

Masters of Ceremony. Two years old, it was Simon Tremont's most recent book and the fifth installment in the Thibodeaux series. It had been—until *Resurrection*—his best book and her favorite. It had given readers everything they had come to expect from Simon: a marvelously intricate plot where nothing was what it seemed; characters so real that you'd swear you knew them and so exquisitely drawn that you shared their pain, their pleasure, and their sorrow; villains so fearfully normal; terrors so innocently called to life, and writing that flowed so smoothly, so effortlessly, that reading it was sheer delight.

Her own copy of the book, the one she had read and reread until the pages were dog-eared and the spine was creased, was at home in her living room, sharing shelf space with all the other Tremont novels. This one was new, barely touched. It had been taken from one of the bookcases in the parlor only a few months ago and placed right here, in the middle of her deskpad, where she would find it when she returned from an afternoon dental appointment. She might have missed meeting her idol that day, but she'd gotten a souvenir of the visit all the same: this book that Rebecca had asked Simon to autograph for one of his greatest fans. Ordinarily, it held a place of honor on the upper shelf of her desk, but her last work day before leaving for New Orleans, she had locked it away in her drawer. It wasn't that anyone in the office might develop a case of sticky fingers; if they wanted an autographed copy, Rebecca would get them one. Still, it was one of the very few Simon Tremont autographs in existence and her most prized possession. Better to be safe than sorry.

She fingered the artwork on the jacket, a street scene easily recognizable as the French Quarter: a corner building, a shop below, an apartment above, the elaborate wrought-iron balcony, the lush plants trailing down, the spires of St. Louis Cathedral rising into an ominously colored sky in the background, and, hardly noticeable on first glance, second, or even third, the voodoo doll in the dimly lit apartment window. Even now, months since her last reading of the book, a brief glance at the small doll, made of Spanish moss with sticks for arms and dressed in black and red cloth, was enough to send shivers down her spine. Simon Tremont, whoever he was, had worked his magic extraordinarily well.

With a sigh, she opened the book, turning to the title page, and laid the sheet of notepaper John had signed above the blue-inked message. The first part of the autograph was easily read: *To Teryl, with best wishes.* The signature—Simon Tremont—wasn't. There was a swooping *S* and a recognizable *i*, a *T* that slashed across the page and a decent *re*, but the remaining letters in both names deteriorated into a series of loops and curves.

They looked absolutely nothing like the Tremont signature John had done for her a few hours ago. But why would they? John had learned the Smith signature before Simon's coming out. Before Simon had autographed anything with his pseudonym.

"What is that?"

Before she had a chance to react to the question or even to process the realization that she was no longer alone, John reached over her shoulder and picked up the book. Abruptly, she scooted her chair to the side and stood up as he flipped the cover shut. Harsh lines formed at the corners of his mouth when he recognized the book. They etched deeper when he opened it again, when he saw the paper with his own versions of the signatures, when he read the note inscribed on the page.

"He can't do that! Goddamn it, he can't take credit for my work! I won't let him!" The notepaper fluttered to the floor as he grasped the title page and ripped it out. He'd caught the next few pages, too, and Teryl, in shocked stillness, watched the Chapter 1 heading drift to the floor in a rain of paper fragments. "Do you know how hard I worked on this book? Do you have any idea how many weeks I spent researching the story, how many weeks I spent writing it? And this bastard comes along years after the fact and says, 'It's mine; *I* wrote it,' and everybody believes him. Well, goddamn it, it's *not* his, it's *mine!*"

Filled with fury, he threw the book with all his strength. It crashed against the opposite wall, making her flinch; then it fell to the floor, pages opened and bent back, the jacket half-off and creased, the binding weakened and torn near the top. She flinched again when he turned toward her and drew back with fear in her eyes. It drained his anger and left him looking guilty and ashamed. Even though his rage had passed as quickly as it had come, even though he was calmer now, she couldn't relax. She couldn't force her muscles to loosen. She couldn't fill her lungs with air. She couldn't rid herself of the sudden, aching need to cry for the loss.

With a weary sigh, he retrieved the book from where it had come to rest after bouncing off the wall. Crouching in front of her, he picked up the ragged pieces of paper, and he offered the pile to her. "I'm sorry, Teryl."

She made no move to accept it. She simply stared at it, her most prized possession, at the wrinkled jacket that hung loose, at the scrap of paper on top of the pile, the one bearing the great curling *S*.

"I had no right to do that. I know it was important to you."

She didn't say anything. She had no thoughts to put into words, no words to express the numbness left by sudden fear and greater shock.

"I'll get you another copy. He'll be happy to sign it for you again."

She still said nothing, did nothing.

He got to his feet. "Damn it, Teryl, please . . ." There was a frantic tone to his voice now, a pleading that she ignored. She knew he had acted out of frustration and anger, and she believed he had genuinely meant it when he'd said he was sorry, but, at that moment, she didn't care. She didn't give a damn how *he* felt. All she cared about was how *she* felt. Sorrowful. Dismayed. Heartsick.

Abruptly she took the book and all the little scraps, turned toward the corner behind her, and dropped them all into the wastebasket there. The book landed with a thud. The papers didn't make a sound as they floated down. Then she grabbed her bag off the desk, switched off the lamp, and left the office.

She left him standing there alone.

He had screwed up again. Teryl had finally stopped looking at him as if she were afraid he was going to do something awful, and with one stupid outburst, he had brought the fear back into her eyes. He had frightened her. Worse, he had hurt her, not physically—not even anger could drive him to that—but spiritually. He had destroyed something that she treasured, had committed a wrong that could never be put right. Even if she got another copy of the book, even if the bastard posing as Tremont signed it again in exactly the same way, it would never replace the original. It would never mean the same thing to her.

He felt like a bigger bastard than Tremont could ever be.

Muttering a curse, John left the office and the house. Teryl's key was stuck in the dead bolt; she was waiting, her back to him, beside the Blazer. He locked the door and pocketed her keys, then hesitantly approached her. "Teryl."

She stiffened and lowered her head.

"Jesus, I'm sorry."

"It doesn't matter." Her voice was thick, husky, a little bit quavery.

Oh, hell, it sounded as if she were crying. He couldn't deal with that, with knowing that he'd upset her badly enough to make her cry. Laying his hands on her shoulders, refusing to be shrugged off, he turned her to face him and saw that, damn it, yes, she *was* crying.

He had never made a woman cry before. His mother had never cared enough, and Janie had been too strong. No one else—from Chrissy when he was a teenager to Marcia, the waitress—had ever cried because of him. He didn't know what to say, what to do. He didn't know how to offer comfort.

"Please don't cry, Teryl." Tilting her face up, he clumsily brushed her hair back, then dried her cheeks. "Please . . . I'm so damned sorry."

She made a visible effort to stop the tears, to clear her throat, to regain control. The effort failed when she spoke. "If I had to give up everything I own and could keep only one thing, it would have been that book. It was *mine*."

He dried her tears again, then cupped his palms to her face. "It was *mine*, Teryl—mine with someone else's signature in it. When this is over, you can have all the Tremont autographs in the world. When I prove to you that that man is a fraud, that *I* wrote those books, I'll sign anything you want, from books to checks."

"What if you don't prove it?" she whispered. "What if you can't?"

"I *have* to."

"Why?"

He stroked her cheek with his thumb, wiping away one last tear, before bleakly replying, "Because without my books, I'm nothing. Because my writing has been my sanity. It's been my life. Without it, I have no life. And because if I don't prove it, you're never going to look at me again the way you did that first day, without the wariness, without the doubt. I *need* you to look at me, Teryl. I need . . ."

Letting the words trail away, he leaned closer, until his mouth was brushing hers. He waited, expecting her to pull away, so sure she would that it took a moment for the realization that it wasn't happening to sink in. Then he kissed her.

It wasn't hot and erotic, as their first kiss had been, or so damned desperate, like the last kiss in that North Carolina motel room. It was tentative. He kept waiting for her protest, for her to push him away, disgusted with him for kissing her and with herself for weakly letting him do it. He waited for her good sense to kick in, to remind her that the last thing she needed or wanted was to endure this with him.

It was sweet, as purely innocent as a kiss between two adults could be. It lacked passion and hunger, but it stirred them, just a faint little need buried deep inside him, just enough of an ache to make its presence felt. He could stop kissing her right now, and everything would be perfectly normal, or he could continue and slowly but surely bring to life an arousal as sharp and raw as any he'd experienced in the last week.

It was comforting. Soothing. He didn't know if it was doing much for her tears, but just being close to her, touching her, sharing this small contact with her, was working wonders on his spirit.

At last, when he was starting to enjoy it too much, to kiss her harder, more greedily, to draw her closer and hold her tighter, the rejection he'd been expecting came. She pushed against his chest, trying to work her way free, and reluctantly, having no choice, he let her go.

Her cheeks were flushed, her lips red, her expression troubled. She liked kissing him. He had enough experience to recognize that. But she didn't want to like it, didn't want to want him. He was smart enough to recognize that, too.

Christ, everything he did made her feel bad. She really needed him out of her life . . . while he desperately needed her *in* his.

She turned away, using the side mirror to comb her fingers through her hair, to check her face and to wipe away a bit of eye makeup that her tears had smeared. When she finished, she faced him, but she couldn't quite meet his gaze. "I'd like to go home now."

"What about lunch?"

"I'm not hungry."

"I am," he lied. Faced with food, he imagined he would be able to eat, but the only appetite he was harboring right now was of a sexual nature. It would be safer dealt with in a restaurant, surrounded by other diners, than at her house, just the two of them alone.

"You can drop me off at the house, then go—"

He touched her hair, and she abruptly stopped speaking. "It was just a kiss, Teryl," he said softly, regretfully. "You don't have to feel guilty for letting me kiss you. You don't have to feel guilty for anything."

"Please . . . don't . . ." She moved away, her hair tangling briefly around his fingers before sliding free.

Once again he let her go. He gave her the space she wanted, the distance she needed, the distance that he thought just might drive him crazy. "All right," he said reluctantly. "I'll take you home."

Back at the house, Teryl tossed her keys into a basket on the kitchen counter, laid her purse beside it, and turned toward John. "I'm going to go upstairs," she said, and right away a new layer of guilt darkened his eyes. He obviously thought she was retreating to her room because she was still upset over what had happened at the office—the damage he'd done to her one and only signed Tremont and the kiss outside. It was true. She *was* upset. But that wasn't the reason she wanted to be alone in her room.

She had phone calls to make.

As she started to walk past him, he extended his hand, blocking her way. "Teryl, I'm—"

She cut him off. "Don't apologize again, please. I just want to be alone now."

He stepped back, as she'd known he would, and she slipped past. She felt him watching her all the way down the hall, and when she turned at the end to climb the stairs, she could see him, just standing there.

Upstairs in her room, she closed and locked the door behind her, then turned on the stereo. After a moment's hesitation, feeling sneaky and guilty, she sat down on the bed, pulled the phone book and a notepad from the nightstand drawer, and reached for the phone. It was a simple matter finding the area code she needed for Florida; for Colorado, she made a note of the two numbers that covered the entire state. Locating Rapid River without a map would be a matter of trial and error, but at least the choices were limited.

First she dialed information for Verona. There was no listing for Jane or Janie Smith, but there were seven J. Smiths, and she coaxed the disinterested operator into giving her the numbers for every one of them. What were the chances, she wondered as she doodled around the numbers on the notepad, that one of these was John's Janie? What were the odds that his thirty-something sister had never married or, if divorced, was still using her maiden name?

Hell, even if she was married, even if her name was no longer Smith, she was a high school Spanish teacher in a small town. How difficult could it be to find her?

With the first two calls, she was informed that there was no Janie at those numbers. The third netted her a recording: *Hi, this is Jack. I'm not home right now . . .* The fourth was another wrong number, and the fifth was busy. Luck was with her, though, on the sixth. The message on the tape was standard, the voice feminine but no-nonsense, as befitted a teacher, and the accent was indistinct—a result of growing up on the West Coast, perhaps, tempered by living on the East Coast? *Hi, this is Janie. I can't take your call right now, but if you'll leave your name and number at the beep, I'll get back to you as soon as I can. Adiós, amigo.* A Spanish farewell. This had to be the one.

The machine beeped, but it didn't register with Teryl. She hadn't thought ahead to what she would actually say to John's sister if she reached her. She couldn't very well announce to the woman that her brother had gone around the bend and kidnapped an innocent woman or blurt out that he was delusional and thought he was a famous author and needed psychiatric intervention before the police were brought into the matter. She hadn't prepared for actually talking to Janie at all, and before any words popped into her head, the machine beeped a second time, stopping the tape.

Muttering a curse, she redialed the number, listened to the four rings and the message again, then cleared her throat. "Hi. My name is Teryl Weaver, and I—I'm looking for the

Janie Smith whose brother John lives in—used to live in Rapid River, Colorado. If you're the right one, I need to talk to you as soon as possible. It's really very important. If you're not the right one, I'd really appreciate it if you would let me know. Call me any time between nine and five, Monday through Friday." She gave the agency number, briefly considered adding her home number, then decided against it. If Janie Smith could verify John's story, receiving her call at home was no problem. But what if his story wasn't true? What would he think when his sister, who would surely tell Teryl that it wasn't true, called her home? What would he do?

She hung up, then, just to satisfy her own curiosity, dialed the fifth number again. That J. Smith was Jennifer, and the seventh and last one, a man, offered no name. He simply said he didn't know a Janie Smith, then hung up in the middle of Teryl's murmured apology.

Now on to Colorado. Hoping that Rapid River shared Denver's area code, she tried it first and was right. This time a friendlier operator gave her the name of the county—Grant—and the number for the sheriff's department. The sleepy-sounding young man she spoke to told her no, he didn't know anything about a recent house fire and that she needed to speak to the sheriff himself, who wouldn't be in until the next morning, and no, he couldn't track him down for her for anything less than an emergency. Wishing she could lie and say it was, she left her name and, again, the office number with him, then returned the phone to the table, rolled onto her side, and stared moodily out the French doors.

Did it mean anything that the man hadn't heard about the fire? Maybe he'd been on vacation, or maybe he simply wasn't as well-informed as a deputy or dispatcher for a county sheriff's department should be. But either excuse was hard to believe. Rapid River was a small town, and people in small towns were supposed to know everybody's business. Heavens, house fires that totally destroyed everything were news even in a city the size of Richmond. And John's hadn't been a simple fire. It had been arson, if he was to be believed—arson involving three bombs that were supposed to have killed him. How could anyone living in the area not know about it? How could an employee of the law enforcement agency investigating it be ignorant of its occurrence?

She knew the answer to those questions, the logical, reasonable, rational answer. She didn't want to face it, but she forced herself to let it form, to put the words together into sentences in her head. Maybe the young man hadn't heard anything because nothing had happened. Maybe the tale was just another part of John's story. Just another part of his fantasies.

Maybe it was just one more part of his delusions.

Afternoon passed quietly into evening. John saw little of Teryl, considering that they were spending all of their time in a house so small that he wouldn't have believed two people could share it without tripping over each other. She stayed in her room, the door closed, the CD player kept busy. They had much the same taste in music, he'd noticed in the times he'd passed by: Louis Armstrong, Ella Fitzgerald, and Duke Ellington. They had similar taste in movies, too, he'd discovered in the hours he'd spent alone with the television and VCR. Many of the old Hollywood greats that he'd lost in the fire were duplicated in her private collection. It was one of those old movies from the fifties, a bittersweet romance, that he chose to pass the time that evening, and it was the movie that finally lured Teryl back into his presence.

She came down the stairs and was on her way to the kitchen when she detoured into the living room. He glanced at her, standing there in the doorway, but said nothing. If she wanted to ignore him and pretend he wasn't there, the least he could do was make it easy.

But this time she wasn't ignoring him. She edged into the room, going to sit on the arm of the sofa, a fairly safe distance from the chair where he was sprawled. "You like old movies?"

"I like her." He gestured to the star whose face filled the screen in a tight shot. "She was a beautiful woman."

"Hmm." She slid down onto the cushion without taking her gaze from the television. "The camera certainly loved her."

"Everyone loved her. She ranked right up there with Marilyn Monroe, Carole Lombard, and Grace Kelly. She was gorgeous and incredibly talented. Too bad she quit so young."

"Maybe she found something else she'd rather do."

He looked at her again. "What else could possibly have compared to the fame, the money, and the adulation that came with being a movie star back in the days when that was really special?"

"Gee, I don't know. Maybe having a life of your own? Maybe getting married and having children? Maybe being able to gain ten pounds or quit bleaching your hair without it being treated with the importance of a national scandal? Maybe being able to go to the grocery store or to church or out to lunch without being mobbed by rabid fans?" She gave him a dry look. "You tell me. Why *would* someone rich and famous choose anonymity over life under a very big microscope?"

He would like to take her question as a sign that she was leaning at least a little toward believing him. After all, John Smith, some poor crazy schmuck who was, at best, delusional, would live anonymously because that was who he was, because he had no claim to fame. On the other hand, the John Smith who had given life to Simon Tremont, legendary author and mysterious millionaire, knew a few things about fame, adulation, and rabid fans.

But he didn't believe her question was an indication of anything, other than the fact that after an afternoon and evening of virtual silence, she was willing to talk to him again.

And after an afternoon and evening of her shunning, he was willing to settle for simple conversation. He was grateful for it.

"I moved into the mountains because I thought that was the best place for me. I wasn't doing well at dealing with the world, and the world—or, at least, the people I knew in it—wasn't dealing well with me."

Her expression turned somber. "You mean because of the accident."

The accident. She made it sound so simple, so blameless, so damned *accidental* and therefore undeserving of guilt. *He* had a tendency to think of it in harsher terms, such as the day he killed his brother and crippled his sister. The day his own life should have ended. The day he destroyed his family and his future.

Lately he'd discovered that he wanted a future. He wanted it a lot.

"Yeah," he agreed at last. "Because of the accident." Picking up the remote control, he stopped the tape, then muted the volume. "I'm the luckiest bastard in the world. I walked away from a wreck that, by rights, should have left me as dead as Tom, and I didn't have a scratch. I spent six years drinking too much, looking for ways to die, living as dangerously as I could, and nothing ever happened. I made it through school by the skin of my teeth and was about to flunk out of college because I was too damned stupid, and a few years later I lucked into a career that has earned me more money than I can spend in the next fifty years. I'm damned lucky . . . and my life is still the pits. Moving into the mountains was both my salvation and my punishment. I couldn't hurt anyone up there, and no one could hurt me."

"It must have been lonely." Her voice was soft, her expression distant. "What did you do?"

"Watched movies. Read. Until the last year or so, wrote." He saw her gaze flicker disturbingly, and he sighed. "No, Teryl, I didn't read Simon Tremont's books. I didn't need to; I *wrote* the damned things. I didn't get fixated on my favorite author. I didn't delude myself into thinking that I *was* him."

"Did you ever travel?"

"Only occasional trips into Denver."

"Then how could you write all those books? One of Simon Tremont's strengths is the atmosphere, the sense of place. If you never went to any of those places—"

"I didn't say that," he disagreed. "I said I didn't do any traveling after I moved into the mountains. I spent the six years before that doing nothing but traveling. When I left home, I hitchhiked to the Texas coast and got a job delivering a boat to the Keys. From there I worked my way north. I spent some time in Georgia and North Carolina, in Philadelphia, New York, and Boston, and I wound up in Maine. When I got tired of New England, I headed back south and didn't stop until I'd hit Mexico. From there I went to New Orleans and settled down for a while, until I got the job on the freighter. You know what happened after that."

"So the locations for all these stories were written from memory."

"Memory, an occasional travel video, and a few calls to local tourism offices just to find out if anything in particular had changed since I was there. What can I say? I'm observant. I have a great eye for detail." Sensing her disappointment, he smiled persuasively. "Isn't that at least a little more satisfying than the answer that bastard gave you in New Orleans? I've actually camped out in Acadia National Park off the coast of Maine. I've gotten drunk in Key West. I've been damned near eaten alive by the mosquitoes in Okefenokee. I've been thrown in jail down in Mexico, and I've hiked the Appalachian Trail in North Carolina. I *haven't* relied solely on travelogues or travel magazines, and I don't believe imagination, understanding, and talent are enough to make up for actually experiencing a place."

"I have to admit that when Simon said—"

He interrupted her again. "Do you have to call him that?"

The look she gave was drily admonishing. "I only know two names for him—John and Simon— and you insist that neither one belongs to him. That may be, but I still have to call him *something*, and since you're John, he gets Simon by default."

Her reasoning made sense . . . although he didn't quite agree that the son of a bitch needed one of *his* names. Until they knew his real name, John could think of a number of names to call him that were perfectly appropriate. "All right," he agreed grudgingly. "You can call him Simon for now. You have to admit what?"

"That I wondered about it when Simon said he hadn't spent much time in New Orleans. The books make the city seem so real. Reading them truly is like being there. There's a sense of intimacy to them that, maybe I'm being naive, but I would have sworn could come only from intimate knowledge of the city, not from guidebooks or videotapes or phone conversations with people a thousand miles away."

"Actually, Teryl, he didn't say he hadn't spent much time there." When she started to protest, he raised one hand to silence her. "I was eavesdropping, remember? You commented that he must have spent a lot of time in the city, and he said, 'You can learn an awful lot about a place without ever going there, Teryl.' For all we know, that could have been his first visit."

Settling against the high arm of the sofa, she rested her chin on her hands and glumly sighed. "What a disappointment if that's true—if the books that introduced me to the city that could easily become my most favorite city in the world had been written from travelogues and magazines."

By sheer will, he kept the frustration her remark aroused out of his voice when he replied. "There's no reason to be disappointed. Your Simon didn't write those books. *I* did. And in the time I lived there, I became intimately familiar with the place—at least, with my small corner of it, and that's what I used in writing the Thibodeaux books."

After one moment of silence extended into two, then three, he pressed the play button, and the movie began where it had left off. He didn't turn his attention to it right away, though. First he fixed his gaze on Teryl. "I did write those books, Teryl," he said quietly. "Someday . . . you're going to believe me."

Chapter Eleven

*P*ulling the key from the lock, Rebecca opened the front door of the Robertson Literary Agency and strolled inside, leaving her briefcase and handbag on Lena's desk before turning back to close and relock the door. For a moment she simply stood there, enjoying the peace of the old house. Ordinarily, she used the back door, like the rest of the staff, but on Monday mornings, she always walked around to the front and climbed the steps to the broad porch. She always took a moment there to smell the fragrance of the flowers, to listen to the tinkle of the crystal wind chimes that hung from a gingerbread bracket, to admire the inviting picture of white wicker chairs separated by pots of bright red geraniums. She always took a moment to savor the sheer pleasure that all of this was hers, to marvel over how far she had come.

She had begun her career twenty-five years ago working for an agency in Manhattan, a big one that filled an entire floor of a high-rise office building. The offices had been purely functional and totally lacking in grace and charm. She had opened her agency in equally impersonal, charm-free quarters in a lower rent neighborhood a few miles away, always with the intention of someday moving to a place like this.

Someday had been a long time coming. After eleven years she still remembered the morning it had arrived in the form

of an unsolicited manuscript from an unpublished writer in
Denver. The mere size of it—some seven hundred pages—
had been daunting, and if she'd had an assistant, she would
have passed the thing on to her. But after five hard years on
her own, it had still been a struggle just to make expenses.
Hired help was a luxury she couldn't yet afford.

She had sat down with the manuscript, intending to read a
chapter, two at most. If it was like the majority of unsolicited
work she received—unpublishable—that was a more than
fair reading. If this unknown writer had a spark of genuine
talent buried underneath the usual first book mistakes, two
chapters was enough to find it. Hours later, she had left the
office for home in a daze, overwhelmed by emotion and utterly astounded by her good fortune. She had carried the
manuscript with her, clutched to her chest like some magical
talisman with the power to change her life.

That was exactly what it had turned out to be. That extraordinary manuscript and the once-in-a-lifetime talent that
had produced it had made both Rebecca and its author rich
beyond their dreams. It had turned three relatively anonymous entities—the agency, Morgan-Wilkes Books, and John
Smith—into major-league players.

And John had blindly picked her agency out of a book.

Such incredible good fortune.

Retrieving her briefcase and bag, she turned toward the
back of the house and her private office. She liked coming in
early Monday mornings so she could make this quiet, undis-
turbed walk through the business she had worked so hard to
build. In another hour, her staff would be at their desks, the
phones would be ringing, and there would be a dozen things
for her to attend to, but for now, the place was all hers, and
she had nothing to do but enjoy it.

When she reached the office before her own, she paused in
the open door. She had arrived home from a dinner date with
Paul Saturday evening to find Teryl's message on her machine. It hadn't been much of a message—a brief apology
and a promise that she would make up the days she'd
missed. Rebecca had assumed that her assistant was so unfamiliar with being unreliable that she hadn't known exactly

what to say. This morning Rebecca wasn't quite sure what *she* was going to say. She would decide, she supposed, when she was face-to-face with Teryl, who would be, if she was back in her routine, the next one in.

Judging by the looks of her office, she had already come in over the weekend, perhaps to get caught up. The disreputable chair that she loved so much was pushed off to the side, the pillows she kept neatly stacked on the window seat were scattered carelessly across the cushion, and a scrap of paper was caught underneath the chair's wheel.

Rebecca bent to pick it up, recognizing it as part of a page torn from a book. That was odd. Teryl loved books. While she might bend the corner of a cheap paperback, if there was such a thing these days, to mark her place, she would never tear a page out.

With a shrug, Rebecca pushed the chair into its proper place, then bent to drop the paper into the wastebasket. What she saw there made her stiffen.

It took only a moment to retrieve the scraps and the book underneath them, only a moment longer to fit the ragged pieces of the title page back together. *To Teryl, with best wishes, Simon Tremont.*

Pulling the chair back again, she sank down and studied the pieced-together message. On the day of Simon's visit to the office, she had taken that copy of *Masters of Ceremony* from the bookcase up front and asked him to autograph it for Teryl. She had thought it might make up to her assistant at least a little for missing out on meeting the man she had so admired all of her adult life. Simon had been flattered by the request, had joked that it was the first autograph he'd ever signed and maybe if he wrote that as part of the message, it would be worth something someday. But he hadn't written it. He had settled for a pretty generic sentiment. *To Teryl, with best wishes, Simon Tremont.*

After he had gone, Rebecca had left the book on Teryl's desk, with a slip of paper sticking out to draw Teryl's attention to the title page. Rebecca had been back in her office, on the phone with Simon's editor at Morgan-Wilkes, when she'd heard Teryl's delighted shriek. The girl had been thrilled, had assured Rebecca that she would treasure it forever.

And now she'd torn it to bits. Forever had lasted only a few months.

Had something happened with Simon in New Orleans? Had he been such a tremendous disappointment to Teryl that she'd lost all her admiration for the man *and* his work? Rebecca had to admit that he wasn't exactly what *she* had expected after eleven years of working together. He was egotistical, but that wasn't uncommon. In her experience, most writers had tremendous egos, offset by tremendous insecurities. He was arrogant, but that wasn't an unusual trait in a rich and powerful man. What was unusual was the creepy feeling he gave her. As if he weren't quite safe. As if he weren't quite sane.

She had tried to tell herself that it was simply a reaction to his books; when it came to creepy and eerie, his were the best. But she knew plenty of other authors who wrote psychological thrillers or straight horror, nice, normal people whom she wouldn't hesitate to invite to dinner. It wasn't the books.

It was Simon himself.

Maybe Teryl had picked up on his peculiarities. Maybe she'd been turned off by his arrogance. Or maybe something else had happened. Maybe he had somehow been part of her decision to stay over in New Orleans. Maybe he'd made a pass at her or had made demands of her that she'd needed time to deal with. Or maybe . . . *Maybe* he was the mystery man Debra Jane Howell had been talking about. Granted, Sheila Callan had accompanied him from the hotel to the airport; in fact, she had flown as far as Charlotte with him. There they had separated, Simon making his connection to Richmond, Sheila continuing to New York. But maybe Simon's connection hadn't been to Richmond. Maybe he had simply turned around and flown back to New Orleans, where Teryl was waiting.

With a sigh, Rebecca slid the scraps of paper inside the book, then took it with her when she went to her own office. Teryl would be in soon, and she would find out then exactly what had happened last week. Until then, she wouldn't let her imagination run wild.

John was in the kitchen drinking a cup of instant coffee when Teryl came down. She was dressed for work in her favorite dress—cool and comfortable, red linen, businesslike but stylish enough to make her feel pretty whenever she wore it. She had pulled her hair back and fastened it off her neck with a gold clasp, had put on her favorite gold jewelry and added a pair of heels. This morning, facing John now and Rebecca later, she felt the need for whatever confidence she could muster. Like a protective suit of armor, the clothing helped.

"You look nice."

She accepted his compliment with a brief smile, thinking at the same time that he did, too. He was wearing his usual faded jeans, and the shirt this morning was a polo shirt in deep crimson. He looked better than nice. He looked damned good.

He offered her a cup of coffee, which she refused, and half of a toasted bagel spread with raspberry jam, which she accepted. Waiting until she took the first bite, he said, "I'll take you to work today."

She shook her head as she chewed; finally managing to swallow, she disagreed. "I'll drive myself. You might get lost, and there's no need for you to be out in rush hour traffic."

"I have an excellent sense of direction. I know exactly how to get to your office and back."

"I need my car. Sometimes I run errands for Rebecca, and she doesn't like to let me use her car."

"So you can call—"

After those phone calls yesterday—one checking out his story, the other seeking his sister's help in getting rid of him and getting help for him—she felt guilty asking for his trust, but she interrupted him to do just that. "Except for that first night when I tried to escape, I haven't done a thing to make you suspicious. I've been good. I've talked to strangers without asking for help. I've talked to D.J. and my mother without hinting that there was something weird going on. I've let you move into my house, and I've gone through confidential records with you. I've cooperated as much as I possibly could. I've trusted you, John. Now you've got to trust me."

He stood motionless for a long time. How long had it been, she wondered, since he'd trusted anyone, even himself? How long since he'd let anyone get close enough that trust had even become an issue? Years, she would bet. About seventeen of them.

She couldn't blame him for being reluctant now. In the last five days they hadn't been more than a hallway and a stairway apart. Now she was asking to travel halfway across the city alone. Of course, in those hours apart here in the house, she could have called for help at any time, but he'd still held the trump card: her. She could have called the police, and they would have come, but she still would have been John's hostage. If she called the cops today, she would be miles away, safely out of his reach, when they came.

Didn't he see that it wasn't any easier for her to trust him? He had kidnapped her, for heaven's sake, had taken her against her will on a cross-country journey, had tied her to the bed every night they were on the road. But she had come to believe that he wouldn't hurt her. She had learned to trust him.

But she had more faith to give, she suspected, and gave it more easily than he ever would. His parents and that damnable accident had seen to that.

When he finally spoke, his misgivings were clear in his voice. "All right. You can go alone. Just don't . . ."

Don't let me down, he had whispered in her ear before leaving her alone with D.J. Sunday morning. As soft as his voice had been, she'd heard the pleading that had underlaid the soft words. She heard it now, unspoken between them. "I won't," she promised. For a moment, she held his gaze, seeing no sign of the trust he was offering so reluctantly. With a sigh, she stopped looking for it. "What are you going to do today?"

"Get in touch with my bank."

She nodded once in acknowledgment, then opened the junk drawer next to the refrigerator and sorted through its contents until she found what she was looking for. She offered him the key, crossing the few feet necessary to lay it in his palm. "Here's my extra key in case you need to go out. I get off at five, and I'll be home shortly after that. If you need to call, the number—"

"I know the number."

It was an honest assumption that he wouldn't. Whether he was Simon Tremont or just a deluded impostor, he'd had no occasion to ever call the agency. It was only fair to expect him not to know the number.

"I usually go to lunch about noon. Why don't I come home and bring some sandwiches?"

His smile was very faint, practically nonexistent, when he nodded.

Taking her keys from the basket, she said good-bye and left. She walked quickly to her car, parked beside the Blazer, and climbed in, backing out as she adjusted the air-conditioning vents, the stereo, and the mirrors.

Since she'd awakened nearly two hours ago, she had resisted thinking about Rebecca, but now she couldn't avoid the nagging worries. The idea of facing her boss after the stunt Rebecca thought she had pulled last week made her muscles clench and stirred more than a few butterflies in her stomach. Rebecca would surely be disappointed in her. Would she also be angry? Unforgiving? Quietly censuring? Would she fire Teryl?

That would be the worst possible outcome. Teryl might downplay the importance of her job to others, but she loved it. It was the best use she could make of her English degree; she liked the others in the office; she admired and respected her boss. She enjoyed talking to and occasionally meeting the authors the agency represented, and she liked reading their books. She especially liked discovering new authors in the manuscripts sent to Rebecca for consideration. It was a tremendously satisfying feeling to read and like a brand-new author's work, to recommend him or her to Rebecca or one of the others, and, a year or two later, to see that book on the shelves at the local bookstores.

She loved her job. She didn't know what she would do if she lost it.

Maybe she would help John prove that he was Simon Tremont, and he would be so grateful that he would reward her in some outrageous fashion. Maybe he would hire her as his assistant or secretary. She could answer mail, do research, run errands, and make coffee for him as easily as she did it for Rebecca.

Of course, if he *was* Simon, chances were good that he would be looking for a new agent when all this was over. Chances were very good that whatever trust he'd placed in Rebecca would be lost. Maybe she was naive, but Teryl liked to think that she was as capable of acting as his agent as anyone else. Simon Tremont was such a valuable commodity that there was little negotiating to do. Morgan-Wilkes came to the contract table with one simple question: What can we do to keep Simon happy? Rebecca always gave a reasonable answer, and Morgan-Wilkes always agreed. After all, if they didn't, there were plenty of other publishers out there who would. Over the years, John—Simon, she corrected herself—had shown no inclination for making unreasonable demands, and she was perfectly capable of presenting whatever requests he did have.

Or maybe, her thoughts continued, maybe John would offer something else, something better than working for him or with him, something far more personal and, potentially, far more satisfying. Maybe he would offer her an affair. Maybe she could be his lover . . . his mistress . . . or more.

If he was sane. *If* he really was Simon Tremont. *If* she helped him prove it.

Pulling into her usual parking space, she turned off the engine and got out. Rebecca's Mercedes was in the space closest to the house. It was as beautiful and flawless as the day she'd driven it off the lot. The only thing it shared in common with her own beat-up little Honda was four wheels and two seats. The Mercedes was pure luxury, while the Honda . . . She glanced at all its dents and dings as she circled around it. The Honda had definitely seen better days.

She let herself in the back door, then locked it once more. The neighborhood was as safe as any in the city, but keeping the doors locked was never a bad idea for six women working alone in a big house. The lock secured, she turned down the hall toward her office, but the closer she got, the more her steps slowed. No doubt Rebecca was in her own office, which, like Teryl's, faced the parking lot. No doubt she had seen Teryl drive up and was waiting to pass judgment on Teryl's behavior of the last week. As anxious as Teryl was to find out if she still had a job, she was equally anxious to put off finding out that maybe she didn't.

She was through her office door and almost in her chair when the summons came. "Teryl, could I see you in here?"

With a sigh, she left her purse on the desk, then went the few yards down the hall to her boss's larger, more elegantly appointed office. "Good morning, Rebecca," she greeted her gravely.

"Have a seat, Teryl."

"I was just going to start the coffee," she fibbed. "If you'll give me just a minute . . ."

"The coffee can wait. Please sit down."

Oh, jeez. Rebecca never started a workday without a cup of her special blend of coffee. It was one of her little luxuries. Expecting the worst, Teryl moved away from the door and seated herself in the chair directly across the desk from her boss. "I know you're upset," she said, launching immediately into her apology. "My behavior was inexcusable, and you would be perfectly justified in firing me, but—"

Rebecca interrupted. "Are you all right?"

The question surprised Teryl as much as the solicitous tone it was voiced in. "All right?" she echoed. "Uh . . . yes, I'm fine."

"You enjoyed New Orleans."

"Yes, it—it was wonderful." Her smile was uneasy and tinged with guilt. "I didn't want to leave."

"Obviously." Rebecca's own smile was brief and gave away nothing. "What did you think of the great Tremont?"

Teryl felt a little of the tension that stretched her muscles ease away. "I thought the interview went pretty well, considering. I thought—"

"Considering what?"

The tension returned. "That it was his first interview ever. That he's been such a loner for the last eleven years. That it was such a high-pressure situation to be thrown into without experience."

"And that he's a pompous, egotistical ass who's nauseatingly full of himself." Rebecca laughed at Teryl's surprise. "Sheila Callan told me that he blamed the failings and problems in the interview on Tiffany Marshall. She wasn't bright enough, talented enough, or good enough to show him at his best. Naturally, none of the fault was *his*. Other than the interview, what did you think?"

Teryl searched for just the right words. What she came up with was less than impressive. "He was . . . interesting."

"Ah. Damning with faint praise. He was a disappointment to you, wasn't he?"

"He wasn't quite what I expected."

"Did you talk to him much?"

What was the point of all the questions? Teryl wondered. Had Simon complained to Rebecca about her behavior in New Orleans? Had he been more annoyed than he'd let on by her failure to show up for breakfast as he had directed? That was just what she needed—the agency's single most important client personally unhappy with an assistant who could be replaced in the blink of an eye. While Rebecca just might overlook Teryl granting herself two days off, there was no way she would forgive the incredible rudeness Teryl had shown in standing up the client who kept them all in business. The only conditions Rebecca had placed on her when okaying the trip was that she stay out of the way, not cause trouble, and not act starstruck. Well, she hadn't acted starstruck, and she had certainly stayed out of the way—unfortunately, even at a time when her presence had been required. If Simon had complained to Rebecca, then she had certainly caused trouble.

"No," she replied, her voice quiet and unsure. "Only for a

moment before the interview, a moment after, and a little in the lobby the next morning before he left."

"Did you see him alone?"

"No, not really. He started to suggest that we go sight-seeing together Tuesday evening, but Sheila said they had to go over the tape."

Rebecca paused as if it were now *her* turn to seek the right words. "He didn't make any . . . improper advances, did he?"

"Advances?" Teryl's throat was tight, and her following response completely tactless. "Thank God, *no*." Then she blushed. "I mean . . . No, he didn't, not at all."

"So it's safe to assume that *he* wasn't the reason you decided to stay over in New Orleans."

For a moment Teryl simply stared at her; then, struggling against a giggle, she replied, "No. No, he had nothing to do with my stay." But that wasn't true, she realized, and the urge to laugh faded. Simon had everything to do with the events of the last week. He was the reason she'd gone to New Orleans. He was the reason John had approached her in the first place. Simon was the reason John had gone back to the hotel with her, the reason he had gone to bed with her, the reason he had kidnapped her. Everything that had happened to her in the last week led straight back to one person: Simon Tremont.

In spite of Rebecca's apparent concern, Simon hadn't made any improper advances to Teryl . . . but he *had* gotten her laid.

"You can't blame me for wondering," Rebecca was saying in her own defense when Teryl forced her attention back to her. "In your heart you've been a Tremont groupie ever since you picked up his very first book. Being worshiped and adored by a pretty, young thing like you is a powerful aphrodisiac to a man, and Simon does like wielding his power." She paused. "Then Debra Jane didn't exaggerate. There *was* a mystery man."

Teryl's blush returned, but she said nothing.

"I'm trying to imagine the man who could make you change your plans on the spur of the moment, forget about your obligations, and spend a few reckless days with him. He must have been incredible."

Teryl thought about the conversation she and John had shared Tuesday evening, about the kiss he'd given her on the street, and the caresses in the backseat of the cab. She thought about the way they'd made love—his passion, her hunger, his need—and the way he'd held her afterward until she'd fallen asleep. Yes, incredible was a perfect description for that John. Handsome, sweet, charming, incredible.

It wasn't a bad description for the John she'd found herself with the next day. He was all those things and more—delusional, criminal, desperate—and yet still incredible.

"Do you think you'll ever see him again?"

"Yeah, I think I might." She tried not to squirm or look guilty. It wasn't a lie exactly; she *would* see John again. But in not saying so definitely rather than hinting at the possibility, in not admitting that he had come home with her, that he was, at that very moment, living in her house, she was definitely misleading her boss.

"With my luck, you will get together again, you'll fall in love, and you'll move off to New Orleans with him." Rebecca laughed again. "Only you, Teryl, could turn a one-night stand into a relationship."

Oh, she and John had a relationship, all right, just not the sort her boss was referring to. She seriously doubted that any two people in the world had exactly the sort of relationship she and John were currently sharing. Only she could get herself into such a mess.

"Now . . ." Rebecca's tone was brisk and professional. "About last week . . ."

Was this where she got fired, warned, or simply admonished? She didn't wait to find out. "I'm sorry about that, Rebecca. I behaved irresponsibly. I don't even understand why. I've never done anything like that in my life, and I'm so sorry, but I can promise it won't happen again."

Her boss studied her for a moment and evidently found her sincere. "Everyone's entitled to a mistake now and then. Yours didn't really cost us anything. But if there's a next time—"

"There won't be."

"If there is, it'll also be the last time. Do you understand?"

She nodded unhappily.

"All right." With those two words, Rebecca put the issue behind them, then smiled. "How about that coffee you mentioned? I've been dying for a good cup for about a week now."

On her way to the kitchen, Teryl whispered a silent prayer of thanks. With her job secure, that meant one less problem with John. If she'd gotten fired, she would have blamed him, would have probably told Rebecca everything in an effort to hold on to her job, even though her boss probably wouldn't have believed her. John would have felt guilty for it and would have promised that he'd make it up to her when all this was over.

As she measured coffee beans into the grinder, she wondered exactly how he intended to make things up to her, as he'd repeatedly said he would. Yesterday he'd said something about money, about giving her Tremont's signature on anything from books to checks. If he really were Simon Tremont, he could reward her richly out of his pocket change . . . but if he really were Simon, she wouldn't want any rewards merely for doing what was right.

She doubted, though, that he had the wherewithal to pay even a small reward. He didn't exactly fit her image of an obscenely rich man. His wardrobe consisted of faded jeans and cotton shirts. He didn't drive a luxury car, didn't wear any jewelry other than an inexpensive wristwatch, didn't spend money any more freely than she did on her tight budget.

But then, the other Simon, the one who had appeared on "New Orleans Afternoon," hadn't seemed conspicuous in his spending, either. Oh, he'd taken advantage of the best suite in one of the city's best hotels and the limos and the expensive meals, but that had been at his publisher's expense. It was always easier and more fun spending someone else's money. Teryl had thoroughly enjoyed her room in that same fine hotel at agency expense . . . but if she'd been there on her own, paying her own way, she would have been riding the bus in from the nearest Motel 6.

So spending habits didn't prove anything. A lot of rich people lived frugally, and a lot of people without money managed to live the good life.

That, she thought with a dreary sigh, was her single biggest problem these days. *Nothing* proved anything.

When he heard Teryl's car in the driveway, John closed the legal pad he'd found underneath the kitchen phone book, capped the pen, and got to his feet. It had been a productive morning. While waiting for the bank to open in Denver, he'd gone out and located a place that did quickie passport photos. The resulting picture had been grim, but it had looked like him. It had been more than adequate for his purposes.

Back at Teryl's—how easily he could come to think of it as home—he had called the bank and spoken to Frank Zarelli. He hadn't wanted much in the way of personal attention when he'd opened his accounts there eleven years ago, but the bank had been unwilling to let a major depositor go totally ignored. Zarelli had made it a point to meet him, and, for the first time, John was grateful for it.

He would be happy to help him, Zarelli had said, once he received John's letter and the photograph. As soon as he'd gotten off the phone, John had written the letter, gone to the post office, and sent it and the photo overnight to Denver. The banker had promised to respond in the same manner. John would have his answer—his proof—Wednesday. Then Teryl would *have* to believe him.

Wouldn't she?

With business taken care of, it had been a quiet morning with no interruptions—perfect for writing, provided that a person wanted to. *He* hadn't been so inclined in longer than he cared to remember. Oh, he had sat down at the computer day after day. He had edited the pages already written and had tried to write new pages, but the words had been hard to come by. Passages that had once flowed as swiftly and effortlessly as the river that gave the nearby town its name had become exercises in futility. Sheer, undiluted torture. He couldn't remember the last time he'd written anything and, when he went back to reread it, had thought, *Hey, this is good.*

But today he had written—not much, nothing brilliant, just a few pages that had been much more of a struggle and much less of a success than they should have been. But the point was he had wanted to write something, and he'd done it. For the first time in months, he'd done it.

Maybe it was being alone, really alone, for the first time since taking Teryl from the hotel last week. Maybe it was the tranquillity of her house—the rounded lines, the soft colors, the summer scents. Maybe it was her presence that touched the rooms even though she was gone.

Maybe it was the regretful words she had murmured in her office yesterday afternoon. *I don't know if you can write anything other than your name.* He had never cared much about accepting challenges. Tom and Janie had both had that sense of competition that made a challenge impossible to ignore, but not him. If he had, maybe his relationship with his parents would have turned out differently. Maybe, if he had accepted his father's challenges—to earn better grades, to be an outstanding athlete, to push hard and succeed at all costs— his family would still be intact.

But, no, he couldn't have let things be so easy. Whenever his father had started a conversation with Why don't you, Why can't you, or Why aren't you, John had immediately tuned out the rest. He'd known all the variations; he'd heard them practically since he was a baby. Why don't you try harder to make the team? Why can't you make good grades like your sister? Why aren't you as popular as your brother? Why won't you practice, work harder, study more, play less, be nicer, quit arguing, concentrate, work out, grow up, stop being difficult, act your age, show some sense, quit playing dumb? There were dozens of them—all negative, all hurtful, all pointing out just what a disappointment he was.

In a perverse way, he supposed, he *had* accepted his father's challenges. George Smith had wanted his second son to be as talented an athlete as the first; John had deliberately

cultivated a lack of physical prowess. George had wanted a
popular child—a class president, active in clubs, well liked
by students and teachers alike; John had looked for and
found his friends among the tough kids, the punks who had
little respect for themselves and none for anyone else.
George had wanted a kid to be proud of; John had given him
one to be ashamed of.

Today he had accepted Teryl's challenge. *I don't know if
you can write anything other than your name.* He had about
fifteen pages here to prove that he could. It wasn't the best
writing he'd ever done, but it was far from his worst. Who
knew? With a little revising and a little editing, it could turn
into the beginning of a new book. He didn't know where he
would go with it, but that wasn't unusual. He often didn't
know exactly where a story was headed until he'd done a
tremendous amount of work on it—notes, plots, and hours of
thinking. He did know who that unnamed female character
would become, though—knew whom he'd had in mind when
he'd begun writing hours ago, knew that Teryl would also
recognize her: Liane, the sister from the Thibodeaux books
who interested Teryl far more than the more popular character of Philip.

What would Teryl's reaction to the pages be? Would she
like the writing? Would she recognize the style? Would she
be intrigued by the situation he'd placed her favorite character in? Or would her first thought be to point out to him that
he couldn't write about someone else's characters, that the
Thibodeauxs belonged to Tremont and were off-limits to
him?

Around the corner the back door opened, then closed
again with a bang. "Jeez, it's hot out there," she said with a
sigh when she came into the kitchen. "I wish summer were
over and fall was on the way."

Reaching to the side, he turned the pad upside down.
"How would you ever manage New Orleans if you don't like
hot weather?"

She laid the plastic bag she carried on the table, hung her
purse by its strap over the back of the chair, then gave him a
smile as a belated greeting. It was a friendly smile—sweet,

pleasant, nothing more—and it was damned near enough to bring him to his knees. "I think living in New Orleans would be special enough to make putting up with the heat and humidity worthwhile. If you have to be hot, I can't imagine a better place to do it." As she began unwrapping the two sandwiches, she looked at him again. "Besides, it's all hypothetical. I'll probably never leave Richmond, and even if I do, I'll certainly never have the kind of money I'd want to live in New Orleans."

He wanted to contradict her, to inform her that, yes, someday soon—if this ended soon, if he was able to prove his identity and to do it without getting himself killed—she would have that kind of money. He would see to it.

But those were some mighty big *if*s.

"Did you call your banker?" she asked as he got two sodas from the refrigerator, then sat down opposite her.

He nodded, but she didn't say anything. She simply waited for him to elaborate. "I'll get the statement from him on Wednesday."

She didn't look at him as she began unwrapping one of the two sandwiches she'd removed from the bag. "Where is this bank?"

"Denver."

"Do you plan to go back there when this is over? To Colorado?"

They hadn't talked much about the future, although he wasn't surprised that she was thinking about it. Of course, they faced two totally different futures and with two totally different attitudes. She was looking forward to getting her life back to normal, to reclaiming her home and her peace of mind, to being left alone to live the way she wanted. She was anticipating the day he would be gone, the time when she would never have to deal with him again.

He wasn't.

And he didn't think, when that time came, when his life returned to his own sad version of *normal*, that it would happen in Colorado. At the moment, he couldn't imagine returning to his mountaintop. It had provided exactly what he needed those years he'd lived there—solitude, a measure of peace, a few good memories—but not anymore. What he needed in his future would be nowhere to be found—at least, not for him. He had promised her that he would make things right, and at the top of that list was getting out of her life. After all he'd put her through, she deserved that and more. "I don't know. Maybe I'll find some place even more remote. Maybe I'll buy an island."

"And surf all day."

"And write all night." He watched her gaze shift to the legal pad. The edges of the pages he'd filled with scenes were ruffled, a few of the corners bent in crooked triangles. She studied it a moment as she chewed a bite of her sub, but she didn't ask what it was. She didn't ask if she could see it. Part of him was glad because, other than the proposals he'd submitted to Rebecca and Candace Baker, he'd never shared any part of a work in progress with anyone. It seemed too personal, too intimate—and, of course, he'd never had anyone to share it with. At the same time, though, he was more than a little sorry that she didn't ask. He wanted her to see that he *could* write. He wanted her to know that he was writing Liane's story, wanted her to know that he was doing it especially for her. He wanted her to get a little personal, a little intimate.

Even if she did ask, he acknowledged, he would have to say no. Those were possibly the most important pages he had ever written. They could go a long way toward convincing Teryl that everything he'd told her was true. They could make her believe in him. Before he gave them to her to read, they needed more work. They had to be polished. They had to be perfect.

"Caribbean or Pacific?" She was looking at him now, the pad and the remarks about writing apparently gone from her mind.

It took him a moment to get his mind back on the subject of islands. "Surfing's better in the Pacific." And the Caribbean was too damned close to New Orleans. It would be too easy to break his promise to her, to just show up there one day, to torment himself with what he couldn't have.

"Someplace around Hawaii or farther south?" she asked.

"Farther south. Someplace exotic."

At that she laughed. "When you're never traveled outside the southern U.S., *all* islands seem exotic. Have you ever been in that part of the world?"

He shook his head.

"Then how do you know you'll like it? How do you know you won't be bored silly by ocean waves, tropical breezes, and all the scantily clad native girls?"

"Liking it has nothing to do with it." Putting distance between himself and all the significant places—and people—in his life did. Staying away from Janie in Florida, his parents in California, Teryl here or in New Orleans or wherever she settled—those were the important things.

"Liking it has everything to do with it," she disagreed. "How can you be happy in a place . . ." Abruptly, her voice trailed away. Her cheeks tinged pink, she focused her attention on her lunch.

What was she thinking? That happiness didn't rank very high in his life and never would? That he'd known so little happiness that he'd grown used to its absence? For a long time, he *had* been accustomed to it. Over the years he'd found his own substitutes—satisfaction with a well-written book, enjoyment in a climb up his mountain, relaxation in a summer storm, pleasure in making love, exceptional pleasure in making love with *her*—but he still missed being happy. He missed the overall sense of well-being that came from fitting properly into all the spaces of your life and sharing it with people you cared about. He missed waking up in the morning and thinking, This is going to be a good day, instead of, Here's another day I have to struggle through.

"You adjust," he said quietly, watching as she slowly brought her gaze back to his. "If you have what you need, you can adapt even to a place you detest."

Her voice was just as quiet when she responded. "And what you need is to be Simon Tremont."

What he needed was *her*. Didn't she know that yet?

With a shrug, he rose from the table, threw the wrapper from his lunch into the wastebasket, then leaned against the counter. "Simon is mine. I created him. I have a right to be him."

She started to speak, then broke off as the phone beside him rang. When she made no move to get up, he answered on the second ring, and what he heard in response to his greeting immediately drew his attention away from her.

"Teryl Weaver, please. This is Sheriff Logan Cassidy of the Grant County, Colorado, Sheriff's Department."

Although he'd spoken to the man on only one occasion, he recognized the voice even without the name. His first reaction was surprise. He had intended to call the sheriff today, to give him Teryl's address so the arson reports could be forwarded to him. Had the sheriff somehow tracked him down? But that was impossible; no one was that good. That meant Cassidy wasn't initiating this contact. He was returning a call he had missed presumably earlier in the day. It meant *Teryl* had called *him*. It meant she was checking up on John.

His gaze locked with hers, he replied in an even voice. "Just a minute, Sheriff. I'll get her."

She looked startled and guilty as she approached to take the phone. She must have given Cassidy her office number, John presumed, so he wouldn't accidentally take the call, so he wouldn't find out that she was trying to prove or disprove his story. Someone at the Robertson office must have given him this number.

Taking the phone from him, she wrapped her fingers tightly around it. "Do you mind?"

Why did she want privacy for the call? Because she simply wasn't comfortable discussing him while he stood there in front of her? Because she felt guilty for telling him this morning that she trusted him, then going to work and calling the sheriff to see if he *was* trustworthy? Or because she expected the sheriff to substantiate her suspicions that he was mental? Because she didn't believe Cassidy would support anything John had told her. Because she didn't want to try to hide her doubts and misgivings. Because she didn't want to give him cause for anger.

Fighting the same peculiar stubbornness that had so often gotten him into trouble with his father, he started toward the door. There he looked back. "I want to talk to him when you're finished." When she nodded, he walked away, down the hall and into the living room. He went to stand at the French doors, staring out at flowers wilting under the day's heat. From the kitchen, he could hear Teryl's voice, a soft murmur, the words indistinct.

He wasn't angry with her for calling Cassidy. Under the circumstances, it was the smart thing to do. But he was a little disappointed. He'd wanted her to do something no one had done since he was nineteen years old: to have faith in him, to believe him because he said so, not because someone else did. He'd wanted her to trust him, to take him at his word.

Obviously he was asking for too much. Despite the intimacy they had shared, they were still strangers. He had begun their relationship with half-truths and clouded motives. He had kidnapped her, had subjected her to nights of misery and terror. He had made claims too outrageous to believe and had forced her into helping him try to prove them. He was a fool to think she might ever overlook all that. He was a damned fool to hope she might ever forgive it.

After a while he realized that the hum of her voice had ended. The awareness of that fact brought with it acknowledgment of another: he was no longer alone in the room. She was standing in the doorway, arms folded across her chest, watching him. "He's waiting."

He followed her back to the kitchen, picking up the phone from the counter. He identified himself before asking, "When do you think the reports will be ready, Sheriff?"

"I'm waiting on the final report from the state's investigators. I should have it in a few days. Where do you want it sent?"

"To Richmond, Virginia. The address is . . ." He glanced at Teryl, standing now next to the table, and she murmured her address, pausing so he could repeat it to the sheriff.

Cassidy read it back for confirmation, then asked, "Do you want me to go over what I told Ms. Weaver?"

"No, thanks. Teryl can tell me. I appreciate your help, Sheriff." He hung up, then watched Teryl. Her hands were gripped tightly around the chair back. "When did you call him?"

"Yesterday afternoon. When we got back from the office." She raised her head, her posture and manner becoming defensive, but she didn't look at him. "I won't apologize for it."

"I wouldn't ask you to."

"There's so little you've told me that can be verified by someone else. I had to ask the sheriff about this."

"What did he tell you?"

She drew a deep breath. "That you bought the land eleven years ago, that the house was built a year later, that you paid cash for both. He said most people in the county never knew the place—or you—existed. He said the first time *he* met you was a week and a half ago, when you walked into his office and said your house had been destroyed by an explosion."

He wondered if the sheriff had told her how much the land and the house had cost, if he'd given her some idea of just how much cash had been involved. A hundred acres of mountaintop land with some of the best views in the state, a location so isolated that he'd had to pay premium prices just to get a construction crew up there, a twenty-five-hundred-square-foot house with no expense spared, getting the power lines extended miles from the nearest terminal point—none of it had come cheap. Most people would never see that much money at one time in their entire lives. But a best-selling, overnight-success, first book wonder using the name of Simon Tremont had.

Deliberately he argued with her. "He told you that John Smith had bought the land, that John Smith's house had been destroyed. How do you know he meant me?"

"He described you, down to the truck you're driving and the shoes you're wearing right now. He said the house burned a week and a half ago. The official cause is arson, the means three incendiary devices." She stumbled over those last two words, unfamiliar, a complicated way of saying bombs. "He said the fire burned so hot and the house went up so quickly that everything was lost. He said you were incredibly lucky to escape with nothing more than the laceration on your arm."

John felt tension he hadn't even been aware of draining from his body, felt the muscles in his jaw loosen and his fingers relax. He had been afraid that Cassidy wouldn't support his story, he realized, stifling the bitter urge to laugh. In the last ten days he had come to doubt himself enough, just enough, to secretly wonder if it *was* all in his head—the books, the money, the fire, the impostor. Someplace deep inside he had wondered if he was, indeed, crazy. Now he knew he wasn't.

He would sell his soul if Teryl could be even half as sure.

"The state arson investigators were able to identify the type of bomb used," she went on, her voice flat and unemotional. "They were glass jars, like canning or mayonnaise jars, quart size. They were filled halfway with gasoline, and some sort of filament was suspended over the gas. The jars were sealed and set with timers. When the timers went off, the filaments got hot and the heat ignited the vapors trapped in the jar. That caused the explosions." Pausing again, she gripped the chair even harder. "He said you had told him that, just before the explosions, you had smelled something inside the house that was familiar and didn't belong, but you couldn't place it. He thinks it was the seal. The jars were sealed with modeling clay."

Her last words brought him a chuckle. "They say smell is one of our most powerful senses. Just a whiff of a particular scent can take you back years. Play-Doh dinosaurs were my only creations of any note in kindergarten art class. I never got to keep them, though. My mother didn't allow the stuff in her house because Tom and Janie made messes with it." He gave a shake of his head. "It's hard to believe I've grown up so much that I didn't recognize it when I smelled it." After considering that for a moment longer, he moved on to a more important issue. "You have to believe my house burned down, and you have to believe I told the truth about the bombs because the sheriff told you so. What else do you believe, Teryl? What's your verdict? Am *I* responsible for the fire? Did *I* set the bombs? Or did someone else?"

Finally she looked at him. Her expression was grave, her eyes shadowed and more than a little concerned. For him? Or herself? "Sheriff Cassidy doesn't have any doubts."

He didn't give a damn what Cassidy believed . . . but obviously she did. Because Cassidy was a sheriff, because he was a lawman with years of experience and the authority of the Grant County Sheriff's Department behind him, she was willing at this point to believe whatever *he* believed. John hoped before asking that the sheriff's opinion was good news for him. "And what does he say?"

Her gaze locked with his as she quietly, somberly replied, "He thinks someone's trying to kill you."

Chapter Twelve

Back in her office, Teryl settled in at her desk to work, but her conversation with the sheriff made concentration impossible. Someone wanted John dead, and the most likely suspect was the man claiming to be Simon. The man who'd done the interview in New Orleans. The man who had given her the willies from the moment they'd met.

Okay, so the man was self-absorbed. He was the center of his own world and saw no reason why he shouldn't be the center of everyone else's, too. He seemed to feel an extremely strong sense of entitlement, as if all the fame, fortune, and adulation were no less than he deserved. There was his intensity, not quite reasonable, not quite normal, and the way he looked at people, measuring them, judging them, exposing them layer by layer with his less than pleasant gaze. Taken one by one, there was nothing wrong with those traits. Even combined, they didn't automatically add up to murderer potential.

In Simon, though, maybe they could. Especially if he wasn't really Simon. If he had become so obsessed with the real Simon Tremont's work that he had learned to write like him, if he had come up with this outrageous scheme to take over his idol's life, if he had managed to steal the outline for *Resurrection* from the real Simon and had somehow written the book . . . *If* he was capable of doing all those things, then, yes, he was capable of killing. What was it John had said that day in the storm in South Carolina? *The son of a bitch can't claim to be Simon Tremont if the real Simon Tremont is around to prove him a fraud. In order to continue being Simon, he needed—needs—to get rid of me.*

According to the sheriff, only a week and a half ago, someone had tried to do just that.

Only a week and a half ago, when Simon had made his changes—the move, the visits, the phone calls—four months ago. Why the delay? Once he'd devised his scheme and put it in motion, why had he given the real Simon Tremont four months to possibly destroy everything? How had he known that John wouldn't contact Rebecca or Candace during that time? How had he known that John wouldn't turn in his own *Resurrection*? Why had he put his great elaborate hoax at such risk?

Maybe it had been arrogance. Maybe he had believed that his plan was so perfect that no one could ever discover the truth. Or maybe it had been the book. *Resurrection*. He had begun the process of claiming Simon Tremont's life four months before the manuscript had been completed. Without *Resurrection*, he could have sustained the lies for a time— long enough to cash a few of Tremont's checks, maybe long enough to bask in a little of Tremont's glory—but eventually he would have been compelled to produce something. Without *Resurrection*, though, his plan eventually would have failed and there would have been little reason to destroy the real Tremont.

And so he had waited, had worked and written, and only when the book was completed, only when he had proven to himself that he could, indeed, write Tremont's book, had he turned his attention to Tremont himself. Two weeks ago the manuscript had been turned in to both Rebecca and Morgan-Wilkes. A few days later someone had tried to kill John. Was the timing coincidence? Or part of Simon's plan?

Her gaze settled on the space occupied for a few months by her autographed copy of *Masters of Ceremony*. It was gone, her treasured possession ruined, destroyed in a fit of rage. Sunday, watching John, she had been stunned, unable to fully comprehend what he'd done. This afternoon she couldn't find it in herself to care much. Even if Simon really was Simon, he wasn't the man she had idolized all these years, and if he wasn't really Simon, she certainly wouldn't want his forgery. She would never want a book signed by a madman who had tried to kill another man all for the sake of his career.

She sighed wearily. All she'd had for the last week was suspicions and doubts, and they were growing every day. But the focus of those suspicions had changed, the target of the doubts shifted. In the space of a few days, she had gone from labeling John's claims outrageous and unbelievable to very nearly accepting them. Deep inside there was still a small doubt—there was still the matter of *Resurrection*, after all— but even that wasn't hard and fast proof. It was possible— not likely, but remotely possible—that one extremely talented author could thoroughly mimic the style of another extremely talented author. If the first author were dedicated enough. Brilliant enough. Obsessed enough.

All three descriptions certainly could apply to Simon.

Maybe it was time to talk to Rebecca, to get everything out in the open. After all, she had a lot at stake here—her reputation and the reputation of the agency, the money that might have been paid to the wrong man, the future of her biggest client, which would, of course, affect the agency and everyone who worked there. She had a right to know what was going on . . . even if, most likely, she wouldn't believe a word of it.

So how should Teryl approach her? Straightforward? Go in and say, "Rebecca, this man who's staying with me says that *he's* Simon Tremont, and he knows enough about Tremont and about *Resurrection* that he's made me won- der"? Rebecca would probably wonder, too—not only about John's sanity but also about Teryl's.

Perhaps it would be better if she spoke in hypotheticals. *What if*'s. She could feel out her boss, see if she was at all open to such possibilities. She could get a better idea of how to handle it when the time came for specifics.

Her gaze settled on one of the manuscripts sitting on the

corner of her desk. Her favorite books were mysteries and romances; this one, a romantic suspense, combined the best of both genres. The author was unpublished, but, if the remainder of the book lived up to the promise of the chapters Teryl had already read, she wouldn't remain that way long. Her story involved a classic case of mistaken identity, her romance writer heroine stalked by killers because she had the same name as and fitted the general description of the woman who was their real target. The writing was stylish and polished, the story twisted enough to hold a reader's interest.

It would be a perfect icebreaker.

Leaving her desk, she went to the kitchen, pouring a cup of almond-flavored coffee for Rebecca and a mug of the regular brew for herself. Coming to a stop in Rebecca's open doorway, she interrupted her boss at work. "I thought you might like a fresh cup," she suggested, lifting the delicate china in offering.

Looking up, Rebecca smiled and removed her reading glasses. "Your timing is perfect. I just finished the last one. Come on in and sit down."

Teryl delivered the coffee to her, then took a seat as instructed. After taking a sip from her own coffee, she wrapped her hands around the pottery mug. She wasn't really thirsty; she simply needed a prop to keep her hands occupied.

"What have you been doing this afternoon?"

"Reading," she lied. It sounded so much better than "Sitting at my desk, gazing off into space, and brooding over whether the man we know as Simon Tremont is, indeed, one of the most talented authors in the country or a devious, warped lunatic who's fooled us all."

"Anything interesting?"

"As a matter of fact, yes. A romantic suspense."

"Promising?"

"So far, but I've only read the first three chapters."

"Which often outshine the rest of the book."

Teryl nodded in acknowledgment. Unpublished writers in the habit of entering contests or submitting partials—three chapters and an outline—to editors or agents had a tendency to write and rewrite those first three chapters, polishing them until they gleamed. Without the same attention and work, the remainder of the manuscript often suffered in comparison. "I don't think that will be the case with this one. She's very good. Her story is about mistaken identity, and her heroine's a writer." Wetting her lips, she took a shallow breath, then continued. "It's interesting. With all the millions of people in the country, so many people have exactly the same names. Even with Social Security numbers, it can be so easy for one person to get mistaken for another. Like Simon."

Rebecca's laughter was soft and amused. "I doubt there are too many Simon Tremonts running around out there."

"But you're forgetting: his real name is John Smith. There must be thousands of John Smiths."

"Yes, but how many of them can write like a dream—or a nightmare, depending on your outlook?"

Maybe one more than she expected, Teryl thought. She hadn't seen any proof yet that John could write, but she wouldn't be surprised if he could. He was bright. He had a strong vocabulary and a nice way with words. Sometimes on the trip from New Orleans to Richmond, when he'd talked about his brother and sister or his home in Colorado or other things important to him, his language had been purely lyrical—not just words, but imagery, emotion, sensation. She wouldn't be at all surprised if he could translate that power from the spoken word to paper.

In fact, she wouldn't be surprised if he'd already done it. She had seen the legal pad on the kitchen table at lunch, had seen all those much-handled pages. She had wanted so badly to look at it, to reach across the table and pick it up and read what he had written. But he had seen her looking, and he hadn't offered to let her see it, so she hadn't asked. Soon she would. She wanted to read the pages. She needed to.

"Wouldn't it be interesting," she began slowly, watching the coffee in her cup vibrate from the unsteadiness in her hands, "if the John Smith who came into the office, the one who did the interview in New Orleans, wasn't the same John Smith who created Simon Tremont?"

Her boss apparently decided to humor her. "If he discovered that he and Tremont shared the same name and he decided to pass himself off as Tremont? If he thought that he'd discovered the easy way to fame and fortune?" She shook her head. "How could he hope to pull it off?"

"No one had ever met Tremont. No one knew what he looked like, how old he was, how he sounded. He'd cultivated such an air of mystery that the world knew only one thing about him: he could write the most incredible books."

"And what could such an impostor hope to gain from this?"

"You said yourself it would be the easy way to fame and fortune. It's not so unusual, Rebecca. One of the daytime talk shows did an entire show some time back about people who routinely claim to be someone they're not. They even made a movie about one of them. People were *thrilled* to meet Simon Tremont. You should have seen the way everyone at the hotel and the TV station treated him, as if he were visiting royalty. All he had to do was lift one finger, and they jumped to fulfill his every wish. And fortune? He's received only one check since coming out of hiding, but we both know that every check Tremont gets is a fortune in itself."

"And where is the real Simon Tremont during all this?"

"The same place he's been for the last eleven years: at home in Colorado, hiding in his mountains, and absolutely unaware that anything unusual is happening."

Rebecca considered the scenario, and for a moment, Teryl thought, plausibility was evenly balanced with skepticism. The moment passed, though, and skepticism won out. "But sooner or later the impostor has to get caught. He meets someone who knows who he really is, or someone who knows the person he's posing as. In this case, sooner or later the fake Simon would have to write another book. His fans haven't even yet seen *Resurrection*, and they're already drooling over the prospect of the *next* Tremont novel."

"But, realistically, no one expects another book for at least a year or two or even longer," Teryl pointed out. "He can bask in an awful lot of celebrity—and spend an awful lot of the real Simon's money—in two years."

"Speaking of books, that shoots down your theory right

there. The man who came to the office, who did the interview in New Orleans, wrote the most incredible of those incredible books. He wrote *Resurrection*. Only the real Simon Tremont could have done that." Replacing her glasses, Rebecca shuffled through the contracts in front of her. Before she turned all of her attention to them, though, she gave Teryl an affectionate smile. "This new author certainly fired your imagination. I like that in a book. Go back and finish reading it, then let me know what you think."

Even though she had clearly been dismissed, Teryl remained where she was for a moment. Then, with a faint sigh, she left, returning to the privacy of her own office, sinking once more into the leather chair, gazing off into space, and brooding once more.

All right, so she had broached the subject with Rebecca, who had, at least, listened and hadn't laughed her from the room. But she hadn't been particularly open to the possibilities, either. She'd never gotten beyond the interesting-idea-but-could-never-happen-in-reality stage. How much less open would she be when Teryl tried again, not with hypotheticals but with details, with facts, with John's claims and her own doubts? If Rebecca didn't believe such a scheme could work in a talking-about-books-and-make-believe scenario, how much more skeptical would she be when Teryl tried to present it as reality?

She would probably be convinced that John was crazy and would have serious doubts about Teryl. She wouldn't for more than a moment consider the possibility that John's claims had any basis in reality. Like any good businessperson, she would go on the defensive, would take whatever steps were necessary to protect the agency, herself, and her most important client, including firing a disloyal employee who had violated the confidentiality of that client's records. John wouldn't prove a thing, and *she* would be out of a job.

All things considered, she thought glumly as she reached for the manuscript on the corner, for the time being, at least, she would rather not say another word.

*   *   *

The computer screen glowed royal blue in the dimly lit office, the cursor an annoying blink of white. Type, it seemed to command with its agitated flutter. Type something, anything, but, damn it, type! But Simon, seated in his high-tech, top-dollar, designed-for-your-spine chair, had nothing to say. He'd had nothing to say for days.

He leaned back in the chair, anchoring his feet on the floor, and twisted slowly from side to side. Every day he came in here, and every night, too. He turned on the computer, and he faced this empty screen, and he tried to write. At first, his goal had been a new book, one that would top *Resurrection*, one that would convince the world that he was, indeed, the greatest writer that lived. Soon that had become a desire to write a chapter, just one chapter, twenty-five or thirty pages. He'd written that and far more in a day, especially there toward the end of *Resurrection*.

Today his goal had been to write one well-crafted sentence that could lead to another. Here it was, the middle of the afternoon, and he hadn't yet succeeded.

Maybe it was still too soon. After those last frantic weeks of obsessing over the last book, maybe he hadn't given his creative self time to recharge. Maybe he needed more rest . . . more public appearances . . . more adulation. Maybe he was feeling the pressure of having to follow up his masterpiece with something at least as good, preferably better. Or maybe he just needed to tie up a few loose ends in his life. Loose ends tended to get messy. They could trip a man up if he wasn't careful.

Still turning from side to side, he reached out and, with the caps lock feature turned on, typed the name of one of his loose ends. TERYL. She was back in town, back in the office at last, and rumor was that she'd brought her lover with her. Just how good could the guy be, to merit an invitation to come home to Virginia with her and move into her house?

IS. He pressed the spacebar, then slumped down and propped his feet on the low stool underneath his desk. His posture at the computer had always been awful, resulting in backaches, stiff fingers, and an occasional nagging worry about carpal tunnel syndrome. Was there an author in the world who didn't worry? Of course, it didn't matter to him now. If sitting at the desk got to be a strain, he would simply hire a secretary. He would make himself comfortable, dictate his books, and let her ruin *her* back and wrists.

Picking out the letters, he finished his first full sentence of the day. A SLUT.

Funny how things could change. In New Orleans and following his return home, he had found himself all too often thinking about sex with Teryl. There was something terribly appealing about slutty sex with someone as sweet, innocent, and pure as she had seemed to be. But the key word there was *seemed*. She might still be sweet, but apparently she was neither innocent nor pure. Being bad with a good girl was a tremendously erotic prospect. Being bad with a bad girl was merely boring.

He would be a liar if he said he wasn't disappointed. Claiming her as his own, he had thought, would be one of his greater achievements. Now he would still claim her, at least for a night or maybe—if she was very, very good—for a weekend, but it would be no great achievement. Apparently, if her affair with this stranger was anything to judge by, just about any man in the world could have her. She was theirs for the taking . . . when, damn her, she was supposed to be *his*.

But maybe the affair wasn't anything to judge by. Maybe there was more to it than met the eye. Maybe the guy hadn't been a stranger but someone she'd once known. Maybe his coming to Richmond with her had been nothing more than coincidence. Maybe he had ties to the area, and she had simply been the impetus he'd needed to bring him home.

Maybe she'd had her fling, and there was nothing between them now but friendship. It could happen. He'd known women who could turn it on and off like that, who could have a steamy hot relationship with a man today and be just pals tomorrow. Maybe she'd been using the guy so she could stay longer in her precious New Orleans and was returning the favor by bringing him back here for a while. Maybe the fact that he had come home with her meant nothing.

And maybe hell had frozen over.

The truth was, most likely, very simple: Teryl really was a slut.

Damn her for that.

Returning the cursor to the beginning of the line, he pressed the delete key and watched as the letters disappeared from the screen. It was so easy to make the words disappear and, lately, so damned hard to make them appear. So damned hard to craft them in a logical order, to infuse them with life, with feeling, with power. So damned hard to string them into sentences, to build sentences into paragraphs, to turn paragraphs into chapters.

He could do it. He had tremendous talent and incomparable skill. If anyone could do it, *he* could. But not today, he thought as he leaned forward and pressed the button that shut off the computer.

Not today.

When John had made the decision eleven years earlier to move into the mountains, he'd had several reasons. Many of his happiest memories involved the California mountains where his family had spent much of their free time hiking, camping, and skiing. He had hoped to recapture some of those good feelings, even though he'd known it would be all but impossible, because his worst memories involved those same mountains—a family camp-out, an argument with his father, a narrow, winding road, and a car out of control.

He had also hoped to find peace in the Rockies, and he must have succeeded in some small measure because he'd finally stopped trying to kill himself. At the same time, he had in a very real sense been punishing himself. He had banished himself from society. He'd done such harm to the people he cared about that he'd believed the only fair thing was to have no contact with anyone. All alone on top of his mountain, he couldn't hurt anyone. He couldn't destroy someone's life, someone's future or dreams.

But all alone was no way to live. Even if it was the only way he could live.

Sometimes—usually after trips into Denver, where life was rushed and the city crowded—he'd thought he had been alone so long that he couldn't adapt to living with someone else. He had thought that the mere presence of another person in the house would make him uneasy, that the loss of total privacy would grate on his nerves. He knew now, of course, that it depended on who the other person was. He wouldn't mind feeling Teryl's presence more often. He would have no objection at all to giving up more of his privacy to her, even if it was only temporary.

Maybe what he felt was a false sense of ease, since they weren't intimate, but they made good roommates. She was a little on the sloppy side, but that was all right, because he liked neatness and order and he honestly didn't mind being the one to restore it when she'd finished scattering the sections of the newspaper around the living room or when he found her damp towels in a heap on the bathroom floor. They liked the same TV shows, had similar tastes in music, and shared a fondness for the same old movies. They both liked to read, and she seemed as fond of quiet times at home as he was. They got along well.

Platonically well. He wished he knew how to change that, but this sunny Monday afternoon, there were no easy answers to tough questions just waiting around to be discovered.

He'd spent most of the afternoon seated here at the kitchen table, adding to Liane's story—in addition to thinking about Teryl—but he had reached the point where he needed to stop writing and start thinking about the plot. He had no routine for the way he put his books together. Sometimes, like now, he started with a character and came up with a story to fit. Sometimes the story came first, and he had to develop characters to go with it. On rare occasions he'd been blessed with the gift of a fully developed book, characters and plot, that seemed to write itself. On other occasions—*Resurrection* came to mind—the creative process was a torturous one.

Liane's story, although not yet plotted, was going to be one of the easier ones.

He had Teryl to thank for that. Because she wanted this story. Because he felt a tremendous desire to give her exactly what she wanted. Because, maybe if he *did* give her what she wanted, she might feel generous enough to fulfill a few of *his* desires.

After their brief conversation that had followed the sheriff's phone call at lunch, she had gone back to work, leaving him with no clue as to what she thought or how she felt. Cassidy believed someone was trying to kill him, and that was reason enough for her to believe, also. But that didn't mean she believed it was Tremont. It didn't mean she believed he *was* Tremont. It just meant that she was willing to accept that someone out there didn't like him enough to want him dead.

And that wasn't enough for John. He wanted more. He wanted her faith, her trust, her acceptance.

Too tired mentally to work any longer, he returned the pad to its place underneath the phone book and headed outside. He had just settled down, sprawled in one of the weathered wood chairs at the end of the patio, staring morosely into the heavily leafed branches overhead, when the sound of a finely tuned engine broke the silence. There was no way Teryl's little economy car could purr like that and no reason for her to be returning home from work more than an hour early. D.J. Howell's car, however, sounded exactly like that. He hoped he was wrong, but the uneasy knot in his stomach suggested that he wasn't.

He wasn't. The car that came around the curve in the driveway was black, shiny enough to gleam, and powerful enough to roar. If he owned it, he would tint the windows, would add an air of mystery to it, but he knew why D.J. hadn't. Tinted windows wouldn't show her to her best advantage, and she cared tremendously about her best advantage.

He wondered why she had come when she must know Teryl was at work. Did she want to question him about his involvement with her best friend? Did she want to find out his intentions, to look out for Teryl's best interests? Or did she have something a little more self-serving in mind? Seduction, perhaps, or the offer of a playmate for the rough games she was into and believed that he was, too?

Climbing out of her car, she spotted him right away and walked toward him with enviable grace. For all the polish and elegance of her movements, though, there was nothing about her that spoke of class. The wild look of her hair was overdone, her dress was too short and clung too tightly, her heels were too high, her moves too practiced. She looked like exactly what she was: a breathtakingly beautiful, exotic, erotic whore.

She didn't stop until she was right in front of him. Only his legs, stretched out straight, prevented her from coming even closer. "Don't you look comfortable," she said in her throatiest, most seductive voice. Just the sound of it, he imagined, was enough to make most men thankful they were males.

He didn't respond to her greeting. He simply remained as he was, slouched down, spine rounded, hands folded across his belly, and watched her.

"My sister's not here, is she?"

"Your sister?"

"Teryl," she said drily.

"Teryl says you're not really her sister, just a foster sister." His tone was mild to bring such a dangerous glint to her eyes. Obviously, being thought of as a real sister—as a real member of the Weaver family—was important to D.J. . . . but not important enough to keep her away when she knew damned well her foster sister wasn't home.

"Teryl teases." Her voice was cool, her body stiff, her annoyance poorly hidden.

"What's to tease about? Either you're a Weaver . . . or you're not."

"And either you're a bastard or you're not. I'd vote for the former." She shifted her weight from side to side, a sensuously natural movement that drew his gaze lower. Her dress was so short that it retained any measure of modesty only by virtue of its tightness. Every single man-made fiber was stretched so tautly across her body that the sheer tension kept it from riding up. It was appropriate, he supposed, for a night on the town in the trendy sort of clubs D.J. probably preferred, but he couldn't think of many other places it would belong. It certainly didn't strike him as appropriate for a visit to your best friend's supposed lover . . . unless you were looking to get laid.

He nearly smiled at that. He would bet his next royalty check that Debra Jane Howell was *always* looking to get laid.

It *was* an option, he admitted, the moment of humor disappearing. With even the slightest encouragement, D.J. would be stripped down bare in a matter of seconds. Living in a perpetual state of unsatisfied desire as he was, with any encouragement at all, he would be hard and throbbing in even less time. In the hour or so before Teryl returned home from work, they could get down to some serious business. He could work off a hell of a load of sexual frustration and maybe lose a little of this obsession over making love to Teryl.

Less than an hour. That was all it would take to turn his life into sheer hell. He would destroy whatever chances he might ever have with Teryl. He would feel too damned guilty ever to look her in the eye, would be too damned scared of what D.J. would tell her to ever let his guard down. Hell, he would probably be too damned busy fulfilling D.J.'s blackmail demands to even spend any time with Teryl—and he had no doubts whatsoever that D.J. was the sort of woman who would blackmail a man. She would have him by the balls, and she would never let him go.

"You don't like me much, do you, John?" Stepping over his feet, she approached him from the side, not stopping until the broad arm of the chair blocked her way.

"Not much," he agreed, forcing himself to remain still, not to surge to his feet and put a safe distance between them. A thousand miles or so sounded about right.

"That's all right. We don't need to like each other to get along."

"We don't need to get along," he disagreed. "We don't need to ever see each other again."

She draped herself over the chair arm, a sexy sort of settling in. He knew it was calculated, every movement studied and planned, but knowing the effect was deliberate didn't stop him from feeling exactly the response she wanted to provoke. It didn't stop him from thinking, even if only for an instant, how easy it would be to pull her down across his lap, to peel up that silly excuse for a dress, to open his jeans and slide right inside her. It didn't stop him from wondering, since he had no real chance of ever developing anything permanent with Teryl, if it wouldn't be all right to blow it now and at least get *something* for his troubles. It didn't stop him from getting just a little bit hard.

"Don't be ridiculous," she practically purred. "We're both a part of Teryl's life. Of course we'll need to see each other."

Forcing himself to control the almost-desperate need to escape, he got to his feet without touching her and retreated a half dozen feet to lean against the nearest tree trunk. He felt a tremendous sense of relief with the distance that now separated them. "Explain that to me, D.J. I'm here because I like Teryl, and you're here because . . . ?"

That nasty glint reappeared in her eyes. "Because she's my best friend," she said icily.

He forced a laugh. "Right. Correct me if I'm wrong, but isn't one of the prerequisites for best friendship actually liking the person whose friendship you're claiming? You like Teryl even less than you like me."

For a moment she simply stared at him, the vaguely surprised look in her eyes confirming what he'd said. Then, abruptly, the surprise disappeared, and she smiled coolly. "You're right. I don't like you at all. I think you're taking advantage of Teryl's kind nature. I think you're using her. I think you're abusing her. I think you're seducing her into things she would never ordinarily do, things that she's ashamed of, things that she'll have to cope with by herself once you've gotten bored and moved on to some other innocent fool. I think you're playing games with her, games that she doesn't know how to play."

Now it was his turn to feel surprised. Although, with her focus naturally on the sexual aspect, she had the details all wrong, overall, her guesses were accurate. He *was* using

Teryl, forcing her to do things that shamed her, things like cooperating with him, going through her boss's files, and lying to the people who cared about her. "But you know how to play the games, don't you?"

"Every one of them."

"And you're willing to play them with me—to save Teryl's pride, of course."

Her only response was a faint smile.

"I never would have pegged you for such a generous woman."

Her smile thinned; then, brushing off the insult, she rose from the chair and took a few lazy steps toward him. "I *am* a generous woman, John. I'll play your games. I'll let you do whatever you want—domination, submission, discipline. I enjoy it all. And to show you just how generous I am, I'll promise you that Teryl will never know."

"And I'm supposed to simply accept your word."

Her look this time was sly, sexy, and full of promise. "I'm good at keeping secrets, especially from Teryl. I've been keeping secrets from and about her since we were kids. This? This is nothing. In all the times it's happened before, she's never suspected a thing."

"All the times?" he repeated. "You make a habit of sleeping with Teryl's lovers?"

Her gaze was steady on his. "Every one of them."

John took a moment to process that information. This was no simple case of sibling rivalry. Bitterness and resentment must run as deep in D.J. as affection and caring did in Teryl. Did Teryl have any idea how little D.J. actually liked her? Did she feel any of those negative emotions seething behind her foster sister's bright smiles and phony concern? Probably not. While she had acknowledged that D.J. had a few problems, Teryl loved her dearly. She didn't see D.J.'s jealousy. She didn't recognize D.J.'s deceit, her manipulation, her betrayal.

He moved away from the tree and came closer to her. When he was close enough to feel her, to smell her, to damned near crawl inside her, he stopped, gazing down at her, his eyes intense, his mouth thin and hard, his derision palpable in the heavy afternoon air. "Not in this lifetime," he said, the soft huskiness of his voice unable to disguise one bit of the steel underneath. "Not if you were the last woman on earth."

Disappointment crossed her face, followed by disbelief and anger, hot and ugly. She raised her hand to deliver a stinging blow to his cheek, but he caught her wrist before she made contact. "You bastard."

"Run along now," he advised, using his grip on her to force her a few steps back, "and maybe I won't tell Teryl how her best friend betrayed her today and how often she's done it in the past."

Yanking free, she rubbed the slight pain in her wrist. "She would never believe you."

For the first time since she'd arrived, he smiled. It was filled with malice and taunting and felt damned good. "You think so? When I'm in bed with her? When I'm inside her, doing things to her that have never been done before? When I'm teaching her things she never realized she was dying to know, when I'm making her writhe with need, when I'm giving her pleasure like no other man she's ever known, do you honestly think Teryl won't believe anything I choose to tell her?"

She didn't answer. She didn't need to. He could read it in her scowl, in the hatred that darkened her eyes and the underlying shadow of fear.

"You can't afford to lose her, D.J. You need her far more than she needs you. So stay the hell away from me, and don't try to cause trouble, because, in the end . . ." His voice dropped a few levels, became low, soft, and threatening. "You'll be the one to suffer."

For a long moment she simply stood there, staring at him. He could see the thoughts running through her head, could see the subtle shift of emotions. Anger gave way to speculation; hatred slid easily into faintly amused satisfaction. He wished he knew what she was thinking, wished he knew what it would take to move her from rage to amusement in a few quiet moments, while at the same time he didn't want to know. No doubt it was something perverse, something hurtful and sick. That was all he needed to know.

She offered him a smile, nothing seductive or sensual, just a cool acknowledgment one to another. "Okay. If you want to belong to Teryl exclusively right now, I have no problems with that. But don't underestimate me, John. Don't underestimate my influence on her. I've been a part of her life—the closest part of her life—for twenty-one years. I know her in ways you never can. I can control her in ways you'll never manage. Don't make me turn her against you just to prove it."

The quiet words sent a chill down his spine, but he hid it well. "You could give it your best shot," he said with a careless shrug as he started toward the house. "But don't count on succeeding."

D.J. watched him as he let himself into the house. Once the door closed behind him, it was impossible, of course, to tell where he'd gone, but she would bet upstairs. She had no sensation of being watched through the sheer curtains on the French doors, and John-boy's blue gaze was so intense that she imagined she would always know when he was around.

Jeez, she hadn't had to work so hard to get any man besides Rich into bed in longer than she could remember. Even Paul Robertson—Rebecca's ex and, according to Teryl, one of the sweetest and most devoted men a woman could ever hope to meet—had been easier than this. He had been too naive to recognize that she wanted an affair with him until the day he'd come home from work and found her waiting, naked and willing, in his bed. He had protested, of course—weakly—but by the time she'd gotten his pants open and started to blow him, words like no and stop had ceased to exist within his vocabulary.

John obviously still had command of all those words. For a moment, when she had sat down on the chair arm, she had thought he might falter. She had thought that, any time now, he would draw her close for a kiss, would pull her dress up and take her right there or maybe invite her inside. She would have liked that—doing it in Teryl's house, maybe even in Teryl's bed.

She would have loved it.

And hated it.

And gotten off on it like never before.

But the moment had passed, though not, she suspected, without some effort, because he had immediately moved away from her. Maybe she shouldn't have let him. Maybe she should have been more brazen. Maybe, as she'd done with Paul, she should have initiated some action and seen how quick he was to stop what was already started.

And then he had threatened her. *Do you honestly think Teryl won't believe anything I choose to tell her?* Of course she would, D.J. thought with a scowl. She knew that from her own experience. She'd been a child when her parents had first taught her, when they'd done things to her and whispered things to her, and she had believed. *This is how a good daddy shows his little girl he loves her, Debra Jane. Quit crying, Debra Jane, and let me teach you what a good little girl does to make her mama happy.* Oh, yes, she had believed, and so would Teryl.

With a sigh, she sat down in the chair he had vacated, feeling the wood slats, sun-warmed and rough, against her bare thighs. Maybe John could turn Teryl against her . . . for a time. But he couldn't make it last. After all, *she* was Teryl's best friend, her sister, a part of her family. Who the hell was he? Some guy that Teryl had picked up on an overnight trip, a summer fling who was introducing her to the darker side of her soul. He didn't understand that, while Teryl might be indulging his taste for the kinky and depraved, she wouldn't settle for a lifetime of it. She couldn't handle the guilt and the shame. She was experimenting, getting off on the thrill of how bad she was being rather than truly enjoying the pain and degradation. Soon the thrill would pass, and she would want to return to straight, plain, boring sex, to normalcy, to being good. After all, Teryl made an art of being good.

When that happened, John would be gone, because to get rid of the shame, Teryl would also have to get rid of the man who'd taught her the shame. She would force him from her life, and she would try desperately to pretend that the entire nasty little interlude had never happened—and that would mean coming crawling back to D.J., pleading for forgiveness, which D.J. naturally would offer . . . eventually.

Until that happened, though, it couldn't hurt to be on guard. It couldn't hurt to keep an eye on John, and the best way to do that was to find out more about him. Right now she knew nothing except that he had more in common by far with her than with her friend and that he had more strength of will than any man she'd ever known besides Rich. Hell, she didn't even know his last name.

Her gaze shifted from the house to the Blazer parked beside her car. You could tell a lot about a person from the car he or she drove. Hers was sleek, fast, flashy, like her. It was her most prized possession, immaculate outside and in, the glove box cluttered only with the manual that had come with it, a box of condoms, and a couple of her favorite CDs. Teryl's car, on the other hand, was nothing less than junky. It had suffered dents and dings on every surface, the tires were bald, and the engine was always in need of a tune-up. She cleaned it only once in a blue moon and relied on rain to rinse off the worst layers of dust and dirt. The glove compartment and console were stuffed with receipts, deposit slips, napkins from fast-food restaurants, breath mints that were inedible, and junk mail intended for but never making it to the garbage. Food wrappers, empty Coke cans, and an occasional M&M littered the floorboards.

The only item the two vehicles shared in common resided in their respective glove boxes: the vehicle registration. It was a handy little piece of paper, full of interesting information like names and addresses.

If John was like virtually everyone she knew, his registration was in his Blazer. It would tell her his name and exactly where he lived in New Orleans. With that information and the vast resources a lifetime of affairs had given her, she could find out almost anything.

She glanced at the house as she stood up, then casually made her way past the fountain and toward the truck. If John discovered her, she would make some excuse or, better yet, create some distraction and be on her way. But there was no sign of him at any of the windows or French doors.

She always locked her car doors, even here at Teryl's house, but her friend, she knew, usually left her own doors open here. Teryl thought that location alone would protect her from thieves and prowlers. Granted, the big house on the other side of the trees did have an elaborate security system and intelligent thieves, realizing that, wouldn't bother with the estate at all. But who said all thieves were intelligent? Most of them were just desperate, and while Teryl didn't have much worth stealing, what she did have, even her old car, could be taken and sold as easily as anyone else's property.

As she circled behind the truck, her steps slowed. Somehow the green and white tag on the Blazer had escaped her notice on her last visit. Chalk it up to surprise, she thought drily, due to all Teryl had done—turning wild and unpredictable and just the slightest bit kinky after a lifetime of sainthood. But that was no Louisiana tag on a truck belonging to a man who claimed to live in New Orleans. The license plate was issued by the state of Colorado and, according to its corner stickers, had recently been renewed, which meant that John had very recently left Colorado for the steamier environs of New Orleans . . . or he had lied.

Feeling grim and more distrustful than ever, she tried the door on the driver's side of the Blazer. It was unlocked.

Opening it, she climbed inside, automatically grimacing at the heat. The truck wasn't spotless, like the Camaro, but it was relatively clean. There was dust on the dash, and a few potato chip crumbs in the passenger floor—most likely Teryl's, she thought uncharitably—but there was no trash. No belongings. No mail bearing a convenient address. There was a little vinyl sticker on the window advising that the Blazer was due for an oil change at sixty-four thousand miles; according to the odometer, he was just over a thousand miles late. There was a handful of coins in the change tray and a pack of cigarettes, a book of matches, and a flashlight in the center console.

Leaning across the stick shift, she opened the glove compartment. Inside was the ever-present manual and—good luck—the registration slip. As soon as she committed the name and address to memory, she would head home and make a few phone calls. There was this cop she knew . . . or maybe the private detective she'd dated a few times would be a better choice. She had kept him occupied on more than a few long, boring surveillances, so he owed her a favor or two. Besides, he lacked the cop's ingrained sense of right and wrong. As long as there was something in it for him, he didn't care if it was legal, fair, or . . .

As she stared at the registration, her mind went blank, and the hairs on the back of her neck stood on end. They had lied to her. Teryl's lover, her summer fling whom she'd picked up on a two-day trip to New Orleans, didn't live in New Orleans; his address was Route 4, Rapid River, Colorado. But his name was John, all right.

John H. Smith.

Chapter Thirteen

After his shower that night, John dried off, drawing the towel carefully over the stitches in his right arm. They should come out after ten days, the doctor had told him, and today was day ten. He could get the name of Teryl's doctor and make an appointment tomorrow, but it would be a waste of time better spent working. The laceration was healing on schedule. There was no sign of infection, and the wound edges had come together nicely. All he needed was a pair of tweezers and some sharp-pointed scissors, and he could take care of it himself.

He found both items in the drawer, tossed in with a jumble of brushes and combs, razor cartridges, and a broken emery board. It took only one try to realize that he needed something else: an extra hand. He could use the tweezers to pull the suture taut or he could snip the thread while it was being held taut, but he couldn't do both.

He needed Teryl's help.

She had come upstairs more than an hour ago, leaving him with an old Lorna Terrill movie. He'd paid little attention to the movie, though, and far too much to the sounds Teryl was making upstairs—a trip from the bedroom to the bathroom, the water running while she showered, and a return trip to the bedroom followed by the closing of her door. When he had finally come up for his own shower, the door had remained closed, a thin line of yellow light seeping underneath it. He had felt thoroughly shut out.

Dropping the tweezers on the counter, he pulled on his jeans, then picked up the tools once more and opened the door. Her light was still on, so she was still awake. She probably wouldn't appreciate being disturbed, particularly when she had retreated to the privacy of her room, but he was going to do it anyway.

There was a rustle of movement inside the room that stilled when he knocked at the door. He could imagine her standing there in the thin tank top that he'd fantasized about, wishing he would go away, wondering if she could stay quiet enough to convince him that she'd fallen asleep with the light on. He knocked a second time and heard movement; then she pulled the door halfway open and faced him from behind it.

She was ready for bed, with her hair brushed back, her nose shiny with moisturizer, and the bedcovers turned down. She *was* wearing the tank top and, over it, a cotton robe that reached only to her knees. The robe probably gave her some measure of modesty, he thought with a mirthless smile. After all, it was as demure as any dress. But it was worn and thin and concealed only enough to remind him of what it was covering. As if he needed reminders.

When she continued to hide behind the door, he eased into the room, forcing her to give up its security and back away. "I need a favor. It's time to remove the stitches from my arm, but I can't manage with only one hand. I want you to do it for me."

Her gaze moved to his arm and the row of sutures there, long, red, dotted with small scabs and the black tails of stitches, fourteen in all. "Don't you think you should see a doctor?"

"I don't need a doctor. You can do it."

After a moment's hesitation, she agreed and took the tweezers and scissors from him. "All right. Sit down."

The only choices were the wooden chair in front of the makeup table or the bed. He chose the bed.

Standing in front of him, she took a deep breath, braced

the heel of her hand against his arm, and used the tweezers to grasp the top suture. She gave the slender black thread a slight tug, snipped it just above the skin, then drew it out the other side, leaving behind only the two small needle marks. He hadn't known whether to expect a small prick of pain, but all he felt was a curious pulling sensation that couldn't begin to compete with the feel of her hand on his arm or the heat radiating from her body or the smell of shampoo that scented her hair.

The next sutures came out just as easily. The fifth one, though, tugged at the scab that had crusted around it, making it bleed. So did the next one, and, in spite of her obvious efforts to be gentle, the next.

He was in a pathetic state, he thought, fixing his gaze on the French doors behind her, when he could savor such attention. It said something about how rarely he had allowed himself the pleasure of a woman's touch, about how needful he had become. And he sure as hell was needful. His entire body was starting to tingle, craving the attention she was giving his arm, wanting her fingers, soft and warm, to stroke there, to caress here, to curl around him there. If she took much longer with this, she was going to make him hard, which would make her uncomfortable.

He was damned sick of making her uncomfortable.

He would sacrifice his soul for another evening like the one they'd shared in New Orleans. For the pleasure of her smiles. For the arousal in her eyes. For the heated kisses, the desperate desire, the incredible tightness of her body gloving his. He would give up a few years of his life to stretch the evening into an entire night, to sleep beside her, to know that she was only inches away, to awaken when the sun came through the French doors and find her against him.

He would even consider giving up Simon Tremont if one evening could become a night, if one night could become a lifetime. He would give up damned near everything if he could have Teryl in return.

Teryl, who was still dealing with the turmoil he'd brought to her life. Who wouldn't thank him for the doubts he'd created. Who would never accept him without absolute proof.

Who wouldn't forgive him all that he'd done. Who had been perfectly happy before she knew he existed and wouldn't be that way again until he was once more out of her life.

Jesus, he wasn't asking for much, was he?

In front of him, she was leaning forward to reach the lower stitches. The movement directed his gaze downward as the ratty robe she wore gapped at the top, and the loose neck of the tank top fell open, too, giving him a tantalizing glimpse of the beginning swell of her breasts. The skin there, he knew, was creamy and soft. It smelled of powder and perfume and tasted of heat and desire. He had fondled her breasts on a French Quarter street, had suckled them in the backseat of a hired cab and in the cool, dim privacy of her hotel room. He could touch them again now—could raise his hand, slide it between the folds of old, well-worn fabric until he reached the contrast of satiny smooth breast and spiky, hard nipple. He could give her pleasure, if she would take it, and could feed his own hunger. He could ease her desire and satisfy his own craving—at least, for a while. Nothing could ever satisfy him permanently, nothing short of spending the rest of his life with her, and he knew that was impossible. She deserved much better than he could ever give her . . . and he deserved far worse.

"I have some antiseptic in the bathroom. Let me get it and clean that before you go." She straightened, backed away, and left the room before her words completely registered. She was almost finished. Another moment or two, a swab with a cotton ball, and she would be done. She would expect him to go to his own room and to leave her in peace.

He wasn't sure he could. Not when he wanted her as desperately as before. Not when he needed her in a way he had never needed anyone.

In only a moment, she returned, a small brown bottle in one hand, a thick pad of cotton squares in the other. She twisted the lid from the bottle, saturated the pad with the cool, clear liquid, then bent to dab it along the length of the laceration. Her hair fell forward to hide her face, casting shadows across his chest as it swayed with her movements, tantalizing him with its scent. He liked bathing after her at night, liked going into the bathroom when the air was steamy and redolent with her fragrances. He liked using the same shampoo himself, liked rubbing the same soap over his own body. He had never thought of showering as an erotic experience until his first time here, when he had walked into the hot, damp bathroom, smelled her scents, and felt his cock swelling.

Like now.

Sweet hell, he wanted to pull her closer, to bring her to him, to nuzzle the robe and that damned shirt aside and bury his face between her breasts. He wanted to seduce her with kisses and caresses across her breasts, down her spine, over her belly, between her thighs. He wanted to arouse and weaken her, to make her body crave his. He wanted to make her want him in spite of herself, wanted to prove to her and to himself that he held some power over her, some small measure of the power she held over him. He wanted to punish her . . . and please her . . . and pleasure her. Christ, he wanted the pleasure.

He shifted awkwardly, seeking a more comfortable position. Tight jeans weren't made for relentless erections. But immediately he regretted the movement because it made Teryl's gaze swing up to meet his. "Does it sting? I'm sorry. I didn't think . . ."

"No," he said, his voice too hoarse, too thick. "It doesn't sting."

"Then what . . . ?" Awareness slipped over her slowly. He could actually see her realization that their position was a little on the intimate side, that the entire damned situation was more than a little intimate. He could see her response: her eyes growing shadowy, her lips parting on a faint puff of breath, the flush that seemed to rise straight up from her breasts to spread its warmth up her throat and color her face, and the slight tremble in her hand.

Awareness. Acknowledgment. Arousal. God help him—God save him—she was aroused.

Slowly she straightened and laid the antiseptic and the pads on the night table before turning back to face him. Refusing to consider the right or wrong of what he was about to do, he raised his hand, gliding it along the front closure of her robe, hovering just above, not actually touching her until he reached her throat. Only his fingertips made contact there, rough calluses against powdery soft skin, before he withdrew his hand.

He was a fool. This was wrong. She deserved better. He didn't deserve anything at all. All the arguments raced through his head, demanding his attention, but every one of them disappeared the instant she clasped his hand in hers and guided it inside the robe to her breast. His fingers naturally curved to fit; his palm naturally moved against her erect nipple with just enough pressure to make her breath catch. Her head was tilted back, her eyes hazy, her expression exquisite.

All his life, he had failed at everything he'd ever tried. Surfing and writing Tremont novels—those were his two big accomplishments. His only talents. Those—and arousing Teryl.

Together those just might be enough for a lifetime's satisfaction.

Reluctantly giving up the caresses, he untied the knot in the cloth belt, working it loose, and let the robe fall open. The tank top she wore underneath was as shabby as the robe—thin, worn, stretched out of shape, never intended to adequately cover *her* shape. It dropped straight down from her shoulders, too soft to cling, too threadbare to conceal. Her breasts were clearly outlined, as were her nipples. Soft and hard, sweet and wicked. The damned shirt was the sexiest garment he'd ever seen.

When he laid his hands on her stomach underneath the top, a shudder rippled through her. He pushed the fabric up enough to reveal her panties—gray cotton with a broad elastic band, cut high on the thigh and low over the abdomen—and her belly, pale, flat, delicately contoured. One of his regrets from New Orleans was that he hadn't seen enough of her, that he hadn't turned on every light in that hotel room and conducted an intimate survey of every inch of her body. He didn't know what shade of brown the curls between her thighs were. He didn't know if her nipples were pink, rose, or brown, didn't know if a delicate web of veins was visible across her breasts, didn't know if she had any imperfections, any scars or freckles or birthmarks.

But he had learned other things. He knew the taste of her nipples, knew the feel of her breasts in his hands. He knew those curls between her thighs were soft, knew they had rubbed like silk along the length of him each time he'd entered her; he knew that right now they were damp and fragrant with the silky, starchy powder she used. He knew that his hands fitted so perfectly where her waist curved in, that her hips cradled him just right, that they fitted together as if they'd been made for each other, that she could take no more than he had to give. He knew that being buried inside her was exquisite pain and incomparable joy. He knew he'd never felt that way with any other woman in his life. He knew he would never feel that way with any other woman.

He knew he was damned. But at least he could have her again before he had to learn to live without her.

Sliding one hand underneath her panties, he glided his fingers through the curls until he reached the small, swollen flesh they protected. For a moment when he stroked her, he half believed the heat there sizzled, but the little rush of sound was a gasp instead, and it came from Teryl, suddenly gone weak and limp, her hands braced against his shoulders for support.

"Oh, jeez, John," she whispered.

His fingers trapped in the intimate caress, he stood up, wrapped his free arm around her, and took her mouth with his. She welcomed him, guiding his tongue into her mouth, sucking it so greedily that he felt it in his cock, swollen, throbbing, and desperate for her attention.

She was on the edge. He could feel it—could feel the little tremblings rocketing through her, could feel her body closing hard around his fingers, could taste the desperation in her kiss. She couldn't get any tighter, any hotter, any wetter. He knew she couldn't possibly endure one more second, one more stroke, one more caress.

"Tell me what you want, Teryl," he murmured just before his teeth closed on the lobe of her ear, tugging gently.

Her voice was thin and insubstantial. "I want you."

"You've got me. Now tell me what you want me to do."

"Please," she whispered, twisting so her mouth was against his, her voice hoarse, her words underlaid with torment. "Please, John . . . want you . . . inside . . ."

If there was a single reason why he shouldn't give her just that, he couldn't think of it. He hadn't done everything he wanted—hadn't touched her everywhere, kissed her all over, or satisfied his endless curiosity about her body. He hadn't laid her on the bed, hadn't settled between her legs, hadn't gotten a taste of her in the most intimate of kisses. Hell, he hadn't even seen her naked yet. But the night was long, and there was always tomorrow, and she was pleading, and he was feeling pretty damned desperate himself.

Clamping his mouth to hers in a hard kiss, he maneuvered her around so the bed was behind her, guided her down, and joined her there. Her breathing was coming faster, and the helpless little cries she was making deep in her throat cut through him as he struggled with his jeans and her panties. When he finally dispensed with their clothing, when he parted her thighs and pushed inside her, she was so close to coming that her body had gone tight, clinging to him, fighting his long, hard intrusion. Then at last he was inside her, deep enough to feel everything she felt, every quiver, every tremble, every heartbeat, and she was shuddering, her wordless cries raw and begging, as he thrust once, twice, three times, before erupting.

Through the haze of his orgasm, he was dimly aware that she was moving beneath him, rubbing against him, seeking her own orgasm, finding it not more than a breath later. It made her go rigid, her body as taut as his own, and made the muscles in her belly clench around his penis, sending exquisite little shivers up his spine and all the way down to his fingers and his toes, curled tightly against the intensity.

Relaxation came slowly. His breathing, noisy and harsh, slowed as his heart rate dropped, and the bands around his chest loosened, allowing his lungs to fill with air. Her breaths, soft little sobs, quieted, too, deepening, coming easier. His muscles clenched spasmodically, flexing, releasing, quivering. Hers were still tight, too, slowly letting the tension go, still racking her body with an occasional shudder. A sense of ease was seeping through him everywhere . . . except, he thought with a faint grin, where it counted. His cock was as stiff and swollen as if it hadn't just emptied into her, as if he hadn't just indulged in the most intense quickie of his life.

"What are you grinning about?"

He had closed his eyes when he'd filled her, had squeezed them shut tightly enough to see stars. Now he opened them to find her looking up at him, her gaze soft and dreamy. Her voice had sounded soft and dreamy, too. He wondered if she felt that way. She did to him as, shifting to lean on his elbows, he brushed his mouth across hers. As soft and comforting as the sweetest dream.

Ignoring her question, he kissed her once more and felt a twinge of need shoot through him—hers or his own, he didn't know or care. It wasn't urgent—not yet, at least, although he had no doubt it would get there. Even if he did nothing, if he simply lay here, still sheathed inside her body, the hunger would build. The desperation would return.

So would the satisfaction.

Bending, he nuzzled the underside of her jaw, up to her ear, down to the hollow at the base of her throat. He dried the sweat that dampened her face, then combed her hair back, burying his fingers in it, wrapping the fine strands like a web around his hands. "You're a beautiful woman."

"Uh-huh." Despite her skeptical tone, his compliment brought her pleasure. He could feel it in her body's response where they joined.

"You are beautiful, Teryl."

Unclasping her hands from around his back, she smiled just a little as she began rubbing his arms, gentle around the scar, gentle everywhere. "My hair is too fine, the color's too drab, my eyes are too brown, my mouth is too thin, my breasts are too small, and my waist is too thick."

She listed her perceived flaws in such an even voice, as if she were merely reciting obvious facts, that he couldn't help but tease her. "My folks always told me I was one stupid kid, and they must have been right, because here I've been thinking ever since we met that you were one of the prettiest and sexiest women I'd ever seen. Now I find out you're just plain homely. Jeez, thanks for telling me."

Suddenly shy, she blushed and dropped her gaze from his. Softening his voice, he asked, "Who says you have all these flaws?"

When she didn't answer, he realized who, but he didn't acknowledge it to her. He didn't want to bring D.J. into their bed . . . even though he'd been tempted to do just that this afternoon. He had been *so* tempted, and by much more than the sexual gratification she had offered. She could save Teryl from him. She could keep them apart for forever. Having an affair with D.J. would make him so unfit to be around Teryl that nothing in the world could ever persuade him otherwise.

Thank God he'd had the sense to send her away.

He opened his fists and let her hair fall free, then filled his hands again. "Your hair *is* fine," he agreed. "You know some of the synonyms for fine? Fragile, delicate, silky, gossamer, flawless, exquisite . . . Not a negative in the bunch. Your mouth is fine, too, perfectly fine for this . . . " He kissed her, gliding his tongue between her teeth, seeking out her own tongue. She responded exactly the way he would have written it if he could: with passion. Heat. Hunger. She had such hunger, and for tonight—maybe for a while—it was his. Sweet damnation.

When she was breathing hard, when he was barely breathing at all, he drew back, drew out of her all the way, even though she protested with her soft whimper, even though his body protested with every fiber in it. He settled on the bed beside her, one leg over hers, his bent knee resting near her heat, his erection hard and sticky against her thigh, and he turned his attention to her breasts. Maybe they were on the small side, but they could never be considered too small. They were delicately shaped, rounded and full, and heavy in his hands. Her nipples were rosy against her fair skin, caught right now somewhere between soft, flat, and unaroused and pebble hard and erect. All it took was one long stroke of his tongue across the nipple closest to him to make them both swell to a crest. All it took was a gentle bite, catching and holding it between his teeth while he laved it, to make her go taut. When he sucked it roughly into his mouth, she began moving helplessly, feverishly.

He heard her breathing turn ragged again, felt her fingers in his hair, her hand on the back of his head pulling him closer, urging him to suckle her harder, deeper, and he obliged, making her back arch, making her gasp. She returned the favor by sliding her hand lower, over his chest, flicking his own nipple, and lower still, across his belly and past his hip. When she wrapped her fingers around his penis, cool flesh against his own burning flesh, and slid them along the length, somehow it grew even stiffer. When she moved her hand even lower, gathering his balls into her palm, cradling them, he groaned aloud, a wordless, helpless, shameless entreaty.

It was the most erotic sound Teryl had ever heard. Power, he'd told her, was one of the biggest turn-ons around. Now she knew what he meant. She'd never imagined she could draw such a plea from a man as big and strong as John. She hadn't suspected that she could make him beg, but she thought she could . . . if she cared to try. She didn't.

Wriggling free of him, she evaded his reaching hands and rose to her knees on the bed, then pushed him onto his back. Like most women, she'd always had a healthy appreciation for the male form, but it had been a long time since she'd had an opportunity to express that appreciation in such a personal way. Maybe life in Colorado was just healthier— cleaner air, cleaner environment—or maybe it was those California genes, combined with all the years he'd spent drifting and working whatever jobs he could get, but he was certainly in better shape than any other man she'd been involved with. They had all been soft. John wasn't muscle-bound—although the muscles in his arms, chest, abdomen, and legs were clearly defined—but neither was he the slightest bit soft, not anywhere. Especially not where she was stroking him now, she thought with wicked delight.

"Come here," he commanded, reaching for her again.

"Not yet." She caught his hand, lifted it to her mouth for a kiss, then laid it on the mattress at his side. He immediately reached again.

"I won't take over. You can do whatever you want. I just want you on top of me. I want to be inside you."

"Then I can't do everything I want." But she relented this time, let him pull her over, lift her up. He steadied her while she guided him into place; then she slid down slowly, achingly slowly, to take every hard inch. She watched his face—watched the muscles in his jaw tighten as she took it all, watched the beads of sweat form across his forehead as she tentatively moved, shifting, her body readjusting to his, watched his mouth move in a silent curse as she moved again and he struggled to retain control. *Power.* She could learn to love it.

She could learn to love *him*.

Even if he *was* going to break her heart.

Leaning forward, she kissed his mouth, his throat, his nipples, her hips rocking back and forth, shifting side to side, not much, never enough to get either of them off, just enough to make them hotter, needier, greedier. She liked it on top, she decided, liked that the position made it so easy for her, that the natural, easy movement, up and down, in and out, stimulated her as thoroughly as it did him. She liked looking down at him, watching the emotions cross his face, seeing what she did to him. She especially liked seeing the effect she had on him and knowing that those same emotions and that same intense need were reflected on her own face.

At some point, what started out as fun turned into serious business. Sweet, lazy enjoyment gave way to sharp-edged desire, raw and dangerous. Lust grew into hunger that threatened to consume her. Her body was clenching, her rhythm faster and barely controlled, John's thrusts harder, deeper. Too aroused, too violently needy, she clung to him, pleaded with him to help, and he responded. Gripping her hips in his hands, he rolled over, never leaving her body, sliding her into place underneath him, and he took her hard and fast, pushing her over the edge, not stopping even then, not relenting. She lay there, fierce waves of pleasure battering her with such intensity that her eyes grew damp and breathing became impossible. Everything was greatly magnified—the heat they generated together, the friction where their bodies rubbed, the little shock waves where her nipples brushed his chest, the emptiness in her own chest, and the fullness, the incredible fullness, down lower as, with a savage groan and a curse, he came again, pumping into her, filling her.

Hell, yes, she could get used to this.

"Your parents were wrong."

John was lying on his back, Teryl's pillows under his head, her bedcovers tangled underneath him, and she was lying beside him, her head cradled on his chest, her leg over and between his, her fingers moving lightly over his skin. If he moved enough to see the clock on the night table, he would find out that it was the middle of the night, long past the time she should have been asleep, considering that she had to get up and go to work in the morning. He didn't bother to move, though. He was perfectly comfortable right where he was. "About what?" he finally asked, although he knew exactly what she was referring to.

"You're *not* stupid."

He liked the defensive, annoyed, derisive tone of her voice. Wouldn't it surprise his parents to hear someone they would probably like, someone who would probably remind them enough of Janie—sweet, friendly, warm, caring, innocent—to make them relate favorably to her, take that attitude regarding *him*. "I know I'm not." For example, in the last few minutes, the absentminded, lazy caresses she had been spreading across his ribs and stomach had now moved down to his crotch—to his penis, soft and spent from their lovemaking, but more than happy to receive her petting—but no way was he stupid enough to point that out to her. No way was he stupid enough to do anything that might make her stop.

"Any fool can tell that you're very bright."

"In all fairness, I did have a lot of trouble in school."

Resting her chin on his chest, she gazed up at him. "Why?"

"I don't know. Maybe, in the beginning, I just wasn't interested in what they were teaching. Once you get a reputation for being dumb, a lot of teachers don't try very hard. Your teachers probably always expected As from you, and you delivered. My teachers didn't think I was capable of anything better than Cs or Ds, so that's what they gave me."

"Maybe your parents had told you you were stupid so often that you believed it. Maybe *you* didn't think you were capable of earning better grades, so you never did."

He smiled faintly. "Oh, I believed them, all right. I felt like some sort of aberration. Here was Tom, who was absolutely brilliant, and Janie, who was pretty damned close to brilliant, and in the middle was John the idiot child. If we hadn't all looked so damned much alike, they would have sworn I couldn't possibly be their son."

"Maybe it would have been better for you if they had," she said, striving for but having difficulty reaching a lighter note. "Then someone else could have taken you in, someone like *my* parents, who think *everyone's* children are *their* children." She fell silent for a moment, then moved so she could see his face better. Immediately he missed her soft little caresses, but he found just as much pleasure gazing into her soft brown eyes. "Could you ever forgive them?"

"I doubt it."

"But how do you get over it if you can't forgive it?"

"I can accept it. I can accept that they had problems far more serious than a not-too-bright kid who wasn't much good at anything he did. What kind of parents can't love their son because he doesn't like football or can't catch a baseball or doesn't do well in school?" He reached for her hand, needing the contact, focusing on her long, slender fingers. "Whatever failings *I* had were forgivable because I was just a kid. But they were adults. They knew better. They were supposed to protect me, and instead they made my life miserable. As for forgiveness . . . that's not something I can just do. They have to ask for it—they have to earn it—and that's never going to happen. As far as they're concerned, I died with Tom. I no longer exist for them."

"You don't know that. If you haven't seen them in seventeen years—"

"My sister keeps in touch with them," he gently interrupted her, "and she keeps in touch with me. If they ever asked about me, if they ever acknowledged me in any way, Janie would let me know."

She became silent again, her expression troubled; then, once more, she changed positions, sitting up this time, pulling on her tank top, facing him from the side of the bed. "*Can* you accept it?" she asked. "Can you understand that everything they did was wrong? That the way they treated you was wrong? That the things they said to you weren't true?"

He sat up, too, slid the pillows behind his back, pulled the sheet free of the covers, and tugged it to his waist. "Some things are easier to accept than others," he admitted. "I know I'm not stupid or clumsy or irresponsible. I don't ruin everything I do. I'm not lazy or worthless or careless or an idiot." There were tangible ways of proving or disproving those insults. The simple fact that he'd become the best-selling author in the country disproved most of them. You didn't write critically acclaimed books if you were stupid. You didn't build a sizable fortune if you were irresponsible. You didn't spend long, hard hours working if you were lazy. You weren't worth millions if you were worthless.

"And the others?"

Ah, yes, the others. Those were tougher. How did you prove you were worthy of being loved? After being told that you were unlovable for nineteen years, after being told that the people who had given you life wished you had never been born—that they prayed for your death—how could you believe that you deserved to be loved? There was no way to prove it. There was nothing to point to the way he could point to his books and say, "I wrote these; obviously, I'm not an idiot." There was nothing that gave him reason to believe he had a right to love someone and be loved in return, nothing that said the man he'd become was any more deserving of love than the boy he'd once been.

And there were two very good reasons to believe he

wasn't. He had loved only two people in his life, the only two people who had ever loved him, and they had both suffered for it. How could he ever risk making Teryl suffer?

"John?"

Feeling an all-too-familiar ache—loneliness, the kind that ate at a man from the inside out, the kind that he had come to know intimately in the last half of his life—he forced a smile to his lips and his attention to her. "Do you know that ever since I had to leave your bed in New Orleans, I've been having fantasies about you, some of them inspired by this shirt?"

For a moment, there was a silent protest in her eyes, disappointment that he wasn't going to answer her question, that he wasn't going to confide in her anymore. Then she forced a smile, too. "What kind of fantasies?"

"Sexual ones, of course. Are there any other kind?" he teased. But, of course, there were. There was what could very easily become his most favorite fantasy ever—the happily-ever-after one—and its variations. The claiming-Teryl-and-spending-the-rest-of-his-life-at-her-side fantasy. The perfectly-normal-husband-wife-a-dozen-kids-and-a-dog fantasy.

"Tell me about them."

He tugged the neckline of her shirt down until he could reach inside and lift her breast free. He fondled her nipple, making it hard, making her soft, making himself stiff. "I'd rather show you. We start with this." Leaning forward, he drew her nipple into his mouth, flicking his tongue across it, biting it gently, sucking it hard.

"And then?" Already she was breathless.

"Then you do this." He pushed the sheet away and brought her hand to his groin, pressing it to him, and immediately her fingers curved around him. Already, with no more than a kiss and a caress, he was erect. With her sweet touch, he grew longer, harder.

"And then?"

"Then, when we're ready—"

"How long does that take?"

"I don't know. An hour or so."

She gave him a hazy, chastising look. "You couldn't survive an hour of this," she taunted, insinuating her hand between his thighs with a firm, unrelenting pressure and making his hips arch to meet it.

"It's my fantasy, honey," he reminded her.

"You feel ready to me, and I don't have an hour to spare. One of us has to go to work in a few hours, so the other one is going to go to work now. So what's next?"

"Next I take your shirt off . . . " He did that, pulling it up slowly, occasionally stopping to press a kiss to her stomach or to nuzzle her breast. When he pulled it over her head, it tousled her hair, and he used his fingers to stroke it back into sleek order. "Now you come to the middle of the bed . . . facing that way . . . on your knees . . . "

She did as he directed but turned to look at him over her shoulder. Her expression was shadowed with wariness and, underneath it, trust. "Is this going to hurt?"

Cupping his hands to her face, he kissed her gently. "I swear on my life, Teryl, I'll never hurt you—*never*. But if you're uncomfortable with this, just say so. You don't have to do anything you don't want to."

In mute acceptance, she turned around and let him move her into position—her bottom snug against his hips, her thighs apart, her hips tilted back, her spine curving down to where her upper body rested on the mattress. He had spoken of fantasies only to distract her, but he *had* fantasized about making love to her like this in New Orleans. He had wanted her badly enough to feel weak, but guilt and shame had made him walk away. Tonight, right at this moment, he had nothing to feel guilty about, nothing to be ashamed of. Tonight he wasn't lying to her, using her, or betraying her. Tonight she knew everything. She knew his life was filled with questions without answers, and she wanted him anyway. He wondered if she fully understood how important that was to him.

Entering her from behind was easy. She was hot and wet, and he was hot and hard, and they fitted together snug and tight. Bracing his hands on her back, his fingers splayed from spine to hip, he began stroking her, long, slow, easy. It was different from being face-to-face, from having her legs locked around his hips, from feeling her breasts against his chest. He couldn't see her face, turned to one side, her hair tumbling over it, but he could hear her breathing, uneven, rapid, punctuated with soft groans. He could feel the tension in her muscles, could feel it double, triple, when he reached underneath, through the moist curls, to rub her. He could feel it intimately when she came, those incredibly tight, clamping sensations hurrying his own orgasm. It wasn't as shattering as the others had been, but it was powerful nonetheless. It made him tremble. It left him weak.

He held her, supported her, until the tremors passed, until he'd started to soften and slip free of her. Then he rolled her over, turned off the lamp, and settled her beside him. She snuggled close with a long, satisfied sigh, pressed a kiss to his chest, murmured good night, and, within minutes, was asleep. He held her, stroked her—just flat-out *savored* her— and, unwillingly, let his thoughts return to one of those unanswerable questions he'd been trying to avoid earlier.

How *did* a man prove to himself that he deserved to love and be loved?

Before his foot touched the bottom step on his way to the kitchen, Simon knew that someone had been—or was still— in his house. There was no obvious sign—the television wasn't on, he didn't hear a voice using the phone, the front door hadn't been kicked open, there wasn't a stranger standing in his hallway or comfortable in his living room. In fact, it took him a moment or two to realize just what had alerted him: the light. The hallway that should be dark wasn't because one of the doors was open and light was spilling into the hall from the lamps inside.

The door that was open led into his office. Someone was in his office.

He moved from the last step to the floor, then slowly started in that direction. Without resorting to demolition, there were only two ways to open that door when it was locked—and it was *always* locked: by undoing the lock from the inside or with a key from the outside. Considering that he had the only key in his pocket and that splintering a solid wood door would make enough noise to raise the soundest of sleepers, which he wasn't, how did the intruder get in?

Warily, his muscles tense, his hands hanging unfortunately empty of weapons at his sides, he stepped into the open doorway and immediately saw the answer to his question. A pane from the double-wide windows lay in jagged pieces across the padded seat and the floor below. The resulting hole wasn't particularly big, but enough for someone to slide his hand through and twist the lock. The black leather jacket tossed across the bench had probably been used to protect the intruder's hand from cuts and had, as a secondary benefit, helped muffle the sound.

Shit. He should have had a security system put in the day he'd gotten that royalty check, instead of tucking virtually all of the money away in the bank where, if he couldn't literally take it out and play with it, at least figuratively, by way of his bank statements, he could.

He came farther into the room, a board creaking under his weight, and the high-backed chair that faced his computer slowly moved. He'd stiffened and damned near panicked before it completed its slow spin and he recognized the person seated in it. Anger—no, rage, swift and intense, replaced the panic. He approached slowly, his gaze steely, his hands clenching into fists, then relaxing before clenching again. "What the hell are you doing here?"

"I've been trying to call for hours. I left a dozen messages before you took the phone off the hook. Why didn't you answer?"

He hated petulance, hated grown people pouting because they didn't get what they wanted. He'd learned very well that you didn't wait around for anyone to give you anything; you saw something you wanted, and you took it. If you didn't have the balls to do that, then piss and whine all you wanted—but not to him. Not in his house. Goddamn it, not in his office.

"I told you not to come out here. I told you I'm working."

"Working? On your next great Simon Tremont novel? And where'd you get the idea for this one?"

He hated sarcasm, too, especially in reference to his work. For a short, frightening time, he had begun to wonder if he'd burned himself out, if there were no more books inside, but he'd discovered with a great sense of relief that he still had stories to tell. In a roundabout way, he had sweet Teryl to thank for this one. Tiring of debating with himself over whether she was simply trashy or there were extenuating circumstances that made her recent behavior forgivable, he'd begun writing instead. His character—no heroine, Eliza, but a villain and, ultimately, a victim—was a sweet, pretty, damned near virginal young woman who projected innocence and unattainability to the one man who loved her while doing the nasty deed with almost every other man around. Love would turn to frustration, frustration to impotence, and impotence to rage, and soon the man who had wanted only to possess her—only to treasure her—would destroy her . . . but not before terrorizing her. Not before punishing her. Not before making her suffer.

In the end, maybe he would suffer, too. Maybe, in killing her, he would be killing himself. Maybe her death would release him to live a normal life, free of her evil and poison. Maybe he would discover a taste for the suffering and the killing, or maybe it would drive him insane. Simon didn't know. At this point, he didn't care.

All he cared about was that he was writing again and it was good. It was damned good. For pure reading satisfaction, the life and death of Eliza Byrd just might surpass the redemption and rebirth of Colin Summers in *Resurrection*. It just might be his absolute best work ever.

He stopped at the desk and directed his coldest, cruelest stare at the woman on the other side. "My next book is none of your business."

"Maybe not . . . but the last one was. Without me, you never could have written *Resurrection*. Without me, you may never get the chance to write another Tremont book." Her smug smile was an invitation to ask why. He knew the game; she had forced him to play it before. He would have to pry the information out of her bit by bit, and the whole time she would be so self-satisfied that the only thing he would *really* want to do is beat it out of her. The mere thought of slapping that smile away brought some measure of tolerance to him.

"Why do you say that?"

"If you'd answered the phone all those countless times I called, you would already know."

He had listened to the messages as the machine recorded them, but he'd had no desire to talk to her. She'd been excited, so excited that a time or two, she had slipped and called him by his old name. Stupid bitch. She'd known for months that he intended to fully, totally, legally become Simon Tremont, but she still forgot the name at times. She was worthless . . . although she had her moments. It was only because of those moments that he still put up with her. If not for them, he would have gotten rid of her long ago.

And he'd made sure she understood that.

With exaggerated patience, he sat down in front of the desk. "What was so important that you filled up the entire message tape on my machine?"

She smiled that damn sick smile again. "You've got problems, my friend."

"Uh-huh." And the biggest one was sitting across from him now. "What kind of problems?"

"This kind." She leaned forward, and for the first time he noticed the picture frame she was holding. She straightened the easel and set the silver and brass frame in the center of the desk, the photograph facing him. He didn't reach out to take it, didn't show any particular interest in it.

Instead, he waited, and she waited, still smiling, still smug. She outwaited him. "All right, I give in. What's so special about the picture?"

"Him." One long, red fingernail tapped the top of the frame above the figure on the left. Simon's gaze shifted to the fading image of the smiling young man. She was wrong. He wasn't a problem. He couldn't be a problem to anyone because he was dead.

Then Debra Jane Howell picked up the frame and glanced at the picture for a moment before tossing it down again. It slid across the desk, teetering on the edge in front of him before stopping. "Simon Tremont," she said in her most maliciously pleasant voice, "meet Teryl's mystery lover. Meet John Smith."

Chapter Fourteen

❖

*O*ut of the frying pan and into the fire, the old saying went, and that was exactly how Teryl felt Tuesday as she left the deli for the two-block walk back to the office. The air conditioner in the restaurant had valiantly done its best to combat the ninety-degree temperatures and the high humidity, but it had lost the battle. It had been uncomfortably warm inside, but, she admitted, it was miserably hot out. She could think of much better places to spend muggy days like this—and much better things to do. Like sipping iced tea beside a courtyard fountain in New Orleans. Or climbing to the top of a mountain in Colorado. Or lying naked with John in a cool, dark room right here in Richmond.

She hadn't spoken to him today, not since he had so expertly demonstrated his fantasy to her in the wee hours of the morning. She had fallen asleep in his arms, and he had been asleep next to her when her alarm had gone off. After shutting it off, she had crawled out from beneath the weight of his arm over her ribs and gotten ready for work without disturbing him. She had thought he might call her when he awoke, and when he didn't, she'd picked up the phone a half dozen times to call him, but always she'd returned it to the cradle without dialing a single digit. What if she woke him or interrupted him at his writing? Besides, what would she say to him? That even though last night had been the best night in her entire life, she'd found herself having a few small regrets this morning? That she wasn't sure they should let it happen again, because, well, gee, there was still the very slight chance that he was crazier than hell, and becoming lovers with a crazy man didn't seem a wise course of action? That she damned well wanted it to happen again and again, because, while he *might* be crazy, she was too damned close to being in love, and she wanted whatever she could get before he left her, which he seemed determined to do, or got locked up in some mental hospital?

The wisest course of action, she'd decided, was to take her cues from him when she saw him again. If he acted differently toward her—warmer, friendlier, more intimate—then she would act the same. Hell, she thought with a grin, the first time she got him alone, she would strip him naked and do it all over again. She would make up for all the long, celibate times when there had been no man in her life and for all the boring times when sex had been a late-night, in-the-dark, grope-and-fumble that was hardly worth breaking a sweat.

And if he acted as if nothing had changed between them?

Turning onto the block where Rebecca's Victorian was located, she pushed that thought out of her mind. She wasn't going looking for heartache. It would find her soon enough. When John got the paperwork he was waiting for. When he left Richmond for New York City. When he gave up the idea of trying to convince Rebecca of who he was and set his sights on Morgan-Wilkes instead. When he left *her* behind.

He hadn't set any deadlines, but she knew it was going to happen soon. If he couldn't convince Rebecca with the sheriff's report and the banker's affidavit in hand, he would leave. The affidavit was due to arrive tomorrow, the sheriff's report sometime soon after. She had a few days, she figured, maybe a week at most. Then he would leave her. He would take care of his business, prove his identity, and reclaim his career, and then he would buy his damned island and go back to the solitude he craved.

Then she wouldn't have to go looking for heartache. By then it would have taken up permanent residence with her.

Scowling hard, she kicked a stone across the uneven sidewalk, her gaze following it to where it stopped near a pair of scuffed leather tennis shoes. Slowly she looked up, over faded jeans and a white cotton shirt, over long legs, a flat stomach, and broad shoulders that were made for leaning on. By the time her gaze reached John's face, her scowl had almost disappeared; a smile had almost taken its place.

He was leaning against his truck, parked in one of the two curbside spaces in front of the agency. Had he come to see her or Rebecca? she wondered, then decided that she didn't care. He had come. That was all that mattered.

Her steps slowed until she came to a stop about five feet in front of him. Exactly a week ago she had behaved shamelessly and wantonly with him on a French Quarter street, and only last night they had made love until neither of them could have endured more, and yet neither time had she felt even a fraction of the shyness that came over her now. She could barely bring herself to meet his eyes, and she could think of nothing to say, nothing to do . . . besides flinging herself into his arms, kissing him, and pleading for another night like those two nights.

Finally, pushing her hands deep into the pockets of her dress, she spoke. "I don't believe Rebecca's back from lunch yet."

"I'm not here to see Rebecca."

She smiled just a little. "Good. Have you been waiting long?"

He shook his head. "I had just parked when you came around the corner."

"If you had come forty-five minutes earlier, I would have let you take me to lunch."

"Honey, if I had come forty-five minutes earlier, I would have taken you to bed." He moved away from the fender then, going to the passenger door and opening it. "I know it's almost time for you to get back to work, so I won't keep you. I just wanted to bring you something."

Teryl watched as he hesitated, then reached inside. What he came out with sent a little shiver of anticipation down her spine. The little yellow pad was in pretty shabby shape, wrinkled and crinkled from all his handling. He needed to pick up a computer, she thought, one of those little notebook PCs that weighed next to nothing and were capable of just about anything. One that would fit in a briefcase . . . or a suitcase. One he could use at her house . . . or in a hotel . . . or on some remote deserted island.

Holding on to the binding of the pad, he offered it to her, but didn't immediately let go. "Read this, will you? I'm not asking you to show it to Rebecca or anything. Just read it and let me know . . . " Breaking off, he stared at the house next door before finally looking at her again. "With my first book, I thought there was something there—an interesting story, a decent style, something readable—but I couldn't honestly say without doubt that it was *good*. Eventually, I learned. I knew whether what I wrote was worth keeping or just garbage. On the rare occasions when it was outstanding, I knew that, too. Then I started working on *Resurrection*, and I developed this mental block, and . . . " Again, he broke off, sighing this time. "I think this isn't bad. I can't say whether it's good, but it *feels* good. Anyway, just read it and let me know if my instincts are getting back on track or if it really is garbage, will you?"

Her fingers closed around the bottom of the pages. "I don't know that my opinion is worth anything, but . . . "

"This one's for you. Your opinion is the only one that counts."

His smile was uneasy, more than a little embarrassed, and it gentled her own smile. "Do you want me to read it right now?"

"No. Take it to your office."

She pulled the pad from his fingers, but resisted the urge to flip it open right there, to start reading right then. He started to turn away then, but she called him back. "John?"

He gave her a questioning look.

"I have fifteen minutes of my lunch hour left. Want to find a private spot and help me pass the time?" She was teasing, of course, and he knew it. Still, it coaxed a grin from him, and it brought him a few steps closer.

"A request for privacy from the woman who seduced me

on a public street and damned near finished the job in a taxi-cab? Isn't it a little late to develop a sense of modesty?"

"I've always been modest." When he reached for her wrists, she let him take them, let him pull her near. "Besides, you have it backward. *You* seduced *me*."

He raised his hand to her hair, barely touching it, lightly stroking it. "No. You seduced me with your voice and your eyes and your smile. With your innocence and your trust and your openness." Bending his head, he touched his mouth to hers. It wasn't a kiss, not really, just a brush, sweet and gentle, mouth to mouth. It was as innocent as a child's kiss, but it carried a man's promise. It made her ache.

"You'd better go in now," he said, withdrawing, circling around the Blazer to the driver's door. "Be careful coming home. I'll be waiting."

Hugging the pad to her chest with both arms, she watched him drive away, waiting until he was no longer in sight before she turned and started up the walk to the porch. In her office, she closed the door, got comfortable at her desk, and flipped past the top two blank pages to the beginning of John's work. John's story. *Her* story, he'd said.

Half an hour later, she still sat in exactly the same position, one thought circling repeatedly through her head: she had been wrong. Terribly, horribly wrong.

Her chest felt tight, her throat clogged, and her eyes were damp, but not because the pages she'd just read were so touching. There were some bittersweet passages and one particularly effective scene, but that wasn't the reason for her own emotional excess. John was.

I'm sorry, John. Sorry I didn't believe you, sorry I didn't have faith in you, sorry I didn't trust you.

She knew so few things for certain in her life, but she had no reservations whatsoever about this: the man who wrote these pages had also written every single one of the Thibodeaux books. Whatever small uncertainty had survived the last twenty-four hours had vanished in the last thirty minutes. There was no doubt in her mind. None in her heart.

John hadn't lied. He wasn't crazy. He wasn't suffering delusions.

He *was* Simon Tremont.

Sweet Jesus, *he* was the man she had admired, had worshiped and respected and idolized, all these many years. *He* was the one who had written those incredibly touching, real, and very scary books that held the place of honor on her shelves at home. *He* was the man she'd been dying to meet. *He* wasn't the crazy man, the impostor, the fraud. *He* was the stranger who had fulfilled her wicked fantasy in New Orleans.

God help her, *he* was the man she'd fallen in love with.

A knock sounded at her door, but she didn't call out an invitation. She wasn't ready to be disturbed yet. She wanted to simply sit here, absorb what she'd read, what she'd discovered, and think. Feel. Understand. Regret.

But the knock at her door was Rebecca, who wasn't turned away by something so minor as a closed door. After a second series of raps, she opened the door and invited herself inside, taking a seat on the padded bench. "Preoccupied?" she asked, adjusting a pillow behind her back.

"Hmm."

"With business?"

Teryl gripped the pad a little tighter. "As a matter of fact, yes."

"Want to discuss it?"

She hesitated. John had asked only for her opinion. He hadn't given her permission to show the pages to someone else. Still, how could he object to Rebecca seeing it? From the very beginning, she'd been the first person to ever see his work. She was his agent, even if she didn't realize it at the moment. She'd handled all of his books and there was a good chance she would sell this one, too . . . once she was convinced that he had the right to write about these characters. If he could be convinced to stay with her.

After a moment, she flipped the blank pages over, then offered the pad to her boss. "Read this first."

It took Rebecca four pages, maybe five, to recognize the female character, who bore no name in those first pages. Teryl suspected that John had simply intended to write about some anonymous character, a woman who, after a lifetime of normalcy, regained consciousness following an accident to find herself blessed—or cursed—with the gift of a healing touch. He had realized only later that the woman wasn't anonymous at all; she was Liane Thibodeaux.

Teryl had recognized her within two paragraphs, but then, she'd always been partial to Liane. Her first night in New Orleans, when she'd gone to the French Quarter to wander about alone, she'd been unable to shake the feeling that if she could only find the right street, turn the right corner, or walk into the right shop, she would find Liane there, painting her portraits or talking with her brothers or simply roaming the city where she'd been born. She was that real to Teryl.

When Rebecca did realize what she was reading, the muscles in her jaw tightened and a frown wrinkled her forehead. Teryl had to give her credit for not stopping right then and pointing out that this character was the property of Simon Tremont, that whoever had written this had no right to appropriate her for his own purposes. That would come, Teryl was sure, but Rebecca continued reading.

When she finished, she closed the pad but didn't return it. "I'm impressed." After a moment, she hesitantly asked, "You didn't write . . . ?"

Teryl shook her head.

"May I ask who did?"

"The man I met in New Orleans." Teryl laced her fingers together to hide her uneasiness. "I misled you yesterday when I said I *might* see him again. The truth is he's here in Richmond. He came back from New Orleans with me, and he's been staying at my house. He wrote that this week."

There was another long moment of silence. "He's very good. Obviously he's a big fan of Simon Tremont. The style is very similar."

It was much more than similar, Teryl thought. It was identical.

Then came the warning. "But you know he can't use these characters. They say that imitation is the sincerest form of flattery, but this sort of copying comes much closer to infringement. He can't simply take Simon's characters from the earlier books and use them."

Teryl didn't respond to that.

"Has he been published before?"

"Yes. Twelve books. But not under his own name."

Still more silence. No doubt Rebecca was remembering their conversation from yesterday. Wouldn't it be interesting, Teryl had asked, if the John Smith who came into the office, the one who did the interview in New Orleans, wasn't the same John Smith who created Simon Tremont? No doubt she was wanting to ask, And what is his own name? No doubt she was reluctant to hear the answer.

"Is he looking for representation? Is that why you have this?" She didn't give Teryl a chance to reply. "Naturally, I'd want to read more of his work. I would want to see that he can sustain the quality for the length of an entire book, but I would be willing to talk to him, if that's what you want."

"That's not what this is about, Rebecca. He already has an agent." Drawing a deep breath, she launched into her explanation. "I met John in New Orleans. He had driven down from Colorado for the Tremont interview. He told me a very interesting story about how someone had found out all the details of his life, how this person had assumed his identity, taken over his career, moved into his life. I thought it was crazy. I thought *he* was crazy. But I was wrong. He's not crazy, and he's not lying. He *is* Simon Tremont."

"Which makes our Simon Tremont an impostor. A fraud." Rebecca smiled broadly and, laying the pad aside, started to rise from the bench. "Nice joke, Teryl. Funny. Now, we have real work to attend to, so—"

"It's not a joke, Rebecca. Listen to me, please." She waited until her boss sank down again. "I admit it sounds outrageous. I didn't believe it myself in the beginning. But, Rebecca, John knows *everything* about Tremont. He knows the terms and figures from every contract Tremont's signed. He knows the details of your association with Tremont. He knows the names of the assistants who worked for you before me. He's seen all the correspondence between this office and Tremont. He knows all the negotiations on Tremont's behalf between this office and Morgan-Wilkes. Rebecca, he knows things about Tremont's career that *I* didn't know."

Rebecca was staring at her, dismay darkening her face. "You brought him here, didn't you? You opened the records to him. You let a stranger—a crazy, insane stranger who was making outrageous claims—have access to Simon Tremont's files. Teryl, how could you? How could you jeopardize us like that? You know those records are confidential! You know you have no right showing any part of them to anyone!" Rising to her feet, she paced to the bookshelves, found herself face-to-face with a whole shelf of Tremont titles, then turned to Teryl again. "Damn it, do you know what you've done? If Simon finds out about this—the *real* Simon—he'll probably leave the agency and be perfectly justified in doing so! You might have cost us our biggest client!"

"He's *not* the real Simon," Teryl said defensively. "He's an impostor."

"Well, that 'impostor' wrote the single best book I've ever read in my life! Explain that, Teryl."

Resurrection. Everything kept coming back to that damned book. Teryl stood up and slipped her shoes on, just so she wouldn't feel at such a physical disadvantage, then folded her arms across her chest. "I can't explain it. Simon— the impostor Simon—somehow got hold of John's outline. He somehow learned to write like John."

Rebecca's response was sharp with anger and sarcasm. "Oh, I see. He *somehow* got hold of an outline that fewer than a half dozen people had ever seen, and he *somehow* learned to write like one of the best authors in the world, and he *somehow* managed to write the book that even that best author couldn't finish." She paused to let those words sink in, then shook her head in dismay. "Teryl, I'm disappointed in you. I thought you were smarter than this. I thought you were more professional than this. I cannot believe you are so enamored of this man that you would help him try to defraud my agency."

"It has nothing to do with my feelings for him," she protested. "When I agreed to help him, I wasn't trying to prove that he *is* Simon. I thought I could prove that he wasn't . . . but I couldn't. He knew too much. He knew everything."

"If he's Simon Tremont, then he can prove it. He can bring in his copies of all the contracts Simon has signed over the years. He can show me his royalty statements, his correspondence, his fan mail, all the records he's collected in the last eleven years." Rebecca waited a moment, then went on. "He can't do that, can he? He can't show me his contracts or anything else because he doesn't have them. Because he's not Simon."

"His house burned down over a week ago. Everything was destroyed."

"How convenient," Rebecca said snidely.

"The fire was caused by bombs. About the time your Simon decided to go public, someone blew up John's house in Colorado while he was inside. Someone tried to kill him." The look her boss was giving her made Teryl want to squirm. She rushed on before the other woman could say anything. "I spoke to the sheriff there, Rebecca. He has no doubt that the intent was murder and that John was the intended victim."

"And does he also believe that *my* Simon Tremont was responsible? Does he believe that your John is the *real* Tremont?"

Teryl looked away, unwilling to answer.

"So what does the sheriff actually know? That someone blew up a house. Unless he has witnesses, who's to say that John was inside at the time? Who's to say that the intent was murder? Maybe John's intent was that it look like attempted murder."

"He was *injured*. His arm was lacerated."

"Ah, but he wasn't killed. He was inside a house that was ripped apart by bombs, and yet he survived with only a minor injury. He must be an extremely lucky man."

"He has other proof," Teryl said, stubbornly continuing. "All those checks you sent John Smith in the last eleven years went into *his* bank accounts. They were all sent to *him*. They were all signed by *him*. If he's not the real Simon Tremont, how did he get the money? How did the checks wind up going to him and not to your Simon?"

"You've seen this proof?"

"No," she admitted reluctantly. "He doesn't have it yet. The bank is sending him a statement, an affidavit. He should have it tomorrow."

Rebecca's smile was chilly. "Unless, of course, it gets lost in the mail. And, unfortunately, for some reason, the bank won't be able to duplicate it. Who knows? Maybe the branch where his records are kept will be blown up by bombs." Her manner turned scornful. "You have no reason to believe that such proof even exists."

She was wrong, Teryl thought. She had *every* reason to believe.

Returning to her desk, she sat down, then tried another tack. "The only events in Simon's career that John is unaware of are the things that have happened in the last four months. Do you realize what's significant about that? It was four months ago that the Simon we know sent us a change of address. Four months ago that he moved to the Richmond area. Four months ago that he gave us a phone number and began conducting business for the very first time in his career the way people normally do."

Teryl broke off to take a few deep breaths, to calm herself before going on. "John is more familiar with the first eleven years of Simon Tremont's career than you and I are, but he knows nothing about the last four months—not about the correspondence, the phone calls, the visit to the office. After eleven years of abiding by his own very strict rule that the only contact he would have with us or Morgan-Wilkes was by mail, that he would do no promotion, no interviews, that he wouldn't sign even one autograph, within the last four months, your Simon suddenly decided that he wanted to meet us. He wanted to talk to us. He wanted to do interviews and book signings and meet fans. He wanted to give up the privacy that he treasured so very much and live in the public eye. He wanted to bask in the adulation."

"So he's tired of privacy," Rebecca said stiffly. "He watches TV. He reads. He sees other big-name authors being treated like stars, and he wants a little of that for himself. There's nothing wrong with that."

"You've corresponded with John for eleven years. When

you met Simon, was he what you expected? After spending thirty minutes with him, did you find yourself wondering how in the hell *that* man could have written *these* books?"

Her boss looked away and refused to answer, but Teryl didn't need an answer. Just yesterday, Rebecca had described Simon as a pompous, egotistical ass who was nauseatingly full of himself. No one, *no one*, who had read and enjoyed Simon Tremont's work ever could have imagined describing him that way. No one could have dreamed that he would be anything less than wonderful.

Turning to her desk, Teryl found a piece of paper and offered it to her boss. "John wrote this right here in this office Sunday. Take it to the file room and compare it to the signatures on the contracts."

"I suppose you've already compared it while you were letting him go through the files."

"I did compare it. It's identical. And I didn't let him go through anything. I asked him questions and he answered them. He never saw any of the papers."

Rebecca accepted the slip of paper and glanced down at the two signatures, but she didn't really look. Because she didn't want to see, Teryl knew. She didn't want to recognize the signature. "This is crazy, Teryl."

"I know."

"You expect me to believe that some unknown writer out there can teach himself to write like Simon Tremont. Do you know how much talent that would take? How much discipline and dedication? How much obsession?"

Teryl nodded.

"If this man is *that* talented, why does he need to become Tremont? Why not publish under his own name? Why not earn his own recognition, his own fame and fortune?"

"You just said it would take obsession. Certain types of people do tend to get obsessed with the stars, with the legends. Sometimes they stalk them. Sometimes they kill them. Sometimes they want to *be* them. I think this man started out as a fan. I think he admired Tremont's work, and then he became obsessed. I think he wanted to write like Tremont, to be like Tremont. Now he's *become* Tremont."

Rebecca glanced at the signature again. "I don't believe our Simon is obsessed with anything but himself. I don't believe he's crazy. Unlikable, yes. A disappointment, absolutely. Self-centered, narcissistic, and egomaniacal, undeniably. But not crazy. Not insane. And not a fraud." With a cool, controlled smile, she folded the paper in half. "It's an interesting proposal, Teryl, but that's all it is. It has no basis in fact. You have no proof, and your John has no proof because there is none. *He's* the one who's become obsessed with his favorite author. *He's* the one wanting to become Simon Tremont, and he's seduced you into helping him. Watch out for him, Teryl. He could be a dangerous man, and I'd hate to see you get hurt."

With that, she walked out of the office and closed the door.

Rebecca forced herself to walk slowly down the hall. At least this conversation explained why Teryl had destroyed the autograph in *Masters of Ceremony*. She believed that the man they knew as Simon wasn't, and she was offended by the idea of owning a forgery signed by a man impersonating her idol. The girl was a fool.

As she turned the corner at the end of the hall, she unfolded the paper she carried and looked—really looked this time—at the signature. She would compare it to the contracts, just for her own peace of mind, but she didn't need to. She'd seen it often enough over the years. She recognized it. But it didn't prove anything. Forgeries weren't uncommon. Learning to copy someone's signature was far, far easier than learning to copy someone's writing style. As for learning to copy someone's talent . . . that was damned near impossible.

But what if . . . She didn't want to face the possibility, but she forced herself to put it into words. What if, by some bizarre, incredible, remote chance, Teryl was right? What if her John *was* Simon Tremont? What if the man who lived here in town and was passing himself off as the great Tremont *was* a fraud?

She couldn't *afford* for him to be a fraud—in more ways

than one. After withholding her fifteen percent commission from Tremont's last royalty check, she had forwarded the remainder to the man. It wasn't the largest single check Tremont had ever earned, but, as Teryl had pointed out yesterday, every Tremont check was a small fortune.

But even that would be surpassed by the cost to her reputation. How highly would her clients think of her when they discovered that she had released a client's money to the wrong man? She would undoubtedly lose a number of them if Teryl's John truly was Simon Tremont. The damage to her reputation and her name would be irreparable. The agency, this business that she had devoted herself to, that she had sacrificed much of her life and even her marriage to, would never recover from such a scandal.

She would be destroyed.

At the end of the hall, she walked into the file room, then closed the door behind her. For a moment, she simply stood there, signature in hand, not wanting to look and compare, not needing the doubt. Then, with a strengthening breath, she pulled one of Simon's contracts from the drawer and held the papers side by side. As she remembered, the signature matched. But it didn't prove a thing, she reassured herself.

Not a damned thing.

Teryl was halfway home from work that afternoon when she got caught in traffic. Ordinarily, she didn't mind waiting; she was used to it. She listened to her favorite tapes or, if it was really stop-and-go, as opposed to the usual tortoise crawl, she read short articles in one of the magazines scattered around the car. Today, though, her air conditioner had chosen to stop working. She was hot and sweaty, and she was anxious to get home. She was anxious to see John.

After an eternity she finally turned onto the street where she lived. It was quiet there, and cool. Giant live oaks lined both sides of the street, and only an occasional shaft of sunlight was powerful enough to cut through the dense web of branches and leaves to touch the street. Slowing, she passed two young girls riding bikes, a collie who sat at the curb every day waiting for his master to arrive home, and a parked blue sedan; then she turned into the brick drive of the Grayson estate.

Her pretty little house looked the same as always, but it felt different. It seemed to be adapting to John, she thought fancifully as she followed the drive around to the back. Instead of being just *her* house, *her* home, it was now also his.

But not *theirs*.

Parking beside his truck, she climbed out. She was halfway to the door before she saw John, sprawled in the old wooden chair in the shade of the patio, his legs outstretched, his head back, his eyes closed. Leaving her purse on the first chair she passed, she headed in that direction, her steps slowing when she took in the scene behind him.

Two chairs had been drawn close to the iron-and-glass table, which had been draped with a sheet and, atop that, her one and only tablecloth. Pillows had been brought from the living room to cushion the chairs, and plates, silverware, glasses, and napkins were laid out on opposite sides of the table, separated by a centerpiece of flowers from the garden. A carafe of iced tea, sweating in the heat, sat beside the flowers, and in the corner a layer of smoldering charcoal was burning down in her little grill.

"You're making dinner?" she exclaimed when she reached him.

He replied without opening his eyes. "Don't sound so surprised. I'm a hell of a cook, although all you're getting tonight is steak, baked potatoes, salad, and ice cream. You like chocolate?"

"I love chocolate. This is so nice." No man had ever cooked for her before, not even something so simple as heating a can of soup. Gregory, when he'd lived there, had never set foot in the kitchen for anything more than a beer, and not even that if she was home to get it for him. "I'm impressed."

"Good. Then thank me." He reached out and unerringly located her hand, using it to pull her down into his lap. Before she even got settled, his mouth was on hers, his tongue coaxing her teeth apart.

When he finally ended the kiss and raised his head to look

at her, she caught her breath. "I like the way you say hello," she said, feeling more than a little weak.

"I like the way you say thanks." He lifted her, got more comfortable, then drew her head over to rest on his shoulder. "Your dress is damp in back. Why?"

"The air-conditioning went out in my car."

"Take the Blazer tomorrow, and I'll take yours in to get it fixed."

"That's okay. I don't mind taking it. Besides, I can't drive a stick shift."

"You're kidding." He worked open the clasp on the big wooden clamp that held her hair off her neck, then combed it free. "I thought everyone learned that when they were kids."

"Maybe out West," she teased, "but not necessarily around here."

"My first car was a stick—an old Chevy convertible that I got for a hundred bucks. When I bought it, it didn't run at all. The doors didn't close, and the windows wouldn't roll up. We had to replace virtually everything on it, but by the time Tom and I finished with it, it looked and ran better than new. We loved it." He gave her a teasing grin. "All the girls loved it."

"I bet they did," she murmured in agreement, although she doubted the car had had anything to do with all the feminine attention he'd gotten. She'd seen a photograph of him when he was a teenager; she remembered how teenage girls' hearts fluttered over big, handsome, six-foot-plus, blue-eyed, blond-haired boys. In fact, though she was far from adolescence, her own heart was doing more than a little fluttering right now. "Do you wish you still had it?"

Underneath her weight, she felt him tense a little. "I wish I'd never laid eyes on it."

So it was the car—his first car, the convertible that all the girls loved—that he was driving when he'd had the accident. So much for sweet memories of that particular rite of passage, she thought grimly. Still, after a brief silence, she spoke. "Do you want to talk about it?"

* * *

John gave her question a long moment's consideration before finally replying, "I don't think so. Not today." Then, in a voice that was determinedly lighter, though just as serious, he remarked, "What I really want to do is slide my hand under your dress and see if I can make you turn that sweet shade of pink that you get just before you come."

"I'm sure you can," she said, her voice throaty from the sudden heat that he knew was building inside her. "It'll probably help if you kiss me again, like you did last night when we were standing beside the bed."

"Like this?" He brushed his mouth across hers. "Or like this?" Catching her lower lip between his teeth, he tugged at it and gently sucked it. "Or—"

"Like this?" she interrupted. Holding her hands to his face, she kissed him hard, thrusting her tongue inside his mouth, mimicking the actions that had aroused her so thoroughly the night before. It was working, too; when she twisted closer to deepen the kiss, he felt his erection swelling against her hip.

All day he had been thinking about this—touching her, kissing her, wanting her. He had awakened with one hell of a hard-on this morning, only to discover that she'd left for work hours earlier. He could have gotten off so easily, lying there in her bed, surrounded by her presence, her combined fragrances light in the air, not quite masking the musky scents of their sex. Oh, yeah, he could have gotten off with no more than a stroke or two.

But he hadn't. He had tolerated the discomfort until it finally went away, but it was so easy to call back. Simply seeing her at lunch had brought it back. The talk about seduction, about finding someplace private, and that nothing little kiss before he'd left ... All those things had made him remember, had made him feel again, had made him want again. Just now, all he'd had to do was look at her when she'd gotten out of her car, and he would swear he had started getting hard right then. Right now he was hard enough to break ... and she was hot enough to burn. She had turned until she was across his lap, and his hands were underneath her skirt, high on her thighs, and their kiss was getting damned near desperate. Forget the coals that were burning down, the meat that was marinating, the potatoes ready for baking. Cooking dinner hadn't been a good idea, not when he was feeling like some randy sixteen-year-old kid offered the once-in-a-lifetime chance of all the sex he could endure.

He was pushing her skirt up, moving his hands to her hips, preparing to open his jeans and slide her slowly down the length of his sex when something—a small sound, a prickly feeling, whatever—made him stop, made him remember where they were and open his eyes. "Uh, Teryl?"

"Hmm." She was leaving kisses along his jaw at the same time her hands tried to pull his shirt from his jeans. He would have stopped her, but his hands were buried deep underneath her skirt and he wasn't quite sure, under the circumstances, how to remove them.

"Teryl, there are kids watching us," he murmured.

She became utterly still, met his gaze, then turned just her head to where he looked at the three round, unsmiling faces only a few yards away. Then she became even stiffer. "Oh, gee," she said, sounding half-strangled. "Hi, guys. Look, John, my mother has brought some of the kids to visit."

"Your mother?" he whispered fiercely. Looking past the children to the driveway, he saw the van and the graying, plump woman approaching them with a baby on one hip and leading a second child by the hand.

"Let me up."

"Oh, right." He gripped her legs when she would have wriggled free. "Honey, I have an erection here like you wouldn't believe," he reminded her in a harsh, hushed voice, and, damn her heart, she grinned at him.

"Of course I would. I'm sitting on it. Let me up. I'll help her with the kids, and you can go sit at the table. With the tablecloth."

Reluctantly he let her go, taking advantage of her distraction as she hugged all three kids at once to rise from the chair and slide into the distant chair at the table. It wasn't comfortable—sitting like that, wearing tight jeans, aroused enough to hurt, and meeting Teryl's mother. He had the damnedest luck.

Then some part of him acknowledged how lucky he was to even be here. He never should have met Teryl, never should have come here, never should have gotten close enough to her to get aroused enough to hurt. He *did* have the damnedest luck.

Leaving the kids, she met her mother halfway, gave her a hug and a kiss, then took the baby from her while she greeted the other child. She wanted a half dozen kids of her own and to take in a few dozen more, she'd said once, and he could believe it. She was obviously comfortable with the children, especially the baby, and they seemed to adore her. The baby nestled right in, and the other little one clung to her skirt while she and Mrs. Weaver talked.

Someday in the not-too-distant future she would have her babies, while *he* had never even considered the possibility of fathering children. If pressed for a reason, he would say it was because he would never marry, but there was more to it, he knew, than that. In his research, he had learned much about the adults that emotionally abused children became— and that was the only label, much as he disliked it, that described what his parents had done to him. Many of those adult children became perfectly normal parents themselves who loved their kids and did the best they could by them. Some abused their own children, the way *they* had been abused, and many others made a conscious choice not to have kids. They were afraid that they *might* be like their parents, that they might treat their children the way the parents had treated them, that they might inflict that sort of damage on another generation of helpless kids.

He hoped he wouldn't—was pretty damned sure he wouldn't—but he couldn't be positive. He couldn't say unequivocally that he would never hurt someone who was dependent on him for his emotional well-being. Hell, he'd never even had any exposure to little kids, but he knew they cried, they fussed, and they behaved unreasonably. They got on the nerves of the best parents and could probably make even someone like Teryl lose her temper from time to time. How could he even make a guess what a cranky two-year-old on a bad day could drive him to?

"Who the hell are you?"

Drawing his gaze from Teryl, he settled it on the child who had spoken. She was six, maybe seven, with wispy blond curls and steady blue eyes. In a dress with ribbons and lace, she would look like a perfect little angel; even in grubby shorts and a T-shirt, she came close. Her voice fit the image, too—soft, delicate, like glass chimes in the wind— which made her language, jarring from any small child, even more so. "I'm John."

Ignoring the two boys who hung back, she came closer, scuffing her rubber thongs on the stone, clasping both hands over the back of the opposite chair. "Are you Teryl's boyfriend?"

"Sort of." Before she could ask another question, he asked his own. "Who are you?"

"Alex."

"Are you Teryl's sister?"

"Sort of. Are you having a picnic?"

"We're cooking out."

"Why? It's too damned hot."

"It's not so hot in the shade, and I wanted—"

"Are you sleeping with Teryl?"

He felt a dull blush creep up his neck to his face and his command of the English language slip away. "I don't . . . uh, that's not . . . we . . . "

"That's what boyfriends do, you know. They spend the night, and everyone has to do what they say, and they yell if you bother them, and if you really bother them, even if you don't mean to, they hit you and do things."

John simply stared at her, cold inside, understanding all too well the situation she had come from, knowing more than he wanted about the yelling but nothing at all except from books, thank God, about the hitting and the "things" that were done. He had no idea what to say to her, but fortunately Teryl's mother saved him from having to try. Reaching the table, she sat down in the chair and scooped the little girl into her lap, holding her with both arms around her waist.

"No, honey, that's not what boyfriends do," she said gently. "That's what some bad people do. When two people like each other a lot and want to be together, then they become boyfriend and girlfriend. They have fun together, and they do nice things for each other. They don't hurt each other, and they don't hurt anyone else. Do you understand?"

Nodding, Alex slid to the ground, her shorts twisting at her waist, her shirt hanging crooked. She stood still long enough for Teryl's mother to straighten her clothes, then she placed her hands on her hips and looked directly at John. "I understand," she said. "But I'm still not ever having any damned boyfriend."

As she ran off to join the two boys, Mrs. Weaver sighed. "I'm sorry about that. We've had Alex only a few months, and she's still dealing with a lot of hurt and anger and guilt."

And she would be dealing with it, he suspected, for many years to come. As *he* had and still was. But she had something he'd lacked: Teryl's mother and her father and, to some extent, Teryl herself. The Weaver family just might be enough to heal anything.

"So, Teryl, aren't you going to introduce us?" She looked from him to her daughter, and John followed her gaze. Teryl was cuddling the baby to her breast, her smile soft, her voice softer. She was definitely good mother material; he thought with a pang of envy that some other man would be the father to her children.

She came closer, standing between them, swaying from side to side to rock the baby. "Mama, this is John Smith. John, my mother Lorna Weaver. And this—" She moved closer to him, bending to put him and the baby on the same level. "This is Kesha."

He acknowledged Lorna with a nod and a polite, "Mrs. Weaver." Although he didn't speak to the baby, he did look at her—her ebony skin that smelled of powder, her soft black curls, her round brown eyes, and her single-toothed grin—and he touched her, stroking her clenched fist with one fingertip. She was so small, so fragile, and yet she wrapped her fingers around his with surprising strength.

"It's a pleasure meeting you, John," Lorna said, leaning back in the chair. "I'd like to say Teryl's told me a lot about you, but since I've hardly seen my daughter in the last few weeks, I don't know anything."

From the corner where she had gone to make a set of brass chimes tinkle for Kesha's pleasure, Teryl sent a chiding smile her way. "John's from Colorado. He's got business here. He grew up in California, he's got a sister who teaches school in Florida, he used to live in New Orleans, and—" her smile turned into a grin—"he likes old movies. He was watching *Summer Splendor* just last night."

"Ah, *Summer Splendor*. That was an interesting time—when movies told stories and weren't merely showcases for special effects. These days actors don't act; they simply *re*act to whatever effects the computers will put in later."

John studied the woman across from him with an intense frown that slowly turned into recognition. "You're Lorna Terr—" He looked from her to her daughter, who was still grinning. "Terrill. Jeez, I never made the connection." He shook his head in disbelief. "I used to have every movie you ever made."

"I'm flattered . . . I think. That 'used to' doesn't sound so complimentary."

He gave Teryl a chiding glance for keeping her secret before turning back to her mother. "I lost them in a fire and haven't had a chance to replace them yet." He looked again from mother to daughter. There was no family resemblance that he could identify. Lorna's hair, bottled blond all through her career, brown and graying now, was lighter in color and coarser in texture than Teryl's. Her eyes were blue, Teryl's brown. Her bone structure, concealed now by the extra weight she carried, was strong, clean, while Teryl's was more delicate. The only thing they shared in common wasn't physical: they were both generous, warm, loving women.

So Teryl took after her father or perhaps one of her grandparents.

"You had tremendous talent. I always thought it was unfortunate that you chose to retire so early. *Summer Splendor* was your last movie, wasn't it?"

Lorna nodded. "Philip, my husband, and I wanted children. The studio wasn't interested in letting me play other kinds of roles, and they certainly weren't interested in seeing me pregnant, so, as soon as filming ended, we came home to start a family. We started with Teryl, and twenty-nine years and over two hundred children later, we're not finished yet."

"I lived in L.A. then," he said. "I can still remember some of the fuss about your retirement. No one wanted you to go—except all the young actresses who were hoping to take your place. None of them ever succeeded."

She reached across the table and patted his hand. "That's sweet of you to say. Heavens, you must have been just a child. Six? Maybe seven?"

"A little older." At the time, the news hadn't meant much to him. But as he'd grown older, as he'd become more of a fan, he had remembered. It had been quite a story: the beautiful young starlet, as big a sex symbol as Monroe and ten times more talented, giving up the fame and glamour of Hollywood to go home with the husband none of her public had known existed.

The two women continued talking as a faint uneasiness settled in John's stomach. The timing, he realized, was off. If *Summer Splendor* had been the last movie Lorna had made before Teryl was born, the film should be, depending on the month of Teryl's birth, twenty-nine or thirty years old. But it wasn't. He was a hard-core fan of the actress and the movie; he knew the stars, the producers, the directors. He knew the studio and when and where it had premiered. He was sure of the filming dates, as sure as he was of his own birthdate.

Summer Splendor had been made only twenty-seven years ago.

Why would Lorna lie? Why would she claim that the movie had been made two to three years earlier than it actually had? Why would she claim that Teryl had been born after the filming had been completed instead of two years before?

The obvious answer sent a chill down his spine. If Teryl had been born two years before the movie, there was no way she could be Lorna's daughter. *None.* Lorna had worked steadily, rarely taking off more than a few weeks at a time, completing eighteen films in a ridiculously short few years.

She had played sexpots and society belles, the seducer and the seduced. She'd been sexy, steamy, sophisticated, and glamorous. There was no way she could have been pregnant during those years. No way, in the wardrobes the studios chose for her, that she could have gained so much as five pounds without it showing.

There was no way she could be Teryl's biological mother.

Maybe her husband was Teryl's father. Maybe he'd grown bored and lonely all those months Lorna had been on one set or another location. Maybe he'd had an affair that had produced a pretty little baby girl and Lorna had been willing to accept the child as her own as the price to save her marriage.

Or maybe Teryl hadn't been born to either of them. She had called herself the only Weaver by birth, but maybe she wasn't. Maybe she was just the first in a long line of other people's kids that the Weavers had taken to love as their own, and she didn't know it.

She didn't even have a clue.

"I can't believe you never told me that Lorna Terrill is your mother."

"I'm named for her, you know. They were expecting a son, and they intended to name him Terrill, but when they had me instead, they just changed the spelling to make it more feminine." Teryl gazed up into the night sky. The stars overhead lost much of their brilliance to the city lights, but she could still pick out a few constellations, a few wishing stars. Wishing on stars had long been a Weaver family tradition, and Lorna had long been their favorite star for wishing. "I meant to tell you, but it's not the sort of tidbit you just drop into the conversation. 'Dinner was wonderful, the dessert was delicious, and the lovemaking was sinful, and, oh, by the way, did I mention that my mother was once a famous movie star?"

He scowled at her. "The dessert was supposed to be sinful."

"Oh, pardon me. Then the lovemaking was delicious." And wicked. Wild. Wonderful. It had definitely been a new

experience for her—damp grass, a soft quilt, moonlight and
starlight, the night-heavy fragrances of the flowers. By the
time they'd finished, she had thought she just might lie there
forever. Every need she'd ever had had been fully sated,
some to overflowing. If she had died then and there, she
would have died a foolishly happy, enormously satisfied
woman.

Then John had suggested this walk, and from somewhere
new reservoirs of energy had appeared. They had gotten
dressed, locked up the house, and followed the winding brick
drive through the grove of oak trees to the rise where they
could look down on the Grayson house. Now they were approaching the ornate gates that led to the street and the city
beyond.

"I did intend to tell you about my mother," she said softly.
"I was just waiting."

"Until you trusted me enough?"

She didn't want to answer, didn't want to risk hurting him,
but she forced the words out anyway. "She was a *star*, John,
one of Hollywood's legendary sex symbols, and you're—"

"Just a fan, Teryl. I'm not deranged. I wouldn't stalk her. I
wouldn't hurt her. I wouldn't confuse what she is today with
what she was thirty years ago."

"I know."

He gave her a sidelong glance. "Do you?"

Crossing the driveway to one of the gates, she ran her fingers along the bars, still warm from the day's sun, then
leaned back against it to face him. "Yes," she admitted
evenly. "I do."

He remained where he was for a moment, hidden in
shadow, then started toward her, not stopping until his body
was pressing against hers. He lowered his head, close enough
that she could feel his breath on her mouth, but he didn't kiss
her. "Don't start trusting me too much tonight, sweetheart,"
he muttered gruffly, "or we'll both wind up in jail."

"Why do you say that?"

"You look damned appealing standing here. If you trust
me too much, I might be tempted to tie your hand up here
like this . . . " He raised her right hand to a point above and

away from her body, curving her fingers around the bar to hold it there. "And I might be tempted to tie your other hand like this . . . " Nuzzling her jaw, he repeated the process, then took a few steps back to look at her. "And if you trust me too much, you might be tempted to let me."

She curled her fingers tightly around the bars, feeling their heat and their strength. Even though she was free, even though she could move at any time, some small part of her was frightened by the mere suggestion of restraints, and that fear made her tremble. Or was it lust, she wondered, that made her body weak? The appeal of the forbidden, the guilty pleasure, the wicked desire. Her head knew that bondage was wrong. But some curious little place inside her wondered how it would feel to be bound to these bars, to be naked in the moonlight, trapped without chance of escape, open and totally vulnerable to John's whims. She would be afraid, of course, but would she also be aroused? Thrilled by the risk? Turned on by the sense of danger but secure in the knowledge that he wouldn't hurt her, that he would protect her and keep her safe?

What would it take, he had once asked, to persuade her to let him strip her and tie her to the bed for pleasure and play? Absolutely nothing, she had replied, but he had disagreed with her. If she trusted him implicitly, she would let him do it, he had insisted. At the time she'd been adamant that he was wrong.

Tonight she wasn't so sure. Tonight she was beginning to see that maybe, just maybe, she *could* let him do it.

And—although the idea shamed her, intrigued and bewildered her—tonight she suspected that she just might enjoy it.

The life and death of Eliza Byrd. Simon had referred to the new book in that way so often that he'd decided tonight to title it that. *The Life and Death of Eliza Byrd*. He wondered if anyone would catch the significance, if anyone would ever notice the similarities between the book and the real-life story unfolding right here in Richmond. He doubted it. That stupid bitch Debra Jane wouldn't, even though she

knew how he felt about Teryl. She knew Teryl's middle
name was Elizabeth, knew that once long, long ago she had
been called Eliza for short. The Byrd would escape her,
though. She wouldn't recognize a robin if it wore a name tag
around its neck; how could she ever know about the existence of an African bird whose woven nests earned it the
name of weaver?

What are you going to do? she had demanded at the house
this morning. You're not going to hurt them, are you? After
all these years, she still didn't understand the difference between business and pleasure. Pain was pleasure. It was sexual. Hurting Teryl, slapping her, bruising her fair skin,
making her cry, tormenting her—that was pleasure. *This* was
business. Much as he would like to mix the two, he couldn't.
He wouldn't.

So what *was* he going to do? He'd been sitting here in the
dark, watching, waiting, thinking. Obviously, he hadn't
planned well enough in Colorado. This time he had to be
more cautious. He had to choose his time and place with
more care. This time he had to succeed.

Leaning across the seat, he silently rolled down the window on the passenger side, then sat back once again. It was a
still night in a quiet neighborhood. There had been occasional cars passing by, but, thanks to the century-old trees
that formed a canopy overhead, the street was so dark he
would bet none of the drivers had even noticed his car, much
less him sitting in it.

It was for damned sure that the two people he was watching hadn't noticed him.

Smith moved up against Teryl again, bringing her hands
down from the bars, guiding them around his neck, and kissing her. He was grinding his hips against hers, fucking her as
surely as if they were naked and he were buried in her to the
hilt. They didn't even care that they were right there in plain
view, the moon like a spotlight, visible to anyone who drove
by. Simon could even hear her little moans. Shit, he thought
scornfully, he could make her moan. He could make her cry
and scream and beg, and he could make her come so hard
that she would think she was dying.

Not that he would bother now. Unlike his unnamed protagonist who continued to covet Eliza Byrd long after confronted by her slutty ways, he'd lost his desire for Teryl. He already had a whore in Debra Jane; sweet Teryl had provided a necessary balance. But Teryl wasn't so sweet, after all. She had fooled her family, had fooled him and everyone else, and that made her a worse slut than even Debra Jane. Her deceit and deception made her impure. Vulgar. Contemptible. If he sought pleasure with her now, she would infect him with her filth, and he would never be able to rid himself of her poison.

He no longer wanted her, no longer needed her. She could fuck with John Smith wherever she wanted, whenever she wanted. It was only fair, after all.

Because she was going to die with John Smith.

Chapter Fifteen

_A_ crash of thunder rumbled through the house, vibrating the windowpanes, sending a shudder up through the bed that woke John from a restless sleep. Finding himself tangled in the covers and with Teryl, he wriggled free, slipped from the bed and into the cutoffs he'd discarded nearby, and made his way to the French doors, unlocking one and opening it only wide enough to slip out onto the balcony. The wind was whipping the trees around, blowing the rain sideways at times, ripping blossoms from their stems and sending them sailing. The balcony rail was scattered with the bruised petals of yellow roses from a bush thirty yards away.

It was 6:10 on Wednesday morning, but the sky was midnight-dark, and what last night's weathercast had predicted as hot and sunny was coming down violent and wet. Lightning flashed with enough brilliance to make him wince, and the thunder and wind combined to sound like a rushing freight train.

He liked storms, liked the intensity and the power. He liked the energized, electrified way they made him feel. He liked the fury, followed always by calm. Maybe _that_, he thought, was what he really liked: the knowledge that the storm always ended. The wind blew itself away, the rain stopped, and the sun always came out again. Calm was always restored.

Most of his life lacked such guarantees. There were no promises that everything would turn out all right, that the sun would come out again and life would once more be good.

Unmindful of the rain that blew against him, he leaned on the rail and gazed across the garden. Teryl would be getting up soon, ready to go to work. He would take her, he decided. She didn't like storms and didn't need to be driving in rain. Besides, it would give him an opportunity to meet Rebecca. After that, he would come back here, make arrangements to get the air-conditioning on the Honda fixed, and wait for an express mail letter from Denver.

In bed last night, Teryl had repeated her conversation with Rebecca to him, had relayed every bit of her boss's skepticism, had told him the accusation that he was seducing Teryl into helping him defraud the agency. Damn Rebecca, and damn her agency. When they got this straightened out, the second thing he was going to do was fire Rebecca, more for that cheap shot than anything else.

The first thing he was going to do was take care of Teryl.

And the last was get out of her life. Even if he didn't want to go. Even if she didn't want him to go. Even if it killed him.

Behind him the door swung open a foot or so, and he saw Teryl, sleepy-eyed, tousle-haired, wearing that tank top, standing there. She looked adorable. Sweet. Beautiful. "What are you doing?" she asked, her voice small, sleep-roughened.

"Watching the storm. Come join me."

She shook her head. "I can't."

"You're safe here." The roof overhead covered him from the worst of the rain, and the L shape of the house protected him from much of the wind. He was at risk of nothing more dangerous than getting a little wet. "Come on out."

Again she shook her head. "Come to bed."

He needed only a glimpse of her discomfort, clearly visible in the lightning, to make up his mind. Returning inside, he locked the door. By the time he reached the bed, she was already under the covers, already snuggling in. Before he could even settle in, she began burrowing against him, wriggling as close as was physically possible. "What is it with you and storms?" he asked, wrapping his arms around her. He had asked her once before, the day they'd run into a storm after crossing from Georgia into South Carolina, and she'd had only a vague answer. *I don't know. They're violent and dangerous.* Now that she knew him better, maybe she would offer the real answer.

"When I was a kid, I used to have nightmares. Thunderstorms were almost always a part of them. I'd wake up in a cold sweat, sometimes crying but usually too scared to make a sound. I never remembered any details, just that horrible things were happening and I couldn't stop them." She rubbed her cheek, warm and soft, against his chest, chilled from the rain. "The dreams had no basis in reality—at least, not *my* reality. Other than having a mother who was a famous movie star and living with anywhere from ten to twenty kids at a time, I had a perfectly normal childhood—nothing to explain nightmares. I always thought they were because of the other children. Some of the kids Mama and Daddy took in were fairly normal, but a number of them had been emotionally, physically, or sexually abused. I knew some of their stories. I'd heard some of the things that their families had done to them. I thought I was dreaming *their* dreams. Reliving their nightmares."

For a time John said nothing. He simply lay there, his muscles taut, his thoughts full of doubt and suspicion. The more he'd thought about the discrepancy in Lorna's story last night, the more convinced he had become that Teryl was adopted, that she was quite likely one of those kids who had been emotionally, physically, or sexually abused. She must have been very young when she went to live with the Weavers, too young to remember those first frightening years. But not too young for nightmares where horrible things happened that she couldn't stop. Not too young to become irrationally afraid of thunderstorms. Not too young to develop an unhealthy terror of being restrained.

Every night they'd been on the road, he must have stirred some terrifying memories hidden deep inside the protective recesses of her mind.

God forgive him.

"I know it's silly to be afraid now," she went on. "I'm nearly thirty years old. I know storms aren't evil. The only damage they can cause is from the force of the wind or flooding from the rain or getting struck by lightning. I know they don't call for anything more than common sense." Reluctantly she sighed and pulled out of his arms. "I'd better get ready for work. With this weather, traffic's going to be awful."

"I'm going to take you."

She looked at him for a moment, probably thinking that she needed to act like a nearly thirty-year-old woman and turn him down. No doubt she considered it, but with a rueful smile, she simply accepted his announcement. "I appreciate it."

It didn't take her long to dress, pull her hair back, and put makeup on. John waited with her until she was done, then they went to the kitchen together for breakfast. Finally, sharing the shelter of an oversize umbrella, they left the house and made a dash for the Blazer.

They were only a short distance from the old Victorian that housed the offices when he announced his secondary motive for bringing her. "When we get to the agency, I want to come in and meet Rebecca."

Teryl gave him a sharp look. "I don't think that's a good idea."

"I won't be difficult. I won't bring up Tremont. I just want to meet her." He offered her a rusty smile. "I've been paying this woman fifteen percent of my income for the last eleven years. She's helped make me a rich man, and I've made her a wealthy woman. I think it's time I at least got an idea what she looks like."

She was hesitant, and he couldn't blame her. He wasn't even being totally honest with her. There *was* one other reason he wanted to meet Rebecca. He wanted to remind her of something she'd once written in a note to him, wanted to see if he could jog her memory. It had been a handwritten note, one of little importance; he'd read it, forgotten everything except the last line, and thrown it away. Unless she was thoroughly compulsive, there wouldn't be any record of it in her files. She and the real Simon Tremont were the only two people who could possibly know about it.

As he pulled into the drive that led around to the parking lot, Teryl shrugged. "All right. Just don't expect her to be happy to see you."

His grin was dry. "I don't ever expect anyone to be happy to see me." But that wasn't true. He'd come to expect it of Teryl.

Once again they shared the umbrella from the truck to the back door. Inside, Teryl started a pot of coffee first, then led the way to her office, where she tucked her purse away in a drawer and changed from the damp loafers she wore to a pair of dressier sandals she'd brought. Finally, with a tight smile, she beckoned him to follow her down the hall.

Rebecca's door was open, all the lights in the office on, the drapes behind her desk drawn shut on the dreary day. Music was coming from the stereo on the shelves, something New Age and soothing, and she was sitting with her head back, her eyes closed. She looked cool, elegant, and impossibly polite, but John knew she was tough as nails. She might appear every bit the well-bred lady, but she was, first and foremost, a businesswoman.

For eleven years her business had been selling *his* books. Unless she'd changed her mind in the last few days, though, she'd now thrown in with the enemy. She intended to help the man claiming to be Simon steal his career. And if she hadn't changed her mind recently, maybe he could help her.

Teryl rapped on the door, then cleared her throat. "Good morning, Rebecca."

The woman didn't startle, as many would have done. She opened her eyes slowly, looking first at Teryl, next at John, then raised her head. "Teryl." Just as slowly, she stood up and came around the corner of the desk. "You must be John. I'm sorry. Teryl didn't mention your last name."

"Smith." As if she didn't know it damned well. He took the hand she offered, and she gave him a strong shake.

Rebecca's smile was tightly controlled and more than a little mocking. "Oh, yes, John Smith. What a coincidence. I'm Rebecca Robertson, but you probably know that. Are you here to discuss Simon Tremont with me? Because, if that's the case, let me save us all some time and tell you that I won't discuss my client's business with anyone."

"Actually, I gave Teryl a ride this morning because of the weather, and, as long as I was here, I just wanted to see if you lived up to my image of you."

She gave him a long look. "And what's the verdict?"

"You do." He had envisioned her, for no reason he could recall, as a brunette instead of a graying blond, but, other than that small detail, she was pretty much what he'd expected.

"I must say, you're nothing like I expected."

"And what did you expect? A raving lunatic? Wild hair and wild eyes?" He smiled faintly. "Sorry to disappoint you, but the only thing I'm crazy about is Teryl."

Rebecca leaned against the front of her desk, crossing one ankle over the other. At his side, Teryl was standing behind one of the two chairs, resting her arms on the high, curved back, clasping her hands together. Neither woman looked particularly comfortable. "I understand you're visiting here from Colorado by way of New Orleans," Rebecca remarked. "How long will you be staying?"

"I don't know yet."

"Where will you go from here? New York?"

It was the obvious choice, John acknowledged. If he was intent on playing out this scam—or if he really was crazy enough to believe that he *was* Simon Tremont—the next likely target, Candace Baker at Morgan-Wilkes, was in New York. "I haven't decided that, either," he replied, fixing his blue gaze on her. "But, you know, I always thought New York might be a nice place to visit—see the Statue of Liberty, catch a Broadway show, maybe take a tour of the house that Jack built."

There was a moment of utter stillness as Rebecca went stiff, her smile frozen on her unmoving mouth, and her eyes widened in shock. So she did remember that long-ago note. John allowed himself only the faintest smile of triumph as he went on. "You lived there a long time, didn't you? If I decide to go, maybe you could make a few recommendations—you know, hotels, restaurants, sights to see." He paused. "Maybe a lawyer."

She was still staring at him as, without waiting for a response, he claimed Teryl's hand and began pulling her toward the door. "It was nice meeting you, Ms. Robertson. I'd better be going, Teryl. Come and walk me to the door."

Teryl didn't speak until they were at the back door again. Looking puzzled, she offered him the umbrella, but he refused it with a shake of his head. "What did I miss back there?" she asked. "What gave her such a shock?"

"Jack is a nickname for John, right?"

She nodded.

"And Morgan-Wilkes is a publishing house that was pretty small-time until they bought the first Tremont book."

"Which made a name for them and helped turn them into one of the big boys in the publishing world. Hence, the house that John built—or, in keeping with the nursery rhyme, the house that Jack built. I assume this is a private joke between you and Rebecca."

He shrugged. "Not exactly. It's just something she mentioned in a note a few years back, and it stuck in my mind."

"Apparently, it stuck in her mind, too."

Nodding, he opened the door and stood there for a moment, watching the rain. The storm had passed, although if the black clouds off to the west were any indication, another system was moving in fast. The rain didn't look as if it ever intended to stop. He knew he should leave, should go on home before the next storm hit, but it was still early. No one else was in the office, and he wasn't keeping Teryl from work.

She stood beside him in the doorway, leaning her shoulder against the wood frame on the opposite side. "Did anyone ever call you Jack?" she asked, her voice soft, her curiosity idle.

"No. Sometimes Tom and Janie called me Johnny, usually when something else had gone wrong between our parents and me." When they were trying to cheer him up or calm him down. When they were trying to make him forget that, no matter what kind of kid he was, no matter how good or bad, their folks were never going to love him the way they loved their older son and younger daughter. He had often wondered whether they had ever loved him at all. Today he knew it didn't matter. His parents were a long-ago part of his past. They had no place in the present and no place at all in his future.

"Johnny." She tilted her head to one side and studied him, then grinned. "I can see that." Before he could fully savor the sound of the nickname in her voice, she gestured outside. "The rain seems to be letting up a bit. Go now so you don't get soaked."

He gave her a kiss, then started for the truck. Halfway across the parking lot, he turned back and found her watching him. "Hey, Teryl?" Feeling suddenly awkward, he hesitated, then blurted out, "Thanks."

"For what?"

"Believing me. Trusting me. Helping me."

She smiled in response, and he turned again, skirting a puddle at the back of the truck. A moment later, he heard the door close, but just before it did, he swore he heard a soft murmur.

"Any time, Johnny."

Given a choice, Rebecca never would have left her office for lunch on such a miserable day, but thanks to Teryl and this crazy man she'd gotten hooked up with, she didn't have a choice. She had to keep the appointment she'd made this morning. She had to reassure herself that her suspicions—Teryl's suspicions and this John Smith's claims—were unfounded.

This crazy man. Truth be told, John Smith didn't strike her as mentally unstable. She had certainly understood her assistant's attraction to him. He was handsome, and he seemed nice enough, friendly enough. And, face it: there was something about a big man that made a woman, feminist or not, simply feel safe. Cared for. Protected. She would bet that John Smith made Teryl feel cared for in every way.

Funny how, at the same time, he made *her* feel that her world was at risk of coming apart.

The house that Jack built. As a woman who was always all business and serious work, she occasionally had a clever moment, and just such a moment had produced that description of Morgan-Wilkes. Although she had often thought of the publisher that way, beyond the one time she'd included it in a note to her client, she had never repeated it to anyone else. That meant there were only two ways John could have learned it: if her client had repeated it to him, or if he *was* her client.

Oh, Christ, don't let that be the case, she silently prayed. Please let the man approaching her now be the real Simon.

He drew no attention as he crossed the dining room. If anyone recognized him as the man from the "New Orleans Afternoon" interview, they didn't show it. Maybe it was his appearance; he wore a baseball cap that covered most of his light brown hair and plastic-framed glasses that gave his eyes an overlarge owlish look, and he looked as if he hadn't shaved in two days or more. Or maybe it was simply that the other diners didn't expect to find the great Simon Tremont in their midst for lunch. Whatever the reason, he seemed to be traveling pretty much unrecognized.

From what little she knew of him, that probably didn't make him very happy.

"Rebecca." He sat down across from her and laid a black folder on the table. "I was surprised by your invitation this morning. I figured a luncheon appointment would be scheduled at least a few days in advance."

She responded to the chastisement in his voice with an apology, even though it annoyed her. "I'm sorry for the short notice, Simon. It won't happen again. I had intended to clear this with you last week, but there was a mix-up," she lied.

"It seems your assistant isn't very reliable. It would probably be in the agency's best interests if you replaced her."

She gave him a long, unwavering look. She wasn't feeling kindly toward Teryl this morning, but her employees were rather like family: *she* could criticize them, but she didn't care to hear someone else do it. "My assistant is *very* reliable, Simon. I would find it very difficult to replace her."

Picking up the menu, he shrugged as if he couldn't care less. "It's your business. So . . . what was it you wanted that required a trip into town in weather like this?"

"It's nothing important, really. I just thought that, since you're ready to give up all the mystery, it would be a good idea for us to get together periodically—you know, to discuss the future, look ahead, make plans."

He gestured with a nod toward the folder he'd brought with him. "There's the future."

"What is it?"

"The first two chapters of my next novel."

"May I see it?"

He shrugged and continued to study the menu. She reached for the folder, withdrawing the stack of pages tucked inside. She delayed reading only long enough to order a salad and iced tea when the waiter came; then she turned her attention to the chapters. Moment after moment passed. She was only vaguely aware of the waiter bringing their drinks and of Simon, passing the time by tapping his fingers on the edge of the table. By the time she finished reading, the young waiter was serving their meal.

"Well?"

"Nice. Very nice." She returned the pages to the folder, then spread her napkin over her lap. "Interesting characters, strong mood. You've captured the futility of the man's feelings for Eliza very well." She offered him a confident smile. "It's your usual outstanding job."

Her words satisfied him, damned near made him preen, and they weren't really lies, she assured herself. The chapters *were* nicely done. They were intense, the atmosphere creepy, the menace building from the very first scene. The story was just *different*. There was a mean-spiritedness to it that she'd never seen in a Tremont book. He didn't *like* the character of Eliza Byrd. He was taking pleasure in setting her up for the fate that was to befall her.

Still, the writing was *good*, and the readers would like it . . . probably. And it *was* just the first few chapters. By the time he finished the outline and showed it to her again, it would be much farther along in development. Eliza and the unnamed man would be more fully fleshed out, and all the emotion, all the understanding and the skill that had made him a master of characterization would be in place.

"I didn't expect you to be working again so soon. I thought that, after the way you pushed so hard on *Resurrection*, you would take off at least a few months, maybe even a year, before starting again."

He shrugged her off. "I don't need time off. I figure I'll have enough of this ready to show to Candace by the end of the week. I want this one to come out as soon after *Resurrection* as possible."

"Morgan-Wilkes will be thrilled." She infused her smile with all the warmth she could muster—a tremendous amount, considering that simply being near him made her cold. "You know, with all the Tremont successes, they really *are* the house that Jack built."

Simon gave her a disinterested look. "Jack who?"

Her smile began slipping, and nothing, damn it, nothing she could do could stop it. Needing a drink to clear her throat, she reached for her glass, but her hand was unsteady. Instead, she clasped her hands together in her lap and concentrated on keeping her voice even, level, and empty of panic. "You know, Jack is a nickname for John. And there's that old kids' rhyme about this is the house that Jack built, and publishers are often referred to as . . ."

He was looking at her, his brown eyes blank, as if he had no idea in the world what she was rambling on about. Trailing off in mid-sentence, she called up the best smile she could manage, but it felt much more like a nervous twitch. "Never mind. It was a bad joke."

Somehow she made it through the rest of the meal, paid the bill, and stood to say good-bye. On impulse, she reached for the manuscript pages. "Can I keep these? I'd like to read over them again."

Still seated, Simon shrugged. "That's why I brought them—so you'd have a copy."

Not for her approval, not for her opinion, just so she

would have a copy. Rebecca curled her fingers tightly around them. "It's been a pleasure, Simon."

He gave her a long, disarming, gazing-right-through-her look, then smiled. It was a chilling thing to see. "Let's do it again. But next time, call ahead. A week's notice should be sufficient." Then, with a dismissive gesture, he turned back to the wine he was finishing.

Leaving him there at the table, she walked stiffly and quickly through the dining room and outside to her Mercedes. She didn't even notice the rain that dampened her hair and ran down the jacket of her suit. Locked inside the car, she dropped the folder on the seat, disliking even the feel of it in her hand. She started the engine, turned the air conditioner on, then reached for a tissue from the box in the other seat to pat her face dry. Her hands were trembling, making the thin paper flutter, and her heart was thudding painfully in her chest.

The man in the restaurant, the man she knew as Simon Tremont—the man to whom she had recently sent a check of John Smith/Simon Tremont's money with more zeroes on it than she cared to count—acted as if he'd never heard her little joke before. Even with her explanation, he hadn't understood it. It hadn't been the least bit familiar to him.

But Teryl's John had known it. He had understood it perfectly.

Could Teryl be right? she wondered, dreading such a possibility so badly that she felt sick with it. Could he be the real Simon Tremont? Could that man in the restaurant right now be a fraud?

Taking a few breaths, she calmed herself. She needed a clear head to sort this out. No panic, no fear—at least, none yet. Not until she was convinced there was reason to fear.

What evidence did John Smith have to prove that he was Simon? None that she could see. Teryl had admitted that the paperwork—all the records that eleven years of writing as a business would have generated—had supposedly been destroyed by an explosion. As far as she could tell, all he had was his claim, an extraordinary knowledge of Simon's ca-

346   *Marilyn Pappano*

to mimic Simon's writing style.

There was surely some logical explanation for the knowledge. He probably knew the real Tremont, had probably been
friends or neighbors with him, had probably been in and out
of his house up there in Colorado. He had probably sneaked
peeks at Simon's work, at Simon's mail. As for the writing,
any reasonably talented author could, with practice, successfully mimic another author's style. The write-like Heming-
way and Faulkner contests held each year proved that.

And what evidence did Simon have? He was also certainly
knowledgeable about Tremont's career. Presumably he had
all the paperwork that John couldn't produce at home in his
office. Granted, he hadn't been familiar with her silly little
joke, but if he hadn't understood it or thought it funny in the
first place, it was perfectly logical that he would have forgotten it by now.

And he had the biggest, most important proof of all: *Resurrection*. No one disputed that he'd written it, not Teryl, not
even her John. There was no doubt in anyone's mind that
only Simon Tremont could have written that book and no
doubt in anyone's mind that the man in the restaurant was
the one who wrote it. Therefore, he *had* to be Tremont.

With *Resurrection* on his side, there was no reason to de-
bate. No reason to doubt. Not that damnable joke that still
bothered her. Not the fact that John certainly fitted her image
of Simon Tremont far better than the real Simon did. Not the
fact that, in comparing John's pages about Liane Thibodeaux
and Simon's pages about Eliza Byrd, John's writing felt
much more like Simon's than Simon's did.

Simon wrote *Resurrection*. He wrote the best book she'd
ever read, and that made him the winner. Her trust, her support, and her agency were behind him.

All the way.

Simon sat at the table, his fingers curled around the stem
of his wineglass, and stared moodily out the window at the
parking lot beyond. More than five minutes had passed since

Rebecca had left the restaurant, and yet she still sat out there in her big expensive car. She couldn't be waiting for the rain to stop; any fool could see that wasn't going to happen for a long time. She could be rereading his partial, but somehow he didn't think so. She seemed to simply be sitting there.

Why?

He tossed down the last of his wine, then pushed his chair back with a scrape. This trip into town had certainly been a waste of time that would have been much better spent at his computer. When she had called this morning insisting that he meet her for lunch—*insisting*, he'd thought at the time with some amazement; didn't she realize that no one insisted anything of Simon Tremont?—he had thought something important was up. He had expected to be given schedules for his next talk show appearances, to be informed of new and more impressive requests for his presence. He had expected to hear how Barbara Walters and Larry King had wheeled and dealed to win him for their shows, had thought *People* might want him on the cover, had considered a preliminary discussion for the major cross-country or international book tours that were inevitable before the end of the year.

Instead Rebecca had wanted nothing. She had wasted his time for *nothing*. Vague talk about discussing the future and making plans—neither of which they'd done—a little luke-warm praise for *Eliza Byrd*, a joke too dumb to be deserving of the name, and small talk. *Nothing*.

Walking out the door, he stood for a moment underneath the canopy that sheltered the entrance. The Mercedes was gone now. Maybe she had seen him leave the table. Maybe she hadn't wanted him to see her sitting out here.

She had gotten weird after reading the chapters. Had she recognized Teryl in Eliza? Maybe he should have changed the description. Maybe he shouldn't have written her as a dead ringer for Teryl, but he found the process easier that way—when he could call a real person to mind, when he could borrow looks, mannerisms, voices, attitudes. Besides, it was so much fun planning Eliza's demise and seeing it in his head happening to Teryl—imagining the fear coming into those big brown eyes, disfiguring that soft creamy skin, crushing that slender, delicate throat, and, ultimately, watching the life drain out of that deceptively sweet, allusively innocent face.

He honestly didn't think Rebecca could have made the connection between her assistant and doomed Eliza. Her mind didn't work that way. She was a bright woman—he wouldn't have her for an agent if she weren't—but she didn't have even a fraction of his complexity. So maybe it hadn't been the chapters that had made her edgy. What had come after? A comment that she'd thought he would take some time off. He'd said the partial would soon be ready to send to Morgan-Wilkes, and she'd made her dumb remark. *You know, with all the Tremont successes, they really* are *the house that Jack built.* She had watched him, waiting for a response, and then she had gone into that edgy explanation before finally, awkwardly letting it drop mid-sentence.

They really are *the house that Jack built.* A private joke? Something she'd shared only with John Smith?

He swore out loud, viciously enough to make a passing customer shrink away. That had to be it. The bitch had been testing him. Something—or some*one*, damn Teryl to hell—had aroused Rebecca's suspicions, and so she had called him, demanding that he meet her for lunch, pulling him away from his work, all so she could test him with her stupid little inside joke.

And he had failed her test. He had acted as if he'd never heard it before—which, of course, he hadn't—and hadn't been interested enough to even understand it.

John Smith didn't matter. He was as good as dead. Teryl's suspicions didn't matter, either, because she was going to die with Smith. As for the younger sister who was the sum total of Smith's personal life, she didn't present much of a threat. Like Teryl, all she knew was what her deranged brother had told her. Like Teryl, if she became a problem, she would be dead.

Rebecca Robertson, though, was another matter. He couldn't afford for her to doubt him. He couldn't afford for her to get skeptical, to start looking into his background and maybe, like that slut Teryl, start spreading her doubts around.

He had planned to wait for the right time to tie up all the loose ends, but already he had waited too long. If only he had known sooner that he had failed in Colorado. If only he had waited around that dreary little town to be sure that John Smith had died. If only he hadn't been so goddamned sure of himself, of his plan, of his infallibility.

He would take care of them tonight. By midnight his two biggest problems would be out of his life forever, and no one would suspect him—with the possible exception of Debra Jane, but he could handle her; he'd been doing it for nine years. If the police looked hard enough, they would find the stores where he would, this afternoon, buy the necessary supplies; they would find the credit card receipts in John Smith's name, would get the clerks' vague descriptions that closely matched Smith's, and they would find out about the strange fire in Colorado recently. It would be such a tragedy, a young woman murdered by the mysterious stranger she had picked up on a trip, but then, these were the nineties. What did a woman expect when she acted without discretion, with such careless disregard for her safety?

There would be questions, of course. The cops might discover that the house in Colorado had belonged to Simon Tremont, and they might question him. They would be intrigued by the coincidences: that this man claiming to be John Smith had been at the scene when Simon's house was destroyed, that Smith had gone to New Orleans when Simon was there, that there he'd met up with Teryl, who just happened to be Simon's agent's assistant, that Teryl's house was destroyed—and both Teryl's and her mystery lover's lives ended—in the same manner that the Colorado house was destroyed.

Simon would have his answers ready. Yes, he'd recently lost his house in Colorado to fire. Yes, he had moved away more than four months ago. No, he hadn't sold the house; he'd intended to return for vacations. No, he hadn't given anyone permission to use the place. No, he didn't know anyone matching this man's description.

He would see to it that Debra Jane's answers were ready, too. She would tell them how she'd met the stranger, how secretive and furtive he'd been. She would tell them how he had controlled Teryl, how her foster sister had had bruises from where he'd tied her up, how he had introduced her to sick, kinky sex games.

He would also make sure that Rebecca had the right answers. They would paint a picture of a mysterious, secretive, deceptive man who had become obsessed with the author he idolized, how he had broken into and destroyed his idol's home, how he had made his way to the city where Simon was appearing for the first time ever, how he had insinuated himself with Teryl, who had some connection to Simon, and had then made his way to the city where Simon now lived. They would show his obsession, his sickness, his derangement, and the cops would close the case.

Murder-suicide. It happened every day. Such a tragedy for the woman's family.

Such good fortune for Simon Tremont.

"Are you ready for bed?"

Resisting a yawn prompted by John's question, Teryl reached for the remote control and shut off the television. Once its noise was gone, the house seemed inordinately quiet. All she could hear was John's breathing, her own breath sounds, and, outside, the gentle drip of the rain. The storms had passed out of the area by noon, but the rain hadn't stopped yet. At least it was gentler now, not those torrential downpours that temporarily flooded the streets and were so hard on her garden. This was the kind of soaker rain that could lull a person to sleep. For the last hour she'd been halfway there already, snuggled in the big chair with John's arms around her, all but the dimmest light turned off, safe, warm, and relaxed. She wasn't sure she wanted to wake up enough to go upstairs and go to bed.

But she got to her feet, stretched, and finally gave in to the yawn. She was putting the remote on the table at the end of the couch when the phone there rang.

"I'm going on up," John said, squeezing past her. "Don't be too long."

She picked up the phone before the first ring was completed. Hearing D.J.'s voice at the other end, she sank down onto the couch, curling her feet under her, settling in for a long chat.

"Hey, girl, how have you been? You still have a job after last week's little escapade?"

"Yeah, I'm still working."

"How's John-boy? Is he still hanging around?"

"Yes, and he's fine. How are you?"

There was a long silence, then a sigh. "I've been worse . . . but I've also been a hell of a lot better." Her voice was uncharacteristically serious and more than a little depressed.

"Anything you want to talk about?" Teryl asked gently, but she knew the answer. D.J. had been only fourteen or fifteen years old when she'd stopped confiding in Teryl or anyone else. There had been an entire area of her life that was off-limits to discussion, involving men—not boys—and sex. She had mastered evasive techniques that any spy could have been proud of, had lied, deceived, manipulated, and maneuvered every conversation away from that side of her life. After a time, Teryl had learned not to pry, but tonight was a special circumstance. D.J. rarely got serious and never got depressed.

The telephone line hummed during another long silence, then the words came out in a rush. "I don't know how I screwed up so badly, you know. I kept thinking that if I just gave him time, if I did what he wanted, if I made him happy, then sooner or later he would *have* to appreciate me, right? He'd have to see how much I'd done for him, how much he needed me. Sooner or later he would have to love me."

Teryl sat in stunned silence. She had never imagined D.J. talking about making one particular man happy, about being needed and loved. All of their adult lives, her friend had made such a show of loving all men, of wanting all men, of never being tied down to only one. She'd had no interest in commitment and thought monogamy was for fools. When Teryl had discovered that Gregory was married and had gone crying to her foster sister for sympathy, D.J. honestly hadn't shared her dismay. Teryl enjoyed his company, didn't she? She enjoyed the sex. So what was the problem? Eventually, D.J. had said the things Teryl had needed to hear, but her heart hadn't been in it. She had only been mouthing the words; she certainly hadn't shared the sentiments.

"Damn it, Teryl, I've fucked up big this time. The things I've done . . . I just wanted . . . jeez, I wanted him to love me, that's all. I never meant for anyone to get hurt. I never intended for anything like this . . . I don't know what he's going to do, I don't know how . . . but I can't stop him. I tried talking to him, I tried reasoning with him, but when he gets like this . . . I didn't mean for this to happen. Do you understand, Teryl? It wasn't supposed to . . . Damn it, he was just supposed to love me!" D.J.'s voice broke, dissolving into a choked sob.

Tears. *Oh, God, something really is wrong,* Teryl thought. D.J. wasn't a crier. Teryl would bet she hadn't shed even one tear in the last fifteen years, and the only crying before then had been involuntary, when she was awakened by a bad dream and couldn't stop herself. She hated tears, thought they were a sign of weakness, and she was too damned tough to ever let herself be weak. But she was crying now, mournful, aching sobs that tore at Teryl's heart. "Are you at home, D.J.? I'm going to come over. We need to talk, okay? Give me a few minutes to let John know, then I'll be there in fifteen, twenty minutes, tops, all right?

The outburst of tears slacked off as quickly as it had begun. "No, don't be crazy. It's eleven o'clock at night, and it's still raining. I'm fine, Teryl."

"No, you're not. Come on, whatever's happened, it can't be so bad. Everything can be dealt with. I'll come over, you'll tell me what's going on, and we'll figure a way out of it. Whatever it is, we can come up with some solution, D.J. Every problem has a solution."

"No," D.J. said flatly. "I'm not at home, and you can't come where I am." She sniffled a few times, drew a deep breath, then spoke in a nearly normal voice. "I'm sorry I dumped this on you tonight. I shouldn't have bothered you. I just needed ... I'm sorry, Teryl."

"D.J., please tell me where you are," she said quickly, frantically. "Please let me know—"

She was talking to a dial tone.

With a frustrated sigh, she hung up, then immediately picked up the receiver again and dialed D.J.'s number. The phone rang three times before the machine clicked on. She hung up without waiting to hear the message. Switching off the lamp on the table, she sat for a moment in the dark.

She knew D.J. better than anyone else in the world, but she never would have guessed that her best friend was involved in a serious relationship. The only thing D.J. had ever been serious about—only two things, she corrected herself—were the family and sex. Men made the short list only because they were necessary for the sex. As for falling in love ... Teryl had honestly—if shamefully—wondered if her friend was even capable of it. Every relationship she'd ever had had been physical; she'd kept her partners at an emotional distance. She'd kept everyone, even the family, at a distance.

And now she'd fallen in love—and with someone who obviously was not healthy for her.

For the first time in their lives, D.J.'s situation, Teryl thought morbidly, wasn't so different from her own. She had fallen in love, too, and while she was now as convinced of John's sanity as her own, she had no doubt that he was unhealthy for her, too. Someday soon he was going to leave— he'd made that clear—and when he did, he was going to break her heart. She and D.J. could be heartbroken and lonesome together.

She was rising from the couch when, from the patio outside, came the sound of wind chimes. It wasn't the gentle brushing of one pipe against another, the way the breeze usually sounded them, but a discordant clang that made her freeze in place. She knew the sound well; she heard it every time she forgot they were hanging there and walked into them on her way to water the garden or to pick a few roses for her desk. It would take a hard wind to produce a similar jangle, but, as hard as she listened, she couldn't detect even a slight rustle in the trees.

She did hear a small thud, though, right in front of the first set of French doors. It made chill bumps rise on her arms, and the little hairs at her nape stood on end. A moment later the sound was repeated, this time in front of the middle set of doors, and only a few seconds later she heard it once again at the third pair. Staring hard at the sheer curtains, she saw a shadowy movement, bending, rising, then gliding silently away.

Her heart pounding, she began edging toward the hall door, sliding first one foot, then the other, over the tile floor. She was afraid to step out into the hallway, afraid to look to her left toward the back door where the outside light always burned and see the shadow of someone there, afraid of somehow being seen. Taking a deep breath for courage, she dashed across the hall, then took the stairs two at a time.

John was on his way from the bathroom to her room; she ran into him at the top of the stairs, colliding with the solid warmth of his chest, and forced herself to swallow back a scream. "There's someone outside!" she whispered, clutching his arms tightly, too afraid to let go, too afraid to speak aloud. "I heard the chimes and some noises, and I saw someone, John, I swear I did!"

For a moment he simply stared at her. He didn't try to brush her off, didn't try to explain away the sounds as the wind or her overactive imagination. "Do you have any sort of weapon in the house?"

She shook her head slowly. "You kidnapped me. Don't *you* have some sort of weapon?"

He smiled tautly. "Just Tom's Boy Scout knife. I'll check outside. You wait right here, and if I don't come back or if anything happens out there, call the police immediately. Understand?"

"Let's both wait here and call the police anyway," she suggested.

He pulled away from her and tugged the shirt he had just removed back over his head. "It's probably nothing, not worth disturbing them with. I'll have a look around—"

Teryl stopped him as he took the first step. "What if it's him, John?"

The look he gave her was sharp and serious.

"He blew up your house while you were in it, but you were lucky enough to survive. What if he's trying to kill you again? What if the noise was just a ploy to get you outside? What if he's waiting out there in the trees with a gun?"

After a moment, he gave her a nervous smile. "Oh, lady, you do have a way of building up my confidence. Go ahead and call 911. I'm just going to look." He gave her a little push toward the bedroom, then he went on downstairs, moving easily, silently in the darkness.

Teryl went into her room and automatically turned out the light before picking up the phone on the nightstand. She dialed the emergency number and was listening to it ring when a shout came from downstairs.

"Teryl!" There was sheer panic in John's voice. "Hang up the damned phone and get down here!"

Dropping the receiver, she raced down the stairs, spun around at the bottom, and turned toward the back of the house, where John had gone. Once again she ran into him in the hallway; this time he was the one to grab *her*. "I was looking out the kitchen window," he said, trembling almost as badly as she was. "He's got bombs out there, Teryl, a whole shitload of them, the same kind he used on my house. He's going to blow this place sky-high! We've got to get out!"

He was pulling her toward the door, but she was hanging back, digging her feet in but sliding along the tile anyway. "What if he is waiting out there, John? What if he doesn't intend to let you escape this time?"

"We've got to take our chances. A gunshot wound can be survived. An explosion fueled by God knows how many gallons of gasoline can't." Still, at the back door, he hesitated. Was he afraid to open the door? she wondered, knowing that *she* was. She wasn't sure she could make her fingers close around the lock and twist it. She was pretty damned sure she couldn't make herself turn the doorknob, pull open the door, and face whatever was out there.

"When I open the door," John whispered in her ear, "stay low, head for the truck, and run like hell. Don't stop for anything."

She nodded, even though it was too dark for him to see, even though he was peering outside the edge of the curtain on the back door instead of looking at her. After a long, silent moment that seemed to last forever, he took her hand in his, unfastened the lock, and yanked the door open. Immediately outside the door, she caught a glimpse of a glass jar, heard the tinkle of glass on stone as one of them—she wasn't sure whether she was responsible or John was—kicked it over on their dash across the patio, then onto the paving stones that led to the parking court.

As they approached the Blazer, he released her hand and sprinted around to the driver's side. In the time it took her to fumble the door open, climb inside, and fumble it shut again, he was already in the driver's seat, starting the engine, shifting into reverse, and releasing the emergency brake all at once. The tires squealed on the wet stones, and the back end fishtailed as he backed up in a tight circle around her car, then accelerated at dangerous speeds down the curving driveway.

They weren't more than a hundred yards away when the first explosion rocked the truck. John didn't stop, didn't take his eyes off the road or even slow down, but Teryl twisted around in the seat to watch. The remaining blasts came within seconds—she counted eight total—and sent debris flying through the air and flames shooting high into the sky. By the light of the eerie flames in the rain, she could catch glimpses of holes where walls used to be, of great gaping places where the red tiled roof had vanished. The entire portion of roof over her bedroom was gone, part of it probably blasted out, the rest fallen in on her dressing table, her floor, her bed.

Dear God, if that call from D.J. hadn't delayed her from going upstairs with John, they would have been in that bed. She wouldn't have heard Simon prowling around out back, wouldn't have seen him on the patio; John wouldn't have discovered the bombs, and they wouldn't have escaped. They would be dead now.

Slowly, numbly, she faced forward again, fastened her seat belt, and sank back into the seat. This attempt on their lives tonight shouldn't have come as a total surprise; John had pointed out that the only way that man could truly become Simon Tremont was by killing the real Simon. After he had tried and failed in Colorado, it was a given that he would try again, that this time he would be desperate to succeed. They should have been prepared for the possibility. Still, she was more than surprised; she was absolutely shocked. Learning the details of the attempt on John's life in Colorado had been unsettling, but also somehow unreal. She hadn't been there, hadn't witnessed the explosions, hadn't felt the concussions, hadn't smelled the gasoline, the flames, the smoke. *This* was real.

This was scary as hell.

Chapter Sixteen

———◆◆◆———

*T*hey were back in familiar territory: a shabby motel in a shabby part of town. But the situation had changed this time, John thought, standing at the window, watching the parking lot through a narrow slit in the drapes. Instead of heading toward a confrontation with Simon Tremont, they were running away. The bastard had almost gotten them tonight, had come within minutes of succeeding. If Teryl hadn't been on the phone, if she hadn't heard the chimes, he *would* have succeeded.

John owed his and Teryl's lives to D.J. Howell, he acknowledged with a wry shake of his head. Sweet damnation.

They had left the Grayson estate through a back gate Teryl had directed him to and had spent the next half hour driving around Richmond, making certain they weren't being followed. Finally they had ditched the Blazer in the parking lot of a nightclub, caught a cab, and come here. He had half expected the clerk to balk at renting them a room—they had both been soaking wet and reeked of gasoline from the jar they'd knocked over, they'd had no luggage, Teryl had no shoes, and they must have looked pretty damned desperate—but the guy hadn't given them a second look. A customer was a customer; as long as they had the means to pay—thank God he hadn't yet taken his wallet or his car keys from his pockets when Teryl had come racing up the stairs—the clerk couldn't have cared less how they looked.

As soon as they had gotten to the room, Teryl had made two calls. She had awakened her parents, telling them about the explosions, downplaying them, making it sound as if it had been a freak accident and not an attempt to kill them. She had called D.J., too, leaving a message on her machine.

Now she was lying in the double bed that stood in the center of the room, stripped naked and scrubbed clean. She hadn't realized she was barefooted until the odor of gasoline had pervaded the Blazer. At first she had found it amusing that she had run through gasoline and rain puddles, across rough rock and paving stone, without noticing that she was shoeless, but then amusement had turned to laughter, which had come too uncomfortably close to tears before she had regained control. Once her phone calls were completed, she'd retreated to the bathroom, where she had showered away the odor of gasoline. Finally, after hanging her clothes to dry, she had crawled between the sheets. She was quiet, but he didn't think she was asleep.

As if prompted by his thought, she broke her silence. "You haven't apologized."

He glanced at her. The lights were off, but enough illumination came through the curtains to allow him to identify the shadow on the bed that was her. "For what?"

"Getting my house blown up. For almost getting us killed."

Turning so that his back was to the wall beside the window, he faced her even though he couldn't really see her. "I *am* sorry. Don't you know that? Or do you need to hear the words?"

"I know it."

"Then why did you bring it up?"

She sat up, drawing the covers with her. "It's just a nice change. In the beginning, you apologized for everything. You were sorry you kidnapped me, sorry you bruised my wrists, sorry before you tied me to the bed, sorry after you did it. You've been that way all your life, haven't you? You've always felt guilty, always accepted responsibility.

Everything that ever went wrong was always your fault."
She broke off, and he saw a faint shrug of movement. "It's
nice to know that you don't feel any guiltier or any more at
fault for what happened tonight than I do."

She was right, he reflected. Of course, if he hadn't
dragged her into this mess, she wouldn't have become one of
Simon's targets; her house would still be standing, and she
would be safe. He regretted that he'd gotten her involved and
that he hadn't been prepared for Simon to strike again, but
the actual attack wasn't his fault. He couldn't take all the
blame for what Simon had done, the way he had always
taken all the blame for his parents' actions. This time he
would have to be satisfied with just a little of it.

"We need to go to the police," she said quietly.

"I called them while you were in the bathroom. I spoke to
a detective named Marcus."

"What did you tell him?"

"That we got out okay. That no one else was in the
house." He paused. "I told him I didn't know what caused
the blast. He said they'll find out, but it'll take some time. He
wants us to come in tomorrow—" He thought about how late
it was and amended that. "Later this morning and give a
statement."

"Why did you lie to him? Why didn't you tell him about
the bombs?"

"Remember when I told you that the fire at my house was
caused by bombs?" His chuckle was dry and unamused.
"You should have seen your face. You thought I was crazy.
If I tell some cop over the phone that the world-famous author, Simon Tremont, blew up your house in an effort to kill
us, *he's* going to think I'm crazy. If I tell him that Tremont's
trying to kill us because he's an impostor and *I'm* the real
Tremont, he's likely to get me locked up for observation instead of going after Tremont." He sighed wearily. "I'll tell
him the truth when we go in, face-to-face. I'll ask him to call
Sheriff Cassidy, and I'll show him the affidavit . . ." His
voice trailed off. The papers from the Denver bank had been
delivered early in the afternoon. He had shown them to Teryl
the moment she'd walked in the door, had given them to her

to read, and then had returned them to their envelope on the kitchen counter. If they hadn't disintegrated in the blast, they had turned to ash. "I'll ask him to call Zarelli at the bank."

Silence settled over the room, and John resumed his stance at the window, his gaze on the parking lot and the street beyond but his thoughts on a pile of smoldering rubble and ash a half dozen miles away. From the moment his house had been destroyed in Colorado, he had expected a second attempt on his life, but Simon had to find him first, and that, he had figured, wouldn't be an easy task. But he'd been wrong. Simon had found him, all right, apparently with little difficulty. How? How had he tracked John to Teryl's house? Only three people besides Teryl herself knew that he was staying with her. Her mother, of course, was above suspicion, which left D.J. and Rebecca.

For his own satisfaction, he would like to lay the blame on D.J., but the agent seemed a likelier suspect. Rebecca was troubled by the discrepancies, especially by the fact that John knew her private joke, but she didn't believe his story. She didn't want to. It was entirely possible that she had called Simon and warned him, that in delivering her warning, she had mentioned that the man challenging him was temporarily living with Teryl. She wouldn't have realized that she was putting their lives in danger, wouldn't have considered for a moment that Simon might try to kill them. She would have simply believed that she was doing what every good agent was supposed to do: looking out for her client.

Her voice soft in the darkness, Teryl spoke again. "Aren't you tired?"

"Honey, I may never sleep again." He was still wired, still running scared.

"The police will pick him up for questioning, won't they? They'll find some proof against him. He must have made some mistakes, left some trail. After all, he's a writer by profession, not a criminal. The pros can't plan perfect crimes; surely Simon can't, either."

"Maybe he can. Crooks don't tend to be the brightest guys in the world, while writers have to be reasonably intelligent. More importantly, a good writer has to be able to weave together complex plots with no loose threads. He has to understand motivation. He has to know human nature. Plotting a good book bears a striking similarity to planning the perfect crime."

"But Simon's 'perfect crime' failed in Colorado. It failed here. Maybe he's not so good a writer."

He stared at her shadow. "You told me in New Orleans that his *Resurrection* was the most impressive work you've ever read."

"I'm not talking about the actual writing. I mean the plotting. You outlined *Resurrection* for him. The outline was so detailed that all he had to do was follow along. He didn't have to deal with the plot. He didn't have to make things fit together. He didn't have to make sense of anything but the writing. I don't have any talent at either one, but I've read a ton of published books and two tons of unpublished ones, and I think the writing would be the easier of the two tasks. Maybe Simon's a better writer than he is a plotter, and that's why you and I are still alive. Maybe that will help the police to catch him."

With a yawn, she slid down into the bed again, snuggling under the covers, and, after a moment, he turned back to the window. He was watching traffic on the street out front when she spoke again, her voice soft and forlorn. "Everything I own is gone."

"I know. I lost everything, too." He sighed wearily. "I don't mind the clothes or the furniture or the videos. I don't care much about the office stuff, either, but I'd give five years off Simon's life to have the diskette and the hard copy of my own *Resurrection*, and I'd give ten years off *my* life to get back the pictures of Tom and Janie that were in the office. They were originals. Even Janie doesn't have copies."

"She never did call me, you know," Teryl said with another yawn. "I left a message on her machine Sunday asking her to please call me about you, and she never did."

This time he left the window and went to sit beside her on the bed. She automatically snuggled close to him. "You called my sister?"

"Hmm."

"How did you get her number?"

"Called information for Verona, Florida. Got all the J. Smiths." Another wide yawn. "There were seven, and she was number six. 'Hi, this is Janie. I can't take your call . . . ' I knew it was her because at the end she said, '*Adios, amigo,*' and you said she teaches Spanish. But she never called."

That was definitely Janie's message; on the rare occasions he had traveled into Denver, he'd always called her, and he had talked to the machine more times than he'd cared to. Teryl had no talent for writing or plotting, she'd said, but she hadn't done badly on this little bit of detective work. "That's because she's out of the country. Every summer she and some friends of hers who teach in other towns take some of their kids to Mexico for a month. The kids get school credit and some new experiences, and the teachers, according to Janie, get a great vacation. This summer they left the day my house burned down, and they won't be back until sometime in July."

"So she's safe." Her voice was soft and fading quickly. In another minute or two, she would be sound asleep.

"Safe from what?" John shook her a little. He was more than willing to let her have all the rest she needed, but first *he* needed an answer to his question.

"Safe from Simon. He has to kill you because of who you are, and he has to kill me because I *know* who you are. If he knows about Janie, he'll need to kill her, too, because she surely won't sit quietly and let him claim her murdered brother's life."

A chill crept over John. A fine writer—and brother—he was. He'd been too single-minded, concerned only with re-claiming his rights to Simon Tremont and the first twelve books. He hadn't considered any of those loose threads—beyond himself—that he'd been talking about earlier. Teryl was right. *She* was one because she had spent so much time with him, because she had come to believe him, because she had spoken to Rebecca on his behalf. Janie was another, because she knew the truth; while she might not be able to prove it, she could stir up some suspicions. She could certainly cause Simon some problems.

They were all three major liabilities to a man who undoubtedly was insane. They were all three in danger.

Was Simon even aware that Janie existed? He would like
to believe the answer was no. Following John's wishes, she
had never told anyone about her relationship to the author,
and *he* had certainly never discussed his sister with anyone
other than Teryl. There had never been any mention of her
anywhere in connection with his career.

But there had been evidence of her all over his house—
photographs and letters, her name, address, and phone number in his Rolodex—and Tremont had been there. Some of
the framed photos had been yellowed newspaper pictures
from her track days; one had even included him, along with a
caption to the effect of Janie Smith being congratulated by
brother John upon winning some race or another. He'd been
hugging her, his back to the camera, so proud of her that day.
It was the same way *she* had felt, she'd told him, years later
when she'd held her autographed copy of his very first book
in her hands.

He knew Tremont had been inside his house; the third
bomb had been placed somewhere inside his bedroom. Had
Tremont simply broken in, chosen the location for the bomb,
set it, then left again, or had he taken the time to look
around? Had he taken the time to notice the photographs on
the walls? John had to assume he had. He couldn't imagine
going to the trouble Tremont had gone through to track him
down, traveling to Colorado, renting a car, and driving the
narrow mountain roads to his house; he couldn't comprehend
Tremont being that close to the man he was so obsessed with
and not snooping through his belongings. Not sitting at his
desk, going through his papers, fondling his awards—hell,
maybe even *taking* his papers and his awards. Not finding
out everything he possibly could about John before putting
into effect his plan to destroy him.

He had to assume that Simon knew about Janie, had to believe that, just as he'd tried to kill John and Teryl, he would
soon try to kill Janie. Thank God she was safely out of the
country. Tomorrow he would make arrangements for her
protection when she returned . . . just in case he wasn't

around to take care of her then. Tomorrow he would make arrangements for Teryl, too, for her safety and for her future. Tomorrow he would face the fact that *he* just might not have a future.

But not tonight. Tonight he was safe, he was lying in bed with a beautiful woman in his arms, and he had a few quiet hours available for sleep. Tonight that was enough of a future to satisfy him.

Teryl felt achy, bruised, and pretty damned battered when she awakened. A glance at her watch showed that it was a few minutes after eight. Time to call Rebecca and tell her that she wouldn't be in, and then time to wake John so they could keep their appointment with Detective Marcus.

Rebecca sounded coolly friendly and professional when she answered the phone.

"Hi, it's Teryl."

Some of the friendliness disappeared from her boss's voice. "I was just thinking about you. There was a message on the machine for you this morning when I got in, and it brought you and our little disagreement to mind. Would you like to hear it?"

"Sure," she replied, wondering if by "disagreement," Rebecca was referring to the situation with John. If so, it was a hell of an understatement, but maybe that would change when she heard what Teryl had to say.

In the background, she could hear Rebecca pushing buttons, then the answering machine rewinding, clicking, starting to play. The voice was only vaguely familiar—she had talked to a number of people Sunday—but the message was clear. "Hi, this is Janie Smith calling for Teryl Weaver. I'm sorry for the delay in getting back to you, but I've been on vacation the last few weeks. In answer to your question, yes, my brother John does live in Rapid River. Is something wrong? I spoke to him just a few weeks ago, and everything seemed fine then. I'd really like to talk to you. I'll call back tomorrow, but if I miss you, you can give me a call any time here at home; I plan to be here all day. Thanks."

The machine shut off, and Rebecca returned to the phone. "This John Smith business has to stop, Teryl," she said sternly. "I know you believe the man's story, which is no surprise. You're sleeping with him, and you're half in love with him. But I won't tolerate it anymore. Do you understand?"

Teryl's temper started a slow burn. "Understand this, Rebecca: somebody destroyed my house last night. He set *eight* bombs outside. What didn't blow up burned down—and he almost got John and me, too. We barely escaped with our lives. If John's the impostor, the liar, why would anyone do that? Why would anyone want to kill him?"

"How do you know *he* didn't do it?"

"He didn't," Teryl said stonily.

"How do you *know*?"

"Because he was upstairs getting ready for bed when I saw Simon out there."

There was a moment's heavy silence, broken at last by Rebecca's small, shocked voice. "You *saw* Simon? You actually saw him, could identify him?"

"No," she admitted. "I just saw a figure. But it was him, Rebecca. He's the only one who can profit from killing John and me. It had to be him."

"That's ridiculous. Simon Tremont is a highly respected, world-renowned, and deeply admired author. You have no reason to believe he was behind this. You have no reason to believe that he's *not* really Simon."

Teryl's fingers tightened around the receiver. "John writes like Simon Tremont. He knows everything about Simon Tremont's career. He knows everything about *Resurrection*. He even knew your inside joke about Morgan-Wilkes."

Rebecca didn't respond right away. More than anything else, Teryl suspected, that one little joke bothered her. Then, her voice sharp, her manner abrupt, she dismissed all that. "Coincidence. Circumstantial evidence."

"And what reason do you have to believe Simon?" Teryl asked sarcastically.

"I have about seven hundred pages of reason sitting on my desk at home. I have *Resurrection*." She sounded triumphant and just a little bit challenging. "Let me tell you something, Teryl, based on more than twenty-five years of experience in this business. *Resurrection* is going to be one of the best-selling books of all time. Right now I don't give a damn who the real Simon is. I'm choosing the book. As far as I'm concerned, the man who wrote it gets to be Simon Tremont, and since even John hasn't been foolish enough to try to claim credit for that, Simon wins."

"But he's not—"

Rebecca interrupted her. "Let me tell you something else. You drop this Smith business and quit trying to ruin my agency and my reputation . . . or find another job."

Teryl grew very still. Her hand where she clutched the phone was clammy, and a funny, empty place had appeared deep in her stomach. "You're saying that if I don't turn my back on the truth, if I don't sell out my principles for your agency, your reputation, and your commissions, you'll fire me."

"That sums it up nicely."

As recently as three days ago, Teryl would have done almost anything to salvage her job. She would have argued, would have pleaded. She would have made promises and compromises. She probably would have begged. But not this morning. This morning she could think of only one thing to say. "Don't bother with warnings, Rebecca. I quit." Then, very quietly, very calmly, she hung up, returned the phone to the night table, and turned to find John watching her. Her cheeks turned a little pink. "I didn't know you were awake."

"Did I just hear you quit your job?" When she nodded, he grimaced. "Then I'm awake. You love that job, Teryl. Why did you quit?"

"Rebecca has decided, for the sake of the agency, that whoever wrote *Resurrection* gets to be the real Simon Tremont. She said that if I kept trying to prove that *you* were Simon, she would fire me, so I quit."

"Screw her. When we get this all straightened out, *I* intend to fire *her*. Then you can be my agent." He threw the covers back and was rising from the bed when Teryl spoke again.

"John, your sister's back in Florida. The only number I

gave her was the agency's because I didn't want you to know I had called her. She left a message there last night, asking me to call her today."

He sat back down and reached for the phone, bracing the receiver between his shoulder and ear while he dialed the number. "Something must have happened to make her cut the trip short. What did she say?"

Teryl repeated the message as close as she could recall it, all the while aware that the phone was ringing endlessly in his ear. How many rings had it taken for the machine to pick up when she'd called before? Three, maybe four. Definitely no more than five.

John disconnected and dialed the number again, with the same results. Holding the phone tightly, he looked at Teryl. "She said she would be home all day."

She nodded.

"Even if she had to go out for something, the machine should have picked up."

"Maybe you're dialing the wrong number."

He shook his head. "She's had the same number for ten years." Still, the next call he placed was to information. Teryl could see by his expression that he had the right number. There had to be some other reason why the call wasn't going through.

Like maybe Simon had already gotten to her.

She tried not to think about that, but her mind kept coming back to it; so, she could see, did John's as he dialed the number again, let it ring ten or twelve times, disconnected, then dialed again.

Setting the phone down with a bang, he got to his feet, grabbed his shirt from the chair, and headed for the bathroom. "Call the airlines. Get us two seats on the first flight to Verona."

"John, we can't just drop everything and go," she protested. "I don't even have any shoes, and we need to talk to the police here. We can call the cops down there. We can tell them that Simon has threatened her and ask them to keep an eye on her."

In the doorway he stopped and faced her. "She's my sister, damn it! She's all I've got! I've got to make sure she's all right." Drawing his wallet from his hip pocket, he tossed it on the bed in front of her. "Reserve one seat on the next flight to Florida. You can wait here and go shopping for shoes."

His sarcasm hurt, but not nearly as much as his message. He would leave her here in Richmond, here in the same city where the man trying to kill them was running free, here to fend for herself from the danger *he* had put her in, so he could go to Florida and look after his precious sister. She's all I've got, he had said. Well, he had *her*, too, and he knew it. He just didn't consider her important enough to rank with Janie. Outside of this very small part of his life—proving Simon Tremont a fraud and reclaiming what was rightfully his—he didn't consider her important at all.

She listened to the bathroom door slam behind him before she reached for the wallet. Flipping it open to his Master-card, she sat down, opened the Yellow Pages to the listing for Airlines, and began dialing. By the time he came out again, she had made reservations for two to Verona and had called for a cab. The flight would leave in ninety minutes; that would give them time to stop and get her a pair of shoes. She might even persuade John to spring for new jeans and T-shirts to replace their rain-stiffened clothing. Considering that, in the last ten hours or so, he'd gotten her house blown up, had almost gotten her killed, and had helped her lose her job, it seemed the least he could do.

They talked very little before the cab arrived. If he was surprised that she climbed into the backseat with him, he didn't say anything. He probably thought she intended to go shopping after dropping him off at the airport, she thought bitterly. He was at least partly right.

She directed the driver to stop at the nearest variety store. Without a word, John handed her a couple of twenties and sent her inside alone. She felt self-conscious as hell as she walked through the doors and down the broad central aisle toward the shoe department at the back. She tried to imagine how D.J. would handle the situation. Of course, D.J. would never be caught in public looking less than her best, but if the world stopped turning and the impossible did happen, she would bluff it out. She would be so brazen, so brassy and bold, that no one would dare say anything to her.

Maybe that was how she ended up, less than fifteen minutes later, hurrying back to the cab in an all new outfit: sandals, a short denim skirt, a T-shirt, a suede vest, and a pair of lace-edged panties that were more lace than panty. Her own clothes, still damp, stiff, wrinkled, and smelling faintly of gasoline, were in the ladies' room where she'd changed after checking out.

He gave her a long look. "Not exactly your style, is it?"

She stared out the side window, her jaw stubbornly set. No, short, sexy, and cute wasn't her style. Jeans were. Tailored outfits. Plain, unspectacular dresses. Long, flowing skirts and concealing jackets and flats and low heels. Nothing too tight, nothing too trendy, nothing that might bring a little attention her way.

Reaching across the seat, John drew his fingertips down her arm from just below the cuffed sleeve of her shirt to her hand. Her expression turned even harder, and she moved closer to the door. His own expression gained a degree or two in hardness, and he pulled back, clenching his hand into a fist on his thigh.

He had hurt her feelings at the motel with that crack about going shopping. He knew, of course, that replacing her ruined clothes was by no means more important to Teryl than Janie's safety, but she needed to understand the stress he was under. If that bastard Tremont got to Janie before he did, if anything happened to her because of him, he didn't think he could stand it. She had already suffered enough for the misfortune of being his sister. He couldn't bear any more guilt.

At the same time, to be fair, he needed to understand the stress Teryl was under. Through no fault of her own, she had lost her house, her car, and everything she owned. In the space of a few minutes, she'd gone from a comfortable home to nothing. Furniture, knicknacks, her mother's movies, family photos, closets filled with favorite clothes, her CD collection, her personal library, all the mementos and keepsakes of her life, had been reduced to ash. She'd been left with nothing but the clothes on her back, not even a pair of damned shoes. On top of that, she'd lost the job she loved, and then *he* had insulted her.

No wonder she didn't want him to touch her.

The cab driver pulled into a vacant space in front of the terminal and waited silently for his fare. John removed all but one twenty from his wallet, added one of his credit cards, and offered it and the cash to Teryl. "I'll be back as soon as I can. How can I find you?"

She gave the money a long look, but didn't take it. "It won't be necessary," she said at last, opening the door. "I'm going with you."

Her announcement sent a tremendous feeling of relief through him. He wanted to hug her tight, to kiss her hard. Instead, he simply paid the fare, then followed her out of the cab.

They checked in, found their way to the gate, and were soon seated on the plane, awaiting takeoff. The seats were first-class, all that was available on such short notice, Teryl stiffly explained. John didn't give a damn how much the tickets cost. He would have paid for the entire damned plane if it had been necessary.

He buckled his seat belt, leaned his head back, and blew out his breath. "Did I ever mention that flying scares the shit out of me?"

Finally, for the first time in far too long, she looked at him, meeting his gaze to see if he was serious. He was. He was so damned serious that he felt sick already, and they hadn't even moved away from the terminal yet. "No," she murmured. "You didn't."

"That's why I drove from Rapid River to New Orleans. That's why we drove from there to Richmond." The pilot started the engines, and John felt sweat beading on his forehead. "My family flew to Florida when I was . . . I don't know, fifteen, sixteen. It was the first time I'd ever been on a plane. I'd never been so scared or so sick in my life." His hands were clammy, and his heart was starting to thud loud enough to compete with the engines in noise level. "The next summer we were going to Hawaii for vacation. Not even the prospect of getting out on those waves was enough to get me willingly on that plane. I pleaded to stay home. I *begged*, and my father said, 'Grow up. Show a little backbone.'" He took a deep breath to ease the tightness in his chest. "I thought I was going to die. I swore when I got back home that I would never, ever get on a plane again as long as I lived, and I never did. Until now."

She reached across the space that separated them and slid her hand into his. "Just remember why you're here," she advised, curling her fingers tightly around his. "Just think about Janie."

He survived the takeoff, the flight, and the landing in Charlotte, where they changed planes. He also survived the second leg of their journey. He walked off the plane in Florida feeling like death warmed over, but he hadn't panicked. He hadn't lost control. He hadn't gotten sick as a dog. Maybe thinking about Janie had helped.

Holding on to Teryl definitely had.

They rented a car for the short drive to Verona, following the rental clerk's directions to Janie's neighborhood. She had lived there ten years, but John had never visited. He had loaned her the down payment for the house—she had refused his offer of a gift but had been happy to accept a loan—but he had never seen the house. Like Teryl's, it was stucco with a red tile roof and plenty of arches, but where Teryl's house was—had been—close to a hundred years old, this one had been new when Janie had moved in. She'd chosen the wallpaper and the paint, the tile and the carpet. She'd made the necessary modifications and had loved every part of it. When it was finished and ready for her to move in, she had pronounced it absolutely perfect.

Perfect. She used the word a lot for a woman whose life, thanks to him, had little perfection in it.

Teryl pulled the car into the empty driveway and shut off the engine, then glanced at him. "Are you feeling better?"

He nodded, even though it was a lie. He felt pretty damned lousy—still queasy from the plane and worried sick over Janie.

Teryl gave his hand a squeeze before climbing out. "Come on. Let's see if she's here."

By the time he got out, she was halfway to the small porch. If she thought there was anything odd about the ramp that replaced the usual steps, she didn't comment on it. She simply walked to the top, rang the doorbell once, waited a moment, then rang it again. She was reaching to press the button a third time when he stopped her. "Sometimes she's kind of slow. Give her a minute."

But maybe this morning she wasn't simply slow. Maybe she wasn't here. Maybe she was here but couldn't answer the door. Maybe she was inside, hurt and unable to call out. Maybe—

The door swung in, interrupting his worries, and for the first time in more years than he wanted to count, he found himself face to face with his sister. She looked at Teryl first, wearing a polite smile, waiting for a greeting of some sort; then her gaze shifted to him. The smile faded, disappeared completely, then returned, brighter, broader, than before. "Johnny?" she asked, her voice sharp and shaky with shock. "Oh, my God, it *is* you! Johnny!"

Teryl took a step back, trying not to stare as John bent to hug his sister. She tried to remember what he had told her about Janie and the accident that had killed their brother. All she'd needed to do to make the Olympic track team, he'd said, was show up for the trials, but she hadn't, because of the accident. But she had survived, Teryl had stated rather than asked, and he'd given a rather cryptic answer that she hadn't pursued. *More or less.*

She had survived in a wheelchair.

That was the other part of John's great grief regarding the wreck. It had been his car, and *he* had been driving. His brother had died, and his sister, the world-class runner, the Olympic hopeful, had suffered injuries so devastating that she would spend the rest of her life in a wheelchair. And John had walked away without a scratch.

Teryl felt a surge of pain in her chest. She wanted to wrap her arms around him and hold him close, wanted to convince him that he'd punished himself long enough, wanted to ease his guilt and his sorrow. She wanted to comfort him, to somehow heal him. She wanted to tell him that she was sorry she hadn't understood his need to come here, to see for himself that Janie was all right. She wanted to simply hold him and love him. But Janie was holding him now. He didn't need *her* when he had his sister.

Turning her back on them, she stared at the ramp. It hadn't really registered with her when they'd arrived; she hadn't noticed that all the other houses on the block had steps. She hadn't noticed the flower beds, either, that ran the length of the house, built up behind pink stucco walls to a height of two and a half to three feet—convenient for gardening from a chair. She was so unobservant.

Behind her Janie sniffled and dried her tears. "Jeez, Johnny, it's been twenty years since you brought a girl around. Introduce us, will you?"

Teryl indulged in her own covert sniff before turning to face them again. She wished he would reach for her hand, but he didn't. She wished he didn't look so embarrassed by the emotion—both Janie's and his own—but he did. He simply, plainly introduced her. "This is Teryl Weaver."

Janie's gaze turned speculative. "Teryl." She offered her hand, and Teryl moved forward to shake it. "We've traded messages." With that knowing, schoolteacher sort of look sharpening, she wheeled her chair back so they could enter the house. "Come on in, you two. I think you both owe me some explanations."

Traffic on I-95 was light when they crossed into North Carolina. It was coming up on 3:00 A.M., and they'd been driving, it seemed to Teryl, for forever. All their worries over Janie, it turned out, had been for nothing. After having the worst luck in the world and facing every misfortune that could have possibly befallen them—from lost luggage to stolen passports, from misplaced reservations to illnesses of every variety—she and her fellow teachers had ended their trip early and returned home. She had found Teryl's message on her machine and called the agency to leave her own message, but it wasn't her fault, she'd said with a shrug, if a fierce summer storm that night had knocked out the phones.

After explaining the situation with Simon, they had moved her into a hotel, and John had made arrangements for security guards to watch her every move. She had protested, but in the end, she'd done exactly what her brother wanted. It was because he didn't often ask favors of her, he had awkwardly teased, but she had disagreed. It was because she loved him.

No wonder Teryl had liked her from the start. They had that much in common.

Once Janie was settled and John had promised to see her again when this mess was over, they had headed north in the rental car. Although she hadn't relished the long drive when she was already feeling pretty ragged, Teryl hadn't even considered asking him to fly again . . . although she would give just about anything if he would find a motel and stop. She had dozed from time to time, but the rental car wasn't nearly as comfortable as the Blazer. There was no room to stretch her legs, and, even with the seat reclined, her position was still awkward. It was only sheer exhaustion that had allowed her to sleep what little she'd managed.

She was lying on her side, staring at billboards in garish, neon-bright colors, when John spoke for the first time in hours. "Are you awake?"

"Hmm."

"You've been extraordinarily patient today. I appreciate it."

She didn't reply. She wasn't like D.J. She didn't *want* to be appreciated. She wasn't that desperate yet . . . was she?

"Today was the first time I'd seen Janie since it happened. The accident," he explained, as if she could possibly need clarification. "She's changed so much."

Turning to face him, she pillowed her head on her clasped hands. "She's a lovely woman."

"She always was. She was the definitive California girl: tall, pretty, blue-eyed, blond-haired, tanned, healthy, athletic." He sighed heavily. "Then she got in the car with me, and all that changed."

"Only the athletic part. She's still tall, pretty, blue-eyed, blond-haired, tanned, and healthy. She seems better adjusted than most people. She's independent. She has a job she likes and plenty of friends. She keeps busy with volunteer work, teaching English as a second language to emigrants. She has a boyfriend." Teryl shrugged. "She's happy."

He gave her a long, measuring look. "I left you two alone for less than an hour while I took care of hiring the security people. You learned an awful lot about her."

"I like her," she said. "She's nice." After a long silence, she asked, "What happened that day, John?" Janie had asked her if she knew the events of that summer day, and Teryl had shaken her head. The other woman hadn't elaborated. She had simply gripped the chair's armrests tighter and fiercely murmured, "It *wasn't* his fault."

A mile or two went by with no response; then he sighed, a soul-weary sound. "It was June, seventeen years ago. We were celebrating Tom's graduation and the end of the spring semester with a family camp-out in the mountains. Our aunts and uncles and some cousins were there and, of course, our parents. I don't remember exactly how it started. My dad wasn't happy with my grades, he didn't like the company I kept, he thought I needed direction in my life, I didn't have enough ambition, I wasn't working hard enough, I wasn't taking school seriously enough. Whatever it was, it led to an argument. *Everything* led to an argument with him. I could be doing something, anything, and he would say I wasn't doing it right. I'd change and start doing it his way, and he would say I didn't have the balls to stand up for myself. So I'd go back to doing it my way, and he would say I was being disrespectful for ignoring his instructions, but, hey, that was what he got for raising a kid who was too stupid to know better. Nothing I did ever satisfied him, and that day was no different."

Teryl thought about her father, sweet, loving, and always respectful. He would never dream of calling a kid stupid, would never have anything but praise for a kid who was trying even if he was always failing. He loved kids—all kids, not just the pretty ones or the smart ones or the easy ones.

Sometimes the kids he loved best were the ones who were the hardest to love. The ones who needed it most. *Like D.J.*

"He'd been on my back all day, and I guess I was in the mood for a fight. I kept goading him, and finally he lost his temper. He slapped me in front of everyone there and told me to get out. He said I wasn't going to ruin the weekend for Tom and Janie. They didn't want me to leave like that, so they got in the car with me. Tom wanted to drive—he said I was too upset—but I wouldn't let him. I *was* upset, and driving fast and recklessly was a hell of a way to deal with it." He broke off for a moment, then continued in that same low, flat voice. "About five miles away I lost control of the car on a curve and drove off the side of the mountain. Tom died right away. Janie's spine was crushed. I was thrown clear."

Tears clogging her throat, Teryl wanted to ask him to stop, wanted to tell him that she'd heard enough. She didn't want to know the rest. She didn't want to hear how devastated he had been, didn't want to feel even the smallest portion of his grief. She'd heard enough sad stories in her life, and she didn't want to hear the rest of this one. But she couldn't stop him. He needed to tell it, and, in some perverse way, because she loved him, she needed to hear it.

"We were taken to the nearest hospital, and arrangements were made to fly Janie to L.A. They sent a state trooper to the campground to tell our parents, but he got the names confused. He told them that Tom was alive and I had died, and he brought them to the hospital. I'll never forget the look on their faces when they walked into the emergency room and saw me standing there."

A fragment of conversation she'd overheard years before came back to her. The subject had been Rico, one of the foster kids her parents had eventually adopted, and the occasion had been the morning after his first night with the family. He had come to them from the hospital, where he'd undergone surgery to repair the damage his mother's boyfriend had done; he had come bearing bruises, scars, casts, and stitches and an unholy fear of physical contact. There must be a special place in hell, her mother had said with a ferocity that had frightened Teryl, for people who hurt children. Twenty-two years later and more than twenty-two years wiser, Teryl could now fully appreciate her mother's sentiment. She hoped John's parents, especially his father, burned there.

"And that's why you left home," she said quietly.

"I had no reason to stay. They refused to believe it was an accident. They insisted I had acted out of jealousy and resentment. They wouldn't let me go to Tom's funeral or see Janie. I had to leave."

Abruptly he changed lanes and exited the interstate. Teryl sat up and looked around at the bright lights of yet another town. "Do we need gas?"

"No, we're stopping. You're tired. You need a bed where you can stretch out and sleep."

She automatically opened her mouth to protest. Instead, all she said was, "Thank you."

They stopped at the first motel, and she waited in the car while he checked them in. The room he rented was luxurious compared to some of the places they'd stayed, but she was too tired to care. Before he got the door closed and locked behind them, she was pulling back the covers with one hand while removing her clothes with the other. She stripped down to her T-shirt and panties, crawled into bed, and laid her head on the pillow with a heavy sigh. This felt like such comfort after last night's shabby motel, the flight, and the long hours in the car.

"Teryl?" John turned out the lights, undressed, then slid into bed beside her. She looked at him in the darkness.

"You know where he lives, don't you?"

Simon. In the hours since leaving Janie in the care of her armed guards, they hadn't mentioned Simon's name even once. Teryl hadn't even thought about him, hadn't wondered where he was or if he knew they were still alive. She'd been too tired to care that he would try once again to kill them, too weary to wonder how or when or where. She just hoped she and John weren't both so exhausted when he did try again. She hoped they had a fair chance of surviving.

Where Simon lived. Yes, she knew. When he had sent the change of address to the office, she had taken the time to locate it. The address was a rural route number, but a little checking had pinpointed for her exactly where that box number was. Feeling foolishly juvenile, she had driven out there a time or two, just to look, just to see where her idol was making his home. The hundred-year-old farmhouse hadn't been exactly what she'd expected, but, she had reasoned, it was probably temporary. He'd moved in the middle of writing *Resurrection*; he probably intended to live in the old house until the book was finished, and then he would probably begin construction on the sort of home she had imagined him living in.

"Yes," she answered softly, knowing what was coming and not wanting to hear it. "I know where he lives."

"In Richmond?"

"Just outside."

"Will you take me there tomorrow?"

"John—"

He laid his fingers over her mouth, silencing the argument she was about to offer. "Please, Teryl."

Sighing forlornly, she pushed his hand away and gave the answer he wanted. The answer she hoped she didn't come to regret. "All right, John. I'll take you there."

The farmhouse sat a few hundred yards off the county road in a shallow depression where the ground dipped low before climbing again on all sides. It was two stories, with a broad porch across the front and a steeply pitched roof in need of repair, with a long, snaking driveway better suited to the Blazer than the rental car that had brought them from Florida. The grass needed mowing, and the porch swing that should have hung in front of the bay window looked silly up-ended in the nearby flower bed.

There was no sign of a car. No sign of life.

He had lived in worse places, John thought, but he had a tendency to prefer better ones. He'd gotten a little spoiled that way.

"There's no one home."

Teryl turned from the house to him. "Now can we go to the police?"

"He's probably got all my stuff in there."

"What stuff?"

"My papers. My records. My contracts. I just assumed everything was destroyed in the fire, but he needed it if he was going to pull this off. If he was going to succeed at becoming Simon Tremont, he had to know all the details of my business."

"So instead of simply blowing up your house and trying to kill you, he broke in first and took the time to carry out everything relating to your work. Then all he had to do was bring it back here, put your files in *his* file cabinets, and *voilà*, instant history. Instant documentation."

"Instant identity." John stared at the house. It needed a coat of paint and an owner interested in upkeep and maintenance. Maybe Simon didn't care about that sort of thing. Maybe, until he'd gotten John's royalty check last month, he hadn't had the money to fix up the place. Maybe since he'd gotten the check, he'd been too busy. Living someone else's life might tend to be a demanding task, especially when that someone was famous. "I want to go in."

"Oh, no, John," Teryl groaned. "The man who lives there wants you dead. Have you forgotten that? What if he comes home and finds us in his house? What do you think he's going to do?"

He gave her a steady look. "I just want to see if he has my papers. I want to know if he's got my pictures." If Tremont had taken the business stuff, he might have taken the personal stuff, too. "You don't have to come with me. You can wait in the car, and if you see him coming, you can honk the horn to warn me."

"The hell I can. He knows me, John, he's seen me and talked to me, and he wants to kill me almost as much as he wants to kill you. If you insist on going inside, I'm going with you."

He looked at her a moment longer, then shifted into gear, pulled into the driveway, and backed out again, heading back toward town. He didn't go far, though, just a couple hundred yards to where another road angled off to the right, curving around before disappearing into the trees. He pulled up far enough that the car was obscured from view from the road, then cut off the engine. "You don't have to do this, Teryl," he said, giving her one last chance to back out. "You'll be safe here."

"I'll be safe with you." Still, as they walked away from the car toward the driveway, she slipped her hand into his and held on tightly.

The front door was locked; so was the back door. John didn't think twice about breaking the glass in the door, reaching inside, and opening the lock. The door opened directly into the kitchen, a big square room with a table in the center, twenty-year-old appliances, and not so much as one dirty dish in the sink. The man who lived there was neat, almost compulsively so. John considered himself a better than average housekeeper, but even he never made things shine like this. Even he never lined up the spices on the counter in alphabetical order or turned the handles on all the coffee cups in the glass-fronted cabinets in exactly the same direction.

Clutching his hand with both of hers, Teryl followed him into the room, the broken glass crunching under her shoes. He swore he could feel her pulse in the tips of her fingers, and it was racing. She had never done anything illegal in her life, and she was terrified of getting caught—of getting killed. He was surprised that she hadn't opted for waiting in the car. He was grateful that she had come with him.

There was no sound in the old house—no hum from an air conditioner or refrigerator, no ticking clock. The place was more than just quiet; it sounded empty. Abandoned. As if no one really lived there. They walked down the hall, past the dining room and an old-fashioned bathroom with a pedestal sink and crystal handles on the faucet. Just before they reached the stairs opposite the front door, they came to the room they were looking for.

There was a sturdy lock on the office door, bright and shiny in contrast to the ancient hardware of the knob and latch. Maybe there was someone in Simon's life—a wife, kids?—from whom he was hiding his new identity. Funny, but John had never thought of Simon as having family or people who loved him. He had automatically assumed that this new Simon was every bit as alone as the old Simon—John himself—had always been. He had assumed that someone as crazy as Simon must be would have nothing to invest in a relationship as, for so many years, *he* hadn't. But maybe he was wrong. Or maybe Simon was simply paranoid.

Whatever the reason for the lock, it wasn't doing its job this morning. The door had been left open. Gaining entry was a simple matter of walking across the threshold. After hesitating only a moment, John did just that, pulling Teryl along behind him. Giving her a little push toward the front, he said, "Watch out the window for visitors, would you? But stay off to the side, out of sight."

She was halfway there when suddenly she froze in place. "Oh, my God," she whispered, staring in such horror that John's blood turned cold. He moved to her side, expecting the worst—finding Simon dead?—but still utterly unprepared for what he saw.

In the recessed wall space between two built-in bookcases were photographs, a dozen or more, a damned shrine of them. Only one was framed, the one in the center, a posed picture of the sort found in college yearbooks. The others were held in place with thumbtacks, and they had been there long enough for the edges to curl, for the sun to fade the wallpaper around them.

And every single one of them was of Teryl.

Chapter Seventeen

She was young in the shots, eighteen, twenty, twenty-two. In this one she was walking across a parking lot, in that one sitting on a bench with friends, in the next one bent over a book in the library. In all of them except the yearbook shot, she was totally unaware of the photographer.

"I thought you didn't know this guy." His voice was little more than a whisper. It was the only way to contain the distaste, the disgust, the fear.

"I swear to you, I never met him before New Orleans!"

"Well, honey, he sure as hell knew you. These pictures are ten years old!"

Raising a trembling hand, she pointed to the yearbook photo. "Eleven. Eight. Seven." The last one she pointed out was the most intimate. It included just enough of her clothing to recognize the gown of a college graduate. She seemed to be looking directly into the camera, her expression distant, pensive.

"Jesus, Teryl, he's been keeping track of you all these years. Why? How could he get so obsessed with someone he'd never met?"

"He's never met you," she pointed out numbly.

"I know, but that's different. He knew me through my books. How did he come into contact with you?"

"I don't know." With a shudder, she turned her back on

the pictures and glanced around the room. Her face was pale, the color drained even from her lips. "Look in those file cabinets. See if what you need is in there."

He watched until she stopped near the window seat before he turned to the tall wooden file cabinets. He hit pay dirt in the first drawer he opened: neatly labeled files held his contracts, his royalty statements, his correspondence with Rebecca and Candace Baker. The next drawer was the same, and the next and the next. Everything he'd thought lost in the fire was right here in Simon's cabinets.

When he opened the final drawer in the fourth cabinet, things got even more interesting. There were no files there, just stacks of books—*his* books—that had been read and pored over until the spines were broken. Passages were highlighted in blue, pink, yellow, and green, and notes had been penciled into the margins. Each of the books resembled nothing so much as a textbook . . . which was exactly what Simon had made them. He had studied them in great depth, had virtually taken apart the stories and put them back together again. A folder of pages tucked between them showed how he had learned the structure, how he had mimicked the style, practicing over and over, never giving up until he got it right.

As John thumbed through *Masters of Ceremony*, a thin white envelope fell to the floor. He picked it up and opened it, removing the card inside. The front was a design of pastel swirls. Inside was yet another photograph, taped beneath the message in flowing black script: *If you can dream it, you can be it.* Underneath the snapshot, Simon had written his own message. *I can be Simon Tremont . . . for you, Teryl.* Christ.

Tearing the picture from the card, he held it up. "Recognize this, Teryl?" It was different from the others. This one hadn't been taken from a distance with a telephoto lens. it was a closeup, taken in her own house by somebody she knew.

She came away from the window, reached out, then decided against touching the picture. "I don't . . . John, he couldn't have been in my house with me. I would remember, damn it!"

"Maybe he wasn't. Maybe whoever took this gave it to him."

"That's impossible. That picture was taken by . . . " Her words trailed off, and the little color that had returned to her face drained away again. Her hand unsteady, she took the photo from him and walked over to stand in front of the nearest bookcase. "Oh, God," she whispered. "This picture was taken by D.J."

D.J. Only yesterday, when he had been wondering how Simon had found him at Teryl's house, he had so easily written off D.J. Rebecca had seemed so much more likely a suspect. She knew Tremont. She knew how to contact him. She had a vested interest in protecting him. For all he'd known at the time, for all Teryl had known, D.J. had had no connection to the man. She hadn't even shown the most casual interest in him.

She had fooled them both. She knew him well enough to give him this snapshot of Teryl.

Helpless and confused, she looked at John, her expression a silent plea that she was wrong. "When she called Wednesday night, she was talking about this man, about how she'd done so much to try to make him love her. She'd never meant for anyone to get hurt, she said. She had never intended for anything 'like this' to happen, but she couldn't reason with him. She couldn't make him stop. Do you think . . . Jesus, John, do you think she meant Simon?"

He opened his mouth to speak, but before he could, another voice broke in. "Go ahead, John, lay it out for her in words simple enough for her to understand," D.J. said coldly. "Tell her of course I meant Simon."

Teryl looked as if she couldn't take any more shocks. She was staring at her foster sister, her best friend—the last person in the world she had expected to run into here—with a total lack of understanding. She knew what she was seeing, knew what she was hearing, but absolutely could not, John suspected, understand it. He knew how she felt. It seemed that his own world had just tilted askew, and he didn't have near the emotional investment in D.J. Howell that Teryl did. Hell, he didn't even like the woman.

D.J. moved away from the door, coming farther into the room. "What the hell are you doing here? You have no right to come here, to break into Simon's house, and go through his things."

"Not much here is actually his, though, is it?" John asked.

Coming across the room, she snatched the card and the book from his hands, returned them to the drawer, and pushed it shut. "It's *all* his. You're fools to come here. Don't you know he plans to kill you? Don't you know he's already tried?"

She was going to be sick, Teryl was sure of it. She had never felt such sorrow, such betrayal, or such hurt. This was all simply a bad dream. She couldn't have broken into a crazy man's house, couldn't have discovered all those creepy pictures of herself here. She couldn't be hearing what D.J. was saying, couldn't be feeling the fear and the sickness she was feeling. Her best friend couldn't be standing there talking so calmly about her own murder. D.J. couldn't be a part of this.

But she was. As much as the idea shocked her, Teryl knew it was true. She felt it on some level deep inside. She felt it with a certainty that made her want to weep.

"You did it, didn't you?" she asked, her disillusionment so great that it seemed to round her shoulders. "You gave him John's address. You gave him the outline for *Resurrection*."

D.J. smiled mockingly. "Honey, I gave him the goddamned idea . . . although, to be honest, at the time I didn't really think he could pull it off. Yes, I gave him the address and the outline—and it was all courtesy of you, Teryl."

"How?" John asked.

"Every day she goes home, and she puts her keys in a cute little basket on the kitchen counter, where anyone who goes into the house could take them. So I did. I pocketed them one evening, I went to the office, and I found everything Simon needed. I used the agency's own copy machine," she said with a laugh. "I made copies of everything, put the originals back, went back to Teryl's house on the pretext of picking up a jacket I'd left, and slipped the keys right back into the basket. It was so easy. No one suspected a damned thing, especially Teryl."

Especially her, Teryl thought miserably. She had no doubt it had happened exactly the way D.J. described, but she didn't remember it. She didn't remember her friend coming over, leaving, then coming back again. She had certainly never noticed her keys missing.

"Of course, the only address in the agency's files was the mailbox in Denver, but Simon's a resourceful man. As soon as he finished the book, he flew to Denver. It cost him a nice little bit of money, but he persuaded the clerk to let him have a look at their records—the ones with John Smith's home address on them. Then it was a simple matter of going to Rapid River and locating Route 4 and the box number."

"Why?" Teryl asked, her voice shaky with threatening tears. "Why did you do this? Why is *he* doing this?"

D.J.'s expression slipped from cocky and sarcastic into pure sorrow. "You don't even know who he is, do you? You went to New Orleans with him, you talked to him and spent time with him, and you didn't even recognize him!"

"I never met him!" she protested. "How could I recognize him?"

Pushing past her, D.J. grabbed a large, heavy book from the bottom shelf of the bookcase and thrust it at Teryl. It was their college yearbook, freshman year. D.J. flipped it open to a section marked with an envelope and stabbed one long red nail at a photograph near the bottom, identified as Richard Martin.

The page was headed English Department, and she recognized the subjects in several of the small photographs as instructors she'd studied under during her four years at the university. After a moment's study, she also recognized Simon—younger, looking very different with dark hair and a heavy beard, but still Simon. Still intense. Still creepy. Even in the flat dimension of a photograph, those eyes were enough to send shivers down her spine. They were enough to make her skin crawl. The idea of facing him in reality, of sitting across from him ... Of sitting in front of him, student before instructor ...

"Oh, God," she whispered. She let the book fall to the desk. The pages fluttered, then settled again, the disturbing picture still staring up at her. "That teacher?" she asked, staring in dismay at D.J. "The writing teacher we had our freshman year?"

D.J.'s smile was chilling. "So you do remember."

Teryl backed away until she bumped into John. Seeking reassurance, she clutched his hand tightly.

"You've met him before?" he asked, drawing her near.

"He taught creative writing at the university. We took it our first year because we thought it would be fun, but it wasn't."

"He had a crush on Teryl from the first time he ever saw her," D.J. filled in. She was still standing at the desk, rubbing her fingertip across the photograph. She was stroking the lifeless image, gently caressing it. "She wouldn't give him the time of day. She said he was weird. Creepy. Spooky. She dropped out of the class after only two weeks. She said that sitting in front of him for an hour three times a week made her skin crawl." Her smile was vague, distant. "He made *my* skin crawl, too, with pleasure. He knew exactly what I wanted, exactly what I needed, and he gave it to me."

"But you couldn't give him what he wanted." John's voice was quietly sympathetic. "You couldn't be Teryl."

D.J. drew a deep breath, then let it out noisily as she looked at them. "No, I couldn't. He used me to keep track of her. I gave him her class schedules, I told him who she was dating and what was going on in her life, and in exchange he let me be part of his life. I loved him, and he loved her, and she forgot he existed. I hated you for that, Teryl." Picking up the yearbook, she studied the picture for a moment, then hugged it to her chest. She seemed suddenly smaller and achingly vulnerable. "Oh, God, I've hated you ever since I met you!"

"I'm sorry, D.J.," Teryl said, her voice catching in her throat. "I never knew . . . I didn't *want* him to like—"

"You should have *loved* him!" D.J. interrupted angrily, slamming the yearbook down on the desk. "But, no, everyone loved sweet Teryl. She had her pick of people to love in return. Some lonely little college instructor who tried to teach no-talent idiots how to write wasn't good enough for her. He wasn't handsome enough. He wasn't rich enough. He wasn't famous enough. Hell, he wasn't the great Simon Tremont, at whose feet she worshiped."

"He wasn't *normal* enough!" Teryl snapped. "For God's sake, D.J., even then we knew there was something *wrong* with this man! He was so intense, so peculiar, so odd. We used to joke about him, that he was probably a serial killer or a deranged stalker or something!"

"*You* used to joke about him," D.J. disagreed, her voice as cold and hard as granite. "You and those stupid bitches you called friends. You were the stupidest bitch of all. You talk about normal. Do you think *you're* normal? After what your grandfather did to you, after what your mother let him do, do you really believe, deep down inside, that you're even close to normal?"

Beside John Teryl became stiff and unyielding. She was barely breathing. "I don't know what you're talking about," she said, her voice unnaturally quiet. "Grandpa Weaver never did anything to me, and I never knew Mama's father."

"Stop it!" D.J. demanded, clenching her hands into fists, squeezing her eyes shut for a moment as if it might stop her from hearing. When she opened them again, she looked at Teryl with such anger, with such pure malice and hatred, that John automatically moved between them. "Grandpa Weaver isn't your grandfather. Lorna and Philip are not your parents. For Christ's sake, Teryl, how can you be so *stupid*? How can you not at least *suspect* the truth? How can you live your entire life with these people and never wonder why you don't look like them? Why there's no more resemblance between you and them than there is between them and every other kid they took in? How can you believe you're so damned special that, of the hundreds of kids they've played parents to, you're the *only* one who really belongs?"

"You're lying," Teryl said, her voice soft but so intense that it quavered. "You've always resented the fact that Mama and Daddy never adopted you. You've always believed that if they had *really* wanted you, they could have found some way to force your parents to relinquish their rights. You've always resented that *I* was their own and you never could be."

"Believe what you want, Teryl, but *I* know the truth. *I've* seen the adoption papers. *I've* read the doctors' and the psychiatrists' reports. They talk about repression and denial, about not forcing Eliza—that's what they called you then—to face the truth." She smiled maliciously, taking such pleasure in her cruelty. "*John* knows the truth, too. Look at him. It's in his eyes."

Teryl whirled around, staring up at him, her eyes pleading for denial, for reassurance that her foster sister was, indeed, lying. He'd never been much good at lying, but, hell, he made up stories for a living. He could give it a try. "Don't listen to her, Teryl. She *has* always resented you. She's always hated you because she's always wanted to be you. If she could be you, then she wouldn't have to be Debra Jane Howell and she wouldn't have to remember all the awful things Debra Jane endured at the hands of people who were supposed to love her. You can't believe her, Teryl. You can't trust her."

She wasn't completely convinced, although she wanted to be. He could see in her expression just how desperately she wanted to believe him. But some part of her knew. Hidden someplace deep inside, someplace that she had kept safely blocked off for most of her life, she knew that D.J. was telling the truth. That she, like the other eight Weaver kids, was adopted. That she, like too many of the Weavers' foster kids, had been abused. That she, like D.J., had horrors in her past. D.J., though, drew strength from hers, while Teryl had had to forget hers in order to survive.

"Bastard," D.J. said; then she shrugged. "It doesn't matter. You can lie all you want, but one of these days she'll remember. One of these days she'll know the truth . . . and I hope it makes you suffer." She directed that last vicious comment to Teryl.

"Why?" Teryl demanded tearfully. "Why are you doing this?"

John slid his arm around her waist and answered with far

more sympathy than he'd believed he could feel for her friend. "Because D.J. never managed to forget. Because she's suffered every day of her life, and just once she wants someone else to feel the pain."

Behind them the boards just inside the door creaked, and, in front of them, D.J.'s expression became panicky. John knew before he turned what he would see. It made his muscles tense, made shivers dance down his spine. Still, he forced himself to slowly turn, taking Teryl with him, until he was finally face-to-face with Richard Martin, dying to be known . . . no, *killing* to be known as Simon Tremont.

There was an unholy light in his eyes, an elation that Martin visibly struggled to control. He must realize that fate, for once, was on his side, that it had delivered to him the perfect opportunity to take care of them and to solidify his claim on Tremont for all eternity. He could kill them right here and bury their bodies anywhere on this sprawling old farm. Only D.J. would know the truth; only Janie and Rebecca might suspect it. Rebecca, for whom the agency was everything, just might look the other way, even on murder. Janie couldn't prove her suspicions, and D.J. . . . .

Hell, D.J. was in love with him; she'd been helping him all these years. She had just admitted that the impersonation had been her idea. John could easily imagine how she had goaded Martin to this point. *Teryl doesn't like Richard Martin; Teryl doesn't know Richard Martin even exists. But she admires Simon Tremont; she worships Tremont. If you could write like him, she would admire you, too.* Her intent, John would bet, had merely been to mock him, to taunt him with what he couldn't have, but Martin had taken her challenge seriously. Somewhere along the way, in his twisted mind, *write like* had become *be like*, and *be like* had soon changed to *be*.

If you can dream it, you can be it. I can be Simon Tremont . . . for you, Teryl. He'd done it all for her, but she still hadn't liked him. To add insult to injury, she'd gotten involved with the very man Martin had tried so hard to become.

All this time, John thought with a humorless smile, he'd

been feeing guilty for dragging Teryl into this mess, when the truth was *she* had unwittingly dragged *him* in. *She* had been the object of Martin's obsession, not Simon Tremont. If she had been a fan of King instead, of Grisham or Clancy, John would probably still be living his quiet life up in the Colorado mountains.

When Martin spoke at last, it was in a mild voice, one that didn't even hint at what was to come. "Jeez, I go to town to run a few errands, and people break into my house. What's this country coming to?" He moved closer, but at an angle, keeping them all a safe distance away. "John Smith. I recognize you from your pictures. And Teryl. Everything I did was for you . . . and it turns out, you're not worth any of it. You're as much a slut as she is." He jerked his head toward D.J. "You don't deserve even a moment of my devotion. You're a whore."

"And you're crazy," Teryl replied, her voice every bit as mild.

Martin smiled, amused by her retort, then turned cold and harsh when he looked at D.J. "Did you bring them here?"

"No." She answered quickly, desperately. "I came out to see you, and as I drove around the last curve in the road, I saw them sneaking around back. I came in to make sure they didn't disturb anything, to make sure they didn't take anything, before you got back." Twisting her hands together, she moved toward him. "What are you going to do, Simon?"

"Kill them, of course." He smiled again—and *crazy*, John thought, didn't come close to describing it. "They've given me no choice."

Although she claimed ownership of the original plan, although she had acknowledged when she first arrived that Martin wanted them dead, D.J. seemed disturbed by the idea now. Wringing her hands again, she looked from him to John and Teryl, then back to him. "I understand him, but . . . do you have to kill her, too? She's not important. Who could she tell? It's all so crazy that she didn't even believe it herself in the beginning. No one would believe her now."

"Don't be a fool, Debra Jane. *Everyone* would believe her. Slut or not, she's not like you. She doesn't lie as naturally as she breathes. They both have to die." Sliding open the credenza drawer, he withdrew a pistol, a hell of a gun, the kind that could undoubtedly leave a hell of a hole in a person, and leveled it at them.

John stiffened, dread turning his skin cold, and Teryl, next to him, shifted behind him. It wasn't a safe place to hide, he thought regretfully. With a gun like that at this close range, the bullet would tear through them both without losing any of its momentum. With a gun like that, they didn't stand a chance in hell of surviving. That meant he had to stall. He had to find some way out, some chance for escape, at least for Teryl. "You're going to shoot us right here. In your office. Where you work."

"Well, I'd rather not, but if it's necessary . . . " Martin shrugged. "Actually, I'd rather not shoot you at all. It seems a shame to change methods so late in the game."

"So you'd rather keep trying the bombs until you get them to work."

"Oh, no, not me. Why, I'm just a writer. I know nothing about bombs." He shrugged again, then used the gun to gesture around the room. "I never cared much for this place. It was fine for somebody like that hack—" with the barrel, he pointed toward the yearbook on his desk, toward the picture of himself—"but it's hardly suitable for an author of my stature. I deserve something a little grander, something along the lines of the Grayson estate, don't you think, Teryl? I can get rid of this place and the two of you *and* throw suspicion your way, all in one afternoon."

Teryl slowly edged out to once again stand at John's side. She might be scared senseless, might be facing death much sooner than she wanted, but she'd be damned if she would do it cowering. Not in front of this crazy man. "And how would you do that?"

Once more he pointed the gun at them—or, specifically, at John. "He's already connected with the bombing in Colorado. Of course, right now the sheriff believes he was the intended victim, but it wouldn't take more than a few well-chosen words to change his perception entirely. He's also connected with the bombing of your house. The fact that he survived both isn't in his favor. Do you know what the odds are of an innocent victim who is truly uninvolved escaping a building only seconds before it blows up not once but *twice*? Walking away once is a miracle. Walking away twice is suspicious. Dying the third time . . . that's justice."

D.J. approached him, coming between him and Teryl and John. "Please, Simon," she said, her voice small and pathetic. "Please don't kill Teryl, please."

He looked at her with enough scorn to make Teryl flinch, but it seemed to have no effect on D.J. She seemed used to it. "You hate her. You've always hated her at least as much as you loved her. Don't beg for her life."

D.J.'s shrug made her hair shimmer. She looked the same as always—beautiful and provocative—but for the first time in her life, Teryl didn't envy her. For the first time she felt nothing but pity for the woman she had believed was her best friend. "I've begged for plenty of other things. I don't mind begging for this. Please, Rich—"

Neither woman was prepared for the sudden blow he struck her. One moment he was apparently calm; an instant later, he was slamming the butt of the gun into D.J.'s face. She was so small and slender, and he struck her hard, knocking her to the floor. Stunned and frightened by her friend's stillness, Teryl instinctively moved to go to her side, but John caught her arm and held her back. "Takes a lot of courage to hit someone half your size," he said in a faintly mocking drawl.

"Takes a lot of stupidity to taunt the man who's holding a gun on you." Martin walked toward the open door and waited there. "Let's go. I've got plans to make. I can't screw around with you anymore."

Teryl went first with John right behind her, his hand resting at the small of her back. With Richard Martin right behind him, she didn't want to think what he felt in *his* back.

Martin directed them to the kitchen, then through a side door into a combination utility/workroom. A battered washer and dryer stood in one corner, a worktable in the middle. Shelves of tools were braced along one wall, and a hot water heater filled the corner. The room smelled faintly of fabric softener and lint and almost overpoweringly of modeling clay and gasoline. The source of those last odors was the items laid out on the table. A five-gallon can of gas. Four one-gallon glass jars. Clay. Timers. Wire filaments.

"Everyone who's come into contact with you believes you're delusional, John," Martin said from the far end of the table. "They know you think you're me. It won't be too hard to convince the authorities that you *were* insane. You became obsessed with Simon Tremont, began having delusions that you *were* Tremont. You blew up your own house and Teryl's to try to convince people that someone was trying to kill you to keep you quiet. When you failed to prove your claims, you became violent, as mentally ill people sometimes do, and you decided to kill me. However, something went wrong, and one of the bombs detonated before the others were in place, killing you and the poor unfortunate woman who was foolish enough to believe in you." He smiled, enormously pleased with himself. "Hey, I'm pretty good at this. I ought to be a writer."

John leaned back against the windowsill, his arms folded over his chest. "Your plot has holes," he said flatly. "For starters, not everyone thought I was crazy. Rebecca *knows* I was telling the truth. For the sake of her reputation, she's not going to do anything about it—so far—but if Teryl and I turn up dead, how long will she stay quiet?" He paused only briefly. "And what about my family? They know the truth. They know about you. Do you think they'll sit back and let you win?" Another short pause. "What about Teryl's family? They'll never accept that she was helping a madman try to kill someone when she died. And D.J. She may hate Teryl as much as she loves her . . . but the same can be said about her feelings for you, can't it? Knowing that you killed her sister will eat at her. It will destroy her . . . and she'll destroy you."

"Minor details. I'll take care of them all once you two are out of the way." He waved the gun again. "Get started."

Teryl looked at John, who glanced at the table filled with equipment, then smiled thinly. "If you think I'm going to put together the bombs that you'll then use to kill us, you *are* crazy. You want to blow us up, you'll have to do it yourself."

Before Martin's movement even registered with Teryl, he was halfway around the table and holding her wrist in a vicious grip. He yanked her to him, holding her tight against his chest, and pressed the barrel of the gun to her temple. "I don't like that response, John," he said mildly. "Come up with another one . . . before I blow her fucking brains out."

Looking regretful as hell, John left the window and approached the rickety table. She watched as he uncapped the gasoline can, then tilted it over the first jar, dribbling it out in a thin stream. When it was half-full, he stopped and looked up at Martin. "You have to give me directions. I've never made one of these before, and I didn't stop to examine them closely at Teryl's house. How much gasoline?"

"That will do. Go ahead and fill the rest."

She wondered what the chances were they would get out of this alive. Probably not very good. She wished she had known the last time she'd seen her mother that it *would* be the last time; there were things she would have liked to tell her. There were things she wanted to say to John, too, starting and ending with *I love you* and with about a million *I'm sorrys* in between. She was sorry she had ever doubted him, sorry she had distrusted him, sorry she had demanded proof, sorry she had thought him crazy, sorry she had gotten him into this in the first place.

Following Martin's directions, John placed the filaments next, suspending them in the space between the mouth of the jars and the surface of the gasoline. Teryl wished there was something he could do to save them. She wished she had the courage to tell him not to worry about her, not to obey Martin's orders simply to protect her. If she had to die—and it was looking very much as if she did—she would prefer a gunshot to the head over the blast of a bomb and the flames that would follow. If she absolutely had to die, it might as well happen right now, before she had to endure Martin's touch any longer.

Almost as if he'd read her mind, Martin drew her even

closer, brushed her hair back, and murmured in her ear, "Do you know how long I've fantasized about you? About what I would do to you and how you would look and act and sound? That's the only reason I ever did it with Debra Jane—because when I was inside her, I felt closer to you. I wanted to be close to you. Do you understand that, Teryl? I only wanted to be close to you. It's *your* fault that he has to die. It's *your* fault that you have to die."

He lowered his head, kissing the soft skin just beneath her ear, and her stomach began churning, bile surging high, threatening to make her ill. On the opposite side of the table, a murderously cold look came across John's face, turning him into as much of a stranger as the man behind her. Before he could act, she did, raising her hand, digging her nails into Martin's face, making him shriek with pain. He hit her in much the same way he'd struck D.J., the clammy steel of the pistol coming into contact with her cheek, creating waves of pain that dulled her senses to everything else, sending her staggering against the table. It swayed precariously beneath her weight, then, suddenly, John was supporting her, holding her against him, warning Tremont, Martin, or whoever the bastard was not to touch her again.

As her vision cleared, she saw that she had knocked over two of the glass jars, their fuel seeping through cracks in the wooden table, dripping to form a puddle on the ancient linoleum. The smell made her sick, and the blow to the head had left her woozy. If John weren't holding on to her, she wouldn't even be able to stand.

Then sheer terror brought her upright in his arms. The floor, as in so many old houses, slanted just the slightest bit toward the outside, and the gasoline pooling there was following its slope straight toward the water heater. "Oh, God," she whimpered, her tongue thick, her voice weak, the words of warning she sought evading her.

It wouldn't have mattered if she could speak, though, because John was muttering his own prayer as Martin, cursing savagely, raised the pistol and pointed it straight at them. The safety was off, and his finger was on the trigger, pulling slowly, squeezing so damned slowly. "Fire," Teryl whispered weakly, and John thought damned right he was going to fire. The bastard was going to kill them both right now.

With a whoosh that seemed to suck the very air out of the room, a wall of fire burst up through the center of the room, engulfing Martin in its flames, muffling his tortured screams with its rush. The heat was intense; in the second it took John to remember the window behind them, it seared his skin and parched his lungs. He fumbled for the lock but couldn't budge it. Grabbing the first tool he found on the shelves, he smashed the window, using the crowbar to rake away the glass, then kicked out the screen. He lifted Teryl to the ground, then, flames licking at his skin, he followed her out, scooped her into his arms and ran like hell.

The concussion from the first explosion knocked them to the ground; it made his ears ring and his chest go tight. A second and a third explosion followed, sending flames out shattered windows, reaching high into the sky, consuming old wood and shingles as if they were paper. John rolled onto his back, feeling the sting of burns on his arms and neck, and pulled Teryl, her expression dazed, her face bruised, into his arms. Together they watched as the house, fully involved now, collapsed inward on itself. She began crying softly— for D.J., he thought, until he saw the slender red-haired woman standing a safe distance away, openly sobbing, obviously heartbroken.

Richard Martin was still inside.

He regretted that the man had to die, even after all he'd done to John and especially to Teryl. He also regretted his own loss. All the Tremont papers were gone for sure this time. All the documentation of his career. Eleven years' worth of work, of suffering, of healing, turned to ash.

Richard Martin wouldn't die alone in this fire. His precious Simon Tremont was dying with him.

But John Smith was coming to life. It was time to stop hiding, time to give up his isolation, time to appreciate all that life had given him, starting with the woman at his side.

The wind shifted, sending the thick, choking smoke the other way, and he breathed deeply, filling his lungs with sweet, clean air. He had a future, and he had Teryl.

Those were reasons enough for living.

Epilogue

━━━◆━━━

*T*wo weeks had passed since the fire that destroyed the old farmhouse. Richard Martin had, indeed, died that day. His body, charred beyond recognition, had been recovered from the rubble hours later by firemen. D.J. had escaped physically unharmed, but emotionally . . . She had answered all of the detectives' questions, had described her nine years with Martin in detail, had revealed his plan and how he had succeeded, and then she had simply stopped talking. She had responded to no one, not even Teryl and her parents when they had paid her a visit in the hospital three days ago. She had simply withdrawn, the psychiatrist had told them. Martin's death, added to all the problems she was already suffering, had been more than she could bear.

Teryl could understand that. Losses and hurts could easily add up until a person's heart simply said no more. She just might be a prime candidate for that condition herself. Already she'd lost her job and her home and had twice almost lost her life. She'd lost her best friend and, in a very real sense, her family. Her parents had confirmed what D.J. had told her, what John had later admitted that he'd already suspected. Her mother hadn't miraculously given birth to her before some vague problem had turned her and Philip to adoption and foster care. Teryl—like D.J., Rico, and so

many of the others—had come from someplace else, someplace cruel, violent, and best forgotten.

Why hadn't they told her? she had demanded. All of her
brothers and sisters had known the details of their adoptions
from the very beginning, and it had never mattered, anyway.
Every child, whether adopted or not, had been treated the
same. Why hadn't *she* been told?

Because the doctors had advised against it. Because she
had been so fragile when she'd come to them. Because they
had feared that telling her the truth might unlock the terrors
still hidden inside her. Because, at the time they'd adopted
her, they hadn't intended to make a practice of it. Because a
year had been too soon, as had five years, ten years, and fifteen. Because they had grown accustomed to thinking of her
as their own, had come to treasure her as their very own.

So many answers, reasonable and logical but not a hundred percent acceptable. Not enough to ease the betrayal. Not
enough to deny this sense of loss.

Soon—a few days, a week at most—she was going to face
the biggest loss of all. Soon she was going to lose John.

She was sure that was why he had brought her to New Orleans. Their affair had begun here, and he probably thought it
appropriate to end it here. He had promised to make up to
her for all that he was putting her through, and on this trip
he'd certainly made a good start. Their hotel suite was, by
far, the most luxurious she had ever seen, and the staff
treated them like royalty. They had eaten at restaurants
known worldwide, had seen a few sights and made a lot of
love, and John had spent more than a little time shut up in
the bedroom on the phone. Even now he had brought her
here to the Café du Monde, then gone off for some bit of
business or another. Arranging for the purchase of his Pacific
island? Determining where he would go and when he would
leave her? Planning his last farewell?

With a forlorn sigh, she took one last sip from her soda,
then stuffed the napkin into the paper cup. She was rising
from the table when she saw him coming toward her. He was
smiling, and even though she'd never felt less like it, she
couldn't help but smile in return. His injuries from the last

blasts had been minor—a few small burns, some cuts from broken glass—and they were healed now. Hers were almost healed, too, the swelling of her face finally gone down, the bruise where Martin had hit her only a shadow that makeup could conceal. Considering what they'd been through the last few weeks—and the heartache she was sure to face in the future—they didn't look too bad. John, in fact, looked pretty damned good.

"Are you ready?" he asked when he reached her.

"For what?"

"There's something I want to show you. It isn't far—just a few blocks."

They crossed Decatur and walked along the uneven sidewalk. It was hot, but the humidity was manageable. The faintly sour smell of garbage perfumed the air, along with exhaust from passing cars and the mingled aromas of food from the restaurants they passed. Hot, noisy, smelly—and she couldn't think of anyplace she'd rather be or anyone she would rather be there with.

Their destination was Chartres Street, an address in the middle of a quiet block. When she would have walked on past, John caught her arm and drew her through an open gate that led back into a courtyard complete with a fountain, sun-warmed stone benches, crepe myrtles in full bloom, and beds of periwinkles and phlox. "What is this?" she asked, slowing her steps until he had to stop or drag her along.

"It's a gracious old home with a courtyard."

She looked around again, taking in the paving stones, the small sections of emerald green grass, the giant live oak draped with Spanish moss near the back wall of the garden. "Whose gracious old home?"

"Yours, if you like it. If you'll have it."

Hers. So this was to be the consolation prize. He was even more generous than she'd expected. She would have been no less happy with a little trip down here, a few more days of his company, a few more nights in his bed, and a plane ticket back home when it was over.

Hers. She took yet another look, this time focusing on the brick-and-stucco house, the broad gallery, the tall windows, the graceful wrought-iron balconies. The house towered three stories over them, plenty of room for a family, for children both natural born and taken in, but much too big for one lonely woman who might live the rest of her life in the same solitude that John had spent the last eleven years.

"You don't like it." John tried to keep the disappointment from his voice. Granted, there were plenty of other places for sale in the city, but when the realtor had described this one to him over the phone, he had been pretty sure it was what he wanted. Seeing it this morning had confirmed his hunch. It had a garden to fulfill Teryl's passion for flowers, high walls for privacy, lots of rooms for all the kids they could manage, and a separate guesthouse tucked in the back corner that would make an ideal office for him. It met the scant requirements she had stated when they were here the first time. *I'd want a place down here in the Quarter, one of these gracious old homes with a courtyard . . .* He had thought she would love it.

"It's a beautiful house." She went to stand near the fountain, watching the water as it spilled from the small bowl at the top to a larger carved basin and landing at last in the pool at the bottom. "Have you already signed the papers?"

"No. I wanted you to see it first."

"It's lovely." Her voice sounded odd, strangled. Teary. "But what would I do with a place like this?"

He went to stand behind her, laying his hands on her shoulders. She struggled against his efforts to turn her around, but he was stronger, though gentle, and finally she was facing him and staring at his chest. "I kind of thought you would live here with me," he said evenly, "and have my babies and raise our kids and anyone else's kids who need two parents to love them."

Her head jerked back, and her gaze flew to his face. He could see the surprise, the shock, and the tears she'd been trying to control. She had thought he'd brought her to New Orleans to say good-bye, he realized, and that the house was her reward for helping him reclaim his career. He gave her his most charming smile. "I can be generous, sweetheart. I can give every last penny I have if that's what it takes to make you happy. But buying you a house to live in alone?" He shook his head. "I'm not *that* generous. I can't let you go, Teryl. I can't walk away from the only woman I've ever loved."

She didn't yield easily. He would have been disappointed, he thought with a grin, if she had. "What about your Pacific island?"

"We can do that, too, if you want. I have a lot of money, Teryl. I never had anyone to spend it on, so after the Colorado house was built, the rest of it has been invested and reinvested for the last eleven years."

"What about living alone?"

"I've spent damned near half my life living alone. I want to spend the rest of it with you."

She was thoughtful for another moment. "*I* don't have any money. I don't have *anything* except these clothes that you've bought me. I don't have anything to give you."

"Except love. And babies. You do love me, Teryl. You can't hide it worth a damn."

Her smile was the sweetest sight he'd ever seen. "Yes. I do love you."

"So will you accept the house as my gift to you? Remembering, of course, that there are strings attached. You have to marry me first."

Turning but remaining in his arms, she leaned back against him, holding his clasped hands with both of hers, as she surveyed their new home. "Strings?" she echoed. "I was thinking of something a little more substantial."

"What do you mean?"

"I have a little gift for you. It certainly pales in comparison to your gift," she said with a self-conscious laugh, then became serious again. "I was going to give it to you when we said good-bye. But . . . " Pulling away from him, she went to sit on a stone bench, opened her purse, and pulled out a small blue box. When he sat down beside her, she offered it to him, then abruptly pulled it back. "Just remember: this is purely symbolic. It's not meant to be used."

She offered the box again, and he took it, sliding his fingertip under the tape that secured the lid on opposite sides.

He removed the lid, then a layer of thick cotton. For a long time, he simply stared, recognizing the significance of the gift immediately. What would it take for her to let him tie her to the bed? he had asked one sunny morning in her bedroom, and she had replied, Nothing. Nothing could convince her to do that. Trust would, he had insisted. *If you trusted me, if you believed in me with all your heart and all your soul . . . you would let me do it. You would trust me to keep you safe.* Knowing that he'd earned that kind of trust would give him a tremendous sense of power.

He'd been right, he thought as he stared at the length of braided cord nestled on a bed of cotton in the box, and he had been wrong. Knowing that she did trust him, that she believed in him with all her heart and all her soul was, indeed, tremendously empowering. It was also tremendously humbling. He wasn't sure that he deserved such an exquisite gift . . . but damned if he was going to give it back.

He replaced the lid on the box, then pulled her to him for a hard, hungry, passionate kiss. When he finally raised his head, he said fiercely, "I love you, Teryl."

She smiled that heart-tugging smile again. "I love you, too."

"Will you marry me?"

"I will. When?"

"As soon as possible." He drew his fingertip across her mouth, then down her throat to the V where her blouse buttoned. "In the meantime, will you fulfill one of my fantasies for me?"

Bless her heart—and her sweet, sweet faith—she didn't remind him that her gift was symbolic, didn't hesitate or falter at all. "If I can. What is it you want?"

"Just once . . . " He undid the top button, drew his fingers lower, and opened the second button. "Just once I'd like to be . . . " The third button slipped free with only the slightest nudge, and he slid his hand inside her blouse, gliding it over the powdery soft skin of her breast to her nipple, already swelling and needy of his caresses.

"Wicked," she prompted him, and then she kissed him,

THROUGHOUT THE NEXT YEAR, LOOK FOR OTHER FABULOUS BOOKS FROM YOUR FAVORITE WRITERS IN THE WARNER ROMANCE GUARANTEED PROGRAM

Win a Romantic Getaway for Two

To show our appreciation for your continued support, Warner Books is offering you an opportunity to win our sweepstakes for four spectacular weekend "trips for two" throughout 1996.

◆ Enter in February or March to win a romantic spring weekend in Hilton Head, South Carolina.

◆ Enter in April, May, or June to win a gorgeous summer getaway to San Francisco, California.

◆ Enter in July or August to win a passionate fall trip to the blazing mountains of Vermont.

◆ Enter in September, October, November, or December to win a hot winter jaunt to Sanibel Island.

For details on how to enter, stop by the Warner Books display at your local bookstore or send a self-addressed stamped envelope for a sweepstakes entry application to:

ⓦ WARNER BOOKS

1271 Avenue of the Americas, Room 9-27B   New York, NY 10020

No purchase necessary. Void where prohibited. Not valid in Canada. Winner must be 18 or older.

Warner Books...
We'll sweep you off your feet.